Intercepting Fate - Book One:
Extinction Virus

Cameron Stewart Miller

Chapter 1:
Welcome To Sellea City

There's something strangely therapeutic about a good punch in the face.

Okay, maybe *good* isn't ever the best word to describe anyone getting punched in the face. It's always nicer to be dishing one out instead of receiving one, but a weak jab will always be enough to send anyone's mind into overdrive.

Only a handful of people in the poorer sections of Sellea City bothered training to become anything let alone a boxer. The sport had been dying out over the last few decades, but it still had a few veterans. I figured most people were afraid to mess up their pretty faces— whatever that even means in a place like Sellea. Still, anyone who trained knew a shot of espresso had nothing on getting tagged by a serious fighter.

"Take it easy, man," Kieran said as he shook a padded hand.

"Here I was thinking you were the toughest guy in your weight class," I said as we squared back up.

"Oh, I am—don't get things twisted." He took a few more of my heavy shots. "You're going about as hard as you did in that last fight. This is called training."

"That fight against Tate?" I changed angles and danced around Kieran. "Please, that was nothing."

"Nothing is one way to describe it."

"I can't help being blessed with a wicked right hook. I did kinda wreck him, huh?"

"No kidding. I dunno why he kept getting back up. He barely landed a single shot by the end of the second round."

Kieran held out a hand and I hit it with another stiff jab. "Everyone wants to be the guy to take me down."

We'd been labouring through the short set of striking combinations from my last big fight. The amount of sweat pouring from us told me that we had been training for more than an hour.

It was part of our daily ritual for the last ten years. We'd trudge through boring days at the academy, and then rush to the gym as soon as we could. The academy's final bell never seemed to come quick enough.

Most days, we'd go train for as long as our bodies would let us. I'd hate to be one of the poor souls that had to crowd into one of the crappy city buses with our collective stench.

"I don't know why I expected to feel different after finishing up," he said as he took a swipe at me.

"What?" I ducked it and danced around him. "At the academy?"

"Yeah. I always figured I'd feel less like—like a kid, ya know? Just—different. I dunno."

"You are different."

"Yeah?"

"You were ugly before—now you're ugly *and* an academy graduate."

As I moved, the flimsy boards of the decrepit boxing ring creaked under my weight. There had been more than one day where I thought I'd end up dropping right through the middle of the ring. Somehow it had been deemed competition ready, so I wasn't about to complain. I was lucky to even have a ring to practice in.

"You're hilarious. I'm serious." He squared up to me again. "There goes all that work, and for what? In a few days I'm going off to become an Interceptor, and then I'll—"

"Oh my god." I took a shot toward his open guard and gave him a soft jab in the gut. "Enough with the Interceptors. Unless it's something about how good Lili looked the other day in those pink shorts—I don't wanna hear it."

Kieran smirked. "Those shorts were pretty great, but don't kill my vibe, man." He took off his pads and tossed them aside. "You gotta lighten up and let yourself get excited about something for once. It sure would make my life a hell of a lot happier."

I stepped back and took a deep breath, the musty air of the gym filled my lungs.

It was easy to be unaware of how exhausted your body was when you're doing something you love. I could have gone for a twelve-round brawl, while Kieran would have been a gassed mess. He spent more energy trying to remember the combinations than he did on actually fighting or on proper breathing. His fights were always entertaining, but they could also be described as an absolute chaotic slugfest.

"Remember the last time I got all excited about something?" He raised an eyebrow as I continued. "The date with Elise? The date that you ended up going out on—that ring any bells—or have you taken one too many shots to the head?"

"Oh, yeah. That was a fun one," he said as he helped me out of my gloves. "Let's not dwell on the past, Rhys. What's done is done."

"Sounds like the words of a guy who made out with his best buddy's date." I picked up my bottle of water from the nearby ring corner and took a swig.

"You say, *made out with your date.* I say, *testing the waters to make sure my best friend is getting himself a good kisser.*" Kieran chuckled. "I still don't understand why you wouldn't let me pay for your application. We both know you want to be one of them as much as I do, and you would have made a great—"

I squeezed my bottle, and a stream of water shot right onto Kieran's face.

He held his hands up. "Okay. Message received. I will now officially be dropping the Interceptors."

My sight set on one of the other guys we trained with from time to time, seated in the corner of the gym. He looked to be done for the day, but instead of taking off, he had started watching an Interceptor feed.

I nearly groaned loud enough for everyone to hear.

They were inescapable.

Sure, they had their fair share of haters—especially whenever they messed up, but it still felt like everyone on the planet couldn't get enough of them. I didn't usually mind everyone gushing about them, but not being able to afford the application fee for the tryout had left a bad taste in my mouth.

What kind of heroes charge a tryout fee?

We packed up our bags, and as I lifted mine, one of the handles snapped off. I'd have to re-stitch it for what must have been the fifth time.

Kieran raised a finger. "It's all good. I'll—"

"If you say you'll buy me a new one—"

"For your birthday."

He knew he had me. I'd always complained and fought Kieran whenever he tried to pay for me. He knew there wasn't anything I could do when it came to my birthday—Lenna would probably kill me if I refused a birthday gift.

"Along with a pair of gloves, new trunks, wrist tape, and a new water bottle?" I asked. "When does it stop being birthday presents and start being charity?"

"What can I say? I'm a giver. Oh, and don't forget the holo-projector so you'll have someone to spar with while I'm out saving the world."

"How could I forget?"

We headed for the door without a glance toward the change rooms. The showers were in a state of disrepair since the day we first signed up at the gym. We didn't have enough fingers and toes for the number of times we begged the owner to fix the showers, but it was a pretty run-down place.

I felt bad that Kieran felt he needed to downgrade to my grungy gym when he could have been training somewhere with access to the latest technology.

He could be a good friend sometimes—I guess.

The bright sun rays caused me to squint as my eyes adjusted. I tilted my head to the clear sky. "Ugh. Sky, if you could just go ahead and rain—ever—or maybe even just pop out one single cloud—that would be absolutely fantastic."

The heat in the gym had nothing on the wave of heat that hit the second we made our way onto the street. The summer had started in full force. The sun's rays felt like someone had set up personal heaters right over my head just to piss me off. Thanks to the heat, our collective stench-cloud would only be made more unbearable. I took a whiff from my armpit and coiled back.

"Rain? Not in our lifetimes—apparently," Kieran said. "Would be cool, though. Oh—or snow."

"What, like in all those ancient holiday movies? Like that's gonna happen."

We made our way across the desolate street to the bus stop. There was more than one boarded-up business and even more graffiti-riddled houses in the area. As we passed through the entryway of the bus shelter, a holographic timestamp for the next bus arrival formed. It would be pulling up any second.

"Since I might not be hanging around too much longer," Kieran said. "I gotta know—when should I tell Lenna that I love her?".

"The bus isn't here yet." I gave him a side-eye. "We could still head back to the gym and do a little proper sparring."

"I'm just saying. Who knows where I'll be next month. It's kind of now or never."

"You're so confident—figure it out yourself."

"Look, it's not my fault your sister's so hot, man," he said as the bus pulled up and screeched to a halt.

The mechanical doors slid open and we walked on, nodding to the driver as we passed by. "I'm gonna let that one slide. Say that again, and there's going to be future Interceptor all over the floor of the bus."

"I knew you believed in me." Kieran grinned.

"Well, someone has to," I said as we snagged the only open seats left on the bus.

I was thankful to give my legs a bit of a rest as I looked around. A feeling of disgust crept up on me seeing all the people on board with their faces buried in their visors. The area was right on the divide for the two poorest sections of the city, so it was surprising to see so many people with visors in the first place. The glowing dull-blue interface that stared back at anyone who glanced toward one screamed that these people were using older—inferior models.

"Since when do so many people in this section have visors?" Kieran asked.

"I guess after the fall of Odrana, all the city's extra tech had to go somewhere. The capital is as good a place as any right?"

"So where's your visor?"

"Why would I need one?" I put an arm around him. "You never leave me alone."

He pushed my arm away. "Really feeling the love, buddy."

All eyes were on us when Kieran pulled out his brand-new visor-tech. He tapped behind his left ear and a small wave of nano-tech crawled across the side of his head. A small green light projected an interface in front of Kieran's face. It felt like it was made specifically to look more expensive than its predecessor as the green glow far outshined the drab glow of the other model.

I caught a few dirty looks from around the bus. "You sure you wanna pull that out here?"

"It's fine. What are they gonna do? Start a fight with two boxers? We'll offend their senses and their faces."

He had a good point.

Kieran's six-foot frame and bulging muscles were more than enough to deter any potential attackers. I might have been a bit shorter than he was, but I had become pretty well known around the city from my viral knockout reel.

Most people knew me as the kid who could take a hundred punches and laugh it off—if my opponent could even hit me. If all that didn't deter someone from starting something—our collective stench sure would.

I peered around and caught more side-eyes from the people on the bus. They'd have had to work for months to be able to afford the older models and here was this kid with the latest and greatest tech.

Kieran had never been shy about his wealth, but he'd never intend to come across as an ass with his money. He knew he was lucky to be born with a silver spoon in the finest section of the city—he just had a tendency to forget that not everyone was so fortunate.

"Who're you calling?" I asked.

"Studying," Kieran said.

Some people used their visors to video call friends or loved ones on their way home from work, but most were tuning in to the Interceptor feeds. As long as people weren't busy working or playing, they had their favourite Interceptor stream up in front of their face or on the holo-device of their choice. I thought it was silly to idolize people all because you could invade their life anytime you wanted.

I'd have joined the team in a heartbeat—the same way any sane person would. However, I suspected that my reason for doing so would be different than most other people's reasons.

He pulled up a newsfeed on his visor and I groaned, "I thought you said you'd drop the Interceptors?"

"I said that back at the gym. Welcome to our new surroundings—" He gestured around the bus. "Public transit. We gotta pass the time somehow, besides it's the news—not a feed."

"A news feed."

"Not the same thing."

"We could talk to each other." I leaned back in my seat. "You know, that thing old people used to do?"

"Shh."

Kieran used his hands to expand his visor for the both of us, and then he slid a finger along the side to raise the volume. Visor-tech was pretty cool, but I could never get into it. Having a little chip that housed nano-tech attached to your head didn't seem all that appealing to me.

"In our next story, a tryout to find the world's next great hero is taking place this weekend," The toothy-grinned reporter said. "One lucky person's life will change forever."

Kieran's face morphed into a cocky smile. "H'oh, whadd'ya know? Perfect timing."

Kieran hadn't let me forget about the tryouts for the last month and a half. He'd eaten, slept, and breathed Interceptor since their inception—and it was finally his shot at becoming one. We'd heard rumours for years about how gruelling the process was, but that didn't deter him one bit. For the first time, the public was going to get to see every second of the tryouts.

He'd been using boxing as a way to train for his moment. The one time he'd missed a training session was a month from the academy closing when he had to show up to a basic fitness test for the whole process. He'd mentioned it being a breeze, but most people weren't able to cut it with something so simple.

"You still haven't mentioned whether or not Lenna and I can come watch you in the first round," I said as the bus halted in a dense area of traffic.

"Everything I've been reading has said that spectators aren't allowed at the facility, but you'll be able to watch one of the—"

"One of the feeds—I know. People won't shut up about this being," I started waving my hands. "*The first-ever televised tryout.* It's just gonna be one big pageant."

"Yeah, yeah, yeah—What's up with the holdup?" Kieran looked out to the wall of traffic. "If we take much longer, you're gonna be dealing with one *hangry* Kieran."

"Probably just another one of those dumb convoy training runs or something."

"Stupid rare tech transfers. Who even needs 'em?"

"Oh, I dunno—maybe hospitals?" I flicked his head. "You know you might have to help out with those if you make it onto the team."

The bus shook, and a pleasant voice came over the speaker. "Now switching to the anti-gravity track." A loud whirring came from under our feet. In the next instant, the bus lifted from the ground as we grabbed onto the poles next to our seats.

There were few feelings worse than when the gravity in the bus would change. The odd floating sensation always made me sick to my stomach. The bus turned until its base faced the wall of buildings that we'd been riding beside, and it carried on like normal over the traffic.

"Anyway, back to your pageant comment," Kieran said. "The people around the world connecting with whoever the team recruits is just as important as them picking someone who's able to run real fast or punch real good," he said, flicking me back on the last part. "The Interceptors can't work if they don't have the trust of the people. Streaming the tryouts live to the world is one of the smartest choices they could have made."

"You just think you'll look pretty up on one of those big holo-screens in your section."

"You aren't wrong." He flexed an arm. "I've been practicing my victory poses."

"Why am I not surprised?"

I looked out the window across from me and watched as we zoomed by the various car roofs stuck in the traffic below. These buses were new in that section of the city, but they were making the poorer people's lives a hell of a lot easier. Not having to show up to the gym in Kieran's fancy hover-car helped cut down on the number of fights we'd nearly had with some seedier people in the area.

The news feed on Kieran's visor switched from coverage of the upcoming tryouts to coverage of an old Interceptor mission. Some people called it the day the Interceptors died, and in a way, it was kind of true.

Footage played, showing the original member of the team, Chase, as he stood alone against overwhelming odds. I didn't care about the Interceptor team members in general, but I could respect the sacrifice of a guy like that.

"You gonna be a big hero, like Chase?" I asked.

"Bigger."

The voice came over the speaker again. "Now switching to the gravity track."

The bus shook once more, and without stopping, it floated back down onto the clear road. The queasy feeling in my stomach started to fade as the gravity returned to normal.

"You'll get used to it one of these days," Kieran said when he saw how ready I was to hurl.

"You keep saying that, and I just keep on waiting for that day to come. I'm starting to think you keep saying that, so I'll keep getting on this thing," I said as I kicked a nearby pole.

Kieran put his visor away as the news feed switched to coverage of the madman known as Zeal. The accompanying headline had something to do with something called the Extinction Virus.

Zeal was the world's most sought-after criminal. Anyone would have recognized the crazed face of that terroristic mad scientist from a glance. Seeing his face brought that sick feeling right back, full force.

"You know, if I become an Interceptor, and you'd stop being so proud—I could use the money to buy you two a better place," Kieran said.

"Hilarious."

We had arrived back to my shabby section of the city, which also happened to be the poorest. Most folks referred to it as the slums since there really wasn't a better word to use. Most of the houses were made up of boxy housing complexes that were far too small for the people they housed. It was all Lenna and I could afford, but we made it work. It helped that people in the poorer sections tended to stick together.

"Think Lenna decided on something different for dinner tonight?" Kieran asked.

"Well, let's see—we have that awful mina-gunk and more of that awful mina-gunk. If you close your eyes real tight and imagine you aren't eating something so gross—you might actually be able to get it down a bit better."

Kieran stared at me. "I'll order a couple burgers—my treat."

"Good call, but I'll still owe you."

The bus screeched to a stop, and we made our way off. "We're family. You don't owe me anything—"

There was something in the air. It wasn't the typical disgusting smell of burning trash. Something smelled like a kind of chemical bonfire. We looked up to see a wall of thick black smoke rising into the air—right in the direction of my house.

I broke into a sprint.

"I'm comin' Lenna."

Chapter 2:
Dirty Conks

The flames shot into the sky from the far side of the street, and as I approached—they only continued to creep higher. The entire complex Lenna and I lived in was engulfed in blistering flames. With every step, the harsh tar-like smoke that filled the air became denser.

Some people were fleeing from the scene, but a large crowd had gathered as well. I had a feeling they were hoping to catch a glimpse of their favourite Interceptor as they came to save the day. That's *if* they deemed a fire in the slums a big enough issue to respond to. Kieran had caught back up to me, and waded his way into the crowd. My heart raced as I pushed my own way through the crowd, trying to spot my sister.

"Lenna?"

If she wasn't out here, that meant one thing. I turned my attention back to the inferno that engulfed the countless homes. It wasn't a mundane electronic malfunction that started the fire. Something so simple couldn't start a fire as big as that. The fire had to have been started by the small squad of Conks that lingered out front the complex.

Two of them started shooting more flames at the building, and another two were armed and ready with cyber-swords. Occasionally Conks would teleport into Sellea City and cause mayhem to draw out the Interceptors, but I never thought it would end up affecting me yet again. Then again, I figured everyone thought the same thing until something horrific happened to them.

A group of police officers pointed guns from their vehicles, but they knew there was nothing they could do without some big-time backup.

I had to do something.

I launched forward from the crowd. If those cops weren't going to try to save anyone in the building, I was going to.

"Hey, stop that kid!" someone yelled—probably one of the cowardly cops.

It was too late for anyone to stop me. I had already made it through the small line of police, and the one thing—or four things keeping me from the blaze was the squad of Conks. Two of them had their backs to me, which made it more of a two-on-one situation. Without any kind of a kit or Interceptor training, the situation probably wasn't going to end well, but I wasn't about to let a couple of Conks keep me from saving my sister.

"Here goes nothing." I gritted my teeth as I got in range of the dopey robots.

The Conks with cyber-swords readied themselves in front of me. I tossed my gym bag at them, but they slashed right through it. It's a good thing that they weren't the brightest machines in existence because they both swung at the same place as I dove past them. A metallic clank let me know that they bumped their arms in the process of trying to turn me into some thinly-sliced Rhys.

As I hit the floor, I rolled and scrambled to my feet. Mechanical footsteps pounded behind me—gaining on me fast. There was no way I could stop now. I could hear the people from the crowd screaming for someone to help me, while others cheered me on.

To some people, my ordeal was nothing but a spectacle. It made me sick.

I knew I only had one shot at making it into the building, but it was going to be risky.

I ran as fast as I could for one of the Conks that was shooting fire. The footsteps behind me grew closer, and the whooshing of their cyber-swords grew louder with each step. I grabbed the arm of the Conk ahead of me and whirled it around as it shot another blast of flames.

"Please work." I winced as the heat from the Conk burned my hand.

The flames torched one of the sword-wielding Conks, and it fell to the floor. I stared down at the blackened robot in awe.

The other Conk managed to jump out of the way without a sound. When I came back to my senses, I threw the hardest punch I could muster to the back of the fire-wielding robot with a loud CONK, and it staggered forward. My hand felt like it was broken, but I couldn't put on the brakes for something like that.

I shook my hand out. "That was a bad freakin' call."

Across from me at the front of the crowd, I saw Kieran staring at me, dumbfounded. "I'll be back." I knew he couldn't hear me, but I needed to say it before I ran into the fiery complex without any help.

My skin stung from the flames that danced all around me. Luckily, the remaining Conks didn't seem to have followed me into the building. That probably should have been my hint as to just how stupid an idea running into a burning building was.

I jumped over bits of burnt debris and made my way up to my home on the second floor. I tried the knob and burnt my hand from how hot it had gotten. I couldn't be sure about some of the other units, but mine had to be on fire on the inside.

"Lenna, if you can hear me, back away from the door. I'm gonna kick it in."

It was getting hard to breathe and it felt like a bedsheet had been pulled over my eyes. I remembered back to when we all took turns trying on an academy members' glasses, and the headache I received from the eye strain was the exact same.

I took off my hoodie and held it over my mouth to filter out some of the smoke. I had no idea if it would work, but it felt like it helped.

I kicked the door as hard as I could, and it bowed slightly. I threw my shoulder into it over, and over until I fell inside the unit. The door was ruined, but I had a feeling the rest of the apartment was worse. I was lucky I fell to the floor because the wall of black smoke that poured into the hallway would have been enough to choke me out.

"Lenna?" I called through gasps and coughs. "Where—where are you?"

I listened hard, but the crackling of walls and furniture going up in flames was all I could hear. I crawled through the apartment calling out and listening for any sign of her. My eyes fell on the kitchen—she was on the floor.

She had to have been trapped inside by the flames if she hadn't been able to make it out. I scrambled toward her and tried to find her pulse.

"Be okay—be okay—please—please, be okay."

Her pulse was weak, but she was alive. I tore a sleeve from my hoodie and gently wrapped it around her nose and mouth. I pulled off the other sleeve and did the same for myself before getting ready for the hardest part.

"I'm gonna get you outta here, sis."

The walls were coming apart, and crumbling from the intensity of the flames. We needed to find a way out of there before the flames made it through a gas line.

I cradled her in my arms and did my best to rush back out of the building. The flames burned my legs as I carried her back down to the first floor, but my adrenaline kept me from caring about the pain. The ceilings around us started to give, and furniture from the second-story units started falling to the floor. As a couch broke through the floor, I took a slight hop to the side, narrowly avoiding it.

The light from outside beckoned us closer like an old friend as I fell out of the building. The crowd cheered when they saw me coming out with Lenna, but stopped in a hurry when the Conks started advancing on us. There were rare occasions where average citizens managed to take down a Conk by themselves. I had already managed to take one down, but three wasn't something anyone had ever accomplished alone and unarmed.

"Oh, yeah—I forgot about you guys." I glared up at the Conks as I tried to catch my breath "Crap."

The two fire-wielding robots created balls of flames in their hands as the other remaining Conk approached with its cyber-sword pointed toward me.

There wasn't anywhere for me to go, and no one in the crowd was stepping forward to help me out—freakin' cowards. Kieran tried to fight his way through the cops, but they were holding him back. I held Lenna close and closed my eyes, waiting for the end.

Chapter 3:
Meet The Interceptors

"I think we'll take it from here." A woman's voice came from behind the Conks. "Good job, kid."

I opened my eyes and stared at the team of Interceptors that had teleported in to save the day. The whole team had shown up to battle the blaze, and I couldn't help feeling relieved that I had some kind of backup.

Each of them had a small spherical camera that followed them around as it flew through the air. It was odd that they deemed that situation enough trouble to send the team, but maybe things looked even more dire than I thought.

The crowd was cheering and even I was happy, but I could almost feel a hint of fear radiating from the Conk in front of me.

"Look—he took out a Conk on his own," the Interceptor named Diggs said with a whistle. "Atta-boy."

The two women of the group were Cleo and Lili. Cleo was kitted out in light blue and Lili was in light green. They both zipped up to buildings on opposite sides of the blaze with grappling hooks. The little cameras that constantly accompanied them whizzed through the air after them to capture different angles of the action.

The suits glowed—one blue and the other white before each one started to channel their elements. Cleo pulled enormous waves of water, from what I guessed were the buildings underground reserves. Lili created smaller gusts of wind that were destroying chunks of flames.

"It's open season," Cleo said as she put out a section of the fire. "Get hunting."

The only man in a purple kit, Kiyoshi, rushed forward and took out one of the flame-wielding Conks with one swing of a huge war hammer. I wasn't sure if the crackling electricity came from his element or the sparks from the chunks of destroyed robot.

I stared at the heap of sparking robotics. "Whoa."

"Weak." Kiyoshi looked down his nose at the robotic heap in front of us.

A Conk that had been camouflaged against a nearby electrical box leaped forward with a cyberknife raised. Kiyoshi ducked its swing and replied with one of his own. The top half of the Conk flew into the air, and Kiyoshi caught it with a bolt of lightning. Kiyoshi's camera whirled around to snap the best angle of what looked like a victory pose.

The other two—a man and a woman each kitted out in light red suits dashed forward. The man—Diggs—wrapped a cyberwhip around the wrists of the other flame conk. The woman—Pegs—cut it in half with a throw of her flaming circle-sword.

"Nice throw, babe," Diggs said as he pulled his whip back.

"It was pretty sweet, huh?" Pegs replied.

Two other camouflaged Conks came out of nowhere to rush at the duo. They each flipped over the attacking Conks, and Diggs launched his whip again. The whip wrapped around one of the Conk's waists, and he threw it into the other one. Pegs dashed forward and caught her sword as it finally circled back to her. She tossed it into the air, hopped upward with a flip, and kicked the sword down through both the Conks.

"How was that?" Pegs asked as she landed in a heroic pose.

Diggs teetered a hand. "Four outta ten."

"*Excuse me?*"

The last Conk hadn't moved until it lifted its sword and spun around, ready to bring it down on me.

I shot up and threw an uppercut right in its jaw. It didn't do much other than add to the punishment my hand had already endured, but it was enough to stagger it.

It took a moment to look at its surroundings. All that thing's robo-buddies were goners. The Conk let out a kind of robotic chirp before it turned and ran, no doubt sensing the danger it was in.

The three Interceptors stood there and watched as it tried to disappear into the crowd of people. As it reached them, another Interceptor materialized in a shadow being cast by a fire engine that had arrived on the scene.

It had to be Mickey. With one swift cyberknife strike to the head, the final Conk was dispatched.

"Kieran's gotta be freaking out right now," I said to myself as I gawked at everything going on around me.

I turned around and watched as Lili launched another Conk into the air with a huge wind blast. It must have been lurking on a rooftop nearby, but a surprise attack by one Conk wasn't going to be enough.

Cleo threw her spear right through the chest of the robot, before jumping to it and kicking the Conks body into the burning wreck of a building below.

Cleo and Lili finished putting out most of the flames that surrounded the building, allowing the firefighters to head inside and contain whatever fires remained. They grouped up back on the ground in front of me.

I picked Lenna up. "Please, my—"

"Don't worry," Diggs said as he took Lenna from my arms. "We'll make sure she gets medical attention." He rushed to a nearby ambulance with Pegs in tow.

"You were brave back there, kid," Cleo said.

Kiyoshi scoffed. "An idiot."

"True," She shot him a stern look. "But brave."

Kiyoshi shook his head and walked off to survey the area with Mickey. I watched them go and saw that the cops were still holding Kieran back from running toward me. His face was filled with excitement rather than concern.

Cleo stepped forward, while Lili hovered behind her. It was what I imagined it would be like to be approached by a lioness and her cub.

"What's your name?" Cleo asked.

"Rhys. Rhys York."

"Not many people would have jumped into a fight with a group of Conks *and* a raging fire—" She looked over to the ambulance they were treating Lenna in. "Even for a girl."

"My sister—she's all the family I—what about the other people? Shouldn't you guys be saving anyone else trapped inside?"

"You want to tell him yourself, Alfie?" Cleo's AI appeared beside her.

"All scans for life within the complex have come back negative." Alfie adjusted his glasses, something that felt weird for a computer program to do. "Your sister was the last living being left inside."

"I guess I can't argue with an AI," I said as I tensed my injured hand.

"I wouldn't suggest it," Cleo said with a chuckle. She opened up her visor and started scrolling. "I can't find your name on the tryout list. Did you not sign up?"

"I couldn't pull the money together to pay for the entry fee." I rubbed the back of my neck. "I don't even know what I'm going to do about my—"

"Ugh. Those slimy bastards really set up an entry fee for the tryouts? Alfie, could you—?" A slight chime came from her visor. "Thanks. You're on the list. I better see you at the first round this weekend."

"Wait. Seriously? What about the physical test?" I asked. "I didn't show up to—"

"Seriously. Don't worry about the physical test, if you are willing to go toe-to-toe with four Conks on your own, you can show up to the tryouts. I have a feeling that you can do more than a few push-ups." She sized me up. "I'll go set up someplace for you and your sister to stay while you figure things out. We'll be in touch." She walked off with her visor still up.

I hadn't dreamed about joining the Interceptors the same way Kieran had, but I would have been first in line to try out if it wasn't so expensive. Kieran had offered to pay for my tryout, but I'd been so tired of relying on him to help me with everything in the city. I couldn't ask for one more favour. At least now we could do it together—regardless of the outcome.

"Hey," Lili said. "Can I ask you something?"

"Go for it."

She was a lot prettier in person—which was saying a lot. Something about the way she approached me made me feel shy. If I had to pick a celebrity crush it would have been her every—single—time. She'd been the newest addition to the team, but she made an impact fast.

"Has she always been like that?" she asked as she nodded toward Lenna.

I looked to the ambulance, and she was up and moving. She waved at me with a bright smile that shined through the oxygen line she had on her face.

"Sorry if that's too personal or something."

"You mean her arm?" I waved back to Lenna. "No —an attack when we were young."

"That's awful."

"You should see her draw. It's a good thing she's always wanted to be a singer."

She laughed and it felt like my heart almost leaped out of my chest. How could someone have such an endearing laugh?

"What about that scar? A white-streaked eyebrow can't be natural. Was that from the same attack?"

I ran my fingers along the scar that ran from my hairline to my cheekbone. "Yeah, it's from the same accident. I'm Rhys, by the way."

"Aliya, but most people just call me Lili."

"Well, I know who you are."

"Oh, right. I still kinda forget I don't need to introduce myself to everyone I meet anymore."

I nodded to the camera following her around. "Perks of having your whole life on display."

She crossed her arms. "Perk—is certainly a word."

A loud whistle pierced through the murmuring crowd, and I turned in time to see Kiyoshi and Cleo teleport away. One by one each of the Interceptors teleported back to their facility until Lili was the last one remaining.

"I guess—" She looked almost nervous as she spoke. "I'll see you this weekend?"

"Yeah, totally. I can't really miss it after Cleo went through all that trouble"

"Good luck."

Just like that, she was gone. The force of the teleport caused dirt and ash to kick up from the ground. The kicked-up dust made me gasp right into a sneeze.

I wiped my nose. "Glad she didn't see that."

I started toward Lenna as Kieran put an arm around me. "You're an absolute madman, you know that?"

"You woulda done the same thing if the cops weren't holding you back."

"You okay? We should get you looked at too."

"Lenna, first." I could feel Kieran wanting to ask more. "Alright—let's hear it."

"DUDE THAT WAS SO COOL! The way they came in and smashed those Conks like—WAH!" Kieran made a smashing motion with his hands. "Then Cleo and Lili put out the fire in no time at all—like, what?! That was the biggest fire I've ever seen! The way Kiyoshi smashed those Conks in one hit, and then the Diggs and Pegs combo too—they were flipping all over the place! Plus Mickey came out of nowhere there at the end to finish it all — I've never seen a cooler android! Then you got to talk to them—what did you say?"

"Not a lot." I coughed a bit and realized how badly my lungs needed to be cleaned out after all that smoke. "I got to see Cleo's AI, that was kind of cool."

"Alfie? Oh, man. I'm so jealous. He's the lamest of all the AI, but that's still so cool."

"Cleo added me to this weekend's tryout."

Kieran stopped in his tracks. "No way."

"Yep."

"You let her—but you wouldn't let me—"

"I'm not exactly going to say no to an Interceptor. It's not like it cost her anything anyway," I said as I kept walking. "Can we please go check on Lenna?"

"I've got so much to process," he said as he caught back up.

As soon as I made it to the ambulance I wrapped my arms around Lenna. It was so relieving to see her up and moving after finding her motionless.

"You're hurting me, bro." She squeaked out.

I held her face in my hands. "You're okay?"

"I'm okay. Promise." She raised an eyebrow at Kieran. "And where the hell was my knight in shining armour on that one, Kieran?"

"The only thing that kept me from saving you was a whole team of burly cops. They wouldn't let me through to help." He spotted a spindly cop and ducked behind the truck a bit. "Speaking of which—"

Lenna looked over to the wreckage that was our home. "What are we gonna do now?"

I sighed, "I dunno. Cleo said the Interceptors would set something up for us while we got back on our feet. Not that I even know how she's going to get in touch with us."

A tap on my shoulder caused me to whirl around and come face to face with the same news reporter Kieran and I had watched on the bus. She stuck a microphone in my face as she grinned at me. Her camera floated by her head, and dozens of other tiny cameras were flying around snapping pictures.

"Holliday Berkley from *This Just In's* Twenty-four Seven feed, I'd love to interview you about what just transpired."

"Uh?"

Kieran nudged me. "I guess it won't be too hard for them to track you down, huh?"

People swarmed all around, and every single one wanted to talk to me. How in the world could the Interceptors deal with their entire life being streamed all the time?

Someone shouted about me being an honorary

Interceptor, and I thought for a moment that I could see a look of disdain on Kieran's face.

I never asked for it, but that was my moment.

Chapter 4:
Ayla's New Partner

We met up out front of the Moore family mansion and waited for the shuttle to come grab us. We were both jittery from nerves, but we were looking forward to the challenge ahead of us. Lenna decided that rules were for losers—as she tended to do—so she planned to at least tag along with us on the ride to the tryout.

When the huge shuttle finally landed in front of us, we all packed into it before it took off into the skies of Sellea City.

It was a long ride, but that gave me the time I needed to ask Kieran as many questions as possible about the Interceptors. He was an encyclopedia for their history, gear, elements, and anything else someone could have thought of. I was worried about what might happen between the two of us at the tryouts, but I knew Kieran would do well regardless.

"This whole being an Interceptor thing sounds really complicated," Lenna whispered.

That was an understatement. Many people from the slums either didn't really care about or didn't really like the Interceptors. My connections to them came from whatever feeds I caught throughout the city, from Kieran, and from the attack all those years ago.

I puffed my cheeks and blew out the air. "Sounds like I'm seriously not going to understand any of this without experiencing it first-hand."

"Yeah, you're probably coming into this with the biggest handicap possible." Kieran slapped my back. "Shoulda let me talk your ear off about the Interceptors more often."

"Kieran." Lenna narrowed her eyes at him.

"I'm just speaking the truth."

"Good ole Kieran—" I said, oozing sarcasm. "Always filling me with so much confidence."

I looked out the window and down to the city below. I was never a big fan of heights, but the nerves of the day were bothering me more than the thought of being hundreds of feet above the city. As I looked at one of the many armed guards on board, the thought had occurred to me that the tryouts were always incredibly secretive.

What if that was because the losers were tossed back down toward the city?

That couldn't be it—right?

Across from us sat a cute punk girl that had been staring at us. We locked eyes when I noticed her, but she turned away in an instant. It even looked like she scoffed at me. I couldn't help but wonder if she was sizing up the competition.

Kieran nudged me. "Some cheery people on the shuttle, huh?"

"So what's up with those robots being called Conks?" Lenna asked.

"It's what Chase affectionately started calling them after he figured out the best way to bust them up was a solid conk in the head," Kieran said as he tapped his own head. "Ever since, the name's kinda just stuck."

"Truly the greatest hero of our time," I said.

The shuttle slowly pulled to a stop, and a loud DING

chimed as the doors slid open. We stepped out, and in front of us was the Interceptors headquarters.

It was a huge complex made up of enormous high-tech buildings. I'd seen it on the news a lot. I knew it came complete with indoor and outdoor training facilities, barracks for potential recruits, extra homes for each team member—and of course, it's massive command centres that the team worked out of.

I looked out at the sea of other people who had stepped off the shuttle with us. Some of these people looked like they'd be serious contenders to become the next Interceptor. When I had met Lili in person—she looked so small, and must have barely been over five-feet tall. If someone like that was able to be picked as an Interceptor, what kind of tests were we gonna be going through?

I tapped Kieran. "Isn't that last year's Launch-Bowl MVP?"

"Holy crap. It is."

I gulped. "You didn't mention any guys like that from the fitness test."

"He—he must have been at another one somewhere else. I haven't seen any of these people before."

The first thing I asked on the ride over was what to expect, but that was the one question Kieran didn't have an answer for. He mentioned that every single recruitment session had apparently involved entirely different challenges for people to overcome. The tiny buzz of energy that I could feel coming from him had to do with the uncertainty of the tests.

"You two are going to be great," Lenna said.

"These guys all look pretty serious."

"Not as serious as my two studs. If one of you isn't the next Interceptor I'm gonna show up to that gym of yours for twelve rounds with each of you. Got it?"

We nodded and she kissed us each on the cheek. She

stepped back into the shuttle along with a few other people.

"You stay safe while we're gone, okay?" I said.

"Call my folks if you need anything," Kieran added.

"As if someone could mess with me." Lenna flexed her scrawny arm. "I'll be alright."

We all had one last laugh as the shuttle door slid closed. Lenna waved and blew us kisses through the window. After a few moments it pulled away, and all that separated us from a couple hundred-foot fall to the city below was a few steps.

"Have my baby!" Kieran called toward the shuttle.

"Watch it." I bumped him with my elbow. "We're pretty close to the edge."

"Someone had to lighten the mood. I hate when everything's so serious."

"No kidding."

"Once the tests start it's every man for himself. Nothing's personal, right?" Kieran asked as he held out a hand.

"Right." I bumped his fist. "Just like a fight—it's just business."

We headed up the steps in front of us toward an open area where everyone was gathering. There were a couple of people that stood out to me as we moved into the crowd.

The first to catch my attention was a clear group of friends, and each of them looked confident that they'd be the next Interceptor. They stood out partly because they were the one group of people talking amongst one another, but also because they all looked—*interesting*.

The group was made up of a guy that was built like one of those huge Brute Conks, a tall girl with a horse face, a short guy with long swept-back hair, and a guy in a wheelchair.

I pointed a thumb toward the group. "Does someone

like that even have a real shot at becoming an Interceptor?"

"The dude in the wheelchair? Yeah, he's probably got some kind of augment in his legs."

"I've never heard about those." My mind snapped right to Lenna. "How much does something like that cost?"

"You don't wanna know. Let's just say it's a lot—even for me and my family. Why do you think I've never mentioned augments? That guy must be pretty loaded."

"Could something like that work on Lenna?"

"I think so," Kieran scratched his chin. "But I think it would be even more expensive than whatever that guy has. Y'know, cuz of the whole missing limb thing."

I could feel my face grow hot. I wished I could have given Lenna the life she deserved. She always insisted that she was going to be the one to support me until I became a *boxing superstar*. She'd come to terms with living a one-armed life, but maybe things could be easier if I could give her something similar to what that guy had.

"If I make it, it's something we could look into, but let's forget about it for now. We need—"

BEEP!

"Looks like we're jumping into things quick." I looked up and saw the entire team of Interceptors standing on the roof of the nearest building.

Ayla, the AI of the original Interceptor, warped above the crowd. "Welcome to everyone who's registered for a chance to not only become the newest member of the Interceptors but also—*my new partner*. So excited to see who it'll be."

The comment about her new partner sent the crowd into a frenzy.

Even I had an in-depth knowledge of who Ayla was. She was one of the most sophisticated AI programs ever created. She had been Chase's partner from day one, and it hadn't occurred to me that whoever joined the team would be receiving her as their new partner. It would be the first time an AI would ever switch owners, and that had to be a big deal.

"Yeah, I'm gonna need everyone to shut up so I can finish up the rest of this speech," Ayla said with a bolt of feedback to quiet everyone. "Thank you. I will now initiate an ID scan to ensure everyone in attendance is registered."

A green light moved from our feet to our heads before disappearing. There was some high-tech equipment throughout the city, but that was on a whole other level. There wasn't anything that I knew of that could ID people without any kind of prior data or DNA.

Bright red lights shot out from the walls of the surrounding buildings and landed on various people in the crowd. Ayla's voice distorted into something more demonic. "All of those with a red light are not registered. Vacate the premises now or face the consequences."

I didn't know what the consequences were, but I was happy that whatever Cleo did to add me to that list had worked.

Most people with the red lights made their way out of the crowd to a line of armed guards. Kieran and all the *interesting* people I had noticed before were fine, but someone right next to us had a red light overhead. He didn't budge an inch for whatever reason.

"I dunno what they'll do to you, but I'm gonna assume you're gonna wanna move, dude," Kieran whispered without looking at the guy next to us.

"I will countdown from five. Those of you who won't leave will be dealt with swiftly." Ayla's form morphed into the number five.

The guy beside me still didn't budge, and he was the only one left with a red light. No one said a word, but every eye was locked on him. Sweat started pouring down the guy's face, probably due to a sense of shame and fear. I had a feeling he was wondering the same thing I was about a good toss back down to the city.

"Five. Four—"

The guy darted out of the crowd.

Ayla changed back to her normal appearance and her voice flipped back to normal. "Thank you! There are currently two-hundred and sixty-four of you, and we need to whittle that number down to one-hundred for basic training."

I looked around at some of the more massive attendees. "I'm not liking our odds."

Kieran bumped me. "Shh."

"Your first task is simple," Ayla held her hands out, and a button appeared in front of her. "Do whatever it takes to hit one of the one-hundred buttons on the opposite side of the facility—but be careful, that pesky team of mine wanted to have some fun too."

The crowd piped up back into a murmur.

"We're going to have to fight everyone?" I asked.

"Looks like it's not every man for himself yet. Let's snag some buttons." He held out a fist again, and I bumped it.

"You will all now have ten seconds to make any preparations for yourselves. *Good luck,*" Ayla said in a sing-song fashion before shrinking and floating over to the Interceptors.

Chimes started as the seconds passed. I looked over to the group from before who were psyching themselves up. The guy in the wheelchair tapped a button, and the metal of the chair wrapped around the lower half of his body. He stood up and started to stretch.

"That was so cool," I whispered.

Five chimes left.

"You ready to do this?" Kieran asked.

"If I said *no*, would it change anything?"

"Nope."

The last chime went off, but before anyone could move a muscle, everything changed.

The concrete floor and buildings around us morphed into a rocky forest, and different obstacles were constructed along with them. Everyone was still for a second as they stared at their new surroundings. A dozen camera drones hovered around in the sky capturing everyones reaction.

Kieran gawked at our exciting new surroundings, "Holy shi—"

Chapter 5:
Just Snag A Button

"C'mon." I grabbed Kieran's arm and pulled him forward through the crowd of dumbfounded people.

A couple of others used the chance to dash forward as well. It was a good idea to be at the front of the group, but the back was just as advantageous. Anyone who hung back would have the advantage of learning the best way to move through each obstacle.

Kieran and I were always going to be the guys to try to dive in headfirst without thinking, but he was a bit distracted with trying to live out his dream.

In just a few seconds, we had made it to the front of the pack. I looked back to where the Interceptors had all been standing, but they had dispersed. We didn't need to be first, we needed to be in the top one hundred. I gave Kieran a light tug back so we could see how these guys were going to tackle the obstacles.

"Good call." We slowed to a jog as we approached a mountainous hill.

As we made it to the base of the hill, the air became thinner. It was like there was some kind of invisible line in the ground and as we passed it, all the air tried to escape our bodies. Somehow the obstacle was simulating some kind of high-elevation oxygen levels. The scene was almost beautiful if it wasn't for the foreboding hill ahead of us.

The craggy hill had portions covered in running water, portions covered in a slimy substance, and portions that were dry—dry enough that someone could easily run up.

That's exactly what one man did until a boulder came rolling right at him from over the hill. He jumped out of the way in time, but the steep hill caused him to roll most of the way back down. Kiyoshi stepped onto the top of the hill with his war hammer crackling with electricity.

"So did we pick the wrong path or what?" I asked.

"Don't blame *me*—" Kieran said. "*You're* the one who picked the path with the big rock hill."

"It's not like we could see the other path, and I was talking about—" A bolt of lightning whizzed by my head. "Kiyoshi."

People had caught up, and many of them were heading up the hill at the same time. If we didn't decide what to do, we'd be eliminated before we managed to earn a real shot.

Kieran pulled me toward a section of the rock that had water running down it. The entire section was wet and slimy.

"It'll take longer," He pointed to a section of wall that was raised up to cut off Kiyoshi's view. "But we have more coverage."

As we moved closer, I studied the water and watched how it ran right off the top of the hill in one steady stream. There wasn't a single break anywhere. I stopped Kieran. "Wait."

"What? What's wrong?"

"Look at the source of the water, I bet he's got pools up on either side of him that he can use his electricity to send a current through. We need to go head-on."

Ayla warped right behind us. "Good call." It scared the hell out of us, but she giggled and disappeared again.

"What the hell was that?" I asked.

Kieran shrugged. "It is a good call. How didn't I think of that?"

"Who cares? Let's go."

We shot up the middle of the hill with a few other people. Kiyoshi kept up the boulders that forced people back down the hill. I looked to the top of the hill as that punk girl from the shuttle made it over. It was clear that she would be a good ally to have.

Toward the bottom of the hill, people had formed a line to make their way up the water-covered section that was free of boulders. The line had managed to reach the top of the hill.

Kiyoshi teleported to the section where the water was coming from and bashed his hammer into it. The crackling electricity flowed from the top of the water to the bottom, frying anyone dumb enough to make their way through what they thought was safety. Every single person in the wet section fell to the bottom of the hill.

"Did he kill all those people?" I asked as I gasped for more of the thin air.

Kieran grabbed the back of my shirt and tugged me over to him as a boulder rolled right by. I hadn't paid attention as it barrelled right for me. We looked up the hill and Kiyoshi stared down right back at us.

"Thanks." I watched as the boulder continued down the hill, taking a few people with it.

"Look at his hammer—" Kieran pointed at Kiyoshi. "His blue electricity stuns, the white electricity is the kind you want to avoid."

We continued our rush up the hill, and right before we reached the top, Kiyoshi stepped in front of us with the fat end of his hammer pointed at our faces. He was so close that he could have stomped the hand I brought down onto the top edge of the hill.

Ayla warped right next to us as if she had crawled up the hill with us and wagged a finger at Kiyoshi. "*Nah-uh-uh*, 'Yoshi. You know the rules—they're in the top section, so they're safe."

He looked down his war hammer at us before walking away, probably to send more boulders at the unwitting people behind us.

"Thanks—" I turned to Ayla, but she was already gone again.

"I can't tell—" Kieran pulled me to my feet at the top of the hill. "If she's creepy or not."

"I'm kinda getting creepy vibes."

"Okay, so it's not just me then."

We moved past the hill and took a look at what we had the pleasure of tackling next.

The next obstacle was a smoke-filled field full of Conks. We had a vantage point to look across the field and make a game plan before jumping into the thick of it. That group of friends from before had already made it most of the way through the field of Conks.

About forty people were ahead of us, so there wasn't any time to waste.

"Well, out of the two of us—you're the one with a Conk takedown so what do you think?" Kieran asked with a pat on my back.

"Me? You're supposed to be the expert in all things Interceptor."

"I am. Conks aren't Interceptors."

"That's a lame technicality and you know it."

I looked across the field at all the chaos. There were a ton of different kinds of Conks, but in one small section, there was a group of the two kinds I had already dealt with. I figured my best bet was with what I knew. Something about them felt different from how I remembered them, but I chalked it up to them being some kind of training models for the team.

Thankfully, the air had returned to normal as we entered the area of the second obstacle. We were capable of a multiple-round fight, but neither of us was able to train at any kind of high altitude. I figured Kieran was as worn out as I was, and we'd only made it through one obstacle.

I started down toward the field and Kieran followed right on my heels. "Hey—whoa, whoa, whoa—plan? Do you even have a plan?" he asked through laboured breaths.

"We're gonna run, and dodge." I huffed. "I don't know what else you're expecting."

"That is a bad plan. A bad—bad plan."

"Beats just standing there staring at everything."

"Dang it—you're right.

We entered the field of Conks at a reckless speed. We dodged slashes from a few Conks with swords and slid under jets of fire being shot at us by the elemental Conks. The reaction speed of these robots was different from the ones I had dealt with. They were sluggish, and it was like their dials had been changed from eleven to a solid two and a half.

That punk girl came barreling toward us faster than I would have thought possible. She may have made it up the hill faster than us, but the thin air must have taken all her energy if we had managed to get ahead of her. I couldn't blame anyone for needing a good breather after dealing with Kiyoshi.

A jet of fire launched toward the girl just out of her field of view. If I didn't do anything, she was going to get torched pretty bad. I rushed forward and tackled her to the ground, sending the air out of the both of us. The fire passed right over us.

"Rhys!" I heard Kieran call.

The light of the flames danced across the girl's face.

Something was different about this fire, though.

"Ugh. It's not real," The girl said with a deep breath.

"What do you mean, it's not—"

"None of this is real. It's hot, but there's no real heat from the fire—no whoosh of the swords. Can't you tell?"

She was right. Something was different, and that was exactly it. There was no heat coming from their flames at all. If there was, my back would have been burned pretty bad.

"Amateur." She pushed me off of her and scrambled back to her feet. She disappeared through the field of smoke and Conks in no time.

I looked over at Kieran as he dodged a few swings from a Conk's cyber-sword

"It's not real."

"What?"

"Trust me."

"You sure about this?"

"God, you ask a lot of questions." I sprinted right through one of the Conk's flames to demonstrate what I meant. "Don't worry about dodging unless you swear it's real."

We made our way straight through the field of Conks and caught up to that girl. As she said, they were all convincing holograms to freak everyone out and slow us down. A field of holograms felt like a bit of a weak obstacle, but it had fooled everyone else so far. The smoke must have made a serious difference in the charade working.

I wondered what had been going on over on the other side, and what kind of hell the other Interceptors were putting those people through. For all I knew, Mickey was terrifying people in a field of shadows or Cleo was dashing around in a make-shift skating rink.

"Remind me to thank that girl," Kieran said as he rushed through holographic sword swings.

"Let's grab those buttons first, then you can thank her all you want."

We were lucky we'd made our way to the flame-wielding Conks since the flames covered our sprint. I had a feeling that's the reason that girl had chosen to run down the same side. We'd managed to catch up near the front of the pack at the third obstacle.

It looked simpler than the two before, but it was going to be the hardest one yet.

We could see the wall of buttons, but guarding them was two Interceptors, Diggs and Pegs as they fought with multiple people. Down guarding the other side were Lili and Mickey. People rushed forward and were tossed back just as quickly. Somehow some people had managed to slip by.

I thought we were doing really well, but about thirty buttons were all that remained. Making things worse, the people were piling in behind us, and on the other side of the trial field in a hurry. People were going to start trickling through by luck due to the sheer number of people rushing the team members.

"So which side do you think is worse now?" I asked. "Because it's looking like I picked us hard-mode compared to the other side."

Someone rushed right between the two of us and was blocked by the pair of Interceptors. Diggs launched his whip upward, and Kieran shoved a hand over my eyes before I was blinded. He moved his hand as the flash died down, but the guy that had run ahead was clutching his eyes.

Pegs gave her sword a graceful toss. It circled him as it caught fire, creating a fire vortex that sent the man backward across the course.

"Hard-mode. That's one way to put it," Kieran said.

We both pushed forward as a group of other people rushed the duo. Pegs rolled her sword along the ground creating a great wall of fire, causing a girl toward the end of the line to fall to the ground. Everyone kept rushing forward, but I darted across the line to see if she was alright. Diggs started launching his whip to keep people back, but he hit Pegs' sword and sent it straight at the girl who had fallen backward.

"Aw, crap." I heard Diggs say.

I made it to her and launched an uppercut on the flat side of the sword. The fire it had been engulfed in was real, and my hand stung from the flames and hot metal. I clutched my hand, as I leaned down to the girl.

"Nice save, dude!" Diggs called as he battled.

I took a look over to the buttons and saw that Kieran had managed to make it past the duo in all the confusion. There were a couple open buttons left, and he had one open right beside him. I saw him mouth the words, *I'm sorry*. I felt a bit betrayed that he went on without me, but I couldn't be too mad—I had a tendency to wander off.

I reached a hand out to the girl, but it went right through her. I fell backward in surprise. A little camera had flown down and was aimed at the two of us.

She turned to look at me, and once again it was Ayla.

"*You just won a freebie!*" She sang.

"A what?"

"A freebie!"

"You have way too much energy for me."

"Oh, shut it. I've been involved in this round all over the place. You've been the only person to stop and help me on either side, so you can walk to a button."

"I can walk to a button? No hassle?"

I didn't know what to expect from the whole process, but I would have never thought it would be anything like that.

She got to her feet and pretended to dust herself off.

"Yep."

"Well, that's not—"

"That's not what?"

"I dunno. That's not very *super*?"

She gave me a dull look. "Take it or not, but there are two buttons left if you want a spot in basic training. I'd take it."

I turned to look at the free button beside Kieran. "That ain't gonna happen." My gaze shifted to Pegs and Diggs. "Me against two Interceptors—I wouldn't be me if I didn't do everything the hard way."

I looked back to Ayla, but she was already gone again. I could see people making their way through the field of Conks. If I was going to make it to a button, it had to be in the next few moments.

I had one way to slip by the two of them, but I'd have to move right in between them to do it. My one saving grace was that Pegs didn't have her sword anymore, but that wouldn't stop her from getting up close and personal, or using more of her fire.

I baited a swing from Diggs' cyber whip and juked the other way to slip in between them. Pegs blocked my way forward with a stream of fire and squared up to me.

"Bring it, fire-boy."

"Uh—that was my *home* that was on fire."

"Whoops." She threw a jab at me. I dodged it along with a few more swings. "What? Are you afraid to hit a girl? That's sexist—"

I took a wide swing to catch a part of her face that was covered in her kit, and she staggered back. "Not afraid to hit a girl—just waiting for an opening."

The people at the buttons all *oohed* after the heavy hit. I shook my hand as it radiated with pain. Her flames had done a number on my fist, and punching the nano-tech armour didn't do me any favours.

She turned back toward me with narrowed eyes.

"Alright, tough guy—"

The rustling of Digg's whip came from behind me, and I dropped to the floor. His whip shot past me and wrapped around Pegs' wrists.

She shook her wrists. "Diggs!"

"Crap. Sorry, Pegs. Kid's good."

"Thanks!" I shouted as I scrambled to my feet.

As I stood back up, I looked to the far end of the course and saw Lili watching me with wide eyes and a happy smile.

I rushed toward the open button, but someone was doing the same. I gave it everything I had to sprint toward the button. I ran into the wall, but I made it to the open button beside Kieran, and I slammed my hand down onto it.

I placed my back along the wall and slid down as I tried to catch my breath for the first time in what felt like forever. I looked over to Kieran, and he flashed me a big thumbs up with a cheesy grin.

My eyes fell onto the facility once more, and all the Interceptors had made their way back to the roof. I wasn't sure exactly why, but it looked like they were all staring right at me. A siren signalled the end of the round as all the buttons had been claimed.

"Congratulations to the one-hundred candidates that have made it to basic training," Ayla said as a group of those small cameras flew over and panned amongst all of us. "Say hello to your adoring public."

A huge visor-like display popped up on a wall across from us. It showed a huge crowd of people watching us on screens in the city down below. They cheered as the feed cut amongst each of us. I laughed when it cut to Kieran and me. The both of us were gassed, but that didn't stop Kieran from striking his best heroic pose.

I hoped Lenna was able to watch a feed of the tryout from the shuttle. I knew she'd be proud of both of us.

Somehow we both managed to make it into basic training.

We were one step closer to becoming an Interceptor.

Chapter 6:
A Not-So-Warm Welcome

Without a moment to breathe, we were rounded up and led into the facility by a group of facility workers. I was surprised that some of the most athletic-looking people from the first round weren't moving on.

A sudden feeling washed over me that what we had gone through was only going to be the easiest of all the tasks we'd have to push through.

Kieran hadn't said a word to me until we reached the entryway to the building. "Sorry 'bout ditching you like that."

It had bothered me that he had decided to grab a button while he had a chance. I couldn't be too mad, though. I would have done the same thing if I didn't think someone had been hurt.

"We did say every man for himself." I shook my head. "It's all good."

He gave me a look that told me he didn't believe me, but with how fast everything was moving, there wasn't time for either of us to dwell on it. We had to focus on the barrage of things that could be coming next.

The facility was one of the most high-tech buildings I'd seen in my entire life. Huge pillars created a walkway to a foyer where everyone bunched up. The pillars had waves of what looked like words flowing up and down them, but they were moving so fast that I couldn't read them.

"You ever seen anything like this before?" I asked.

"Not outside of the feeds."

We surrounded an ornate fountain that had a statue of Chase in the middle. On the steps behind it stood the team of Interceptors with Ayla as they surveyed the crowd. Further behind them were four separate enormous doorways. Cleo was standing next to Lili when the duo spotted me. Each of them gave me a cheerful two-finger salute.

Above them all was a balcony, where a lone seemingly battle-ready woman stood. Everyone became quiet when thunderous steps came from that direction. It was the last remaining original Interceptor, General Odon.

I remembered he'd retired from in-field action early in his career so that he could start a family. During the rare severe threat, he'd step in to assist the current team, but that had only happened a handful of times before. It was pretty rare for things to get *that* bad.

He looked down across the sea of hopefuls. "So, all of you believe you have what it takes to become the next Interceptor—to live up to Chase's legacy," he sneered down at us. "I don't see it—but you'll have a month to prove me otherwise. You may all think this is some kind of game for a chance at your childhood dreams, but this is far more than that. The world is entering a dire state, as we have reason to believe that Zeal is currently working on a new strand of the Extinction Virus. Work hard—stop Zeal."

The mention of the Extinction Virus sent everyone into a frenzy. There had been news coverage and murmurs about what Zeal may be planning, but no one really believed the news. Who would when they stretch the truth so much? Nobody knew the stakes were really that high.

When I looked back up to Odon, he'd already disappeared as quickly as he had come.

"Well, that was cheery," I said, causing the people around me to chuckle. "Who's the—"

"She's Odon's right-hand man—woman—Ramona —she's a total badass. Pretty sure she's in charge of everyone in the facility that doesn't have a kit or AI," Kieran said as if he had read my mind.

Ramona gave the crowd a final look before she followed General Odon.

Ayla floated over to the fountain. In an instant, she grew to the same size as Chase's statue. "Like Odon said, basic training starts tomorrow. Every one of you will be taught and judged by the very team that you hope to join. How well you do in their training sessions will affect your ranking. At the end of the month, only the top ten candidates will be moving on to the final round of cuts."

I looked at Kieran who had a surprised look on his face. The first cut was already massive, but it had more to do with being able to improvise on the fly. The next cut was going to come down to nothing but skill and determination.

"You're all one step closer to becoming a hero like Chase." Ayla looked at the statue of her old partner with a solemn expression. "When we data-scanned you, we gave you one of four symbols. Check the visor above each doorway to find which group you're in. Those are the people you will spend the rest of the month learning alongside. Go get some rest."

"What if we end up against each other?" I asked.

"Being put in a different group doesn't mean we're against each other, right?" Kieran responded, but I had no answer. He looked at the people around us. "Right?" They all shrugged and looked amongst one another.

We headed over to the screens to take a look at where we'd ended up. Some people had already figured out which group they were in and had headed through their doors. The guy in the wheelchair from earlier had spotted where he and his friends each belonged, but they'd each been split into separate groups.

The four separate groups were marked with symbols of the four elements. Swaths of flames, gusts of wind, a drop of rain, and a solid rock.

Fire? No.

Water? Nope.

We checked earth, but neither of our names showed up. "Aw, man. I thought it woulda been cool to be in the group that matched up with Chase's element." Kieran's shoulders slumped.

"At least we're together, besides wind's pretty cool," I said as I cocked my head to spot our names.

"You're just saying that because that's Lili's element, and you think she's hot."

"Heya, Rhys," Lili said with a laugh from right behind us. "Looks like you and your buddy ended up in the wind group."

What a time for her to show up.

I whirled around as my face turned the brightest possible shade of red. "Hey, Lili. I—"

"Yeah, I was wondering," Kieran cut in. "Does that mean anything?"

"You'll see." She turned her attention back to me. "Nice moves against Diggs and Pegs. Most people lucked out and ran past them while they focused on other people." She finished with her gaze on Kieran.

He let out an awkward laugh. "Well, you know, we try to be—"

"Thanks." I pushed Kieren back. "Am I allowed to ask for any pointers? Did anyone stand out to you guys?"

She brought a finger to her chin. "Hmm." She thought for a long time before speaking again. "Nope. Ayla probably would have mentioned if someone stood out to her."

"Crap," Kieran and I said at the same time.

Lili walked off, but what she said lingered in my mind. Ayla had warped to me multiple times during that first round.

Did that not mean anything?

Had Ayla not mentioned anything to anyone?

Was Lili just trying to get inside my head?

Smoke could have started wafting out of my ears with how hard my brain was working to figure anything out.

"Training with Lili sounds fun." Kieran nudged me.

I rolled my eyes and we took another glance up at the wind visor. Our names were one on top of the other. We headed through our door and followed a long white hallway until we reached another door. We opened it and found our barracks for the month.

"Homey—in a boring, OCD kinda way," I said as we walked in.

The other twenty-three members of our group were already inside. Rows of beds lined each wall, with one at the end of the room. Above every bed was a digital plaque that had a name and a picture of the person who could claim the bed.

There were small chests at the foot of each bed that the other people had already explored. They were filled with different coloured training outfits for the month.

"Well, hello to you all, too," Kieran said with a wave.

No one had said anything or even looked at us since we walked in. We made our way down to the two open beds in the room, the one lone bed and a corner bed. Kieran had been assigned the lone bed at the end of the room, while I was stuck in the corner next to him.

He plopped down onto the bed and pushed on the fabric. "Not exactly the life of luxury."

I pushed on the bed and had a moment I'd had many times with Kieran. A moment where I don't understand what he's talking about at all. The bed was comfier than anything I'd ever slept on—unless I was staying at Kieran's house.

Sometimes the Sellea City divisions didn't mean much, but it was always the weird little things that showed how different people were able to live.

A sudden push on my back sent me forward, but I caught myself on the bed. "Oh, this is happening now."

"What the hell?" Kieran leaped from his bed.

I whirled around and wound up in the face of the huge brute from that group of friends I kept noticing. "I'm gonna give you one chance to apologize before—"

"People are saying that Ayla appeared for you during that first round," The brute said as all eyes fell on the two of us.

"So what?"

"She warped in front of the two of us *multiple* times," Kieran said as he stepped beside me.

The brute didn't take his eyes off of me. "What's so special about you two? As far as my buds could tell, you two are the only ones that made it through that had help from Ayla."

"She didn't help us. She just kept scaring the crap out of us," I said.

"Yeah, Rhys tried to help *her* before he even knew it was Ayla." Kieran grinned.

"All I'm gonna say is you've made yourselves targets. I don't know if we're going to end up going group against group, or if we're all supposed to bond or some rah-rah friendship crap like that, but the two of you— are on your own."

He turned around, but I grabbed the back of his shirt and tugged him back around. "I don't care if it's the two of us against you, or two of us against a hundred other people, We're getting to the next round—" The monster of a man looked down his nose at me, but the others in the room looked impressed. "And if you push me again, you're gonna have a rough headache just in time for the first day of training."

A chime sounded and Ayla's voice filled the room. "Attention candidates, the cafeteria is now open. Follow the green lights for a bite to eat—but be warned, you're always being watched—even when you don't think you are, so watch the attitude you two." A chime sounded again, and all was quiet.

You two?

Was she talking about us?

Little cameras rotated out from the wall. It was clear that we were going to start getting the Interceptor treatment early. It was a good idea. I'd rather become accustomed to the cameras sooner rather than later.

"You're lucky I don't feel like embarrassing you in front of the whole world," The brute said before heading out of the room with most of the other people.

"Not that I don't think the *both* of us could take that guy, but do you really think you could take him *alone*?" Kieran asked.

Probably not.

I shrugged. "Probably."

The only other person left in the room, a cute blonde girl made her way over. "Hey, don't worry about Raysean. Anyone who needs to put up a macho act like that probably isn't the most secure guy around." She held a hand out to me. "Phoebe."

As I reached out Kieran bumped me out of the way and shook her hand. "Kieran."

I cleared my throat, and Kieran backed off with an awkward laugh. "Rhys." I shook her hand. "Nice to meet you, Phoebe. You got to know that guy?"

"Oh, god no. I overheard him and his friends. Aside from your—*eager* friend, I'd rather associate with people that don't radiate the fact that they're an asshole. I went around the other side of the course, but I watched what you did with Ayla, and I saw what happened the other day with the fire on the news. I hope your sister's okay."

I looked into her dark brown eyes and felt a kind of comfort from her. She was far prettier than most of the women from my section of the city, but something about Phoebe felt familiar—like an old friend.

"She's as sassy as ever, thanks for asking. How about we go find some grub, and you two can try to help fill me in on everything I should already know about the Interceptors," I said as I headed to the door.

"Again?" Kieran asked. "Wasn't the shuttle ride enough?"

"Yeah, but I didn't think I'd make it through the first round. I figured I was there for emotional support for you. I clearly don't know enough about what's going on here."

"Wait, what do you mean? Have you not always wanted to become an Interceptor? That's pretty much everyone's dream," Phoebe said.

I walked out into the hall. "It's not that I don't want to, it's more—"

"It wasn't in his cards." Kieran cut in.

"Basically."

"A money thing?" I nodded, but I must have made a face because Phoebe piped back up. "Don't feel weird about it. It took me forever to scrape the money together for the application."

We started following a glowing green stream of data to the cafeteria. Walking the halls of the facility felt like being in the middle of one of those old sci-fi holos Kieran liked to watch. There was something menacing about the halls, but the looks on Phoebe and Kieran's faces told me that they thought the complete opposite.

"Should we even bother trying to set things right with Raysean?" Kieran asked.

"Probably not." Phoebe shrugged. "One month stuck together shouldn't be too bad."

"I guess you're right. The three of us can stick together and make it to the finals."

"I'm already included in the finals with you guys? Love it."

"What do you mean?" I asked.

"I was terrified I wasn't going to make any friends here," Phoebe said as we rounded a corner and passed by a few facility workers.

I nodded to the workers as they went by. "In the slums, everyone's family—until they stab you in the back. That's how I live my life—minus the backstabbing thing."

"How—quaint."

"It's not as bad as it sounds," Kieran said as we walked through a set of giant doors that opened to reveal the bustling cafeteria.

The huge room was packed with all the new potential recruits and various facility staff. People seemed to have grouped up into small pods of recruits they thought they could trust.

I watched a group of people snag an empty table, and wave a hand to bring up a huge menu of food. They each selected what they wanted, and in a matter of seconds, a tiny pill dropped in front of each of them. The pills broke open and slowly changed from a sandy material to the food they had selected.

I looked at Kieran. "You guys don't have anything like that at your place."

"More crazy expensive tech. My parents have been thinking of splurging for something like that."

"I hope the food doesn't taste like sand," Phoebe said as she headed toward an open table.

We joined her at the table and selected our own dinners. I couldn't remember the last time I had such an incredible selection. I selected a meal made up of fresh veggies and a fish that I'd never heard of before. The same pills I'd seen at the other table dropped down in front of each of us, and our meals pieced together before our eyes.

Phoebe took a bite of her chicken. "Hmm. Definitely not sand."

After that confirmation, Kieran and I both dug into our meals. It was refreshing to have something so filled with flavour after eating the bland vitamin-filled gunk I was used to.

"So—either of you guys spot anyone you think has a shot at making it?" Phoebe asked as she peered around.

"Yeah. There's one big guy that looks like he coulda come fresh out of the academy like the two of us. He musta been on your side, Phoebe. I watched him make it through Micky and Lili—it was pretty badass. He's probably got a pretty good shot." Kieran flicked his eyes toward another table. "Check it out, he's next to that chick that kept staring at you."

I turned around and looked at the table Kieran was talking about. The guy oozed charisma, and it wasn't surprising to see that his table was the most populated.

"I think that girl's going to do well too. She was able to tell one of the obstacles was a complete fake. I dunno why, but she's really familiar for some reason," I said as I turned back. "What about you?"

"Something tells me Raysean is gonna do pretty well." Phoebe stared off toward his massive frame. "That guy's a monster. We're going to have to work hard to stand out against him—"

"What a bunch of losers," The guy in the wheelchair said as he passed by with the horse-faced girl. "You guys should be afraid of all four of us, not just Raysean. He's part of our group, and the four of us are going to win the whole thing."

"We're the losers? You're over here talking like a bully from one of those old holo-vids. You're lucky you can even participate in this, sit-and-spin." Kieran fired back.

They shot us a dirty look before heading over to join Raysean and the short guy with the swept-back hair at their table.

I narrowed my eyes at Kieran. "Do you think—"

"I know. I know. That comment woulda got me slugged by Lenna." He stuck out his shoulder. "Let me have it."

I cocked my fist back and gave him a solid shot in the arm. "I feel like we're back at the academy already."

"They do realize that only one of them can win, right?"

"People with egos like theirs forget about things like that. Let's finish up so we can go get some sleep," Phoebe said as she took another bite of her chicken.

"Good idea. I have a feeling they're gonna throw everything at us—even on the first day," I said as I popped a piece of broccoli in my mouth.

"It better not be one of those crack of dawn type deals. I'm not a morning person," Kieran groaned.

One by one all the tables cleared and the facility fell quiet. The next day was going to be the start of the rest of our lives.

Chapter 7:

Day One Is Always The Worst One

Chaotic jazz music jolted all of us from our sleep at what I assumed was the ass-crack of dawn. Since there weren't any windows, we had no idea what time it was when the near-blinding lights flicked on. Lili had arrived to kick our butts into gear for the day, and that meant getting in a nice crisp twenty-kilometre run. We ran around the facility enough times to learn the layout from the outside.

It wasn't any leisurely jog either.

It was a *real* run.

By the time we'd made it halfway through the never-ending torture, my legs felt like they were ready to give up on me and crawl back in bed on their own—the traitors. I'd been able to go the distance in a couple of tough twelve-round fights, but at least those fights included a tiny breather between rounds.

I looked up at one of the many little cameras that followed our group around and rolled my eyes. I couldn't take a break without seeming like a chump to the whole world.

A couple of people slowed into a walk momentarily. "This is your only warning—" Lili called. "Anyone who walks will be sitting out during training. Keep that in mind for each morning."

Every single walker shifted back into a run.

As we all made it back around to the front of the facility, the ground started to shake.

"What's going on?" Kieran asked.

"I dunno. Do floating facilities have earthquakes?" I asked through laboured breaths. "Air-quakes?"

The ground split open in front of us, but Lili kept right on running. She hopped over the newly-formed fissure as the ground around the facility continued falling away. The gaps inched wider as we continued our run.

I thought things were already bad enough. What an idiot I was. The running had nothing on the leaps we had to make across the chasms.

We'd look back whenever we had a bit of a stretch to run. Each time, we'd catch the odd person falling into a hole or climbing their way back out of one. No one was having fun. No one, except Lili.

I made a leap to another section, but as my foot touched down on the edge, the ground crumbled away. I caught the edge and pulled myself up to my back.

"*Oh*, this really freakin' sucks," I muttered to myself.

"Remember, no stopping!" Lili called as I made it back to my feet.

When she finally came to a halt, we all collapsed behind her. No one was going to bother trying to look tough, the world had to know that the run was a nightmare. Phoebe and Raysean were the last ones to catch up, and it looked like they were each ready to pass out. As soon as I saw their ghostly skin, I knew to steer clear of that area if I wanted to avoid the splash-zone.

Lili opened her visor and pushed a button. The ground shook again, but all the holes filled back up. The facility looked as if nothing catastrophic had ever happened.

Lili looked down at all of us. "Good job, everyone. Don't worry, it'll start getting easier from here."

"So you mean this was some kind of extra hard test

to see how fit we all were?" One guy asked as he tried to catch his breath.

"No. It'll get easier because now you know what to expect. I personally think that pitfalls are one of the easier obstacles for our runs—and I have a new one for each morning."

"Each morning?" Phoebe asked as she laid on her back. "Like—we're going to do this every single day?"

"You guys could at least *try* to sound a little excited." Lili nodded with a devilish grin. "Maybe we'll do ice patches tomorrow. Everyone up. We need to head to our first taste of endurance training. Lots to get through today."

Everyone groaned as we peeled ourselves from the ground. We trudged behind Lili toward the doors to the facility, but as we reached them, a group led by Cleo headed outside.

The punk girl I kept noticing locked her eyes on Kieran and I. "What happened to your group?"

I looked over to Cleo as she brought a finger to her lips and then turned back. "You guys don't wanna know."

"Good luck." Kieran snickered as he threw and arm around me. "Those bright-eyed suckers have no idea how much worse their day is about to get."

Lili led our group through the winding corridors of the facility until we came to one of the biggest rooms I'd ever seen. It was the kind of room I figured the military would store all their biggest planes in. The room was an eerie sight as rather than planes, it was completely empty.

"Your daily endurance circuits consist of doing as many push-ups as humanly possible in one sitting," Lili began. "Then squats—and then holding planks for as long as you can—then…"

I nudged Kieran, "Why do I get the feeling that all of this is just more *warming up*?"

Lili cleared her throat to catch my attention. "That would be because there are about fifty other exercises to work through after your body is warmed up."

"Great."

I wouldn't ever think anyone would consider me a whiner when it came to exercise. Quite the opposite. If most people knew how often I was in the gym with Kieran, they'd probably think we were crazy. The issue was, boxing had nothing on Interceptor training

"Isn't it?" She swiped her hand a small screen appeared beside her. After the push of a button, the room constructed all kinds of workout equipment with nothing but a few rays of light. "Get to it."

After a bit of work, I figured that there wasn't a single person who had any idea how long we'd been exercising for. Anyone who wasn't at the peak of fitness had to be aching all over again.

"Dude," Kieran tapped me. "Look."

I turned and stared at Raysean as he hammered through his exercises. He'd thrown on an optional weighted-vest—probably just to show off.

"How heavy are those weight vests?" I asked.

"Pretty sure the one he's wearing is like an extra forty pounds."

"Yikes."

After the second round of torture was over, Lili had us hold sets of weights over our heads for as long as possible. It felt like some kind of sick game, but I was surprised how long everyone lasted after everything our bodies had been through.

I looked over to a shaky Phoebe. "How you doing, noodle-arms?"

Raysean laughed, "I coulda said the same thing to you, pipsqueak."

A camera whizzed over and positioned itself in such a way that must have had the three of us in frame.

"Pipsqueak? Who the hell actually calls someone a pipsqueak?" I asked.

"Will you two shut up?" Phoebe took a deep breath. "I'm trying to concentrate."

Kieran was one of the first ones out for the test, which surprised me. When I looked over to Raysean, he looked as solid as a mountain. There was no way I'd outlast him. The whole exercise could have lasted five minutes—or five hours. It felt like my arms were ready to fall apart piece by piece.

I managed to hang in there until Lili blew a whistle to stop, along with Raysean and another guy in our group. They both played off the challenge like it was no big deal, but I knew their arms had to be rubber at that point. The only way my arms were getting lifted over my waist again was with the help of an elevator.

Lili opened her visor and glanced at our worn-out group. "Break for as long as you need—within reason—and then feel free to work on whatever you need to."

I'd never been so thankful to just sit and do nothing for a few minutes. Kieran and Phoebe were both slumped beside me and they looked just as relieved as I imagined I probably looked.

Phoebe reached across me and gave Kieran a lazy swat. "What was that back there? I lasted longer than you."

Kieran cracked a grin. "I figured we still had a long day to go—gotta be smart and conserve some energy somehow." He flicked my temple. "Can't all be show-offs like Remarkable Rhys."

I would have whacked him if my arms were willing to cooperate. "Shut it."

He nodded toward a boxing ring deeper in the room. "How's about we get back into our element?"

"I honestly don't know if my arms can take it."

"You two can teach me. I'm not exactly the best fighter around." Phoebe shot up and held a hand out toward me. She nodded toward a nearby camera. "You guys can look super sweet teaching a delicate girl to fight, while also looking like hot, sweaty studs to the whole world."

With a groan, I took her hand.

We put Phoebe through some basic drills to show her the ropes. As tired as we were, we were both happy to help her learn something we loved. Being able to take time to explain things to Phoebe acted as a nice break from action as well, so I couldn't complain too much. Once I was rested enough, Kieran and I started sparring with each other.

I ducked a swing and backed up before looking over toward Raysean. "How much is he benching?" He was firing through reps with weights so heavy that the metal bar was bending.

"That's gotta be well over three-hundred pounds." Kieran leaned against the ropes. "Still wanna brawl?"

I shrugged. "He can be as strong as he wants—I know he couldn't catch me if he tried."

"Yeah, he probably wouldn't even be flexible enough to get a good hold of you."

"Guys—hello?" Phoebe threw a couple of limp punches at the air. "Trying to learn to box better here. Keep going!"

After what had to be another hour or so, Lili blew a whistle. "Drop what you're doing. It's time to pick your weapons."

No one said a word, but Kieran's face was more than enough to show how excited most of the group was.

Chapter 8:
How About A Special Weapon?

Lili led us a few rooms over for our next portion of training. The room was filled with every weapon I could have thought of. We all walked around testing out how each weapon felt in our hands, but none of them felt right to me.

"Make sure you're confident in your weapon choice," Lili said. "Once you pick, that weapon will be attached to you every day for the rest of your training—*if* you make it through the next wave of cuts."

Kieran jumped right for twin hand axes and started to practice right away. Phoebe grabbed a spear and twirled it around like she'd been practicing with one for years. Clearly, Raysean wasn't the only showoff.

I poured over all the weapons, but none of them seemed to click with me. It was rare for me to even hold a weapon, let alone practice with one.

"You know you can just go with your fists," Kieran said as he twirled an axe. "You could log some extra combat practice hours with Lili."

"I know that, but I already know what I'm doing with my fists," I said. "Wouldn't it be better to be able to fall back on that if I ever got disarmed or something? You know—maximize the skills and techniques I have access to?"

"He's got a good point," Phoebe said as she felt the tip of her spear.

I continued to stare at the weapons, and at that point, I was the last person to select one. Lili walked over and looked over the weapons with me.

"Can't decide?" she asked.

"Yeah, I don't know what it is, but none of these feel right." I scratched my head. "Probably sounds kinda weird, huh?"

"Not at all." She gestured to herself. "Look at me, I don't use a weapon."

Lili didn't just not use a weapon, she dominated her foes with her bare hands. A quick look at her would have led anyone to underestimate her. That was just an extra factor as to why she was so dangerous.

"Yeah, I've been meaning to ask, why is it that you chose to go with no weapon?"

Lili looked down at a knife. "My mom was attacked by some psycho with a knife one night on her way home from work." She placed a finger on the hilt of the knife. "I couldn't bring myself to pick something, even though everyone warned me against that. Chase was the only one who believed in my choice and supported me."

I looked down at the knife, and then over to Lili. "That's terrible. I—"

"How about a special weapon?" she asked.

That caught the attention of the rest of the group. Everyone stopped what they were doing, and I felt them all cast their eyes on me. If most people didn't already hate me for everything with Ayla, having them all know I picked a special weapon wasn't going to help.

"What's a special weapon?"

"Chase was a hand-to-hand specialist too, but he wore gauntlets that had been augmented. The more damage his kit took and the lower the power dwindled, the more force he could output through his gauntlets.

When his kit was on the brink of a shutdown, his fists became as dangerous as bazookas."

"That sounds so cool," I said with wide eyes.

"Don't get too excited." She examined her wrists. "The team decided we could repurpose his tech for my kit."

I looked down at my fists. How could someone who had been the greatest hero with a weapon like that end up losing?

"Check this out." Lili waved her hand over the wall and a menu popped up. She swiped a few times before selecting something, and the wall beside me opened up.

There were three different weapons. One was a pair of strange gauntlets that had miniature crossbows attached. The second was a staff that was covered in small holes. The third was a sheathed sword with a name beside it—Trigger.

I wondered what it was that made each of them special, but I had some idea from the look of two of the weapons. I scooped up the plain sword and examined its sheath. As soon as I touched it, the sheathe started to glow different colours.

"Whoa—what's happening?" I asked.

"It's trying to figure out what rank you are," Kieran said from behind me.

"That's right," Lili said. "All special weapons are designed to match the colour of your rank. If you choose one now, it'll glow like that until you become an Interceptor—*if* you become an Interceptor."

I looked around at everyone else. "No one else wants a special weapon?"

"If most people did what I did," Phoebe said. "They'd had a weapon picked out for years."

Lili nodded. "Exactly. Special weapons put you at a disadvantage of not knowing what to expect, but if you haven't specialized in a weapon—"

"What a bunch of nerds," I said to myself.

I looked at Kieran, and he chuckled as he tossed an axe. Suddenly all the time he wanted to spend chopping any rare wood he could find made sense to me.

"I guess I'll go with this funky sword." I attached it to my belt and unsheathed it. The hilt and the blade of the sword continued to glow different colours, which gave the blade a kind of hypnotic appearance. After a small step back, I gave the sword a couple of swings in the air. It was heavy, but it felt like the kind of weight that I could adapt to with enough practice. "What makes it so special?" I finally asked.

Lili walked over and moved my fingers so they rested on a small trigger in the hilt before backing up. "Try putting it back in its sheath, and pulling it out again."

I clicked the trigger a few times and stared at the sword. If nothing else, the trigger would give me something to fidget with when I was bored. I slid it back into its sheath and nothing happened.

"I was hoping it would morph into a cool rifle or something." Kieran scratched his head.

I pulled the sword back out, but it had more than quadrupled in size. The weight brought the blade to the floor, and I stared at the enormous glowing sword. It had morphed from a simple one-handed blade to a huge two-handed greatsword with a pull of the trigger, and an unsheathing of the blade.

"This is cool and all—but how am I—supposed to lift—this thing now?" I asked between grunts.

Anyone who had gone back to doing their own thing had snapped right back to what was going on.

"Give the trigger another pull," Lili said.

I looked from Lili, back to the blade, and pulled the trigger. A wave of light passed through the blade, and suddenly it felt as light as it was before the change. I lifted it with ease and gave it a couple of quick swings. I clicked the trigger again, and the sword dropped back to the floor.

"How do I make it go back to the way it was before?"

"You'll figure it out," Lili said as she walked away.

"Will I?" I stared at the blade before clicking the trigger again and tossing the sword from hand to hand. It was the coolest weapon I'd ever held.

"He's a teacher's pet too." Raysean scowled.

Lili blew her whistle and it was time to get started with weapon training. Everyone in our group spent hours getting used to the weight of their chosen weapons and learning or showing off new attack combinations with them. Surprisingly, Lili was more than helpful when it came to pointers for each person's weapons.

It turned out that the trick to making the sword shrink again was to just force it back into its sheathe—something that was far easier than it sounds. However it worked, when the sword came into contact with the sheathe, it shrunk back to its original size.

Phoebe and Kieran showed off their incredible skills for a while. Kieran looked as impressive with the axes as he did in a boxing ring. He destroyed a dummy with an impressive attack before he turned his attention to Lili. "Quick question."

She walked over. "Shoot."

"Is this it? A bunch of physical training? I kinda thought we'd—"

"Well," She became loud enough that the whole room could hear her. "I would have thought you guys would want to avoid the *worst* part of training for as long as possible, but *Kieran* here wants to get moving."

Everyone stared at Kieran, and I couldn't help but laugh. He always was the kind of guy to put his foot in his mouth.

"That's not really what I—"

"C'mon everyone!" She headed for the door. "Time to show you all the final portions of your training. Isn't it fun that you get to do this all day—every—single—day?"

Everyone cursed Kieran as we trudged into a strange classroom. It was a small auditorium with more than enough seats hold a section of the slums. There were two sets of heavy metal doors on the far wall that seemed to catch everyone's attention.

We had to sit and answer questions about what we'd do in specific situations that we might come across in the field. It wasn't the most fun in the world, but it was a cool exercise to have everyone think about the steps to take while saving the day.

It was also good to learn about the different classifications of Conks. There were the standard weaponized Conks, Brutes, Elementals, Executioners, and Fighters. It felt like the more I learned, the less I actually knew. Learning one new thing meant learning five different subtopics.

"You all look so bored," Lili said with a chuckle. "Everyone come down here. Let's get you set up for a real test."

"I'm ready for anything you want to throw at us," Raysean said as he rushed down toward Lili.

"What a kiss-ass," I said under my breath.

Kieran must have heard me, because he nudged me. "Look who's the teacher's pet now!" Raysean glared at him, but Kieran replied by flipping him off.

Lili made her way to the metal doors and they each slid open. "You'll be put in a series of situations in here. They'll generally be catered to each of you in some way —but I think that's all I want to say about it for now." She looked over at the group. "Who's first?"

Kieran stepped up first, and when he came out from the room, the group crowded around him. He wasn't in there all that long, and there wasn't a single noise that had come from the room. He looked as rough as Phoebe and Raysean had during the morning run.

What really worried me was that he wouldn't answer anyone.

"Kieran. C'mon, man." I put a hand on his shoulder. "What happened in there?"

"Not talking about it."

"Ha. Figures," Raysean said. "A guy like that isn't gonna cut it as an Interceptor."

"First fail of the day," Lili said as she exited the neighbouring room. She looked at Kierans' condition and switched her tone. "Don't worry, though. Most people fail their first few tries in there. Raysean, why don't you head in there next?"

"Watch this—first try," Raysean said as he pushed his way to the door.

He ate his words when he went in and refused to talk when he made his way out. One by one, people made their way in and back out of the room. Some were pale like Kieran, but some were entirely despondent. Everyone had one thing in common—no one was sharing what went on when they stepped into the room.

Lili stuck me in a room where she started a simulation that had me on the edge of a cliff as I did battle with an opponent who could fly. It took a while to calm down from the heights, but I managed to make it through the simulation without any trouble.

I walked out, being the one person still in high spirits, but Lili wasn't about to let that stand. "Get back in there, Rhys. We're going to try that one more time."

Everyone stared at me as I raised an eyebrow. "What? Why?"

"I'm not satisfied with how that went. I had two options, and clearly, I picked the wrong one."

I nodded and headed back into the room. A laser came from the far wall and scanned me. I had no idea what to expect, but I had a feeling that my test had been easier than any of the others.

A flash went off in the room, and when my sight came back to me I was in the middle of a familiar burning building. I spotted Lenna as she rushed through an open door, only to be met with a massive explosion from a far wall.

The explosion caused the ground beneath her to give away, and she managed to catch the edge of the floor as she was falling.

"LENNA! Hold on, I'm coming," I said as I rushed through the burning building.

I knew it wasn't real, but the simulation had switched on all of my senses. For whatever reason, it was real in that moment. The simulation was the most convincing recreation of Lenna I'd ever seen, something that made me want to try my best, just in case.

Something caught my eye, and I stopped in my tracks. It was Zeal crouched on the ground. It looked like he was trying to recover after being hit by a blast. If I could hop across the gap and pull Lenna up—I could make it back quick enough to take him down.

"Rhys!" Lenna called. "I'm slipping!"

I rushed through the flames and hopped the gap to Lenna. As I reached out to grab her, Zeal hit her in the chest with a blast. She coughed out some blood before dropping into the fiery innards of the building.

"LENNA!!!"

I looked up to where Zeal had been, but he had moved and was hovering right in front of me. He raised a hand and blasted me. I fell backward as he cackled and teleported out of the building.

Another flash went off and the simulation ended. I felt a hell of a lot more like the rest of the group did.

What was the purpose of that?

Decision making?

Bravery?

Facing fears?

Something to do with attachments?

That first day was pretty much how every single day of training went for that entire month. None of us had the slightest clue how we'd been graded on any of the training. It just didn't make sense.

***

By the end of the month, there wasn't a single person who wasn't concerned about how they had done. Everyone had tried their hardest, and while some days were better than others, I felt like I'd done enough to make it to the next round.

We were all getting dressed for the day ahead when an announcement from Ayla started. "Attention all hopefuls. Today is the day for the next round of cuts. All of you are to report to the front of the facility immediately."

It was time to find out just how well we'd all managed to do.

Chapter 9:
The Eleventh Choice

The groups may have spent every day of the past month together, but it didn't seem like many people had started new friendships. I thought we might all end up like one of those ancient fantasy books from the academy where each group becomes like a family. Boy—were we far from that.

It made sense, the whole thing was a competition that could only have one winner, but a part of me was glad that at least Kieran and I had managed to make one new friend—even if that meant making about twenty other enemies.

We gathered out on the steps of the facility in front of a large stage that had been digitally constructed. The technology the Interceptors possessed amazed me in a new way every day. However the tech worked, the facility was able to use simple beams of light to create tangible objects.

Cleo, Lili, and Kiyoshi were the only Interceptors present—along with a mousy girl I had never seen before. Since she was amongst the team, she had to be important in some way.

Before I had a chance to ask Kieran who that girl was, Ayla stepped to the front of the stage and whirled around. Her clothes changed until she was dressed like the head of the academy when he handed out our diplomas. "For those of you wondering, Diggs, Pegs, and everyone' favourite android Mickey are out on a mission currently, but they send their congratulations to those of you that made it through. You've all worked hard this month, but only ten of you will be moving on to the next phase of this process. If you don't hear your name, you are to board the shuttle behind you, and head home."

Phoebe was in between Kieran and me, and she grabbed onto each of our hands. She squeezed my hand, and I knew what it meant. The whole experience meant so much to her. It meant so much to all of those people.

"Let's kick things off. From the fire group, Claudia McGrath and Bernardo Rosales!"

The tall horse-faced girl pumped her fist. I almost groaned at the fact that one of the group of jerks had made it through.

A nerdy-looking guy that had to be Bernardo broke down in tears. I'd never noticed the guy once during the first test or even around the facility during training. If a guy like that did well enough to pass to the next round, I had no idea how we were being assessed.

"From the earth group, Rowan Wall and Akio Ito!"

A short kid with the swept-back hair nodded his head—cool and collected.

I didn't know who Akio was until Kieran leaned over. "Ito. That means that Akio is Kiyoshi's brother."

I looked over to Kiyoshi. He had a smug smile on his face, a refreshing change of pace to see something other than a scowl. Akio was as stone-faced as I'd expect someone related to Kiyoshi would be.

"From the water group, which did exceptionally well, Fern Huber, Aiden Cisneros, and Keyshawn Greer!"

I scanned the crowd and watched the guy in the wheelchair throw his arms into the air in victory.

That punk-looking girl who'd helped me in the first round pushed her purple-tinted hair out of her face and crossed her arms. Clearly, her cool-girl persona wasn't going to let her show how big of a deal making it through was.

A group of people patted a large athletic guy on the back as he pumped his fist. "WOO!" He was the same guy we'd seen that first day in the cafeteria—the one everyone seemed to gravitate toward.

"I thought the water group had done well," Ayla continued. "But it looks like congratulations are in order for the wind group too."

Phoebe's grip tightened on my hand. I looked over to Kieran, and the look on his face said that she was crushing him just as hard. There were three slots left in the final ten. With any luck, those three spots were for us.

"From the wind group, Raysean Ball."

So much for the three of us making it through.

Raysean burst out with a victorious yell. He might have been a jerk, but it made sense. The team would be crazy if they weren't at least thinking about adding someone like Raysean to their roster. He'd be an even bigger powerhouse than Kiyoshi.

"Kieran Moore." Phoebe and I looked at him, and he looked like he was about to cry. He was one step closer to his dream.

Unfortunately, there was only room for one more person.

Phoebe looked at me and leaned into me while we waited for the final name. "Phoebe Price."

That was it.

I wasn't going to become an Interceptor after all.

I was kidding myself.

At least I could head home and look after Lenna while we cheered Kieran on. My heart sank, but I was happy for Kieran and Phoebe. They had both worked

74

their asses off to make it to the next round.

"Congrats, guys," I said. "I'm proud of—"

"Rhys York."

My attention snapped right back to the stage, and Ayla had her eyes trained right on me. The rest of the crowd was as confused as I was. They had made it clear that only ten people would be moving on to the next round, but my name made eleven.

Kieran and Phoebe wrapped me in a hug as the three of us celebrated. It didn't make any sense, but I wan't about to argue.

"If your name wasn't called, you must leave the premises immediately," Ayla said.

The disappointed crowd dispersed, and before long, there were eleven of us standing there. Eleven hopefuls looking to be the next Interceptor.

"You may all be confused—"

"You got that right," Raysean said. "You told us ten people were moving on. What's up with this bull—"

Ayla locked a death stare on Raysean. "I suggest you watch your mouth before we make it ten by sending *you* home," he shut up, and she continued, "Akio Ito, and Rhys York, please step forward."

Akio looked to be a bit taller than Kieran, and I wouldn't be surprised to find out he was all muscle. It looked like he could have jumped into any professional sport and held his own against elite athletes. If anyone had a shot against Raysean in a one-on-one situation, it was him.

We locked eyes and stepped forward from the rest of the group as Ayla spoke again. "The two of you are the only tied score in the history of this process, and such an occasion calls for something special."

The stage started to morph until it had become a square arena. A number of ruined walls and buildings had sprouted up. It reminded me of an old tech-ball arena. On each side of the arena, cases had been created.

"The two of you will fight for the final spot in the top ten." Ayla started zipping to different points of interest in the arena. "The first person to yield, leave the arena, or be knocked out, will head home. In the cases at your starting position, you will find your chosen weapons if you wish to use them—*I sure would.* Anything goes. Akio, you head to the left, and Rhys, you're on the right."

We each headed toward our ends of the arena, and I opened up my case. I looked down at Trigger and studied its hilt. I didn't know what Akio's weapon of choice was, and I didn't know what his strengths and weaknesses were. Luckily, that meant he was probably in the same position.

I attached the sword to my belt, and looked across the arena. It would have been nice to see what weapon he had before he was trying to kill me with it, but a building had been placed in between us.

The group of hopefuls watching made me nervous, but not as nervous as the Interceptors on the opposite side of the arena made me. Kiyoshi looked from where Akio was, to me with a look of disgust.

"You've got this Rhys," Phoebe said.

I flashed her a thumbs up and took a deep breath. Small blips started, and after ten, a siren sounded.

"Begin!" Ayla called.

I stepped into the arena, and the case behind me disappeared. Everything was quiet aside from the howling of the wind.

I didn't have a game plan. I couldn't use the darkness of the inside of buildings to my advantage as long as the sword kept glowing different colours.

If Akio managed to surprise me, the whole thing would be over before it started. I needed to find him before he found me.

I ran past a couple of the small buildings to what looked like the centre of the arena. There were small walls that had been crumbling, and he could have been hiding behind any one of them.

Footsteps pounded from the gravel to my left. I turned my head—he had to be coming from behind the building there. I backed off and hid behind one of the crumbling walls. There was a small hole, so I peered through it as Akio came around the corner. It didn't look like he knew where I was until he pointed a fist in my direction, and an arrow flew right for my eye.

I leaned back in time for an arrow to fly right through the hole I had been peering through. He had picked those weird crossbow gauntlets from the special weapons case—and he was a great shot.

"There goes the element of surprise." After vaulting the wall, I charged at him.

On his fist, data compiled bit by bit until an arrow reconstructed back in the hand he had fired from. He ran right at me and pointed his hands in my direction. With how fast that last arrow had flown, if he timed a good shot at me from that distance, I'd be done for.

I reached for my sword and pulled the trigger as Akio shot both of his arrows toward me. I drew my sword, and it morphed into the enormous blade from before, but the weight stopped me in my tracks. I clicked the trigger again and held the blade flat against the palm of my hand to block the two arrows.

The arrows bounced off, but as I brought the blade back down, Akio was already a foot away. He rocked me with a stiff left hook. I staggered back and swung my sword in his direction to back him off. He dodged the swing and put some space between us as the bits of data started compiling back onto his gauntlets.

He needed to wait for his arrows to reload.

I had a chance.

I rushed back at him and lashed out with a flurry of sword strikes, but nothing connected. For all I knew, Akio had been training with Kiyoshi since he was a kid. If I was going to take him down, I'd need to start getting creative.

I let the sword hang in my hand, and I waved him over with my other hand before spitting toward him. If he was anything like his brother, that kind of disrespect would piss him off. He looked over to where Kiyoshi must have been before charging right at me with his fists raised.

He was fast and threw his strikes with excellent technique. His strikes were so fast that all I could do was dodge while taking a couple of body shots in the process. I backed up against the wall of a building and he landed a few good hits before I spotted that his arrows were back.

He raised both his fists as I stabbed my sword into the wall of the building above me. I swung forward and kicked him in the chest as he launched his arrows.

He fell back to the floor as an arrow nicked the side of my arm. I followed through on my swing and placed my feet along the side of the building. If I timed my next move perfectly, I'd be the one making it into the top ten.

I pushed off the building as hard as I could, pulling my sword out in the process, and launched myself at Akio. Something I hadn't planned on was my sword morphing back into its smaller form mid-jump for some reason.

I landed short but rolled forward as he rolled backward. We both stood up, but I brought the blade of my sword to his throat, as he raised his fists toward me.

I didn't know why my sword had changed back, but it didn't matter. It was smaller, but it was still sharp.

His gauntlets didn't have any arrows loaded.

I won.

"That's it, Akio," I said. "I got you. Time for you to yield."

Akio cocked his head. "What's that?"

"C'mon, man. That's like—the oldest trick in the book. I'm not falling for that."

He wasn't playing me.

A bright trail of data floated down from the sky a few feet away from us. the way it flowed through the air was strange. It felt chaotic, yet also graceful. We both stared at it as it sunk down, and merged with the ground. I cocked my head wondering if it was some kind of notification of my win, or a piece of data not finding Akio's gauntlets.

"What the—"

"GET OUT OF THERE!" Cleo screamed.

BOOM

Chapter 10:
Blood Puddles And Flaming Swords

The explosion had tossed me and Akio into the side of a building along the edge of the arena. I staggered to my feet, using my sword's sheathe as a kind of cane. My vision was blurry and I had a headache that so bad I was worried I might have cracked my head open. My ears were ringing, and it felt like everything was moving in slow motion.

I picked up my sword and sheathed it while I checked on Akio. In the state my body was in, I couldn't tell if he was out cold—or something worse.

Ayla warped beside me and tried to say something to me, but I couldn't hear her. I had to concentrate just to make out two words.

"He's alive."

"Wha—what happened?" I muttered as I leaned against the building.

"Surprise attack by the Conks. It's not looking good. You need to get out of here, and—"

"Where's Kieran?" I asked, looking back to where everyone had been watching from. "Where's Phoebe?"

"Lili led them all inside, so you need to head in and submit yourself for proper medical attention." Ayla reached a hand out like she forgot she was a program. "We have no idea how hurt you might be."

"So it's Cleo and Kiyoshi against a squad of Conks?" Reaching down, I grabbed Akio's gauntlets off his hands.

"They'll be okay—"

An explosion went off behind one of the buildings, and I darted toward it while I put the gauntlets on. Much like my sword, they too were cycling through different colours. Without doing anything else, they resized to be a perfect fit for my hands. There was a small button in the palm of each of the gauntlets, and I figured that was how to fire the arrows.

"Ugh, you're exactly like him." Ayla floated right beside me. "I'm not gonna be able to say anything to stop you, huh?"

I didn't bother answering. I needed to help out before someone ended up dead.

"Even if I said you'll lose your spot in the top ten?" Ayla asked.

"I'm not letting those two take on a whole squad alone. You can hang back and make sure Akio stays safe."

Out of the corner of my eye, it looked like Ayla cracked a smile. "Alright, alright, but I'm sticking with you—to keep you alive of course." She flew into my sword and then popped back out a moment later. "I'll be linked to you—for a little while at least."

The sword and the gauntlets stopped changing colours and instead turned silver and gold. The same colour as an S-Rank Interceptor's kit.

"Gotta be honest," I started. "Glad we're done with the disco sword."

"For now." Ayla corrected. "Rhys, I really suggest heading to the building for medical attention. Your body is in rough shape."

I rounded the corner of the building and came up behind Cleo and Kiyoshi as they held off a full squad of Conks. Kiyoshi had a hand over his arm, but that wasn't stopping the blood from pouring out. Something cut him, and it cut him bad.

"A little too late for that now."

There were two huge Brute Conks and a ton of Executioner Conks. That would have been enough of a handful for the whole team, but on one of the buildings above the squad was a woman I recognized.

She was one of the first Interceptors, Sable. One of the ones who had joined Zeal—one of the people that killed Chase. Her kit was similar to the S-Rank of the Interceptors, but hers was black and gold, instead of white and gold. In her hands, she held a fearsome flaming katana.

"I was wondering when you'd be making an appearance," Sable said as she stared at me. She brought a finger to the side of her head as if she were accessing a visor to check the time. "Right on schedule."

Cleo and Kiyoshi turned and faced me. "You know her?"

"I was going to ask the same thing," I said. "Personally, no, but I've seen her on—"

Before they had a chance to turn around she had boosted her way right toward me. I launched the arrows from the gauntlets at her, but she deflected them mid-flight. She flew in between Cleo, and Kiyoshi which sent them staggering back as the group of Conks jumped toward them. The Interceptor cameras whizzed around trying to cover all of the action.

I clicked the trigger and pulled the sword out again, but I didn't need to re-pull it to be able to handle the weight. It must have had something to do with Ayla. I raised my sword just in time to block her strike.

She leaned forward so our faces were an inch apart,

somehow the flames of her sword weren't causing her any pain at all. If they were hurting her, she might have been enjoying it.

"You ended up a lot cuter than I'd thought you would," she said with a sideways grin.

She looked like any other mildly attractive woman in the city to me, but she had a defect I'd never seen in person before. Both of her eyes were different colours. One blue, and the other a light brown.

"What do you want, lady?" I asked.

She was keeping a ton of pressure on me, but it was still clear that she was holding back. With a kit like that, she could have sent me flying whenever she wanted to. Even worse, she probably could have sliced through me and my sword.

"The name's Sable—not lady, but don't worry. You'll get to know me a hell of a lot better soon."

"What does that—"

She backed off when a huge blade of air swung between the two of us. It was Lili, back from getting everyone else to safety.

She landed right in front of me with her fists up. "Stay the hell away from him."

"Oh." Sable landed a few feet away. "You like this boy, don't you, Lili? I can see it written all over your face. I can't remember the last time I saw a fire like that in you."

"What? No, I don't." Even from behind her I could tell her face had changed to a deep shade of red. "Shut up."

Lili launched a punch that sent a tornado right at her, but one big swing of Sable's katana cut the wind while blowing the flames out.

"You have no idea what he's capable of." Sable took a step forward. "You don't even know what *all of you* are capable of."

I looked over to Cleo and Kiyoshi. Despite Kiyoshi's injury, it looked like the two of them were going to be fine against the wave of Conk grunts after all.

Lili looked back at me. "Don't worry about them. I'm gonna need your help with her."

"But—"

"Trust me."

"Got it."

"Isn't that precious?" Sable swung her katana and it reignited. "A tiny little D-Rank Interceptor and an Interceptor-to-be think they can take me on."

Sable swung again, and a lion made from fire burst from the wall of flames. It was already terrifying enough, but then it lunged straight for us.

Lili stepped to the side and swung a fist which sent me flying thanks to huge gust of wind. I did my best to control my spin, but I still ended up slamming through one of the crumbling walls.

I stood up in time to see Lili deliver a series of punches to the flaming lion. She whirled around and delivered a huge spinning kick that sent it into the sky. Sable lunged forward at Lili with enough force to destroy one of the small buildings. Once the dust cleared, I could see the two trading swings.

I rushed toward the fight, but Sable must have seen me coming. She booted Lili through another building and away from the arena, before turning her attention right back to me.

"Plant your feet and ready your sword," Ayla said.

Sable boosted over and took a few swings that I almost didn't manage to deflect. She was so fast, and so strong that I felt myself crumbling to the floor with each strike.

"Block left. Spin clockwise—" If it weren't for Ayla flying beside me like a little fairy—guiding me on where to block and how to move, Sable would have skewered me for sure.

She slashed until I was on one knee before rearing back with her katana and bringing it down as hard as she could, knocking my sword out of my hand. Resting the edge of her blade on my throat, she forced me to my feet.

"He must have been too confident," Sable said to herself. "I'd heard you'd put up more of a fight. I guess he meant when you had a kit."

"What are you talking about?" I asked. "I've never worn a kit."

Her eyes flicked to the side. "One more step," Lili was ready to continue the fight, but Sable pushed her blade closer to my neck. "And I kill him right here, right now."

Lili froze. There wasn't anything she could do because I'd let myself get captured. Akio may have been taken out by the bomb, but I had a feeling I'd be the one going home after the situation was done with.

Out of the corner of my eye, Cleo and Kiyoshi finished dealing with the last of the Conks. If I could find a way out of my predicament, the three Interceptors could take Sable, no problem. Cleo turned to look at the situation, and she cocked her head at something.

Look down, Rhys.

It was strange, but it almost sounded like Ayla's voice was jumping around in my brain.

I did my best not to react as I looked down at the pool of what had to be Kiyoshi's blood on the ground right underneath Sable's katana. I slowly started to raise my hands in the air so I could see how close the arrows were to being reloaded.

They'd be done any second.

If Cleo noticed what Ayla had noticed, we could turn the fight around.

"What do you want?" I blurted out, trying to buy time.

"Aside from causing a little chaos? Well—the one I'm looking for doesn't seem to be here, so I'll settle for getting a good look at *you* for myself. Any other final words before I kill you and your friends?" Sable finished in a baby-like voice.

"Other than what a cliché bad guy thing that is to say? Evil people have had thousands of years to come up with something better. I'm a little disappointed."

"You remind me of Chase."

"I'll take that as a compliment," I said with a smirk.

"I helped kill Chase."

"Well, you aren't going to kill me."

The blood on the ground froze, and a stick of blood-red ice shot straight up to knock the katana away from me right as the arrows reloaded. I launched them toward Sable, and she dodged one. The other arrow slashed across the side of her face causing a superficial cut. I moved in and swung with a wild right hook, sending her staggering back.

A few drops of blood fell to the ground from her cut, and she brought a hand to the wound. "You're going to regret that."

A wave of bloody icicles pushed Sable backward as Cleo jumped in front of me. Lili launched wind strikes of her own as she moved beside Cleo. Sable dodged backward and jumped to the top of a building.

As she landed on the building, Ramona led a small team of armed Mercs into the fray, and they all pointed their weapons at Sable.

Ramona cocked her rifle. "Give it up, Sable."

"I suppose that's enough playtime for one day. The good doctor is going to be pissed that I let so many bots get destroyed for nothing, but oh well," Sable said as she fawned over her nails. "Don't worry. We'll be seeing each other again, very soon." Her body twitched. "Oh, and by the way—Cleo, since it's been so long, I hope Chase's funeral was as good a time as killing him was." She laughed hysterically as she teleported away.

Cleo froze the entire building that Sable had been standing on, and Lili crumbled it to the ground with a single punch. That was the real kind of power that the Interceptors had, and it was still hard to fathom seeing it up close.

I snatched my sword, and we all turned in time to see Kiyoshi running back over to where the first bomb had gone off. Kiyoshi came across like a hard-ass, but he cared for his little brother.

The three of us followed without a word. I wasn't sure if there was anything I could say after that. I knew Chase had to be a sore spot for Lili and Cleo. He had meant the world to both of them, and his death had to have hit them both hard.

Kiyoshi was still bleeding pretty badly from his arm, but he was more concerned with his brother. thankfully, Akio was awake and leaning against the side of a building. Kiyoshi helped him to his feet as the three of us caught up.

"We'll have to reschedule their fight until the two of them have recovered," Kiyoshi said.

Ayla popped out of my sword, and it went back to the usual colourful glow.

"Well…" She began through gritted teeth. "It was *your* decision that the match was not to stop for *anything*, and the first one to yield, to leave the arena, or to be knocked out would be the one to go home."

"And?" Kiyoshi narrowed his eyebrows.

"And—Akio was knocked out by the blast of the bomb, which means Rhys is the winner and will be moving on to the top ten."

"That's ridiculous. A winner should never be decided by a bomb blast. Let's put them both through and fall back on our—"

"Rhys did have Akio at the end of his sword before the bomb went off anyway," Cleo added.

Kiyoshi gave me dagger eyes before storming off toward the facility. It was a jerk move to not say goodbye to his little brother, but maybe it was some kind of tough love. Akio hung his head and headed toward the shuttle bay.

I ran over and stopped him. "You were wicked back there. I don't know if I would have—"

"No." He held a hand up to me. "You had me fair and square before the bomb went off. You were the better man. There's always next time." He held a hand out, and I shook it.

Clearly, he was the level-headed one in the family

"You don't wanna come get checked out by a doctor before you go?" I asked. "I doubt they'll mind."

"I think I'll just wait 'till I get home." Akio winced. "You go get looked at. You better win now, though. It's not as bad if I lost to the guy who ends up joining the team."

Akio may have looked like Kiyoshi, but the two of them couldn't be more different. He headed off toward the shuttle, and I returned to Cleo and Lili.

"We've got a lot to discuss, but for now, go get checked into the med-bay and get some rest," Cleo said. "You too, Lili."

We both nodded.

"Come on. I'll show you where the med-bay is," Lili said.

As we both made our way back into the facility I couldn't help but replay the day's events in my mind. I never would have thought I'd have a chance to tryout for the Interceptors, and here I was in the top ten out of hundreds of people.

At that point, it really had become every man for themselves.

Chapter 11:
A Little Bit Of Faith

They kept me in the med-bay for observation for a few days, but it felt more like solitary confinement. No one came to see me aside from the daily check-ups from Ayla to scan my vitals. On the odd occasion, one of the Interceptors would come in to ask me questions about what had happened in the fight against Sable. Unfortunately, I didn't have many answers.

"Seems like you're fully recovered," Ayla said as she finished another scan. "I'm surprised. Even with our tech, I would have thought you'd need another full day or two to be back to one-hundred percent."

Something about the nurse outfit she decided on was making me a bit uncomfortable. It was a bit—tighter than it probably ought to be. If nothing else, Ayla was enthusiastic about playing a part.

"Probably something to do with me being a boxer." I shrugged. "My body is pretty used to getting the crap beaten out of it."

She gave me a dull look. "I don't think getting punched in the face can match the feeling of getting *blown up*."

"I didn't lose any of my limbs," I waved my arm. "We're all good."

"Well if nothing else, you certainly bring Chase's energy to the facility."

"Is that a good thing?"

"Not always," Ayla said before warping away.

I was bummed that I couldn't keep Akio's gauntlets along with my sword. Ayla reassured me that if I made it onto the team I could use as much or as little gear as I wanted. Those crossbow gauntlets would be a neat little piece of gear to have in my arsenal.

The door to my room slid open and Cleo walked in with a camera in tow. There was always something so funny about seeing the Interceptors dressed in everyday clothes, and seeing Cleo in her comfy clothes amused me all the more.

"What's so funny?" she asked.

"I'm just not used to seeing the world's greatest heroes in sweatpants," I said.

"Not a big feed watcher?"

"It's pretty rare for me to watch you guys at all. I mostly catch highlights, or the bits Kieran shows me."

I was worried I had been a bit too honest with that statement, but Cleo's grin told me she was more amused than annoyed. "Now I understand why you're the only one who hasn't been fanboying over us. Mind if I pull up a chair to ask a few questions?"

I gestured to a nearby chair. "Fire away."

She sat down and tossed out a disc that shot out a little blue light. It was so bright that it could have burnt my eyes if I gawked at it for too long. The other Interceptors had used it when they came in to ask me questions, so while it was neat, I was more than used to it.

"Ready?" she asked, and I replied with a nod. "Do you have any idea what Sable meant when she said that we have no idea what you are capable of?"

The way her eyes were fixed on me—she was looking

for a hint of... something. It's possible the team was worried I was some kind of plant by Sable and her friends, but my closest link to Zeal's forces came from the attack when I was a kid.

"No, I have no idea. I've been a pretty normal guy my whole life." I watched as the little disc logged every word I said in real-time. "Unless she's a huge fan of boxing and thinks I can be the next Chase or something, I have no clue what she meant."

"Do you know why Zeal targeted your housing unit for an attack?" Cleo asked.

I stared at her words, now burned into the air. The thought of Lenna on the ground of our unit with flames all around her raged in my mind. I had assumed that the attack was random. There was no telling what Zeal would have wanted with us. Maybe it had to do with whatever his reason was for attacking my parents, but there wasn't a person alive who even knew why that happened.

"Targeted my—? No—I—I have no idea," I finally said. "I'm sorry. I hadn't even thought of that before."

Cleo took some time to think before speaking. "Confidential feed." She brought a hand to the camera. "Five minutes." After a moment, the camera powered down.

"Are you allowed to do that?"

She pushed a button on the disc and it closed up before she shoved it into her pocket. "Not really. I'm sure there'll be some weird rumour in the news that I turned the camera off so we could hook up or something—the usual tabloid crap—*blechh*. We can only turn our camera off for short periods when we need a private moment."

"First, ouch. Second, we need a private moment?" I asked.

"Has anyone made you aware of the connection you have with Ayla?"

That caught me off guard more than the question about Zeal did. I know she had popped up around me during the first round of tryouts more than the others. We also worked together to help out against Sable, but I had no clue what Cleo meant. I'd never seen Ayla before the day of the first tryout.

"A connection?" I asked.

She crossed her arms. "That's a no."

"She hopped into my gear for the fight against Sable, and she said we had a some kind of—temporary link, but she never mentioned anything about a connection."

"Not a connection in that way." Cleo leaned toward me. "Rhys, Ayla knows who you are."

"Well, like I said, my boxing has been pretty public. Most people around—"

"This isn't about fighting. She's been getting—flashes of you in her data. Like simulations—or memories—of the two of you fighting together as an Interceptor. Sometimes you look pretty close to how you do right now, and sometimes you've aged a few years. You look different, but it's clear that it's you." Cleo didn't look curious, she looked concerned. "Do you have any idea why that is?"

I couldn't figure out if the fact that Cleo was asking something like that was a good thing or a bad thing, but the way she asked it didn't feel too good. It had to be some kind of weird malfunction. Ayla probably just had a little AI crush on me or something like that. That made sense to me—or at least that's what I told myself.

"Is that why she—" I started.

"Appeared for you so many times in the first round? Possibly. She was more focused on you than any of the other candidates. We all took note of that."

She looked at me, but neither of us had any words. It was clear to me that she was as confused about the whole situation as I was.

"Do I need to be careful?" I asked.

"I don't think so. If you are in any danger, you're in the safest possible place."

"Well," I rubbed my head. "I did literally blow up the other day."

She rolled her eyes. "You know what I mean. I need you to keep this between you, me, and Ayla. Okay?"

"I can do that." I peered around the room. "What about Alfie? Is it okay that he knows all this?"

"Oh, yeah." Cleo's expression softened. "Anything you say to the team is always going to be known by our AI's. You can add him to the list of people to keep our conversation between."

Alfie warped in front of me on the bed, no bigger than an action figure. "Don't worry. Cleo's scary when she's mad, so I avoid that whenever possible."

"Hey!"

Alfie warped right back out of the room when he saw the offended look on her face.

"Okay," I said with a nod.

Cleo nodded and pushed a button on the camera. It snapped back on, and the lens blinked awake.

"Alright, Rhys." She patted her legs and stood up. "Rest up, because this next month of training is going to be a ride."

"Can I ask *you* a question?" I asked.

Cleo looked at the camera for a second like she wasn't sure whether or not that was a good idea. "Go for it."

I looked at the floating camera. "What's it like having your entire life being streamed to the world?"

She paused for a moment.

"It can be tough."

I could sense a hint of sadness that came with her words, but I didn't want to press her. Asking a million questions probably would have made sense, but if they did have worries of me secretly working with Zeal, it would just make me look more suspicious.

Cleo headed for the door with her camera following close behind. As she stepped into the hall, she poked her head in one more time and waved. I waved back, but I spotted Ramona waiting in the hall as the door slid shut.

"I never expected this place to be this weird," I said with a sigh.

I'd be getting out of the med-bay the next day for the first week of top ten training. It was going to be another month of some kind of intense training. They'd probably add a few more in-depth courses on top of what we had already been doing. My feeling of dread was as strong as my feeling of excitement.

I was finally able to get back up and move around, but I was still relegated to the medical and engineering section of the facility.

Antsy was the only word to describe me after laying in bed all day, so I decided to take a walk. Eventually, I ended up in the engineering labs, but everything seemed quiet. I figured that was where they fixed up any damaged weapons or kits. If someone was busy with work over the weekend, maybe an engineer could give me a few quick pointers with any of the tech.

"Anyone home?" I asked.

Aside from the sound of rows of data being compiled on a computer, all was silent. I moved past lines of computers as I glanced at electronic components that were strewn out on desks. On the far end of the lab, someone was working on a computer.

"Hello?" I called.

Whoever it wasn't didn't turn around. Either they were in the zone, or they didn't care that I had wandered into what was probably a pretty classified section of the facility.

I made my way over and nudged the person. I came face to face with that same mousey girl I had seen the day of the attack—the girl I wanted to ask Kieran about. She looked like I'd terrified her with my approach.

"Oh, hi. You were there for the top ten cuts, right?" I asked. "If I shouldn't be here, I'll leave, but I thought it would be cool to maybe talk to the engineers, and—"

She stood up and started moving her hands, but I didn't understand. It was sign language, but I didn't know anything about it. Her eyes went wide like she had become embarrassed that neither of us was able to communicate with one another.

Despite her small stature, she had rather large features, but not in an off-putting way. She had big endearing eyes and pouty lips that looked like they were doing their best to take up all the room they could from her tiny nose. The thin rose-gold-framed glasses that matched the colour of her hair looked right at home on her nose.

She cocked her head and raised her hands to me with the palms to the ceiling. I stared at her as she jerked her head toward her hands with a kind smile. I didn't understand what she was trying to get at. Kinda weird that she wanted to hold hands all the sudden

"Uh—I don't really understand," I said.

She puffed her cheeks and blew out the air. She carefully grabbed my wrists and moved my hands where her hands had been with my palms facing the floor. She slowly moved her hands to mine and we gently clasped hands.

Can you hear me now?

Her voice had somehow flown into my head. It was like I'd had a thought, but rather than the typical voice I'd hear rattling around in my brain, it was a voice I'd never heard before.

I pulled my hands away and stared at her. I'd never

experienced anything like that before. She clicked her tongue and grabbed my hands again, placing them the same way they were.

Stop doing that. Do you want to talk or not?

"Your voice is in my head," I said.

Yup! Cool, huh?

I clued into the fact that she'd responded to words I'd spoken rather than ones I thought. "How come you can hear me all of the sudden?"

I can't actually hear your spoken voice. Your brain is just repeating what you're saying out loud.

"Whoa. Should I just—think at you then?"

She let out a warm smile. That probably wasn't the first time she'd had to explain that strange form of communication to someone, but it looked like she loved every second of it.

I wouldn't suggest it if you don't want me listening in to all the other thoughts you can't hide.

I gulped. "Speaking it is."

It's a neural-link, kind of like how the Interceptors AI work. Mine only works when I'm touching a person. This is how I talk to most people these days.

"I didn't know tech like this existed."

Well, you shouldn't. I invented it specifically for me.

"You could sell this for millions, though. There's so many different—" Something so brilliant—she had to be the head engineer for the Interceptors. "You're Faith?"

Her eyes bulged, but her surprised look turned into a bit of a blush. The average person probably never thought about where the team got all of their gear, but Kieran managed to sneak in a lecture on Faith about once a month.

You've heard of me?

"My friend might actually be your biggest fan."

The comment made her smile. It was an endearing smile, the kind of smile that could get anyone to follow through with even the toughest request.

Most people don't care about the engineer. People only care about the Interceptors swooping in to save the day.

"They couldn't do what they do without you. I'm just surprised, I didn't know you were so young."

She nodded with a proud smile. Anyone would have guessed she was a brilliant bookworm at a glance, but Faith was on an entirely different level. Her grasp on tech was unlike anyone else around the world, something that had to make her a target of Zeal.

I finished up my academy work here while I worked for the Interceptors.

"Wow." I glanced at her computer. "What's that you're working on? Or is it super-top-secret and I'm not allowed to know?"

I've been trying to figure out a way to upgrade the elements the Interceptors use.

"Upgrade them?"

Yeah. Like how Cleo can control water and ice. I want to let the Interceptors use their elements more in-depth. Use light or darkness for invisibility. Earth for healing. All those kinds of things.

Amazing.

She smiled at that, but that was meant more as a private thought. I'd actually forgotten that she'd be able to hear me think.

Faith let go of my hands and sat back in her chair. She pulled one over next to her and patted the seat. I sat down as she pulled up a new screen on the computer, and we locked hands again. The screen lit her face in a way that made it look like her eyes were glowing.

She gestured toward the screen with her head.

See all that? That's the data for the new trainee kits I've been developing for you guys. I try to make them even better each time we have tryouts.

I looked at the screen and watched as waves of data scrolled down the screen. It had been doing that since I walked in, and it put into perspective how high-tech the kits were. I couldn't imagine how long it would have taken to figure all of that out.

How could it all be the work of one girl?

"So we're going to use the kits? The same kind as the Interceptors?"

Her hands shot away from mine. Clearly, she shouldn't have said that, but it's not like I could tell anyone. I tapped her shoulder and shook my head to try to reassure her, but she raised an eyebrow.

I couldn't help wanting to ask Faith about what Cleo had said, but I couldn't bring anyone else in. I gave her my word. If Cleo thought Faith could be of any help, she or Ayla would have already gone to her.

We linked hands again.

"You weren't supposed to say—think that, huh?"

She shook her head.

I forgot it's supposed to be a surprise, so don't tell anyone. The kits aren't exactly the same—that would be crazy. They're like baby versions.

"Baby's first kit, huh? Don't worry, I won't see anyone until tomorrow—besides it'll be fun to sit back and watch Kieran so I can see his reaction in real-time. He'll probably start to cry."

She laughed out loud. It was the type of laugh that'd never get old to hear. She caught herself, and did her best to hide her amusement.

"Is there anything you are allowed to tell me?" I asked. "Tips for the kits? My nifty sword? How the heck they're grading us? Anything that might help would be great."

She thought for a moment.

Listen. Really listen. Any one of you could be the one to join the team at this point, and they want someone that they'll get along with. Someone who can learn. Someone who genuinely wants to help people and become better. Practice hard.

Someone who genuinely wants to help people.

That struck me.

If I stopped to think about why Kieran and I each wanted to become Interceptors, neither of us would have picked that as our primary reason. Kieran had always dreamed of living his life to the fullest. He wanted the fame and the glory that came with being an Interceptor above everything else. All I wanted was the ability to take revenge.

That's not true.

I needed to stop forgetting she had a weird window into my brain while we were holding hands.

She giggled again.

I saw what you did when your complex was on fire, and when you helped Ayla, and even when you wanted to make Akio feel better after his loss. You may not know it, but you do genuinely want to help people.

"I guess that all makes sense."

She turned away and typed on the computer until a new screen popped up. It showed the top eleven candidates and their scores. I turned my head and didn't believe what I was seeing. At the top of the list right next to Akio, was my name.

It didn't explain how the Interceptors had graded us, but it did have the key criteria listed. Strength, Skill, Determination, Endurance, Bravery, Public Likability, and one that stood out—Number of Interceptors in Favour.

I had scored well in all of the areas, and I was surprised to find that held true for the final one. There were two hold outs and I figured those had to be Kiyoshi and Mickey. Those were the two I've had the least positive contact with.

Faith grabbed my hands again.

This is how you all placed in that round of cuts, but it doesn't matter for this next round.

"What do you mean it doesn't matter?" I asked.

The final round is always the same thing.

"What's that?"

The final candidates fight each other with full use of their gear. It's like one big brawl. The folks at home are gonna love it.

I looked up at the screen one more time. I had thought that the reason I ended up in that fight with Akio was because we tied at the bottom of the top ten, not at the top. The thing that shocked me more was the fact that Kieran was the one who had been down at number eleven on the leaderboard.

I didn't know if I should let Kieran know or hide it away forever, but I knew I'd never forget it. At the bottom of the list, below Kieran's name was a short message.

`We will hold a tie-breaker fight between Akio and Rhys to determine the number one spot moving forward. Both top candidates are exceptional and based on their scores, it is likely that their match will end in a draw. If there is no clear winner, eleventh place will be cut.`

I wasn't only fighting to protect my spot, I was fighting to protect Kieran's.

Chapter 12:
Baby's First Kit

Ayla popped into the med-bay the next morning to drag me to the first day of top-ten training. Thankfully, for the first time in over a month, we didn't have to start the day with a twenty-kilometre run. She led me to the training room where we had first picked our weapons and disappeared as I walked in.

"Rhys," Kieran and Phoebe said as they rushed over and wrapped me in a pair of bear hugs.

"Hey guys, how's it going?" I looked around at the quiet room. "I miss anything cool?"

"Did you—dude." Kieran had a childlike wonder in his eyes. "You fought against one of the original Interceptors—*with the* Interceptors—and you're totally not dead! That's so cool! How was it?"

"Well, being caught in the middle of an explosion for the second time in my life wasn't fun," I said with a shrug.

I did my best to play it off like it wasn't a big deal, and maybe deep down it really wasn't considering I'd exploded before, but the whole situation was scary. Most likely, I would have been nothing but a pain in the ass for the Interceptors if Ayla hadn't decided to hop into my sword to help me out.

"Plus you wrecked the little brother of the highest-ranking Interceptor in a one-on-one fight. You barely even broke a sweat. You're officially my new hero."

Phoebe slapped a hand over Kieran's mouth. "We're glad you're alright."

Keyshawn sauntered over and stuck out a fist. "I ain't saying we're gonna be best friends or anything, but what you did the other day—that was hardcore."

"Thanks, man." I bumped it. "It's Keyshawn, right?"

"The one and only. And you're Rhys—the super fighting—explosion taking—shining star trainee eliminating—badass himself."

"That's a hell of an intro. I'll have to use that for my next fight."

"You better. It'll make me look even better after I win."

I looked around at the other finalists, and to no one's surprise, the usual suspects were giving me the stink-eye. That girl that had helped me out, Fern, was giving me the biggest stink-eye of all. I wasn't quite sure why, though. I hadn't done anything to her.

She marched right up to me and stuck a finger in my face. "Do you think you're some big hot-shot now that you've been able to fight alongside the Interceptors twice?"

"That came out of nowhere." I pushed her finger away. "No, I don't."

"Well, do you think—"

"Do you think this super cool girl act is keeping everyone from thinking you're just as lost as the rest of us in all this?"

"Excuse me?" Fern said with wide eyes.

It was like all the energy had been sucked from the room and concentrated right onto the two of us. Phoebe bumped me and gave me a look that told me another confrontation wasn't the right call. She was right, but it was in my nature to return any shots fired my way.

I held up a hand. "Fern, if it weren't for you and what you did in the first round, I might not be standing here right now. I owe you one."

Something about what I had said threw her off. Her demeanour changed completely. Rather looking like she was ready to kick me square in the nuts, she looked more like my veiled thanks had flattered her. She looked good with bright red cheeks.

"Oh—well—you're welcome," She started shuffling back to where she had been staring at me. "I guess. I— I'm glad you're okay."

"Glad to see she's as weird as she looks," Phoebe said

"Classic girl cattiness," Keyshawn said.

"What?"

"You don't even know her. You two'd probably be best friends if you got to know each other."

For the first time since I'd known her, Phoebe didn't know what to say. The camera that pointed toward her spun and shifted, probably to change focus. Hopefully, the world was going to like how strange each one of us was.

Kieran put a hand on my shoulder. "This is gonna be a hell of a month."

The door to the room slid open, and the Interceptors walked in with Ayla. They each pulled cases that I assumed housed the kits designed for each of us. We all gathered around as they lined the wall of the training room. It was exciting, but I had a feeling anyone else would have been a lot more excited than even I was.

"Congrats to everybody who's made it this far. In honour of each of you making it to this point," Cleo said as she tapped a case. "You will all now receive your own trainee kits."

I looked over to Kieran, and he looked like he was ready to faint as the Interceptors opened each of the cases.

"You can each come up and claim a kit. Be warned, if any of you utilize your kit outside of training for any reason, you will immediately be kicked out of the running," Kiyoshi said.

"We know some of you can get heated," Cleo added as her eyes flicked between me and Raysean. "We don't want to find any of you ready to butt heads with tech like this at your disposal—well, until we say so at least."

Everyone nodded and walked up to the cases. We all stared down at the small pieces of ordinary-looking jewelry in them. Some had simple watches, some had necklaces, and some had bracelets. A few people swapped places for an accessory that they preferred, but I was fine with a necklace.

It seemed a bit weird to accessorize to become superheroes in training, but the Interceptors were the experts so wasn't about to cause a fuss.

Kieran had landed on a watch, and Phoebe grinned at her new bracelet.

"These are our kits?" I asked, wondering how a tiny necklace could house an entire suit of high-tech armour.

"Nano-tech," Kieran whispered.

With a nod from the team, everyone snatched their new accessories and put them on. I looked down at the small gold medallion around my neck and wondered how it was supposed to work.

"Everyone prepare yourself, this might hurt a bit," Ayla said from behind us. "A lot really."

What do you mean it might hurt a bit—or a lot?" Fern asked.

"People have been known to crap their pants if they aren't ready for the jolt."

"What jolt?"

A bolt of energy washed across my body, and by the looks of it, it had happened to everyone else too. It felt like an earthquake was radiating from my body. The jolt went as quick as it had come, and everyone looked down at themselves. Some people fidgeted, and some people twitched for a few moments.

The sudden wave of energy was rough, but not nearly as rough as it would have been if it shocked my bowels loose. Luckily, I was all clear down there.

"Everyone good?" Cleo asked.

"I'm gonna do a scan, but I promise I won't tell." Ayla grinned.

If anyone had crapped their pants, they were selling the idea that they hadn't well.

"I don't feel any different," Phoebe said, looking at her hands.

"You all need to will the kit to come out," Diggs said as he stepped forward.

"It's sort of stupid, but you'll feel like—a kind of little tingle when it's working," Pegs added as the pair let their kits crawl across their bodies.

Everyone looked at themselves again. Some people closed their eyes or even just one eye to focus. Everyone tried to concentrate, but no one knew what exactly they were concentrating on.

To the shock of everyone, Phoebe's kit shot out of her bracelet and wrapped around her body. Soon, her whole body was covered in a grey kit that looked like the kind the Interceptors wore. The one thing it didn't cover was her head.

"First trainee to do it, and with quick coverage too," Cleo said with an impressed nod.

"Trainee armour—so cool," Kieran said as he closed his eyes.

My kit slowly made its way around my body, and soon I was looking down at the incredible grey kit.

Having it on my body felt strange. I felt like I could throw a bus, or run faster than a tech-cycle.

It wasn't all good, though. My body felt cut off from my head because there wasn't any kind of external stimuli coming in at all. Whatever that nano-tech was made of, it had to be state-of-the-art.

One by one each person managed to will their kit to wrap around their bodies, and then back into their accessories. Kieran was the last one to get his kit off, but after a bit of panicking, he managed to pull it off.

"I was wondering—back at the fire," I said, rubbing my hand as I recalled the pain of that day. "You and Lili had full helmets to deal with the burning building. When we were fighting with Sable, she had parts of her body that weren't covered in armour, like her hands. How do we do that?"

"Good question," Cleo said. "The more practice you get, the more control you'll have." Her kit covered her body, and slowly it started to morph into different coverage combinations. "Soon you won't need to concentrate to activate your kit. You'll be able to choose how armoured you want to be or send the armour to a specific body part."

"There're advantages to different combinations from the obvious to the not so obvious." Mickey grabbed a training bag to sit on. "That's not what we're here for today, though."

From the serious tone of the team, I could tell that this wasn't a moment to goof around. There probably weren't all that many people who could say they'd put on an Interceptor kit.

"Right," Lili said. "Today each of you will decide on your element of specialization. Choose carefully though, if you become an Interceptor you'll have to commit to one element."

"You'll be able to swap elements on these trainee

suits since they're weaker than the real deal, so if there's any issue, you have options. We're all here to help you make an informed choice, and to help you learn to hone your skill with the element in question." Kiyoshi finished.

They grabbed the top layer of foam from each of the crates and revealed ten different modules in each crate.

Each glowed with the simple colour of their type. In the ten cases were modules for fire, water, light, darkness, electricity, poison, earth, wind, psychic, and time.

"Holy crap. So many choices. Lemme guess, most of you already know what elements you want?" I asked to a sea of nodding heads.

Kieran jumped right for electricity, and Phoebe jumped right for water, but I had no idea what to pick. Every element type had its own series of advantages and disadvantages. Everyone else chose their elements without a second thought.

Fire for Raysean, darkness for Fern, light for Bernardo, time for Aiden, fire for Claudia as well, poison for Rowan, and psychic for Keyshawn.

"Everyone who's decided, hold the module to your kit to integrate it into the tech," Pegs said with a grin.

Small flashes of light shined throughout the room.

Some of the choices the others had made surprised me, but the thing that surprised me more was that not a single person picked wind or earth.

Seeing the way Lili had used her wind element in a fight up close and personal made me interested in giving it a shot. It would be awesome for movement, and being able to combine that with the sword slashes could be a lethal combination.

I made my way over to the crate of wind and looked down at the modules. The brown glow of the earth modules in the crate beside it caught my eye. The greatest hero the Interceptors had ever known used earth. If I picked earth, it would be a bigger learning curve with no one to help teach me, but it was already proven that it could lead to greatness.

I reached down and took an earth module.

"Oh look," Raysean said. "Mr. big-shot thinks he's good enough to carry on Chase's legacy."

"You know, you don't have to comment on every single thing I do," I spat back.

"Are you sure you wanna do that?" Kieran asked.

"There isn't anyone here with expertise enough to help train you," Cleo said with a look of concern.

"I'll train him." Lili offered. "It's not like anyone else picked wind anyway. I suck when it comes to the time, and psychic modules so, I'll help Rhys with earth. He'll have a chance if one of us is there to help him figure some of it out."

At least someone had my back.

I picked up the module and held it up to the medallion of my necklace. It absorbed the module in a flash of light, and when everyone brought their kits back out, the grey kits were accented with glowing lines of their chosen elements. I thought it was mind-blowingly cool, so I could imagine how quick Kierans' mind must have melted into mush.

"Awesome," I whispered to myself.

While the kits were neat pieces of tech, mine was by far the ugliest. The combination of the dull grey with the earthy brown didn't make for a stunning visual. It was definitely cooler than my usual baggy clothes, but at least I could add some colour with a simple shirt.

Of every kit, the blue glow of Phoebe's was the best.

"Hey, what are all those glowing things along the wall?" Claudia asked as she pointed a finger.

"These?" Diggs said as he pulled a small glowing box off the wall.

She nodded, and he pushed a button. The box morphed into a kit that wrapped around his body. "Single-use kits—good for situations where you can't safely evac' civvies."

"Alright, alright," Cleo said as she rubbed her hands together. "How about we see if anyone can get their element working?"

Ayla reappeared. "I'll check in on how everyone's doing. Gotta keep an eye out for my new partner."

The Interceptors rounded up their new trainees and led each of us to separate sections of the room where we could practice with our new tech. Everyone had paired with the Interceptor that matched their element, but a few of the members took on additional trainees.

Lili led me over to a corner that was filled with training dummies. She waved her hand along the wall and a virtual keypad appeared. She pushed a few buttons and the sleek metallic surroundings of our small section morphed into a vibrant forest. Even the air changed, and I could smell the scent of fresh pine.

"You've got big shoes to fill, mud-boy," Lili said as she walked around me. "Kit up."

"First fire-boy, now it's mud-boy—I really hope that doesn't stick," I sighed. "Big shoes—where do we start?"

It took a minute, but soon, my kit covered my body.

"Everything with your kit needs to be like an extension of your body. The more you practice, the better you'll be, and the more control you'll have over your element. After you have some semblance of control of your element, you'll be able to branch out and do more creative things with it."

I thought back to a mission I had caught on TV with Kieran a few years ago. Chase ended up in a fight against an army of a hundred Conks by himself and used nothing but his element to take them down. He could morph the earth into pillars, and even more creative creations, while getting trees and plant life to help him.

Something told me that sort of thing wasn't exactly beginner-level skills.

"With enough practice, you will be able to control everything that you can see in front of you," Lili said with a melancholic smile. "Chase could move the earth, cause earthquakes, talk to plants, and so—so much more."

"Talk to plants?" I said to myself.

Everyday, things got weirder and weirder.

I raised a hand and concentrated. If I could cause the earth to crack at all, that would be a victory enough for me.

Nothing happened, so I tried to make a root come from the ground from a nearby tree.

Nothing again.

I wasn't doing anything, but somehow, I was already exhausted.

It felt like an eternity had passed before I turned to Lili. "I'm thinking I'm gonna need more of a hint to make this work."

Lili's AI, Walker, warped in—and by the look on his face, it looked like he had been caught in a heavy downpour. "You're gonna need more than a hint."

Lili laughed, "The only person I know of who managed to get any elemental control on their first day was—"

"Don't tell me—Chase," I said as I pointed a hand back at the tree.

"I'm just trying to make you feel better." Lili shrugged.

"Lower your hand a bit," Walker said.

"No back-seat teaching," Lili said as she waved her hands through Walker.

I looked around the room at everyone else as they tried their best to use a hint of their new power. I figured Phoebe or Kieran might have a better chance at getting their element to work since they were knowledge centres for all things Interceptor.

They looked as stumped as I was. Fern and Keyshawn looked confident as they tried, but they too ended up unable to make any significant progress.

"You need to stop thinking about it, and just do it." Lili grabbed my arm and tilted my head slightly. "I know it sounds weird to hear me say *concentrate on it*, and then *just do it*, but it's more of a need. You *need* the earth to move."

She shifted my stance, moving my legs with hers and adjusting my arms. It was nice to be close to her like that, but the slight sense of frustration I got from her wasn't exactly what I had in mind for when we were close.

"I need it to move?" I asked.

She moved beside me and closed her eyes. The nano-tech of her kit made its way across her body and covered her hands. After a deep breath, she swung her arm in an arc, and a blade of wind flew through the forest. The blade bashed into the unseen wall that looked like nothing but more open forest.

"Everything we do is to protect people." Lili opened her eyes and looked at me. "Use that. Imagine needing to protect someone or something you love."

I couldn't help thinking back to when she had told me about what had happened to her mother. Wind made sense to me. If she had the power to save her mom, she could have blown away the criminal that hurt her before he even had a chance.

I looked back down to the ground. Focusing on a hole was easier than willing a living tree to move.

"Don't worry if you can't get it. It took me a week before I was able to do anything with wind and look at me now" Lili leaned closer. "Kiyoshi took two with his lightning. No one's really going to get their element going today."

I filled my thoughts with Lenna. I thought back to the fire, and how desperately I needed to protect her. My mind wandered from her to my parents, and the explosion that changed our lives forever. Maybe if I had the power the Interceptors had, my parents might still be alive. Maybe Lenna would still have both of her arms.

Ayla's voice slid into my head. *You can do it.*

The ground shifted some.

It wasn't a hole, but the dirt was moving.

Like magic, I made the earth move.

I'd managed to turn the hard earth into some kind of sand. The sand folded over itself in a small circle. It was some kind of quick-sand. It wasn't exactly my intention, but a victory was a victory.

"Holy sh——" Walker started.

"I stand corrected." Lili cut in with her arms crossed.

I had been so lost in thought that I didn't notice my eyes had welled up with tears. I wiped my eyes and caught a concerned look from Lili. She walked over and placed a hand on my arm.

I stopped concentrating, and the ground returned to normal. It felt like I only managed to do it because of Ayla's help. I checked my sword, but was shocked by what I saw. The sword was still glowing all sorts of different colours so Ayla hadn't re-established that strange link from the fight with Sable.

I wondered if I had merely thought I'd heard Ayla's voice, or if she really was cheering me on.

Maybe that connection Cleo mentioned was real.

The look Lili gave me felt a bit comforting and even encouraging. When I turned around, I was met with resentful stares from everyone in the room. Ayla was off by Keyshawn, but her sight was set on me with a big grin. The other Interceptors must have seen that I managed to will the ground to move. Each of them—except for Kiyoshi—had come closer to snag a better look.

"Looks like we've got a Chase in the making on our hands," Diggs said.

"That's way too much pressure." Pegs punched his arm. "Don't put that on the kid."

"Good job, Rhys. You've officially joined Chase as the only people who managed to use their element on the first day of training," Cleo said as she made her way back to her trainees.

I couldn't read the room.

Everyone was giving off a different energy.

Diggs, Peggs, and Lili were all excited for me—but Cleo, Mickey, and Kiyoshi seemed irritated. Even the rest of the trainees didn't seem too thrilled for me, but Fern locked her eyes on me with a look of intrigue. I figured landing an accolade alongside Chase might add to her random hatred of me, but apparently not.

What a weird girl.

"Earth must be the easiest one," Mickey said before heading back to the trainees.

"Looks like you all have more work to do," Kiyoshi said as his eyes locked on me. "You want to let him get ahead of you?"

I scratched my head. "Feeling kinda personally attacked right now."

Phoebe and Kieran gave me sideways glances before turning back to their areas. I knew the rest of training was every man for himself, but I thought maybe Kieran would be excited for me.

Every single advantage one person had meant a disadvantage for everyone else.

Lili grabbed my wrist and returned my attention to my surroundings. "Ignore them. Just because you got it to work once, doesn't mean you'll automatically be any good with your element. Do it again." She moved into the corner of my eyesight. "Good job. That was kinda awesome."

"Lower your arm," Walker added again.

Ayla did an excited jog into my view and flashed me two thumbs up. "Clearly you don't need any of my pointers." After a quick wink, she disappeared once more.

I had so many questions.

I brought the memories of that terrible day back into my mind, and after a while, the ground started to swirl again. I had found a great starting point, and if that meant I had a week's advantage over the rest of the recruits. Maybe I did have a shot at becoming an Interceptor.

The one question I had was, would Kieran be able to forgive me if I ended up becoming an Interceptor, and he didn't?

Chapter 13:
Rhys Vs. Lili

After elemental training, we were led into an empty circular room. Compared to the rest of the facility, the room was pretty bland. The bright glow of the facility's various rooms wasn't present there.

Before we reached the room, the Interceptors all headed off on their own except for Lili and Ayla.

As we made our way into the centre of the room, Kieran knew exactly where we were. "Combat training time."

Lili waved her hand to open a menu similar to the one from elemental training. "Where would we like to train today?" She selected a few different choices, and the room changed as she called out the locations. "Sunny beach? Feudal Japan? Ruined city?" She looked over at me. "Maybe, not that one. How about an ancient garden?" She pushed another button, and the room morphed again.

The high-tech room had become a beautiful sunny field of colourful flowers. The sky was an incredible shade of blue, and there was a slight breeze that had to have been coming from somewhere in the room. It looked like it went on forever, but there's no way the room had changed that much.

Ayla whirled around until she was dressed in an old gi. "Most of you have probably already guessed that it's time for combat training. Lili is arguably the greatest hand-to-hand combatant in the world, and she'll be your instructor for combat for the rest of the month. One on one after-hours training sessions can be requested of any of the Interceptors at any time."

"That doesn't make any sense. She's the lowest ranking Interceptor," Fern said a bit harsher than she probably meant to. "How is she a better fighter than the rest of them?"

"Rank doesn't have to do with skill, it has to do with feats that a member has performed," Keyshawn said.

That seemed a bit odd for a group of heroes. Rather than being promoted based on skill, there was almost incentive to pull off crazy moments instead. Whoever made a decision like that had some skewed-ass priorities.

"Plus hand-to-hand skill doesn't have anything to do with weapon, gear, or element skill," Kieran added without taking his eyes off Lili.

Lili made her way to the fields' centre. "So—who's first?"

No one made a move except to back away from her.

It made sense. Anyone who went one-on-one with her first was going to be the example. A guy with an ego like Raysean may never recover after getting wrecked by a small woman like Lili.

"Oh, c'mon." She cracked her neck. "I'll be gentle—maybe."

I stepped forward and the group *oohed*.

Someone had to go first and I was excited to see how I matched up in a fight against a real Interceptor. Despite my excitement, my nerves had built up. I didn't want to do something stupid like hit her too hard and ruin the basic friendship we had.

"I know you have good striking form. What are you trained in? Boxing?" she asked.

"Yeah." I stopped just a few feet away from her. "Boxing." She looked at me like she expected me to keep going. "Just—boxing. Good ole—one-two."

I needed to learn to stop talking a sentence earlier.

"That's a fun one." Lili smirked. "How long?"

"Ten years—same with Kieran."

She looked from me to Kieran, and then right back. "Remarkable Rhys."

I didn't react much when I was noticed by people around the city, but I never would have thought that an Interceptor would have known my nickname. The first thing that sent me into a state of fanboying was Lili knowing my fight-moniker.

"I've definitely seen you fight before all of this, and I didn't even know it." She threw a few slow jabs. "I thought you seemed familiar when I saw you practicing in the training ring. You sure you wanna be an Interceptor? You might end up going down as one of the all-time greats in boxing."

"Well, I—"

She rushed at me with her fists raised and closed the distance between us in an instant. She led with a heavy left hook that I managed to duck. I took a step backward and slipped out of the way of a jab, before countering with a swing of my own.

I wasn't even close to landing my strike.

She laughed as she continued to dodge me without a hint of effort, "You're pretty quick."

I had lost a handful of fights in my boxing career, but I had never had an issue with landing a strike on my opponent. Lili was making me look like a chump with a smile on her face. The last ray of hope in the situation was that she hadn't managed to hit me yet either. We bobbed around the arena before lunging back in, in attempts to strike one another. Flower petals we'd kicked up had filled the air around us.

I launched a straight cross, and she grabbed my arm. She spun along the side of it until she was behind me and nailed me with a hard punch to the back of my neck. I staggered forward and turned in time to dodge an incoming right hook. As I moved out of the way, I twisted my body and returned a right hook of my own straight into her face.

"Way to go, Rhys," Phoebe said.

"I'm so sorry." I blurted out.

Lili rolled her eyes. "*Combat* training."

She took a step back and touched her face to see if there was any blood. There wasn't, so a confident smirk crawled across her face before launching forward again.

I had never had to focus so hard on avoiding getting hit. At least in boxing, the gloves could absorb some of the impact. It was a tough fight, and I felt proud that I was going toe-to-toe with the best fighter in the world.

After a few more strikes she hopped back and held a hand up. "You're better than I thought, but you wouldn't last a minute in a real fight. You need to use everything to your advantage against someone like Zeal. Practice kicks, throw in some jumps, and rolls. You need to be able to utilize every part of your body at any moment to get the advantage."

My heart sank.

She was right.

She'd been fighting in my style the entire time. I may not have known a lot about the Interceptors, but I knew that boxing had never been Lili's style of choice. She was a Muay Thai kinda girl.

"Wanna see what I mean?" she asked.

"What kind of gentleman would I be if I said, no?"

I rushed forward trying to wait for any telegraph of a kick, but it never came. She waited for me to throw a strike, but rather than slip the punch, she dodged right out of the way. She had gotten behind me faster than I could even comprehend.

I turned in time to glance at her in mid-air as her foot came crashing down against my cheek. I dropped to the ground and brought a hand to my face.

That was the hardest kick I'd ever taken. For a moment, I was worried she'd broken my jaw.

"Being an expert in one style of combat is a huge accomplishment, but it's not enough to keep you alive against the kind of people who will do anything to kill you," Lili said without another glance at me. "Next."

"You did great, Rhys!" Ayla said with an over-exaggerated arm swing.

I rubbed my face where the kick had connected. "Thanks, Ayla." I trudged over to where everyone else had been watching from to a round of snickers.

They may have been laughing, but I knew they wouldn't be for long. There was no way any of them would even be able to touch Lili if she went all out.

Chapter 14:
Getting Choked Up

One by one, every single trainee was put in their place.

Kieran did his best against Lili, but she didn't bother indulging him by coming at him in a straight boxing match. Phoebe and Bernardo each had next to no combat training, so they went down pretty quick. Not a single other person managed to land a hit on Lili, but Keyshawn did manage to wrap her in a hold—for a few seconds.

The last person to take a crack at Lili was Fern. She shot me a look before making her way up to Lili.

"What's her problem with you?" Phoebe asked.

I shrugged. "I don't even know if it's actually a problem that she has with me. You've all got me in a constant state of confusion."

"You sure that isn't just thanks to that explosion?" Kieran asked with a snicker.

"Haha—*how funny*—I blew up," I said as I gave him a dull look.

"She's kinda cute if you ignore the thought that she probably told her parents what to do as a kid."

"Any specialities, Fern?" Lili asked.

"Let's let it be a surprise." Fern replied as she took a stance low to the ground.

She looked like a human crab.

It was certainly one way to start a fight. Didn't seem all that effective, but maybe crabs were the most battle-ready creatures on the planet and I didn't even know it.

"Have it your way," Lili said before she shot forward.

Fern remained still until Lili was in range. Lili faked a punch and instead threw a kick. Fern caught her leg and flipped around it using her momentum to send Lili to the ground.

I could tell she had been caught by surprise when she looked back up in time to see Fern rushing toward her.

Fern led with her knee aimed right at Lili's face, but Lili dished out exactly what Fern had dished to her. She slid out of the way of the knee but scooped her off the ground with a hand on her knee and her back. With a swing of her arms, she tossed her backward over her head.

Fern controlled her landing, and they stared each other down.

"Everyone pay attention to Fern. She's done exactly what we want from all of you," Lili said without taking her eyes off Fern.

Kieran, Phoebe, and I looked to one another for any hint at what she meant.

"I can already tell she has a strong grasp of at least four or five different fighting styles." She finished.

If that was true, Lili was more knowledgeable on fighting than I had thought. I wondered how anyone could have figured out someone's mastery of fighting styles from a few seconds-long exchange.

Without a word, Fern lunged forward once again. She led with a flurry of kicks and a straight punch, but it was like Lili knew the punch was coming. As she moved away from the punch—she grabbed Fern's wrist, kicked out her ankle, and flipped her face-first to the floor.

Lili laughed and let her up, "This group has some promising candidates."

We all beamed with pride at a comment like that, but it was clear who she had been talking about from how all the fights went.

If she meant purely hand-to-hand combat, the standouts were Fern, Keyshawn, Kieran, Raysean— more for his sheer size rather than skill, and me. I looked at Phoebe, and the look on her face told me that she knew she wasn't one of the people Lili had been referring to.

"I'm gonna get each of you to do some one-on-one training," Lili said as Fern joined back up to the group. "I hope everyone's ready. The winners can have the rest of the night to relax. The losers will have a twenty-kilometre *swim* to look forward to when training is done."

No one wanted that swim.

We'd been subject to a long swim as a punishment before, but it wasn't any ordinary swim. The pool might as well have just been called a typhoon with how rough the waters were for the duration of the swim.

I shuddered at the thought of another horrible swim.

The first three matches were pretty quick and uneventful. Raysean brute-forced through Claudia's strikes and as soon as he put his hands on her, the match was over. Bernardo barely put up a fight with Aiden. To everyone's shock, Phoebe managed to beat Rowan when a surprise kick caught him on the jaw and knocked him out.

"Alright, Phoebe!" Kieran and I cheered.

Kieran and Keyshawn stepped up and gave each other props before separating. I wasn't sure how the match was going to go. Kieran was an excellent boxer in his own right, but the fight would come down to how he adapted to Keyshawn's grappling style.

Lili whistled, and the pair shot toward each other like two wolves fighting for dominance. Kieran's strikes were fast, but Keyshawn dodged faster. He managed to roll behind him and clamp him in a wrap.

Keyshawn squeezed. "Gotcha."

"Not for long."

I figured that would be the end of the match right there, but Kieran surprised everyone. He bent at a ninety-degree angle at his waist, before hopping and flipping forward. He landed on top of Keyshawn which broke his hold on him.

"Nice move!" I called out.

They scrambled back to their feet, but Kieran stayed right with Keyshawn, landing a couple of body shots to keep him winded.

Keyshawn dropped to his knees and made a *T* with his hands to signify that he gave up.

Kieran checked on him while he caught his breath, and he helped Keyshawn to his feet. They shook hands and made their way back to the group. As he reached me, Kieran gave me an excited high-five.

It was my turn.

Fern bumped me as she walked by. "I'm lookin' forward to this."

She smiled at me, but I wasn't sure if it was a friendly smile or a mischievous *'I'm gonna break you'* kind of smile. We readied up across from each other, and Lili whistled again.

I wasn't going to make the same mistake Lili had made. Whatever styles Fern knew, she was quick and she fought in an unorthodox way. If I was going to beat her, I needed to do whatever I could to read her movements and react in ways she wouldn't expect.

My body tensed and I stepped forward as Fern shuffled toward me. The anticipation in the moment sent my heart racing.

With a quick step forward, I launched a weak southpaw cross toward her. She dodged it, but she was coming in low which was exactly what I had hoped for. I stepped my left leg forward with the cross and shifted my weight. I lifted my right leg and drove my knee right into her chin.

She staggered backward, and I moved in. "Didn't see that one coming, huh?"

If I gave her a second to recover, she'd get the better of me. I caught her with a body shot before rushing close into her body for a clinch. She grabbed each of my arms, but I swept her nearest leg as she went to toss me. We both went down in a heap, our faces inches from each other.

She rolled on top and straddled my body. An elbow flew right for my face and I managed to deflect it. I wrapped my hands around the back of her neck, pulling her head down to my chest. I forced another roll, and we broke apart.

"You're pretty go—"

Fern was already back in my face.

She launched a kick, but I managed to block it as I stood back up. She kept up the attack with a wide left hook. I ducked under and went for a heavy uppercut to end the match. She spun out of the way of my fist and was wrapped around my body.

She wrapped her arm across my throat and wrapped her legs around my waist. She wrenched her arms, and I felt myself fading quick. I wasn't winded, but that didn't matter because she wasn't choking the air out of me, she was cutting off blood flow to my brain.

"Tap," Fern whispered through gritted teeth.

I dropped to a knee, and then to the ground. "No."

I tried to think of some way to get out of the hold, but I was already too drained to pull off a move similar to what Kieran had done.

I was stuck.

"That's enough." Lili called.

Everything went black.

My eyes snapped back open, and the circular tech room had returned. I lost the match, but I'd rather lose fair and square than give up.

"You okay, dude?" Fern hovered in the edges of my vision. "Pretty ballsy—not tapping out. Respect." She helped me to my feet as the feeling returned to my body.

"You're really good," I said while I rubbed where she had wrenched on my neck. "Think we can train together some more sometime?"

She smiled, and it was the first time I'd seen her crack what I was sure was a genuine smile. She had one of those infectious smiles some people had, so it was a shame that she often hid it behind a scowl.

"Yeah! I mean—I'd like that." She nodded as we headed back over to the rest of the group.

I wasn't upset about losing.

I was too busy being upset about the impending natural disaster of a swim I'd have.

"Alright everybody, good work with the physical portion of today's training," Lili said as Pegs and Diggs walked into the room. "These two are going to take over for the rest of today's training, but don't go thinking those of you that lost don't owe me that swim. Trust me, I'll know if you don't do it."

Lili headed for the door but stopped to whisper to Diggs and Pegs before leaving.

"Alright folks," Diggs rubbed his hands together. "Let's see what you can do."

Chapter 15:
Just Another Friday Night

We'd all made it through two weeks of gruelling training, and it was time for the weekend once again. We knew that Monday meant it would be time to learn how to operate our kits properly. Kieran had been drooling over the chance to use the different gadgets all of our suits had.

Throughout the last two weeks Phoebe, Kieran, and I had become closer friends with Fern and Keyshawn.

It was like a split had formed in the class with two separate groups butting heads, with poor, dorky Bernardo stuck in the middle of it all. The hard training and punishments for messing up were made more enjoyable when we were able to do it with friends. Despite that, there still was the odd occasion where one of us would end up stuck with the other group.

"I really thought we'd have today's combat training in the bag," Keyshawn said.

I sighed, "Guys against girls sounds easy until Lili says she wants to be a part of things."

"It's all Raysean's fault—that comment about how easy it was gonna be." Kieran ran a hand through his damp hair. "I feel like I'll never be able to wash away the chemical pool smell."

The three of us were on our way back from the showers after a long day of training. The girls had decided to watch us as we did our swim and taunted us.

Half of the group decided to grab something to eat, while the rest of us cleaned up. Down the hall Fern and Phoebe were headed toward us on their way back from their own showers.

If anyone saw the three of us guys they wouldn't have any issue assuming that we were good friends. At a glance, we were all athletic and pleasant dudes. On the other hand, seeing a girl like Fern smiling and laughing with a girl like Phoebe was strange. They were polar opposites, but they became fast friends as Keyshawn had predicted.

"What-up, dorks?" Fern asked as we met at the door to our common room.

"You guys might wanna head back there and try again." I plugged my nose and walked into the room."
I think you missed a spot—or a few."

Phoebe rolled her eyes. "Ha-ha."

The room was sleek and white like the rest of the facility with glowing lines of data that stretched across the walls. It was equipped with a huge entertainment centre filled with video games, an ancient-looking table for some game called Pool, and a huge video library. A full kitchen was attached to the room, and along the walls were ten doors for each person's room.

Bernardo was sitting on the couch watching a news feed about us on the holo-TV. It cut from various footage of each of us during training before landing on a shot of Keyshawn.

"Ooh—I'm not gonna argue with the public if they think I'm going to be the next Interceptor," he said as he flexed.

"If only we could have walked in a few minutes later —your already swollen ego wouldn't be getting any bigger," Phoebe said as she disappeared into her room.

"You love it," Keyshawn said as her door closed.

The weekend was a nice break from the cameras that constantly recorded us. As soon as Friday's training ended, so did the recording so we actually had some private time to relax without worrying what the world might think of us.

The coverage on the holo-TV switched from us to a group of people called the Vanguard, but before I could hear anything, Fern pushed me toward my door. "Go change before I steal your towel. I have a fun idea for our Friday night."

"*Ooh.* I'm down for some fun—unless you're talking about just the two of you," Keyshawn said with a wink.

"As long as it doesn't involve sacrificing chickens, I'm in," Kieran said as Fern glared at him. "You scare me."

She stuck her tongue out at him. "Good."

Kieran waved his hand over the table and a menu popped up. He made a selection and a small circle in the centre of the table opened up. There was a slight CLUNK, before an apple flew into the air. It was always neat to see fruit since it was so rare in recent years.

Kieran caught it and took a bite. "Fruit on demand is the real MVP."

After heading into my room, I threw on a pair of old jeans and a long sleeve. I tossed my towel into my overflowing clothes bin. Why I procrastinated with my laundry for so long when it was so simple would have been a good question. Flipping the lid down, I forced the overflowing bin shut. On the wall, the facility had set up a plaque of instructions, no doubt for people like me.

"Clothes in—shut lid—turn dial—push start," I muttered to myself.

I activated the strange bin with a BEEP.

It gave a brief shake, before coming back to a rest. I pushed a button on the lid, and it popped back open. A silver tray lifted from the bottom of the bin with all the now-folded clothes smelling of fresh wildflowers, and radiating heat. The tray swung over to the bed and placed the clothes neatly on top of it before returning to the bin.

"Some people have *way* too much money."

I made my way back out to the common room, and Bernardo was nowhere to be found. Fern must have scared him into his room. It was hard to get to know the poor guy since he'd pull a similar disappearing act whenever people were around.

Fern tossed me a pool cue as I looked around. "Where is everyone? I figured I'd be the last one out."

"The ladies must be staring at themselves in the mirror again," she laughed as she pointed to Keyshawn and Kieran's doors.

I made my way to the table that Fern had already started the game on. "Stripes or solids?"

"You're stripes." She shot a solid green ball into a corner pocket.

"What's this *fun plan* of yours?"

"Well, we could sit around eating pizza and arguing with the spastic foursome like always," She missed a shot. "Or we could go on a little field trip."

I took a shot but missed the mark. "What do you mean?"

The others came out of their rooms one by one and joined us by the pool table.

"Wanna play pairs?" Keyshawn asked.

"Hold up." I held a hand up. "What do you mean a little field trip?"

A mischievous grin scrawled across her face. "I'm saying we take a joyride back down to Sellea City, and enjoy some not-so-fresh air for once." We all stared at her. "Oh, c'mon. You're telling me that there isn't one person any of you wanna see? We can pick whoever up and grab a real drink for the first time in forever."

Kieran and I looked at each other, and I knew we were both thinking about Lenna. She'd ended up staying at Kieran's house after the first month was up. That was something we learned when Kieran's dad had a message sent to the facility.

We must have finally been deemed fit to stay with his family since I was in the running to become an Interceptor.

"I don't know anyone in the city, but I'm down to sneak out of here for a little while anyway." Keyshawn joined Fern on her side of the table. "I'm sick of looking at all the endless eye-burningly white rooms in this place. I feel like I'm gonna need glasses after this."

"I'm in too," Kieran said as he too made his way over to Fern. He gave me a look. "Sorry, man. I gotta see my future wife."

Phoebe's eyes nearly bugged out of her head. "You're engaged?"

That was a bit of a funny thought. Kieran wasn't the kind of guy who'd ever been tied to a single girl for all that long. Sure, he always crushed on Lenna, but that never stopped him form stealing my dates.

Kieran scoffed. "Would that be so hard to believe?"

"He's talking about my sister," I groaned. "Saying he has a crush on her would be the understatement of the millennia."

"I'm gonna marry that girl."

I cracked my knuckles. "I hope we get paired for combat training again soon."

"Kieran—that's weirdly adorable for you," Phoebe said.

"Alright, I'm in too," I said to change the subject. "Nothing wrong with a little fun."

We all looked at Phoebe, the one hold-out. She looked down, and grew a bit red in the face.

She turned and paced back and forth. "If we get caught, we're going to be in so much trouble."

"We won't get caught. How'll they know we're gone? It's not like they record us on the weekend," Fern said.

"But what if they do without telling us? What if they kick us out?"

Fern put a hand on her shoulder. "We've been working our asses off. We can sneak off for one night of fun." She leaned in and whispered something to her, before stepping back.

"Okay. I'm in."

Me and the guys looked amongst one another. "What did you say to her?"

"Don't worry about it," Fern said. "So boys, how are we gonna sneak off this flying rock?"

I looked at Phoebe as her eyes flicked from Keyshawn to the floor.

"I don't know about you guys, but I've got one of those self-driving hover-cars." Kieran pulled out his visor. "I can send it here with Lenna—Rhys's sister. We'll have to squeeze, but we can head off wherever we want." Everyone stared at him. Kieran had his moments where he didn't realize how insufferable he could sound when it came to all his family's money. "What?"

"Don't worry, baby-trust-fund. It's just that we don't all come from the silver spoon district." Fern hung up her pool cue.

"I didn't mean it like—"

"We know." I patted his back. "Don't worry."

He didn't look like he believed me. "I'll call Lenna and have the car swing by the back of the facility." He walked to the kitchen with his visor up.

Phoebe sat on the back of a couch. "Where're all you guys from?"

We had all been avoiding the topic.

It was as dividing a question as asking about religion, politics, or pay checks. Most people around Sellea City would give you an evil eye if you dared to ask what section they were from—if their appearance hadn't already made it obvious. Touchy wouldn't even cut it when describing someone's attitude to a question like that.

"I'm from outside of the city actually," Keyshawn said. "My family headed out of there when the tech started getting out of control. Right around when the Zeal attacks started really picking up."

"Isn't it dangerous to live outside the city?" I asked. "You know, with all the—"

"It can be. If you stick to your land, fortify it well, and have more than enough weapons to defend yourself from all those—things. You'll be fine. What about you guys?"

"I'm from smack dab in the middle of the city," Phoebe said.

"Slums, through and through." Fern raised a fist.

Where I grew up, everyone knew everyone else. If there was someone you didn't know—you knew your sibling, friend, or cousin knew that person. I had never seen or heard of Fern before, but something about her attitude told me that we would have been good friends growing up.

"Same here." I placed my cue on the table. "How've we never bumped into each other?"

"We kind of have. I was at your last fight, the one against Tantalizing Tate. We were kind of dating."

"Oh."

"What happened?" Phoebe asked.

Fern poked my gut. "Let's just say, he wasn't so *tantalizing* after Remarkable Rhys was done with him."

That was an understatement. To give Tate some credit, he could take some serious punishment. A few days after the fight I'd learned that I'd left him with a fractured orbital bone, a broken nose, and a serious concussion.

"Tate could take a punch." I admitted. 'He needs to stop leading with his chin, though."

Kieran walked back over and put his visor away. "Alright folks, the vehicle will be here in about a half an hour. Oh, and Lenna told me to tell you that she loves me more than you, Rhys."

"No, she didn't."

"No—she didn't. Thirty minutes should be enough time for everyone to get ready right?"

The girls locked eyes and dashed to their rooms.

"What was that?" Kieran asked.

"Thirty minutes is not enough for the ladies to get ready, buddy." Keyshawn grabbed a game controller from the couch. "You guys wanna run a couple rounds of that racing game before we go?"

"You mean get dusted by me?" Kieran sat on the couch and grabbed another controller.

"We'll see." The controllers in their hands lit up, and the inside of two race cars constructed around them. "That's never gonna *not* be cool."

I headed toward my room. "I'll take a rain check on that one. I'm gonna take a nap. Wake me up when it's time to go."

"*Okay*, but you're gonna have nap-breath."

"I'll take my chances. I'm not trying to impress anyone." I walked into my room and laid down on my bed.

As nice as it would be to head out of the facility for the first time in two months, I was exhausted. I would have just as easily opted to turn in early for the night to catch up on sleep. My eyelids kept getting heavier and heavier.

Chapter 16:
It's Not What You're Thinking

When I closed my eyes, I was expecting the next voice I heard to be Kieran shouting in my ear to wake me up. The second I felt my body relax, I could sense the presence of someone else in my room. I opened my eyes and leaned up to see Ayla standing there looking around.

"Uh—"

"Have you ever gotten a feeling that you couldn't explain?" Ayla asked. "A kind of feeling that you couldn't shake, and you weren't really sure why?"

"Yeah, but—can an AI have a feeling like that—or— just have feelings in general?"

She sent dagger-eyes my way. "You have no idea how sophisticated we are."

"No." I rubbed my eyes. "I guess I don't."

"I'm sorry to ruin your sleep, I needed to see you— to talk to you."

"What's going on? Does this have something to do with what Cleo said to me about you?"

Ayla looked like she was holding something back as she walked toward me. I knew she had full control over her appearance, but she had decided on the girl next door look she was famed for. She was incredibly cute, and it made me feel a bit weird to say I was attracted to a hologram. She stopped in front of me and looked into my eyes.

I felt awkward for some reason. "Are you going to tell me you're in love with me or something? Because that would be *way* too weird."

"What? No. I didn't mean this to seem like that." She moved back to the centre of the room. "I don't understand it, but I've been getting these tiny bits of data that have been coming to me, and it's giving me weird feelings about tonight in particular."

"Yeah, Cleo mentioned that to me. What's so special about tonight?"

Did she know what we were planning to do? Did the Interceptors know? Was it all some elaborate test that Fern was in on? I couldn't wait for the day when I stopped having a thousand questions about literally everything.

"I don't know." She shook her head and looked into my eyes. "Just—be careful, okay? I don't understand it, but I needed to tell you that."

Ayla warped out of the room, and I sat there staring at the wall. "Thanks?" I laid back down. "Someone's not big on goodbyes."

It felt more like a blink than it did a few-minute long nap. At least it was a slight nudge that woke me up instead of Kieran in my ear. I blinked my eyes open, and Fern was hovering above my face for the second time.

"Welcome back to the waking world," she said.

"You better be careful or I'm gonna start thinking you like being in my personal space."

She leaned closer and closer to me until our lips hovered inches apart. "Who said that would be a bad thing?"

Few girls could work the punk look, but Fern had it doing all kinds of favours for her. The light blue glow of her cyber-earrings lit her face in a soft light. She had done herself up with heavy make-up, but it added to her style. Her smokey eyes and dark red lips were so inviting. I had to do my best to keep my eyes from wandering a bit lower.

"I guess you make a good—"

The sharp whir of the door sliding open cam from the other side of the room.

"Oh my god," Keyshawn said with so much emotion that I could actually feel him smiling. "KIERAN! Your boy—is an ab-so-lute—legend."

I couldn't blame Keyshawn for assuming—what he was clearly assuming. Most people probably would have been embarrassed like Fern, but I was struggling to hold back laughter.

Fern shot up, and I sat up to see Kieran and Keyshawn in the doorway with huge toothy grins.

Fern rolled her eyes. "Uh-huh, it's not what you're thinking."

"Yeah, we *totally* didn't just walk in on anything—I'll get the 'deets from you later, buddy," Kieran said as they walked back out to the common room. "Don't forget to wipe that lipstick off before you come out."

"He's not going to give you any *'deets*, because there aren't any." Fern stormed after them. "We didn't even do any—"

Fern's voice was cut off by the door whizzing shut behind her. I groaned as I grabbed a jacket and followed everyone back into the common room. Kieran and Keyshawn looked the same aside from the jackets they'd also grabbed, but both the girls had dolled themselves up as much as they could in the time they had.

I leaned against the kitchen counter. "I don't know if we should do this tonight, guys."

"But you were in right before your nap. Someone convince you to stick around here instead?" Keyshawn asked with a raised eyebrow.

"I will make you eat your fist," Fern said.

"Okay, I missed something," Phoebe said.

I debated if I should tell them about what Ayla had said. If she had talked to any of them, they would have understood why I said that. For some reason, Ayla had chosen to appear to me to give me that warning. Heading out didn't feel right, but I needed to see Lenna.

I had no idea what to think.

"Forget it. I know this question might be coming at a bad time—but does anyone know how we're going to make it to the other side of the facility without getting caught?"

"*That* is a good point." Fern wagged a finger.

Phoebe raised her hand while she had her arms crossed. "I know a way." We all looked at her in surprise. "Remember that day with all the vomiting?"

Who could ever forget?

Phoebe had eaten a bit too big of a breakfast one morning before training, and is if it were always meant to happen, she took a nasty hit during some early training. The solid shot to her gut had her puking everything she could out for the rest of the day. Everyone still debated about whether it was the hit or some kind of food poisoning.

"I don't need that mental image right now," Keyshawn said with a shudder.

"Shut it. Lili brought me back here through an old service door that's basically one long empty hallway through the facility. Apparently it's used to move deliveries across the facility quickly. She actually told me about a time when her trainee group snuck out to—"

"Wait, wait, wait. Other Interceptors have snuck out while they were in training?" Kieran asked.

"I wasn't supposed to say that." Phoebe palmed her face.

"Looks like we aren't going to get in that much trouble if we get caught after all," Fern said as we all headed for the door. "Vámonos."

"What if it's locked?"

"Locked?" Fern scoffed. "How many doors have you come across in this giant floating facility that are actually locked?"

Phoebe sighed, "Let's go."

As we snuck into the desolate hallway, I couldn't get Ayla out of my mind. Her warning was so out of nowhere that it had been pretty alarming. If she knew what we were planning to do, she would have told the Interceptors. If there was danger of any kind she would have told me.

The Interceptors AI was the most intricate tech I'd ever experienced, so the thought of Ayla not knowing how she knew something put me off.

We opened the old service door at the end of the hallway and stared out into the endless night sky. Warning or no warning, it was a beautiful night to sneak out.

Chapter 17:
Welcome To Shift

When we made it to Kieran's car, Lenna jumped out and threw her arm around me. I missed her, but I had no idea I had missed her so much. I wrapped her in the tightest bear hug I could, and kissed her on her head. After our quick greeting, she hopped into Kieran's arms, and it looked like he was in heaven.

"Everything's been okay?" I asked.

"It's been refreshing to stay at Kieran's place. Mrs. Moore told me I could stay until you guys were back so I didn't have to figure everything out on my own."

"Classic mom," Kieran said.

"Classic mom? Remember when we were kids and she—"

"I know—I know. My parents can be dicks. The only reason they're letting Lenna stay is because you're here with me and one of us might become famous. I know."

"Alright, love the kinda-awkward reunion—can't wait to meet you—lots of obvious questions," Fern glanced at Lenna's arm. "But if we get caught, we might actually die, so—" She gestured to the car.

We all piled in, and after a few menus on Kieran's visor, we were on our way down to the city.

"Any requests for what shenanigans we should get up to tonight?" Kieran asked.

"Make the visor bigger—I know a sweet place where we can grab some food, some drinks, and have some fun," Fern said. "Maybe a little dancing?"

Kieran extended it, and she put in the address. "Are you sure? This place is kind of expensive."

"Kieran's treat."

His eyes bugged out of his head, but Keyshawn tapped him. "I got you, buddy. It'll be our treat."

"Our big, strapping, rich heroes," Fern said in dramatic fashion.

"Uh-huh. I ain't rich so I better earn a kiss like you were laying on Rhys back there."

I groaned as I felt Lenna, and Phoebe's eyes landing on me, "Excuse me—what?"

Fern started smacking him. "That's not what was happening—you—stop—that."

"Get it, bro." Lenna gave me a playful punch in the shoulder.

Fern spun around. "You wanna lose another arm?"

Everyone in the vehicle stopped and stared as Lenna, and Fern stared each other down.

Lenna leaned forward. "Try it."

They both burst into laughter, and thankfully, everyone was as confused as I was.

"I like her, Rhys," Lenna said. "She's not some kind of pushover."

"Oh, he has a habit of dating *those* kinds of girls, huh?" Fern moved over to sit next to Lenna.

"You don't know the half of it."

I brought a hand to my head. "You can see your sister, they said. It'll be nice, they said."

I looked over to Keyshawn while he was whispering to Kieran. He pointed to the same arm Lenna had lost.

Kieran shook his head and waved his hand by his neck. He nodded in understanding.

Lenna's arm wasn't usually a touchy subject, and it was pretty common that she'd been asked about it. I wanted to tell Keyshawn that it was okay to ask, but it wasn't my place to decide something like that for either of them.

"Super quick question for everyone—" Lenna said.

I figured she probably had a thousand questions about the Interceptors and the whole process we'd been going through over the last little while.

"I was thinking about this in the shower—"

"Nice." Kieran smirked.

"That's his sister, man." Keyshawn punched Kieran's shoulder. "I got you, Rhys."

Lenna rolled her eyes. "Anyways—do you guys ever wonder if what you experience is the same as everyone else? Like, if I eat a piece of cheese, does that cheese taste the same to you guys? Does it feel the same? Smell the same? Isn't that weird to think about?" Everyone stared at her. "What?"

"You're so weird," Fern finally said. "It's like you were made for Kieran."

Lenna blushed as Kieran pumped his fist. "Glad someone else finally agrees."

After a while of catching up, and Lenna making a few new friends, we arrived at a bustling skyscraper. I wasn't in the typically expensive area often, but I had come here with Kieran on his eighteenth birthday. It was one of the crazy party spots for younger people in the city.

"Ladies, and not-so-gentle-men, welcome to Shift. The best nightclub in the city," Fern said as she swung a door open.

"Why do they call it that?" Keyshawn asked as we stepped out of the car. "*Shift* is a kinda lame name."

"See all the balconies that are sticking out?" Phoebe pointed upward. "Those are all mini bio-tech domes that recreate any location throughout the history of the world."

"Hence the name, Shift," Fern said.

"It doesn't look any different from here."

"Wait 'till you're up there." I gave him a light push. "They didn't even mention what happens inside."

"Well, what about our—"

"It's weapon-friendly. Most places in the city are now, thanks to Zeal. This place gets lots of out-of-towners and they tend to be the most strapped with weapons—for the obvious reasons. Let's go."

Kieran sent the car off to park itself while we made our way into Shift. Bouncy pop music reverberated all the way down to the lobby of the building, and the girls did a little dance on their way to the elevator. People who'd had a few too many drinks were dancing their way out of the building.

"Where to first?" Kieran asked as we hopped in the elevator. "Dancing and drinks, or a bite to eat?"

"Let's get our boogie on," Phoebe said. "Food can wait."

"Yeah, we don't need Phoeb' puking all over the dance floor." I teased.

"Oh my god."

The club was situated in what was generally a safer section of the city, but the nightlife could attract less than savoury patrons. Allowing in most people with weapons helped the public feel safe—somehow. Our weapons were right at home alongside all the others.

Kieran pushed a button as the girls *wooed* and the elevator shot up to the top floor of the building. My stomach growled as we passed by the floor that sold food.

The doors opened up to a multi-level party that had been packed with people from every walk of life. Music was blaring, and everyone was either on their feet dancing or at a booth drinking.

Fern said something into Phoebe's ear and then grabbed Keyshawn and me by the arm. "C'mon boys, let's go grab drinks. You know Kieran, and Lenna's orders?" I nodded. "First round's on Keyshawn."

The song changed as we made our way through the dance floor and the entirety of the room changed. A laser ran across the room, and anything it passed over morphed. Where it had once been more rustic with bright lasers, it shifted to a soft pink with smoke.

We reached the bar and passed a line on the ground. In an instant, the music sounded like it was miles away. Moving through tech-fields always gave me a sick feeling in the pit of my stomach in the same way the anti-gravity of the city's buses had. None of us could complain—the tech-field did help out a lot.

"That made me feel all kinds of weird," Keyshawn said as he shivered and brought a hand up to his midsection.

"People keep telling me I'll get used to it, but I still haven't," I said.

"Gotta live in a higher-end district for that kind of thing. Go through the fields multiple times a day, and you get used to it," Fern said as she pushed past a few people. "Us lower folks get to almost throw up every time we walk through one of those stupid things."

We made it to the front of the bar and ordered everyone's drinks. Keyshawn opened his old visor and used it to transfer his credits. Once the bartender spotted the finished transfer he turned around and started sliding bars on a huge holo-display.

Fern turned toward Keyshawn. "Word around the facility is you like Phoebe."

He looked from her to me. "Is that so?"

"Don't look at me, man. I'm not interested in anyone's love life."

"Look, I'm not into all the dumb drama either," Fern rolled her eyes. "So I'm gonna make this as simple as possible. You like tall, nerdy blondes. Go ask everyone's favourite tall, nerdy blonde to dance—have a good time —maybe hit her with the lips."

The bartender put two of our smokey drinks down in front of us.

"You sure?" Keyshawn asked with a glance back at Phoebe.

Fern grabbed the drinks and handed them to him. "One for you, one for her. Go get to know her a little better. Think of it like a surprise date."

"You sure this ain't just so you can get to know Rhys a little bit better?"

I didn't hear Fern's response, but I assumed Keyshawn received one of her patented evil eye looks, because he ran off with the drinks. If he wasn't careful, Fern was going to get in some extra combat training with him in the middle of our common room.

She turned around with a cool smile. "You ever been here before?"

I leaned against the bar. "Yeah—once for Kieran's birthday. Places like this aren't exactly my scene. Not to mention, I can't exactly afford to—"

"Not your scene, huh?" The bartender placed two more drinks in front of us, and we sipped on them as Fern continued. "So that has to mean—you can't dance."

"Hey! I can—you're not wrong."

"So basically—we have to dance."

I raised an eyebrow. "You really don't seem like the *go dancing at a club* type."

"I can have my girly moments in between kicking all the boy's asses."

"No promises—but maybe." I turned and saw Kieran chatting up Lenna. "Didn't realize I was going to end up on a make-shift triple-date."

"Don't get ahead of yourself there, mud-boy."

There probably wasn't a nickname worse than mud-boy.

"That can not catch on."

"I haven't decided if it's a date or not."

The bartender dropped off the last two drinks and we made our way back over to the group. We handed Lenna and Kieran their drinks and bobbed to the music. The song shifted into an ancient funk song and the pink room changed to a rainbow of lights.

"Lenna, you feeling a dance comin' on?" Fern asked

She smiled. "What are we waiting for?"

We made our way to the dance floor and the group danced for what felt like hours. I was thankful for the conditioning training because an hour or so of dancing usually would have worn me out. We'd made our way to the bottom of a few drinks, and about a dozen songs when I noticed some guy getting a little too handsy with Lenna.

It wasn't just typical bar handsy either.

I made my way over to Lenna and Kieran as they talked to some guy. His platinum blonde hair had been set back into a whooshing spike.

"What the hell's your problem, dude?" Kieran asked.

"My problem? What's your problem? Bringing some weird amputee chick into the club." The man scoffed. "I can't figure out if she's supposed to turn me on or not."

No one insults my sister.

Not like that.

I cocked back an arm as I pushed between the two of them, but Lenna must have had a feeling I was coming, because she grabbed my arm. "Rhys—don't."

"Oh-ho-ho! Big man over here," the man said to me before turning his attention back to Kieran. "I thought I recognized you. You're two of those goons in the running to become the next member of the super-zero squad. Mess with me and you're messing with the Vanguard, so I suggest you step off."

Whatever that guy said had led Kieran to post up in his face. I knew a comment like that was going to be the thing that launched him into a full-on rage.

I caught his arm as he went for a swing.

Lenna was right. That guy wasn't worth it. If we ended up in a fight, we'd end up getting caught. I didn't know much about the Vanguard, but I had a feeling that assaulting one of its members wouldn't go over well.

"Let's just—just go get some air," Lenna said.

It was clear that the guy had bothered her, but I wasn't about to risk all of our chances at becoming Interceptors over some drunken asshole at a bar. Kieran stared the guy down for a little longer than I was comfortable with so I gave him a strong tug, and the three of us headed for some air.

The room changed to look like we were walking on the sky, with all the chairs and tables becoming clouds. I waved to Keyshawn, Fern, and Phoebe on our way to the bio-tech dome on the balcony. They caught up to us as we passed across the line on the floor, and the music became distant again.

From inside the club, it looked like any other night in the city. Once we crossed the line the entire balcony morphed into a beautiful raised sandy pier overlooking a golden beach.

"Everything alright?" Phoebe asked.

"It's cool. Just some douchebag," I said.

"I'll go grab everyone some fresh drinks and bring them back out here. Then we can head down and grab some food. Fern?" Phoebe waved her over.

They headed back into the bar for drinks and a little bit of gal-pal chit-chat time.

I turned to Kieran. "You good?"

"Yeah, you?"

I nodded.

"It ain't a night out if there isn't one asshole, right?" Keyshawn laughed.

Kieran and I joined in on the laughter—and even Lenna did eventually. It might have been because it was true. It might have also been that we all knew any one of us could have taken that guy with our eyes closed, and a hand tied behind our backs.

"So this is where you super-zeroes ran away to hide. Not so super if you ask me," the platinum blonde man said as he walked out onto the balcony.

"Could you be more of a standard bully?" Keyshawn asked.

I sighed as I glared at the man, "Look, dude. If you'd just shut the hell—"

The scene around us glitched for a moment. Without warning someone flew right by me, knocking Keyshawn away from the group. There was a man in the same kind of kit Sable had been wearing with a hand wrapped around the top of Keyshawn's head. He pushed him up against the wall and bashed his head against the concrete so violently that chunks of rock flew away from the wall.

I couldn't believe what I was seeing.

Chapter 18:
Not Enough Time

It happened so fast.

Crack.

Blood.

Crack.

Blood.

Over and over.

Lenna screamed as I sprinted toward whoever that guy assaulting Keyshawn was, but before I could reach him he had let go of him. Keyshawn fell to the floor in a heap with blood spewing from the back of his head. The sight stopped me in my tracks.

"Awe, I got the wrong one again," the man said.

Wrong one?

Again?

Who else?

Keyshawn.

Was he—?

No.

He couldn't be.

My eyes moved from Keyshawn to the man who had attacked him as the other people in the dome ran the hell outta there. The guy was massive, with a frame that was well over six feet and covered in muscle. He had the same defect as Sable with two different coloured eyes.

It had to be Sable's fraternal twin, Dorian.

"There you are, Rhys," he said as he looked at me with a face filled with rage. "I'm gonna enjoy making you bleed."

"Yeah—we're gonna have to ask you to not," I said as I squared up.

"Who's we?" Dorian chuckled.

I turned to where I expected Kieran to be, but he was still in the same spot—motionless, staring at Keyshawn. It looked like he was frozen in fear, but that wasn't normal for Kieran. Lenna's expression told me everything I needed to know about what was going to happen next.

Dorian launched himself at me, but I managed to swerve out of the way— sending my fist into his midsection in the process.

Delivering unprotected punches to people wearing kits was something that I seriously needed to stop doing.

I clutched my hand, as Phoebe screamed from behind me. I wanted to look back, but I knew if I dropped my guard for a second, Dorian would toss me off the building.

His expression changed from one of anger to enjoyment. It's like he relished every scream he heard. How could a sick person like that have ever been an Interceptor?

"What the hell happened?" Fern rushed beside me.

"This guy came out of nowhere. I'll stick to him. You make sure everyone gets out of here. Don't let him hurt anyone in the building." I turned to Dorian and blew on my fist. "This guy's just pissed that I rocked his sister's world."

His expression morphed back to one of anger. "I was already gonna kill you, but maybe I'll beat you within an inch of your life and let her do it."

Beside us, a terrified couple was in the midst of a slow crawl back into the bar. The only reason I noticed them was because of how much they were shaking.

"Aw, what's the matter?" Fern mocked. "Sis gotta do all the heavy lifting for you? You too afraid to get your hands dirty?"

I didn't know if two Interceptors in training could beat one of the original's—I didn't even know if we could do it if Kieran managed to snap out of the trance he was in, but we had to try.

I grabbed the crawling couple by the backs of each of their shirts and did what I could to toss them to safety.

Dorian launched toward us. After tugging his belt from his kit, it morphed into a huge scythe. He swung it right at my face, but I ducked it—grabbing the shaft of it to swoop over beside him and I landed a clean strike to his face.

It didn't do anything.

Not a single thing.

I stepped back as Fern kicked the platinum blonde guy back into the bar—and caught Dorian with one of the wicked spinning kicks Lili had been teaching us, which staggered him. He brought a hand to his face and started laughing.

"You need help," Fern said as she curled her lip.

From my new angle, I could see Keyshawn and Phoebe on the ground. Her face was cherry red, and she was sobbing uncontrollably, but I couldn't blame her. I hoped they were tears from fear and concern, and not any other reason.

"You need some die," Dorian sneered at Fern.

"*Some* die?" I asked. "Don't you mean—"

Dorian launched at us again. He focused on me and waited for me to make a hint of a move. He must have underestimated me before because he caught me across the leg with a slash of his scythe with ease. He punched me square in the jaw, but Fern jumped in to help me.

She managed to land a couple of quick hits on him, but he grabbed her shoulders and nailed her with a head-butt before tossing her aside.

I could see blood trickle from her head as he tossed her, and it pissed me off all over again. I took a step, but the gash on my leg stopped me.

Dorian looked at me and laughed again. He wrapped his scythe back around his waist as he stalked toward me. I caught him with a quick elbow strike, but I failed to faze him again. I tried to ready myself, but he nailed me with a stiff series of shots before kicking me toward the railing of the building.

My vision was blurry, and my leg felt like it was on fire. The coppery tinge of blood filled my mouth, and I knew all it would take was a bit of pressure to toss me over the rail.

Dorian was back on me in a second, he grabbed the scruff of my jacket in his hands and held me over the railing.

"Not gonna ask me if I have any last words?"

Dorian growled, "Am I supposed to?"

"It's kinda the bad-guy thing to do."

"Sounds dumb."

I spat a glob of blood into his face and after a quick chuckle, he tossed me clean over the rail.

I managed to wrap a hand around the railing, and I swung hard back against the concrete wall. I heard Lenna scream again, and while I hated it, I hoped it would be enough to distract Dorian. I looked down, and thankfully the bio-tech dome made the drop look a lot less scary than it would have been. Something about looking like I'd land in the ocean helped, even though I knew I'd splat on the concrete instead.

I expected Dorian to stomp on my hand or stick me with his scythe, but instead I heard him cry out in pain.

Ayla appeared next to me. "I knew it!" She looked around as she pretended to hang from the railing with me. "What the hell is going on? Where are we?"

"Long story. Dorian's out for revenge for his sister or something. Mind waiting until I climb back up from my imminent death to yell at me?"

"I could tell Dorian was here, I can feel little bits of Pandora's data from all the way over here. It's gross. The Interceptors are on their way. Hold on."

"*Hold on.* Funny." I climbed back over the railing.

Ayla merged with my sword again. "You aren't dying on my watch."

Kieran had broken out of whatever trance he was in and had his axes at the ready. Fern twirled her flail around while Dorian readied his scythe again. His kit had been split across the back, and the cut that accompanied the split oozed with blood.

"How'd you break outta my hold, kid?" he asked Kieran.

"Don't know—don't care."

I clicked the trigger on the hilt of my sword and pulled it out. Once again, Ayla being merged with my sword allowed me to hold it with ease. I readied it in case Dorian made another move, but suddenly, I couldn't move at all. I couldn't speak. Whatever had happened to Kieran had happened to me.

"The three of us can take this guy," Fern said.

"A couple rookies think they can take me out without a kit between them. Laughable," Dorian said.

Kieran looked at me and understood what had happened. "Rhys can't move. Dorian's using his time element to freeze us one by one."

"Found me out." He rushed toward Kieran and Fern. "Time to die."

Kieran swung his axes in an attempt to force Dorian into a swing of Fern's flail, but he dodged them both. He punched Ferns hand which sent the end of the flail shooting toward Kieran. He ducked it, as Dorian caught Fern with a kick, disarming her. Kieran lashed out with his axes, but Dorian slowed him down mid-movement and caught each of his wrists with ease. He head-butted Kieran until he was motionless.

"You asshole!" Phoebe threw her spear right at Dorian.

He narrowly managed to dodge the spear and it landed on the ground by me. Phoebe rushed in to help Fern, but she was met with a huge kick in the chest for her troubles.

Dorian tossed Kieran at her, and the two fell to the ground. Fern had snatched one of Kieran's axes, but Dorian caught her wrist as well and rocked her with another huge kick.

Everyone was down.

I started to sweat as Dorian stalked toward me with his scythe drawn. He'd been toying with us the entire time. Hurting Keyshawn was fun for that guy. He did that to scramble us, and send our emotions into disarray.

"You're going to need to snap out of it real quick," Ayla said as she waved her arms in my face.

How am I supposed to do that?

"Use the kit."

You can hear my thoughts?

"Use the kit! Now!"

If I do that, I'll get kicked out of—

"If you don't do it, you'll be dead—which is worse than being kicked out—unless your name is Kieran."

Lenna ran up and punched Dorian clean across the face. "Okay, ow." She shook her hand.

He gripped his scythe tighter as he turned to face her. There wasn't any time to worry about getting kicked

155

out. I closed my eyes and my kit covered my body. The slight shock of the cold alloy against the cut on my leg snapped me from my daze, and I shot forward with my sword pointed at Dorian.

I caught him off-guard as he raised his scythe. The look of surprise on his face told me that people didn't break out of his element often—and he was annoyed two people had done it in the same night. He barely managed to deflect my strike with his scythe.

Ayla guided me. *Up and over.*

I pushed Lenna away as he swung in a half-circle. After flipping over him, I slashed him across the back where Kieran had before. Dorian stumbled forward with blood seeping from his wound. He turned around and looked angrier than he had before. He had started sweating as well, and I hoped it was because his wound was worse than it looked.

"You're dead meat, kid."

Get some distance and ditch the kit.

I grabbed Lenna and jumped back toward the group. My kit returned back to the medallion of my necklace and the stinging pain in my leg returned. I sheathed my sword as Kieran, Phoebe and Fern made it to shaky feet, ready to back me up for another round.

Ayla popped out of the sword, and I couldn't hear her in my head anymore.

Mickey jumped from the shadows being created by a nearby umbrella and blocked Dorian's path to us. Lili hopped down into the dome and did the same. One by one, the rest of the Interceptors surrounded Dorian.

Cleo pointed her spear. "Drop the scythe and surrender, Dorian."

"Long time no see." He looked around at all of them and growled, "Looks like replacing Chase is going well for you." He turned his attention to me. "You're a fighter. You're going to need to be."

"Take him," Kiyoshi said, as his war hammer crackled with electricity.

Cleo, Diggs, and Pegs all approached him with weapons drawn. Cleo launched a small spike of ice, but Dorian just laughed it off as he teleported away. They all landed on the rooftop and stormed toward us.

"We—"

Lili stopped Kieran. "Not another word."

I rushed toward Keyshawn, but Cleo stopped me. "Is he alive?"

"You all better hope he is," Kiyoshi barked.

I didn't want to imagine what the consequences of our actions would be, but that didn't matter as much as Keyshawn's well-being.

Chapter 19:
A Classic Scolding

Keyshawn survived Dorian's attack.

Barely.

The worst part was the waiting and wondering. We weren't allowed into the med-bay to visit him. Being able to sit with him for a little while to hope and pray to whatever's out there for his well-being would have been better than nothing.

I would have even settled for a quick call to Lenna.

The team had dragged us all back, and locked us into our rooms for hours. They barely spoke a word to us that didn't come in the form of an angry shout. Lili looked like she wanted nothing to do with me, and I wondered if I had blown it with my elemental training partner.

When Sunday rolled around, we were all hauled into General Odon's office. To my surprise Claudia, Rowan, Raysean, and Aiden were brought in as well. The two people that weren't present were Keyshawn and Bernardo.

"What am I to do with a group of insubordinate, ungrateful, pions like you? Not one of you—not one group, but two separate groups sneaking out on the same night? Do you have any idea what kind of light this puts all of us in? We're supposed to be finding the next great hero," General Odon said with a scowl. "Two of you end up suffering serious injuries at the hands of Dorian. The public is going to crucify us."

"I'm fine. It's not like I could feel my legs anyway," Aiden said.

Ramona was lingering in the corner of the office, and her eyes grew wider as Aiden spoke up. General Odon probably wasn't the kind of guy anyone wanted to sass.

"You're just lucky that Dorian thought you were so weak that you weren't even worth killing. Keep your mouth shut or you'll be wheeling your ass out of here right now. Don't go thinking I won't punish you just because you're in one of those things."

"It's a wheelchair—you can call it what it—" The looks from both Ramona and General Odon caused Aiden to shut up.

The other four had snuck out and battled Dorian as well. That must have been what he meant when he said he got the wrong one again.

If we all ended up kicked out, that would mean Bernardo would become the new Interceptor for the team. While he looked like a nice enough guy, he didn't fit the bill.

"I wanted every single one of you out, but Ramona informed me that what we were left with might not be up to my standards either. I'll have you know that two of the Interceptors think you should have all been kicked out of the process as well. We are a team here though, and we went with the majority—including Ayla."

It felt like every person in the room sighed a breath of relief at the same time.

"Had Mr. Greer been killed, you'd all be out of here and on your asses. Thanks to the quick actions of Mr.

York and Ms. Huber, he sustained a fractured skull and mild—repairable brain damage."

It was a relief to hear that Keyshawn would pull through, but I had never heard of any kind of repairable brain damage.

"All of you seem confused by that, so let me explain. We've been experimenting with state of the art healing methods here in the facility, and now anyone bonded with a kit—even a training kit, can be brought back from the brink of death. Keyshawn will be as good as new, but he will not be able to return to training during this session."

I looked over to Phoebe. She'd started to cry.

"I'm glad he's okay sir, but, Kieran and Phoebe did as much as I—"

"Now is not the time for you all to speak up. Now is the time for you to listen." I shut my mouth and stared at a white flower that sat in a pot on the corner of Odon's desk. "You may want to watch how much you piss me off considering you actively used your kit outside of training." I hung my head while Odon continued. "Your punishment will be decided upon individually by the Interceptors based on the recollection of events that played out."

I almost felt thankful that we'd be getting punished by the team rather than Odon, but I had a feeling that the team had much more creative ideas for punishments.

General Odon waved his hand. "All of you, get out of my office and think about how each of you are representing Chase's legacy every single day. Think about how you failed not only him, but the team as a whole."

Without a word, we all piled out of his office.

As we shut the door, Ayla warped in front of us. "Each of you is to report to the Interceptor who is training you on your elements."

We each hurried toward our teacher's living areas without a word. As I passed by Cleo's place, I looked back to see that Ramona had followed me. She waved me over as Phoebe and Bernardo walked into the apartment.

"What's up—ma'am?"

"You don't need to do that. Ramona is fine. I wanted to let you know—I think you did the right thing. You guys deserved a night of fun. What happened isn't your fault." She knocked on Cleo's door and headed in.

I hadn't had many interactions with Ramona at that point, but I was glad to hear that from her. She struck me as the kind of woman anyone would want on their side.

Lili was on the far side of the facility by herself so I was on my own in the hall when Ayla warped in front of me.

"You know it's freaky when you pop up like that," I said. "It's like I'm living with a ghost."

"Well, get used to it. If you end up becoming an Interceptor, you're going to have to learn to love my beautiful ghostly-ass." She tapped a finger to her tongue and made a sizzling sound as she brought the finger to a butt cheek. "I'm kinda the prize, ya know?"

I wasn't having any part of her attempts at jokes. I felt like crap that we had gotten caught, and I felt worse that Keyshawn had gotten hurt.

"They're not angry—they're disappointed."

I turned a corner. "Great. The disappointed parent treatment. The only good thing is I've never actually experienced it first-hand."

"Dark. They're all guilty of sneaking out too—even 'Yoshi. They've all been in your shoes. You should be proud, Rhys. You've stood up to two ex-Interceptors and haven't died. You guys actually did really well against Dorian. You made sure no one at that club died that night, and that means something."

The image of Dorian smashing Keyshawn's head into the wall flashed in my mind. "When can I see him?"

"You won't." Ayla hung her head. "Once he's healed, he'll be taken home. If there's ever another vacancy or we decide it's time to expand the team, he can try again."

Not getting to say goodbye was going to be rough. He'd become a good friend of mine far faster than most. Keyshawn was a good guy, and he didn't deserve to lose his shot like that.

I felt terrible all over again as I reached Lili's door. "Any tips on how I should go about this?"

"Shut up, and don't piss her off more than she already is."

"I thought you said they're disappointed."

"Yeah, but Lili is like Kiyoshi. Those two get disappointed *and* they get mad."

I nodded and reached for the panel, but stopped myself. "Can I ask you one more thing?"

"Shoot."

"Do you appear to anyone else as much as you do with me?"

She paused for a moment before she spoke. "Nope. Huh, what's up with that?"

"That's kind of what I was wondering."

"Who knows? Maybe I like your spunk and plucky attitude—or maybe I think you'll wind up dead if I don't help you out. I'll figure that out later. Right now, I'm still trying to figure out what's going on with these bits of rogue data."

"Don't you think they might have something to do with each other?"

"Probably, but that's for me to worry about." Ayla disappeared, and I placed my hand on the panel.

The door to Lili's quarters opened up, and I was met with a quaint wood-panelled apartment. It smelled like freshly baked cookies, and the warmth of the apartment was inviting. Lili could be tough, but that was exactly the kind of cute place I pictured her living in.

"Lili? It's Rhys. I was told to come see you about my punishment for—well you know." I called.

She stormed out of what I assumed was her bedroom, and marched right up to me, her stupid little camera right alongside her. I'd never seen her so angry. She didn't look that angry the night of the incident. It was like something inside her had been stewing over the last couple of days. The baggy sweats she had on made her look smaller than usual, which managed to make her a bit less scary.

She slapped me across the face and I was lucky her sleeve was long enough to cover her hand. Lili stared into my eyes—she was hurt. I felt like an old lover who had betrayed her trust.

After a deep breath, she wrapped me in a tight hug. "Are you okay?"

"Yeah," I wrapped my arms around her in more of my usual confusion. "They wouldn't let me into the med-bay for my leg, but I'm okay. I've been more worried about Keyshawn."

She let go of me and walked to her kitchen. "Will you have a cup of tea with me?"

"Of course."

"Go pop a squat on the couch. I'll be a sec."

"Sure."

Something about her place felt simple. It wasn't bogged down with entertainment stations or hard to look at thanks to bright white walls. It was cozy, and the little fireplace below her holo-TV looked like the perfect place to curl up after a long day.

Lili walked over with two cups of tea and sat next to me. "I was angry."

"I know, I—"

She held a hand up and shot me dagger eyes. "I was *really* angry, but I think it was because a part of me expected better from you. I was expecting you to be better than me." She took a breath. "I did the same thing with the friends I made when I was joining. I get it."

"We shouldn't have gone out."

"No. You shouldn't have," A menu popped up next to her cup and she selected an option. To my amusement, the tea changed to a lighter colour. "But you did, and now you're dealing with the consequences. Ayla was able to mine your memories when she connected with you, we all saw what happened."

I closed my eyes and saw the moment again. The horrific sight of Keyshawn's head crumbling a wall. The blood splattering everywhere. It was a miracle that he'd managed to survive.

"I can't stop seeing it," I said.

"He's going to be fine."

"What if he wasn't? I didn't have time to react. I couldn't help him. I—"

"If you're going to be an Interceptor, you're going to see a lot worse—but you made the best choice." She put a hand on my leg. "You jumped in to try to save him from someone who could have killed any of you in an instant."

I took a sip of tea and grimaced at the taste. Lili placed her hand over mine on the cup. "Use this to open the menu and pick what you want in it."

I selected some milk and sugar, and the tea changed the same way hers had. "I didn't know what to do."

"You didn't think—you reacted. That's good. I'm happy to hear that, but you're on thin ice now. All of you are. If anything—and I mean *anything* like this happens again, you'll all be gone. I can't defend something like this again."

She looked into my eyes with the most serious look I'd seen on an Interceptor. It made me happy to hear that she had been one of the team members that had defended us. Regardless, it still hurt to know she'd only stick her neck out so far.

"I was wondering—no one's mentioned anything about me using my kit."

"We decided that since you were instructed specifically by Ayla to use it in a life or death situation, it could slide—this time. Like everything else, don't push your luck again."

"Got it."

"You'll probably be happy to know that while not everyone had your back, most of us did—and we all agreed you did the right thing."

"Yeah, Ramona mentioned something like that. I guess that does kinda make me feel better."

"Your punishment is a twenty-K run with me every morning and an additional two hours of combat training each night—one hour with myself, and an hour with Cleo, at her request."

To some people, that might have sounded like a light punishment. I'd already learned that something like that was the worst punishment imaginable. Two hours of getting my ass kicked by women was painful in more than one way.

The camera flew closer to my face—probably to snag a great shot of my reaction. "That does the opposite of make me feel better. My punishment—is more training?"

"You're going to find out how rough training can be. If you thought I was bad—Cleo is going to dust you. Her technique isn't as good, but she makes up for that with strength."

I gulped, and suddenly I wasn't in the mood for tea. I stood up and scratched my head. "I guess I'll let you be if that's it."

"I don't know what they want with you, but it's clear that for whatever reason, you're one of Zeal's targets." She stood up and put a hand on my shoulder. "You need to be careful."

I nodded before heading for the door. "Is there anything I can do—that any of us can do to fix things?"

There was a hint of a smile on her face. "Become the next Interceptor."

The walk back to my room was eerily silent. I fell back on my bed and stared up at the ceiling. My eyes closed, but flashes from the fight with Dorian kept coming back. That cycle repeated for hours, and when I checked the time it was two in the morning.

I headed for my door to grab a glass of water, but when it slid open I found Fern staring back at me. She looked as worn out as I felt. We hadn't said a word to each other since the other night—none of us had, and I still didn't know what to say to her.

"Fern, I—I, uh—"

"I can't get it out of my head. Keyshawn on the ground—nearly getting killed by Dorian. Seeing you flip over the railing. When he was head-butting Kieran over and over. What if you had—what if—what if Keyshawn had—"

She looked distraught, and something told me I shouldn't use the words *die* or *died* at any point. I wanted to wrap my arms around her and comfort her more than anything.

"Keyshawn's going to be okay. I'm okay—everyone's okay. It was a rough night."

"It's all my fault."

"Fern—"

"It was all my idea. You tried to stop us."

"No one could have seen that coming."

That wasn't true.

Ayla had seen it coming. She didn't know how, or what she had seen, but she knew there was some kind of danger headed my way. I wondered again if I should share the conversation I had with Ayla to Fern.

"Could I sleep with you?" Fern asked

"Uh—you want to *sleep* with me?"

"Not in—*that* way. Like, in the same bed. I don't want to be alone. I'll leave before wake-up, so no one gets the wrong idea."

"That won't be much of a problem considering my punishment involves early morning runs," I said with a sigh. "But what about the cameras—in the morning?"

"I'll leave extra early. I promise. Please, just for a little while." I gestured for her to climb in and we slid under the covers. She cuddled into my chest, and it felt like my shirt started to dampen some. "I don't know if I can do this—if this is how I'm going to feel when something like this happens."

"One day at a time. It's always gotta be worse when it's your friend that gets hurt. You can do it."

Part of me said that for her, but deep down, part of it was for me too.

"I don't know."

I didn't know what to say. Fern was always so strong and put together, so it was weird to hear her talk like that. A situation where your friend is beaten within an inch of his life in front of you could change anyone.

"Why are you here? Why do you want this—really?"

There was a long pause. I wasn't sure if maybe she had fallen asleep from how worn out she was, or if she was trying to find the words.

"Aside from beating up the big bad? I want to help the slums. I don't want any kid to have to grow up the way I grew up. The divide between people isn't fair. The

Interceptors' presence in a place like the slums is laughable and I want to do everything I can to fix that."

I smiled. "Then do me a favour and you keep on fighting, okay?"

After a while, her body started to have tiny twitches, but I wasn't sure if it was her falling asleep or silent sobs. I drifted off to sleep wondering why I had been targeted by two ex-Interceptors in the span of a few weeks. I couldn't help wondering exactly how long I had before my luck finally ran out.

Chapter 20:
A Good Ole Hostage Situation

Monday came and after a horrible early morning run—which was really more of a sprint thanks to a still-angry Lili—I shuffled into a group training room.

It was time to learn how to properly use our kits. We'd all grown interested in trying out all the gadgets that our kits had, but I wasn't sure how to activate any of them. Some people were looking forward to learning to use the jet thrusters in their kits legs and trying to utilize their element for mobility.

Everyone in the room looked well-rested compared to me, and I wondered what their punishments had ended up being. No one else was unlucky enough to end up doing more endless runs.

The common room had been looking a lot cleaner when I walked through that morning, so someone must have been forced into cleaning.

"You guys okay?" I asked as I made my way over to Phoebe, Kieran, and Fern.

"Yeah." Kieran nodded. "It's been a rough few days, and I figure we all feel like ass, but we just need to dive back into training."

The door slid open, and Cleo walked in with Akio in tow. "Due to the events that took place on the weekend,

Akio will be taking Keyshawn's place for the rest of your training. He will be at a heavy disadvantage, but he's said he's up for the challenge."

I looked around and Bernardo looked more confused than anyone else in the room. He must have been hanging out in his room tinkering with something all night. He had no clue what had happened, and I doubted anyone felt like telling him about it.

Akio walked over to us as Cleo continued. "It's time for tech and mobility training." Cleo hit a button, and the room morphed into a primitive city complete with high buildings, bustling traffic, and wildlife. "Everyone activate your kits."

My kit covered my body in an instant, and I took a look around. I might have been having the most trouble with my element after my first-day fluke, but I was having the best luck with control over my kit.

Fern also managed to will her kit out quick, but most people had difficulty bringing theirs out immediately. I watched as Kieran's kit slowly crawled across his body.

I figured Akio would be having more trouble than anyone, but by the time I looked toward him he already had his kit on.

"I'm sure all of you have glanced down at the panels on your wrists more than once," Cleo said. "The first button will create an energy shield on the outside of your arm. You can use it for defence and offence." She popped a shield out on each arm.

Cleo turned toward a tree and swung her arms toward it. The two shields left her arms and flew right at the tree. They passed through the thick wood, and the tree came right down. However the energy on the shields worked, it must have created some kind of immense heat or sharp edge. She pushed a button, and the shields returned.

"Do we need to be worried about the shield cutting

us?" Phoebe asked.

"No, your kits create a kind of field against the type of cyber energy our gear uses. The worst you could be hurt is from simple blunt force. They are pretty versatile pieces of equipment. With an AI, you could send power to them to propel them forward—almost like a motor on a car."

"Cleo is the best with those things," Kieran whispered. "She could probably take Dorian or Sable on with nothing but her shields as a weapon."

"The next button is a grappling hook." Cleo pushed another button and two short lights replaced where the shields had been. "If you get creative with their applications, any of the gear you'll see today can be useful as a weapon or as a tool to move around through the city."

She aimed her arm up at a building, and the grappling hook shot out. It landed in the side of the wall, and Cleo flew up toward where it had landed. The hook disengaged, and in mid-air, she pointed her other arm toward another building and flew toward it. She travelled from building to building as fast as any car could have before landing back in front of us.

"Like that old superhero—swingin' around," Kieran whispered to me in excitement. "So cool."

"You can also disconnect the lines to tether two things together or to tie up a target."

I could tell that I wasn't on my own in my amazement. Cleo made using the gear look so simple, but there was no way that any of us would end up doing things like that.

Cleo pushed the third button, and a spherical force field covered her. "This is a last defence shield. It takes a lot of energy from your kit to use it, but it can withstand a nuclear blast. If you activate it, you won't be able to move all that much, though. You need to use it carefully."

171

She pushed the final button, and the shield dissipated.

"That just leaves—" Kieran started.

"The last button activates the thrusters on your legs. They will allow you to move at great speeds."

Cleo dashed around the area, and it was hard to keep an eye on her movements. She pointed at a big building and ran straight up the side of it before making her way back to the ground in front of us.

I nudged Kieran. "Even I'm excited to practice that."

"If you master all the gear your kit offers, you'll be able to throw in elemental twists when using your gear. Nothing is out of the realm of possibility—it's all about what you can come up with. Start testing the gear out. In a couple of minutes, you'll be demonstrating your skill in front of the class against me."

Everyone became a bit nervous when they heard that. Cleo might not have been the highest-ranking Interceptor, but most people thought she was the most skilled member of the team. She'd done so much good for the world. Most people in the city felt like there was some kind of sexist plot keeping her from being an A-Rank or even an S-Rank Interceptor. At the very least, most of the general public saw her as an equal to Kiyoshi.

We all started pushing buttons and trying out our gear. I had some difficulty throwing the shields with any kind of accuracy, while Kieran had blown everyone away in terms of shield skill. He was close to Cleo's level of precision without any practice, but I suspected his axe throwing helped.

Akio started zipping around with the grappling hooks, but I had a hard time getting used to the force of the pull once it anchored onto something. Once again, Kieran was a whiz kid with the gear.

I was about to test out the thrusters when I thought

of something. "Hey Cleo, the other night—with Dorian. I activated the thrusters on my kit without pushing a button. How do I do that again?"

"You *don't* do that again." Cleo glared at me. "The buttons on your kit are meant to give you a way to manually activate your kit's tech. Whoever joins the team will be permanently linked with Ayla, and she'll be able to activate any of your gear for you."

"Then why even have the manual activation?" Rowan asked.

"The AI." Bernardo squeaked out.

The answer came as a bit of a surprise. It was easy to forget that Bernado was ever in the room thanks to his meek demeanour. I still had no clue how he'd managed to make it to this portion of the selection process.

"Correct," Cleo said. "If something were to happen —something like an EMP, the AI in any of our kits wouldn't be able to activate, and you'd be on your own in a fight."

They thought of everything. There was a backup for the backups. Get in a fight? Use your weapon. Get disarmed? Use your your element. EMP knocks your AI out? Manual use of tech. Kit runs out of power? You can still fall back on your fighting skills.

There were always options.

I wasn't any good with the gear—aside from the thrusters, but at least I knew how to use it all. I still had two weeks before the final assessment—that big fight Faith had mentioned.

I felt like I was one of the strongest in hand-to-hand combat. If I didn't make it, I'd at least have a damn good showing.

"Everyone got a bit of practice in?" Cleo asked to a round of nodding heads. "Good. We're going to run a hostage situation. I'll pick a building and spawn holographic citizens. It's your job to locate me and rescue the hostages without any casualties. You may use any and all of the things you've been taught. Phoebe, Kieran, Bernardo, Rhys, and Fern—you're up first. When Ayla says so, you can start."

Cleo disappeared into the small city in front of us. She was good enough to sneak past us, so we couldn't be certain that she would be in a building in front of us. We'd only have a few minutes to make a plan.

"Cleo isn't going to make this easy," I said as I looked around. "Any ideas?"

I wasn't great with the tech, or my element so I was essentially there to brawl. Kieran was great with the tech, but he too wasn't any good with his element. Phoebe was one of the standouts with her element, and Fern was naturally good at everything that came her way.

The wild card was Bernardo. I hadn't been paying attention to him during any of our training. I knew he had no idea what he was doing in a fight, but he was smart. I hoped he was good with his light element.

"Well, we're a pretty rough mix of skills," Phoebe said.

"Bernardo, how's your element training been going?" Fern asked.

"Not the best, but I can make a flash—"

"That's perfect. We'll link our kits, so we can radio each other. Phoebe and Kieran can take the rooftops to locate which building she's holding up in," Fern said.

"Then the three of us sneak in using your element, Bernardo uses his flash, and the two of us take Cleo down?" I asked.

"Bingo."

"Guys, I don't know how—" Bernardo started.

"Your five minutes starts now," Ayla said with a little hop.

"Five minutes?" We all pushed a button on our kits to sync our kit's communication systems.

"Crap. You guys head up high and start looking around. Check for any buildings that have power on, we'll sweep the streets. Radio in if anyone finds anything," I said before activating my thrusters and taking off.

Bernado reached out. "But—hey!"

I looked back to see Bernardo, and Fern each do the same. Phoebe forced water out of a nearby hydrant to create a wave of ice. It lifted her and Kieran into the air, but Kieran jumped off like a madman. He launched his grappling hooks and started swinging.

"WOOHOO!" Kieran's shout echoed throughout the small city.

"Keep it quiet, numb-nuts." Fern's voice came over the comms.

"Sorry. This is so cool."

It was about a minute before Phoebe came over the comms. "Got her. The tallest building, below the top floor. It looks like there's about fifteen hostages to look out for. They're seated around the walls of the floor."

I headed toward the building. "Fern, Bernardo, group up out front the building, I'm down the street from it. Kieran, move over to the building on the opposite side from Phoebe."

Another minute went by and we all grouped up in the street. "We all know the plan?" Fern asked.

Time was ticking.

Bernardo and I nodded. "Phoebe, Kieran, you guys get ready to come busting through the windows to snag the hostages while we deal with Cleo."

"Got it," they each said.

"Give me your hands." Fern held out her own.

We gave her our hands, and everything went black. Bernardo and I were looking around, but we had no idea where we were. The three of us were in a cold void of nothingness. It was terrifying, but Fern looked like she knew where she was going. Her eyes were locked upward, and her body jerked slightly to the left and right every few moments.

We popped out of the dark shape made by a pillar in the shadow-filled room. Hostages were all around, and in the middle of it all was Cleo. Fern nudged Bernardo forward, as I activated my thrusters and ran toward Cleo. I waited for the bright flash to come, so I could get the drop on Cleo, but it never did.

I worried I had blocked the flash somehow.

As I looked back, Bernardo was doing his best to activate a flash that was about as bright as the average visor flashlight.

"You said you could make a flash!" Fern said.

"This is a flash!" Bernardo panicked. "I—I tried to tell you it wasn't a big flash!"

One thing Phoebe hadn't told us was the fact that the floor was covered in water. In an instant Fern, and Bernardo's feet were frozen to the ground.

I turned around in time to take a huge kick from Cleo. She caught me with a series of punches before sending me face-first to the ground with an axe kick.

I looked up, and Kieran and Phoebe had infiltrated the building. "What went wrong?"

"Ask Bernardo," I said as I stood up and took a few swings at Cleo.

Without looking away from me, Cleo froze Kieran's feet to the ground. Phoebe took note of the water and created an ice slide over to us. Cleo gathered up what was left of the water and sent her right back out the window she had come in with a huge wave.

She dodged a few more punches, as the floor refilled with water. We were at a disadvantage if the fight continued in the same place. If I could get a good wrap on her, I could force us out a window.

Cleo came at me with a series of kicks. It was

effortless for her and looked like she was flying. She kept trying to freeze my feet to the floor, but I wasn't about to stop moving. She had a combination of kicks she kept going back to, and when I caught the pattern I was able to grab ahold of her.

As I started forcing her toward one of the windows, I peeked backward at Kieran.

"I got this, guys," he said as he made a tiny spark in his hands.

"Kieran, no—"

My warning was too late.

He let his electricity crackle through the water, shocking me and destroying all of the hostage holograms. Cleo had managed to kick me off and jump into the air. She landed on a nearby desk and shook her head at all of us as Phoebe came back through the window again.

"Fail. I don't know what the hell you were all trying to do, but killing all of the hostages is the exact opposite of what you were supposed to accomplish. If you'd all slow down and communicate a little bit more, you might have avoided fighting me where I had the advantage—and you might have figured out Rhys was about to force me out of the building anyway."

"Yeah, but—" Kieran started.

Cleo hopped back to the floor. "Back down to the group, and tell them to prepare for their turn."

We hung our heads as we all made our way back down to the group. We didn't say a word to each other on the way back. Training was getting more difficult with each day. Our trainers weren't pulling any punches anymore.

"It's your turn. Get ready," I said to the other five.

They had already circled up and were hatching a plan. Raysean waved a hand dismissing what I was saying. It looked like Akio was taking the lead on the plan despite having the least training. I wondered how hard his brother pushed him to train for the position.

After a few minutes, Ayla warped over and the group headed off.

The five of them were lucky. They couldn't see what had happened from where they were, but they had the advantage of all that extra time to make a plan. Those four were friends before any of the craziness so they'd work together without a problem, and something told me Akio wouldn't have any issue adapting.

"Bernardo—what the crap was that back there?" Fern asked.

"Before we started, I tried to tell you that I—"

"C'mon, dude," Kieran said as he let his kit leave his body. "It wouldn't have taken much to speak up."

I looked at Phoebe, but she had nothing to say. Bernardo was taking all the heat for the screw-up, and while he was the biggest part of the plan, it wasn't his fault. It wasn't fair that he was being targeted.

"Guys, it's not his fault." I willed my kit back into its medallion. "He *did* try to tell us. We got interrupted."

"It takes two seconds to go '*by flash I mean flashlight*'."

"If you want to play the blame game, don't forget you're the one that killed all the holo-hostages."

"Well, that's—"

"We're all to blame," Phoebe said. "We *played* Interceptor rather than actually working as a team. I should have caught that the floor was covered in water. Kieran shouldn't have sparked the floor. Bernardo should have spoken up," She pointed at Fern and me. "And you two should have slowed down for the rest of the group."

There was a tense energy in the group. It was different from the energy after the night at the club. It was an angry energy. We all knew that we'd have to shift into looking out for ourselves at some point, but it felt like that point had just happened. I looked to Kieran for anything, but he shook his head and turned away.

A loud horn sounded after a few minutes, and Cleo made her way back to the group with the other team. Their morale was a lot higher than ours was and I knew what that meant.

"How'd you guys do?" I asked.

"Better than you chumps," Raysean said as he passed me.

"The second team succeeded in trapping me after an excellently coordinated plan by Akio. They are the winners of this little test."

We'd be stuck with more drills like that before even more intense training. Regardless, I knew I needed Cleo to teach me that awesome axe kick she nailed me with. That part of my punishment felt more like a reward to me, but I could see how most people would hate it.

If I managed to play my cards right, I could turn my punishment into my ticket to becoming the newest Interceptor.

Chapter 21:
The Day Has Come

The remaining two weeks went by in a flash. Everyone had managed to improve dramatically on all fronts, but I was still stuck with little skill in my element. Luckily, I could fall back on being one of the best fighters thanks to the extra training from Lili and Cleo.

Everyone else being far better with their own elements put me at a serious disadvantage. I had no idea if I could beat Fern in a one-on-one fight if it came down to it.

We gathered in a huge room that was sure to be our final assessment arena. It looked like all the others that could morph into different landscapes or construct various objects, except a lot bigger. The room could have housed a majority of the slums.

All of the Interceptors were present—Faith and Ramona included. General Odon was the only person missing for some reason. I would have thought he'd be there to see who he'd get to yell at some more in the future.

Ayla made her way around the group chatting with everyone who was eager to start. It was refreshing to have people talking amongst one another again after most people had gone into solo-mode for the past two weeks. It was too bad these conversations were the last ones they'd have as trainees.

Kieran barely spoke to me anymore, and it felt like my only friends left were Phoebe and Fern.

"Alright everybody, time to get started." Ayla flew above us and grew to an enormous size. "This is the final assessment to decide who will become the newest Interceptor."

Everyone knew that was the case, but actually hearing it got everyone excited and nervous.

"The task is simple, be the last person standing." Ayla spun around and her clothes morphed into something a train conductor would wear. "You will all be placed onto a moving train filled with civilians. It is your job to battle your peers while ensuring the safety of all civilians at all times."

The group all started looking amongst one another, no doubt sizing each other up. Most people probably had some kind of strategy, but mine was to do whatever I could to win. There were too many variables to make any kind of effective plan.

Ayla swooped down toward our group. "If a civilian dies due to your actions, you are eliminated. If you are thrown from the train and hit the ground, you are eliminated. If you are knocked out, you are eliminated. Anything goes, except for killing. Does everyone understand the rules?"

"Yes."

"You have one minute to prepare."

I looked up to the Interceptors, and Lili gave me a little thumbs up. It put me at ease a bit to know that at least one of them was rooting for me.

I had been able to spend time with all of them aside from Mickey, and Kiyoshi, and I liked them all. I hoped they thought I'd make a good addition to the team, even if I didn't end up making it.

I needed to stop thinking like that.

I was going to make it.

I was going to be the next Interceptor.

Kieran looked at me. "You know I'm going to do whatever it takes to win."

I cocked my head. "Every man for himself, right?"

I meant it as a friendly jab, but Kieran narrowed his eyes and turned away from me.

Fern tapped my shoulder. "Good luck, Rhys."

"Good luck."

She leaned closer to my ear. "Final-two pact?" I looked at her—confused. "I'm saying, we work together until the end, and duke it out to see who really is the best. Between the two of us, we shouldn't have any problem getting rid of everyone else."

I liked the idea of working with someone, and it was the smartest idea to ensure a better chance at winning, but it didn't feel right. It felt like something I needed to do by myself.

The compliment hadn't escaped me either. I appreciated that Fern thought we were that much better than everyone else.

I shook my head. "I appreciate the offer and I really —really wanna take it, but I think this is something we all gotta do solo."

I expected her to react angrily, or at least something similar to how Kieran had reacted, but she smiled. "You wouldn't be you if you didn't make everything as difficult as possible."

"That's what I always say."

A chime sounded, and I was teleported onto a moving train. The air felt musty—like we were in the middle of the desert, and the light rattling of the train made my heart beat faster.

It was my only chance.

If I wanted to use Trigger at all it would have to be in its small form inside of the train. It was too tight inside for the larger version. If I managed to find a way to the top of the train or if there were any open cars I could use Trigger properly. There wasn't exactly any earth inside of the train to utilize either.

The longer I stayed inside, the longer I'd be relegated to half of the capabilities of my weapon and hand-to-hand combat. On the flip side, the longer I stayed inside—the safer I'd be.

There wasn't a doorway behind me, so I must have been at the back of the train. The train itself was about ten feet wide, but I had no clue how many cars long it might be.

I opened the door to the car and stepped into the neighbouring one. It was full of civilians with blank faces.

At least it wasn't a real train with real people.

I'd seen the blank expressionless faces of the training-holo's enough times to know one when I saw one.

"Crazy enough tech to make fake people, but not crazy enough to make them—less creepy."

I continued to the end of the car, and when I opened the door, the sounds of fighting from elsewhere on the train filled my ears. A crowd of panicked civilians rushed by me to escape the car, telling me the fighting was nearby.

Once the crowd cleared, I was able to see Kieran fighting with Rowan. I debated if I wanted to get involved or hang back, but something told me that hanging back and watching wasn't the heroic thing to do.

I rushed in and launched a kick at Rowan. It caught him in the face and sent him staggering backward. Kieran threw a couple of jabs my way, but I was able to avoid them. Rowan reinserted himself into the mix, and the three of us started trading blows.

The train went dark.

We must have entered a tunnel.

I stepped back from the fight slowly, but I could still hear Rowan and Kieran fighting. Pinpointing where I thought they were in the dark, I put a hand on each seat beside me and used it to throw myself forward at the two of them.

I caught them both with my feet, and Rowan went flying into the door of the car. We exited the tunnel and light flooded in from the door he had fallen through.

"Claudia has been eliminated." Ayla's voice rang out.

We all looked around in surprise. Most people would have guessed Bernardo would be the first person eliminated. Somehow, hearing someone had already lost their shot at the team made everything feel more real. It was the last chance for everyone.

Claudia hadn't ever said a kind thing to me, so I didn't care too much. Just made things easier in the end.

Rowan activated his kit and came right back at the both of us. Kieran and I looked at each other. "Rowan?"

"Rowan."

Kieran knew what I knew, if you used your kit too early, you'd risk running out of energy against someone who hadn't used there's yet. We weren't in danger of being thrown from the train while we were inside, but we needed to avoid being knocked out.

He hit me with a huge uppercut that sent me bouncing off the ceiling before catching me with a kick that sent me backward.

He picked up Kieran by his throat, but Kieran slashed at him with an axe. Rowan backed off and shot a grappling hook right at me. I managed to duck it, but it was so close that it felt like it may have sliced through some of my hair.

I looked where his grappling hook had landed and watched as it pierced one of the holo-civilians. As it connected, the civilian burst into a million little blue cubes.

"NO!" Rowan screamed.

Before he even finished screaming, he was teleported out of the train.

"Rowan has been eliminated."

"See ya, shorty," Kieran laughed himself into a groan as he clutched his neck.

I could see a dark spot growing on Kieran's neck, and I realized what the burning sensation in my midsection was. I pulled my shirt up and looked at my own dark mark. Rowan had poisoned us when he hit us. The burning sensation spread out across my body.

"We don't need to do this right now," I said.

"You think so, huh?" Kieran asked.

"We both got poisoned by Rowan. We know that, but no one else does."

"Yeah, but if I can take you out now, my biggest competition is gone."

"Kieran. C'mon."

I didn't want a fistfight with him. We'd end up tiring each other out, and whoever ended up winning would be easy pickings for anyone who came across us.

I rushed over to the open doorway and leaped upward. The harsh rush of the wind stung my eyes as I climbed up onto the top of the train. No one behind me, but there were people up ahead already fighting in their kits.

Raysean was such a hulking mass that he didn't need his kit yet, but he spotted me as soon as I had made it on top. He stalked toward me as Kieran climbed up on the opposite side of the car. Kieran took a heavy punch from

Raysean as he made his way to me, and Kieran barely managed to grab the edge of the train.

Raysean locked his eyes on me. "I was hoping I'd get to eliminate you."

Kieran dangled off the side of the train as Raysean kitted up, and threw a heavy kick my way. I caught his leg and tipped him over, before running toward another duo that was locked in a fight. I looked back as he scrambled to his feet and launched a giant flaming fist at me. My run shifted into a sprint, as I spotted another tunnel coming way off in the distance.

Phoebe had found a water tank on board the train and was using it to combat Aiden. I figured she'd be the best response to any of Raysean's fire attacks. She either saw me coming—or saw the giant flaming fist behind me, and sent a huge water geyser aimed right at me.

"Thanks, Phoeb'." I jumped back down into the train at a small break between cars.

Hot water splashed down as the fist and the water clashed. A bit of hot water was nothing when the other options were a barrage of water or being cooked alive by a flaming fist.

Counting Kieran, that made at least four people on the top of the train. Bernardo and Fern were somewhere inside the train. It made sense based on their size and their elements. Fern wasn't going to be able to use shadows out in the blazing sun, and Bernardo's flash wasn't strong enough to be used in the daylight.

Akio could have been anywhere, but I didn't think a guy like that was going to be at a disadvantage regardless of where he fought.

I held a hand over my body where I had been poisoned as I limped my way through the train cars. Some were filled with civilians and some were empty.

I threw open a door and came face to face with Bernardo in an empty car as he crouched down over a device. It had cables running to the roof of the car, and he was crouched on a rubber mat. We locked eyes as I stepped in, and he frantically pushed buttons.

"What are you—"

His machine started whirring as I hopped backward. Bolts of electricity passed into the metallic car with a low hum. Anyone on the top of the car would have been fried and tossed off.

"Aiden has been eliminated."

I looked around at the car and saw that tons of electronic components, metals, and fabrics had all been torn from various sections of the car.

"Holy crap."

Had Bernardo been eliminating people with that makeshift machine? Whatever was going on, I couldn't fall victim to it, so I threw my sword right through it. He scrambled away to the other side of the car and climbed up to the top.

The lights went out again.

Another tunnel.

"Bernardo has been eliminated."

The poor guy had a great plan. No one else would have been smart enough to create some kind of a strange electrocution machine in a matter of minutes. He must have not had his eyes forward when he climbed up and was knocked off the train.

"Sorry, dude."

Six of us left.

I wondered how everyone else up top managed to avoid the tunnel. Maybe they ducked back into the train, or maybe there was enough room to lay down on the top. I couldn't imagine anyone taking a gamble that they could lay across the top while the train rolled through the tunnel.

Sooner or later Fern was going to find me in the darkness of the train. After denying her deal, she might want to go right for me since she viewed me as her biggest competition. If we were in a tunnel there'd be no way I could beat her. I needed to head back up top, and stay up top.

The light returned, and I dashed back to the top.

As I made it up, Phoebe climb back to the top of her water tank. She had her kit on, and her spear at the ready. It felt like the team knew she wasn't the greatest with hand-to-hand combat, so they provided her with a way to stay in the running.

The truth was, they'd done that for each of us. Phoebe had her water tank. Kieran and Akio could pass their electricity through the metal. Bernardo and Fern had the darkness of the tunnels—and I had the earth along the ground beside the train.

If only I could get my element to work.

Raysean popped up in his kit and rushed toward Phoebe. I wasn't sure if she could take him by herself so I kitted up and rushed over.

He launched a wall of fire at her, and she responded once again with a huge water jet. Phoebe's elemental skill was greater than Raysean's, but he powered through her water and rocked Phoebe with his mace. Thankfully the points had been removed from it, but even with the kit taking a ton of the force, she was going to have a wicked headache.

I drew Trigger in its smaller form and swung at Raysean, cutting him across his arm. The slash managed to cut through the kit, and he dropped his mace off the train.

Phoebe made it back to her feet. "Thanks, Rhys."

I nodded as I pointed my sword at Raysean. "Stand down, and give up."

He smiled. "What are you gonna do? Kill me?"

He had a point.

"Huh."

He lunged at me and knocked my sword off the train. After he caught me with an elbow strike, Phoebe launched a few small icicles into his back. Clearly annoyed, Raysean kicked me in the chest, sending me sprawling backward.

"You good, Rhys?" Phoebe asked.

"Chest-kicked-tastic," I groaned from the floor.

Raysean turned his attention back to her, and Phoebe managed to dodge a few strikes. As soon as he caught her with one, it was over.

He beat her down to the ground and tossed her off the train by her leg. Raysean had beaten her so viciously that most of her kit had left her body. She must have been using her kit from the start of the fight. Phoebe flailed uncontrollably until she hit the ground and disappeared.

"Phoebe has been eliminated."

"That asshole," I said under my breath.

There could only be one winner, but I never would have wanted her to go out like that. She was a good friend—she deserved better.

I made it back to my feet. "After that, I'm making sure you aren't winning this. Even if it means I don't."

"Bring it on, small-fry."

We ran at each other and I ducked a big swing. My best bet was to work the body, so I launched shot after shot into his gut. I could take Raysean on my own. All I needed was to borrow the strategy Kieran had used against Keyshawn. Keeping close, I dodged his swings, always returning a punch of my own to his gut.

With every punch, he was getting slower and his kit was crawling back away from his body. It might not have been hurting him, but at least it was forcing the air out of his body and draining his kit's energy. He was gasping for air, but he managed to tag me a few times.

Kieran thrust into the fight from out of nowhere and nailed me with a hard straight left. I rolled off the edge of the train, but I thought fast. Launching my grappling hook at the side of the train, it caught the metal, and I slammed back into the side.

"Thanks, buddy," I muttered to myself.

I made sure I had a firm grip before reeling my hook back. I may not have been good with the tech, but I was able to use it well enough to avoid elimination.

The few seconds of pressure off of Raysean was enough for him to recover and get the drop on Kieran. He started beating him down the same way he had Phoebe, and he was about to throw him off the train. He picked Kieran up by his neck and dangled him over the edge of the train.

I hadn't heard what Raysean said, but Kieran spat at him, "Screw you."

I flipped back up onto the train and did my best to toss a shield at Raysean. The throw was a bit too wide, but Kieran was able to catch it out of the air and bash it against Raysean's head. He fell to the ground holding his nose as Kieran grabbed the edge of the train. He must have dropped the shield because I couldn't call it back.

I made it over to them and ran my knee across the side of Raysean's face, sending him over the side of the train. A grappling hook shot straight up, but it wasn't going to hook onto anything.

"Raysean has been eliminated."

I grinned. "I got him back for ya, Phoebe."

Six down. Four of us left.

Chapter 22:
The Next Interceptor

I held out a hand for Kieran. If I was going to beat him, I wanted to do it in a fair fight.

I helped him up, and he tried to toss me right off the side of the train. I broke free of his grip and backed up.

"You're welcome," I said.

He wouldn't meet my eye.

That wasn't the Kieran I knew. He was different. He wanted the win so bad, and he was willing to do whatever it took to become an Interceptor.

"I've gotta knock you out," Kieran said.

"If I had a dollar for every time someone said that, I wouldn't be living in the slums."

We ran toward each other, but we were pretty evenly matched. For every hit I landed, he landed one as a receipt.

It was time to break out some of the kicks Lili, and Cleo had taught me. I caught him with a spinning thrust kick, before rearing up and catching him with an axe kick.

I expected the way my body had to move would cause me pain from Rowan's poisoning. The lack of a mark on Kieran told me that my mark had likely disappeared as well. That was the one good thing about us only being trainees—weak elements.

Kieran hit the roof of the car as a bolt of lightning shot through the neighbouring train car. A huge hole— big enough for a car to drive through, had been torn in the roof of it. Fern flipped out of it and onto the top of the train. Akio was close behind her, and suddenly the final four of us were all together.

If the two of them had been using their kits as long as Kieran and I had, they'd be low on energy too. The energy reserves on the training kits weren't the greatest.

Fern sprinted toward us and slid as Akio launched bolts of lightning at her. They flew over her and right towards me.

I had no choice but to use my energy shield. The bolts struck it, but it didn't budge me. Technology was wicked, but my kit's energy dwindled lower. All that was left covered were my hands and sections along my legs.

"Comin' through." Fern called.

She continued her run and nailed Kieran with a kick on her way over. He flew right at me, but I managed to duck him. Fern used Kieran to obscure my vision so she could move in close.

She delivered a huge shot to my jaw, which sent me reeling back. I dodged a series of strikes and pushed her back as an arrow flew our way, courtesy of Akio.

As the arrow flew by, she kicked at me, but I caught it and threw her foot hard at Akio as he arrived. Her foot caught him in the face, but she managed to land a few feet away.

Kieran came back in and the three of us traded shots. Akio rushed up and joined in, and suddenly it was four people kicking the absolute crap out of each other.

It was kind of messed up, but it was awesome.

Kieran managed to run his electricity through his hand as he placed it on my chest, and I exploded away from the fight.

Akio sprinted right at me. He was coming for his retribution from when I beat him in our first fight.

My vision was blurry, and my chest felt like it was on fire. I gasped for air, and I knew my heart had to be beating in an irregular pattern. If Akio made it to me before I recovered, I was done for.

I needed it.

My mind drifted to when Lenna stood up to Dorian at the nightclub. Then I thought back to the night my parents were killed. The horrible explosion that scarred my face and took Lenna's arm from her.

The explosion caused by Zeal and his Conks.

I had to win.

I was going to become an Interceptor—

So I could protect Lenna—

And so I could avenge my parents.

Far in the distance, there was a large rock. My kit glowed a deep brown, and I raised my hand to it. It rose from the ground, and as I clenched my fist it flew closer.

I wasn't quite sure if it counted as some kind of telekinesis or not, but I had a feeling I wasn't going to get that kind of thing working with anything other than the earth.

Akio hadn't bothered to look at what I might be doing. He must not have thought I'd be able to do it. The boulder hovered over the side of the train, and with a sweep of my arm, it knocked him clean off the train.

The boulder whirled, and I spotted him clinging to it. He'd spiked both his grappling hooks into the rock and was waiting for the perfect moment to jump back to the train. He hopped back toward it and extended his arm. I pointed my hand at the ground and lifted a dirt block in front of him as the train sped away.

"Akio has been eliminated."

I looked at my hand, and then over to Fern and Kieran as they brawled.

It was the three of us.

They each looked toward me and jumped to opposite sides of the train car they were on. They each hopped down, and I knew exactly what was coming.

Another freakin' tunnel.

I turned, and sprawled forward, pulling myself into the hole that had been blasted into the car by Akio. Everything went pitch black before I hit the ground.

"*Great.* My *everything* hurts."

Fern had the advantage down there, but Kieran was the unlucky soul who had his hands full. I needed the breather, so I rolled onto my back. I took a deep breath before letting what was left of my kit slide off of me. There wasn't much energy left in the reserves, and the smartest play would be to let it recharge while I rested.

There was no telling how beat up Fern was, and if she was fresh I'd need Kieran to help me take her out. I stumbled to my feet and headed into the neighbouring car to try to help him out.

"However everyone's watching this—you better be rooting for me. I'm gonna end this now."

I couldn't see anything, but I could hear Kieran's grunts as he tumbled around in the dark. My grunts were added to the mix when a hand pulled me deeper into the dark, and I took a strong punch in the face.

She beat the both of us pretty good until we cleared the tunnel. Fern popped back into the light in between the two of us, and we turned the tables on her.

She would have been able to take one of us on, especially with how beat up we were. Luckily, Two expert strikers had no issue forcing someone into another person's strikes.

After a few good combinations, I sent out a straight jab that she redirected into Kieran's face. She capitalized on it and threw me into him. She took the opportunity to sprint out of the train car, and back to the top of the train.

"Later losers."

"Back and forth—up and down," I groaned. "This is the worst."

"You're telling me," Kieran said with a cough.

A bunch of holo-civilians stared at us with blank faces, and after scrambling away from each other, we both headed back to the top for what I hoped was the final time. If either of us wanted to win, we needed to eliminate Fern before the next tunnel. As far as I could tell, if their kits weren't fully drained, they were running low like mine.

We closed in on Fern, and the three of us fought once more. She didn't have her flail with her so Akio must have disarmed her at some point, but Kieran still had his axes with him.

Advantage went to team Kieran since all of us were letting our kits charge.

He slashed toward our legs, and he caught me in the same area Dorian had. I cried out in pain from my reopened wound as I fell to a knee. Kieran and Fern looked concerned, but an explosion of anger from the pain sent me forward at Kieran.

My fist connected hard into his stomach, and it was enough to push him backward. He stumbled and wobbled right on the edge of the train. He knew he was in trouble, so he started letting his kit crawl back onto his body, but he couldn't get it out fast enough.

Fern hit him with a solid kick to launch Kieran off the train.

"Kieran has been eliminated."

"And then there were two," she said.

"And then there were two." I echoed with a sigh.

I made it to my feet and took stock of the hopeless situation I was left in. My leg was cut pretty bad, I had next to no energy left in my kit, I had no weapon—and up ahead, another tunnel was on its way.

"Any chance you wanna just—jump off and give me the win?" I asked

She clicked her tongue. "That doesn't sound like you're trying to do this the hard way."

Fern ran at me and I managed to dodge a series of strikes. "So—that's—a no?"

I had a terrible idea for how to beat Fern, but the only way it would work would be if I could avoid getting knocked out.

I pushed her backward and ran for the blown-out car again. After hopping back down, she did exactly what I had hoped—she put her kit back on. I rushed into the car and let what was left of my kit come on, and stared at the hole. My last hope was that she'd come through it.

—

Nothing.

She had to be waiting for the tunnel.

It didn't matter.

If I could time it right, I'd come out with the win. The train was entering the tunnel ahead, and I knew she'd be coming in at any moment.

She flipped down into the hole and I threw the hardest punch I could, she managed to spin right past it as darkness swallowed the train.

I was done for.

Fern launched a flurry of attacks on me. She swarmed me with punches and kicks that I couldn't hope to avoid. I was thrown toward the hole, but I managed to stay inside the train.

That was her play.

She wanted to toss me out of the hole in the same way I had planned to do to her.

The tunnel was short, and I could see daylight coming through the train. Fern beat me down to the ground, and it must have been to keep me from trying anything once her advantage was gone.

I knew exactly what she was going to do.

As light filled the car once again I turned opposite of the hole and reached out. Fern launched out of the darkness right where I thought she would—what would have been right behind me. Rolling backward, I pushed her out the hole with my foot.

All I could do was hope she didn't have enough time or energy to hook onto the side of the train.

I waited a moment.

—

"Fern has been eliminated."

I did it.

"Congratulations to the newest member of the Interceptors, Remarkable Rhys York."

I laid on my back trying to catch my breath. There was a lone civilian that had wandered into the car with me. He was staring at me and clapping with a creepy smile scrawled across his face.

"Thanks, dude," I said as I nodded to the creepy fake civilian.

Ayla warped in front of me with a tender smile. "Congratulations—partner."

Chapter 23:
My New Partner

The entire train simulation faded away, data strand by data strand. Everyone must have been watching a feed of the people still in contention from a big hologram. I figured the feed I was seeing was likely the same one people around the world were watching, so I got up and waved to the camera.

Anyone who had been hurt during the final round was being looked at by some medical personnel. Various facility staff rushed back and forth on visor-calls. It felt like everyone in the facility wanted to talk to somebody, except for me.

I looked around for Kieran, but he wasn't anywhere to be seen. Phoebe met my gaze from across the room. "Kieran?"

She shook her head and looked at the door. I knew he'd be upset about what had happened, but I hoped he'd be able to forgive me.

It kind of pissed me off that my best friend didn't want to be there to congratulate me.

"I don't know why," Ayla spun around into my field of vision. "But I knew you were going to win. Must be these tiny bits of data."

"Thanks, Ayla. That means a lot—I think."

The team made their way over to me and they each congratulated me. Each of their annoying little cameras flew around to find the best angle of their dedicated Interceptor and me.

"Nice job using that kick I taught you," Cleo said as she handed me my sword. "The punishment training paid off, huh?"

"Plus that reversal roll that I taught you for the finish —so wicked," Lili said. "I was worried when you got poisoned right at the start, but you pulled through."

"That was definitely the most interesting final round we've had for any of our applicants," Mickey said.

As tired as I was, it was nice to see how excited the team was. Rather than wondering if some of them secretly hated me, they genuinely seemed happy to welcome a new member to the team.

"How does all this work?" I asked. "What happens now?"

"There's a congratulatory dinner planned tonight courtesy of Lili and Cleo, and after that, you'll be given your personalized kit," Kiyoshi said, as unenthused as ever. "That's when your neural link with Ayla will become permanent, and you'll be an official Interceptor. If you wish to say goodbye to the other applicants, do so now." He shot a disappointed look at his brother before heading for the door. "Let Lili know when you're done."

Diggs stuck a thumb toward Kiyoshi. "Don't worry about sunshine over there, I think he's got a mission tonight, probably trying to get in the zone. You did a wicked job out there. You reacted—and read what people were doing."

"Much better than Diggs during his competition. He basically won by accident," Pegs said with a laugh.

Diggs rolled his eyes. "We'll give you some time to say bye to your—"

Heavy footsteps caused me to whirl around when Diggs stopped mid-sentence. General Odon had come from wherever he had been—doing whatever a guy like him does—to congratulate me.

He held a hand out toward me as he walked up. "Congratulations, Mr. York."

"Thanks, General Odon." I shook his hand. "Rhys is fine. It's an honour to actually—"

"Yes, yes. I'm sure you did very well. I wanted to make sure I welcomed you to the team. I trust everyone shall make you feel welcome."

"Wait—you mean you didn't even wa—"

"Watch the final round? No. I don't watch any of the feeds. Not much interest to me. I'm a busy man, but I believe my congratulations are still in order," General Odon said with a hearty chuckle as he started to walk away. "Don't you think?"

Cleo stared at Odon as he left, and I couldn't help getting a strange energy from her. She looked angry for whatever reason. It was entirely possible that she was angry about how he'd treated the newest member of her team, but the real reason was anyone's guess.

Ramona came over and shook my hand. "Between the two of us—my money was on you."

It was nice to hear something like that from someone so respected in the facility.

The rest of the team left, with Lili and Ayla sticking around. Rowan, Claudia, Aiden, and Bernardo left without saying a word to me. I expected that though, it was obvious that not everyone would have a graceful exit. To my surprise—Raysean joined Fern, Phoebe, and Akio as they came over.

"Here to tell me I got lucky?" I asked Raysean.

"Nah. You beat me fair and square—man-to-man," he said as he shook my hand. "Congrats, Rhys."

"I appreciate it."

"It won't happen again, though. You better be ready for me to claw my way onto that team. I'm not done bullying you yet."

"I—won't be looking forward to it—at all," I said.

"Plus if you screw up again and get yourself kicked out, I'd love to take your spot." Raysean smirked.

"I wouldn't expect anything less."

He nodded to me and walked out of the building, probably to join his friends so they could complain.

I turned to Akio, and he looked more crushed than he had been the first time I eliminated him from the running.

"Two times—you beat me two times," he said. "You're the better man."

"Everything gonna be okay with you and your brother?" I asked.

"He'll get over it. Who knows? Maybe I'll earn another shot one day."

"There's no way you won't. You're like—some kind of Interceptor prodigy." I nudged his shoulder. "That move with your hooks in the rock was sweet. I didn't see it coming."

He chuckled. "Thanks. I don't think my brother's going to see it like that. You did still get me anyway."

"Get home safe. It'd be good to hangout sometime soon. I think you'd get along with the whole gang."

I knew that sounded like the sort of thing you just say to someone to be nice, but I really meant it. With how tense the final portion of training had been, none of us got to know Akio all that well. He seemed like a cool guy, or at least cooler than his older brother.

"I'd like that." Akio made his way out the door as Fern, and Phoebe wrapped me in a group hug.

"I knew it was going to be you. Thanks for taking Raysean out for me. It was a sweet kind of revenge. Remember, slow down, okay?" Phoebe kissed me on the cheek. "You can't expect to be the best right from the start."

"I'm gonna miss you Phoebe," I said. "I'll do my best —you know it's just how I am."

"I know. I'll miss you, too. You and Kieran are like the annoying little brothers I never knew I wanted." She looked between Fern and me. "I'll let you two say goodbye—alone. *Have-fun.*"

"Hey, are you going to go see Keyshawn?" I called after her.

She nodded. "Yeah, I am."

"Tell him—tell him, I'm sorry—about everything."

There was a lot more I wished I could say to Keyshawn, but that would have to do for the time being. It was probably going to be a while before I could make any personal visits. There was no way to know how busy an Interceptor's schedule was, but I figured it was pretty packed.

Phoebe smiled and backed up toward the door. "You two better plan a time when we can all get together. I'll be watching your feed, so try not to forget you're gonna be recorded constantly. The last thing I need to see is you pickin' your nose or something."

Fern and I laughed as Phoebe left, but we soon fell into an awkward silence.

"You okay?" I asked.

"Yeah. Disappointed I couldn't quite make the cut, but if anyone did, I'm glad it was you. I was way too predictable back there. I'll be fine, though. A girl like me always has options."

I caught Lili staring as Fern moved closer to me, and I wasn't sure how to navigate the situation. "We're, uh— we're going to keep in touch right?"

She grabbed the collar of my shirt. "I'd kick your ass if you didn't at least try to call me once a day." Her eyes flick toward Lili before looking back up at me. She kissed me on the cheek and headed toward the door. "Call me, Mr. Interceptor."

"That's better than mud-boy." I watched her leave and realized I should have been watching her leave more often.

Winning was bittersweet.

I wished Kieran would have said something to me, but at least I knew Lenna wouldn't have to be on her own anymore.

The money I'd be making would let me buy her a place in a good part of the city away from the violence and the drugs. I could finally buy her one of those augments Kieran talked about, so she could have a second arm. Best of all, she could put all of her effort into becoming a singer like she'd always wanted.

The door everyone had left through swung open, and Kieran stormed toward me. It looked like he had been crying, and I knew that whatever was coming, it wasn't going to be good. A little camera swooped down to catch every second of the drama for the world to see.

I braced myself for a shot as he stomped up to me.

"You didn't even want it," he spat.

"Kieran, you know that's not true."

"You didn't even want it—not like I did."

"That doesn't mean I *didn't* want this."

It had been a while since I'd seen him that frustrated. Kieran was always the kind of guy to let things roll off his back, but things were different. That moment was one that I feared he'd never properly recover from.

"Hey, you lost." Lili grabbed his arm. "Learn to lose with grace, or there's no way you'll be welcomed back for future opportunities. You're a strong applicant—you're better than this, and this team doesn't function with people that lash out—most of the time."

"I'm going to take care of Lenna," Kieran pulled his arm free and stormed back toward the door. "But it's not gonna be for you."

Kieran took one last look back into the facility, and left. I was worried about our friendship, but I knew if anyone could talk some sense into him after the cameras caught that, it would be Lenna.

He'd be lucky if the love of his life didn't greet him with a solid whack on the head the next time he saw her after something like that.

I sighed, "Thanks—I guess."

I turned to a big smile and the open arms of Lili, and Ayla. I didn't know what Ayla was expecting, but I headed over and hugged Lili. Ayla positioned herself so it looked like she was hugging me from behind.

"I'm so proud. My little trainee was the one that won it all." She let go of me and cleared her throat. "The rookies are making big moves, you might have just bumped my promotion timeline up quite a bit."

Walker warped beside her. "I guess you did a pretty solid job."

"Thanks, Walker. Not that I'm not *super thrilled* about this whole thing, but is there anyone who can stitch up my leg?" I asked as I pointed down to the bloody gash on my leg.

The adrenaline from the fight had been wearing off, and while it didn't bother me too much on the train, the pain had become unbearable. The cut was probably a lot deeper than I had realized.

"Oh my god, yes." Lili waved over a medic. "I'm so sorry. With all the excitement—"

"No, it's okay. So—you and Cleo planned a dinner?" I asked as a medic came over and started tending to my leg.

"Ayla helped too. We thought it would be a good way

for whoever won to hang out with everyone and be welcomed to our little family."

"I feel like me sitting down and having dinner with Kiyoshi isn't going to go so well after—you know."

"Don't worry it won't be like a sit-down kind of thing. It's little finger foods and drinks. A little intro to the crew. Like Diggs said, apparently Kiyoshi might be on a mission tonight anyway, so you might not have to worry about that."

"Am I gonna be able to call my sister at some point?" I asked as the medic finished up with a sticky gel and some kind of spray.

It had been too long since I'd been able to talk to Lenna. She was probably ready to scream about how excited she was all while scolding me for beating Kieran. There wasn't any winning, but I still needed to hear her voice.

"All the trainee rules are gone," Lili said. "You can do whatever you want, and your kit comes with a built-in visor."

"Sweet, so I can call anyone—"

"Yes, you'll have free rein to call Fern." She almost looked annoyed as she said that.

"I didn't exactly—"

"You just need to keep in mind that starting tomorrow, you'll have a camera on you every single day for the rest of your life from six in the morning until midnight—aside from unforeseen events and missions, which obviously can be at any time."

That didn't sound amazing, but it was a small price to pay. Experiencing the power of the kits firsthand put the cameras into a new perspective. This random group of people had the power to destroy the world if they really wanted to, why wouldn't everyone want to be aware of what it is they're up to?

"You guys haven't made it seem like that big of an issue," I said.

"Nah, you get used to it pretty quick. You'll have the occasional moment where you forget it's there, but it gives you enough privacy."

"Like when you're on the—"

"Like when you're on the toilet, yes." Lili chuckled.

Ayla joined in on the laughter and tried to grab at my hand.

I stared at her. "Did you just forget you're an AI?"

Ayla turned a shade of red. "It happens. I was going to say that you've gotta go get ready for your party."

"Ayla's right," Lili said. "Why don't you two head on back to your barracks to change into something a bit less —battle-worn. She can lead you over to the shindig afterward."

I hadn't realized how shredded my clothes had become until she mentioned it. My threads looked as if I'd just spent the last hour getting cheese graters tossed at me by professional pitchers.

"You don't want to tag along?" I asked as I pulled on a ripped piece of fabric, creating an even bigger hole. "Whoops. You can fill me in on newbie tips."

"So nice to not be the only newbie now." Lili pumped her fists. "I'm sure you'd love it if I tagged along, but you aren't the only one that needs to get ready."

She headed off ahead of me, and it turned out that she was as fun to watch leave as Fern was.

Ayla flew in front of me. "You perv."

"What—no. I—"

"I saw how you were looking at Fern as well."

"It wasn't anything creepy." I stammered. "I just—"

"So which one do you like?"

"I—"

"Relax! I'm kidding," Ayla laughed. "Let's go."

"Are you sure?"

"Even if I was serious, I'm an AI," She shrugged. "What do I care?"

We headed back through the facility, and into the common room. It felt barren and a bit creepy without everyone to add life to the room. The thought of not having dinner with my friends every night brought me down, but the thought of an entirely new group of friends cheered me right back up.

"I don't even remember the last time I was in this common room," Ayla said as she looked around. "I guess it would have been when Chase gave a little pep-talk to Lili's group of recruits."

"You must miss him, huh?" I asked.

"Every day."

"I hope I can live up to his legacy."

"You don't need to do that. You shouldn't even feel you have to do that."

"It's kinda hard not to. He was the best."

She sighed, "He was."

As I made my way into my room, I cocked my head at a pristine grey suit laid out on my bed. Weird. I hadn't brought one with me, and there had never been one in my trunk. Even weirder, It looked like it would fit me perfectly.

"What's up with the suit?"

Ayla spun in a circle and her clothes changed into a suit of her own. "It's for the dinner party. We had suits and dresses made up for all of you, so we were ready for whoever won."

"I have to wear a suit?"

"Well, what did you expect? A welcome party where everyone wears sweatpants?"

"I mean—that would be kinda nice." I got a bit shy when I thought of changing in front of Ayla. "Do you mind—"

She gave me a confused look before she clued in. "Oh! You do know I'm about to have intimate knowledge of not only your entire body, but your entire brain right?"

"Well, let's let the body be unknown for a bit longer," I said.

"Fine."

Ayla huffed and whirled around as I started changing into the suit. Something about the fabric was different than anything I'd felt before. The soft and smooth feel of the suit put everything I'd worn before to shame.

"This is probably the most expensive piece of clothing I'll ever wear."

"Probably," Ayla said as she whirled around again, once again facing me, but also changing into a sparkling dress. "It's top of the line, and there aren't too many people hand-making these anymore."

Everything fit me perfectly, and I checked myself out in the mirror. The suit looked great on me, minus my tired eyes.

I held a piece of fabric in my hands and sighed.

I had no idea how to tie a tie.

"I'll show you," Ayla flew beside me. "Don't worry."

"Thanks, Ayla. I owe you."

She shook her head. "You don't owe me anything—we're a team."

I smiled as she made an untied tie appear around her neck. With some expert patience, she walked me through how to tie my own tie.

It already felt good to be a part of a team.

Chapter 24:
One Hell Of A Dinner Party

The dinner party was incredible, but I was awkward as hell. It felt weird to be celebrating after I beat up a bunch of the closest friends I'd made in years. It didn't help matters that one of them was the baby brother of the highest-ranking member of the team.

That's where I lucked out, Kiyoshi had been called out on official Interceptor business.

The dinner was being held in a room that was like the common room we had access to during training—but on steroids. Everything was sleek and fancy, except for the easy listening pop music that played in the background.

I thought Lili had taken me under her wing, but the whole team had made it clear that they planned on doing that.

As soon as I walked into the room Diggs and Pegs grabbed me and showed me around. Everyone was dressed up like I was, and we all fit into the room perfectly. It would have been impossible for anyone to get bored in the facility.

"So you like the place?" Pegs asked.

"Kinda sucks if you don't, since this is your new home and all. Forever—and ever—and ever—" Diggs added.

"Diggs, Pegs—you guys scaring Rhys off already?" Cleo called as she chatted with Ramona.

Diggs scoffed. "We don't scare people off."

"I dunno," Lili said. "I was pretty close to packing my bags and making a run for it once you two got your hands on me."

"Ignore them. They think they're *so* funny," Pegs said as she wrapped an arm around me. "Drink? You do drink, right?"

They led me over to an enormous wooden cabinet. It was pretty rare to see anything made of actual wood pretty much anywhere. It was refreshing, and it smelled rich and ancient.

The doors popped open, and I was faced with two dozen expensive bottles of alcohol. I had never seen or heard of any of them before. Some glowed bright colours, but the liquor I'd seen in the slums was all dull and grey.

"What's good?" I asked.

"All of it."

"You not a big drinker?" Diggs asked.

"Well I just finished up at the academy pretty recently, so I'm still new to—"

"Oh, you're a baby like our Lili—just a bit younger." Pegs patted my head. "An even littler baby"

"Cool it with the whole calling him baby thing," Diggs said. "He's our new teammate, and he might not appreciate it the same way Lili does." He turned his attention to me. "You go hangout with them, and we'll make you something good. Fizz, or no fizz?"

"No fizz?"

"My man." Diggs flashed me a thumb as he clicked his tongue. "Good call."

Diggs and Pegs were an odd pair, but they seemed like good people. As far as I knew, they were actually the two oldest members on the team, yet somehow, the two exuded the most youthful energy around.

I took the chance to wander around and take in my surroundings. The place was a little over the top, but I could get used to it. Pretty much everything in the room could either be described as ornate or elaborate.

"Pretty neat, huh?" Cleo asked.

I made my way over to the group of Cleo, Ramona, Lili, and Mickey. "It's a bit—much."

"Not exactly home?" Ramona asked.

"No, not really. Where I lived, a place like this would have been torn apart by a bunch of criminals lookin' to make some quick cash."

"Well, now you're here to help make your home a safer place to live." Cleo playfully shook my shoulders. "I know I was hard on you, but I am happy to have you on the team."

"I'd say I'm thrilled to be here," I rubbed the back of my neck. "But I did kinda have to kick my best friend's ass to get here."

"He'll come around." Mickey shrugged. "Kieran seems like a good kid."

"You should tell him that, he might actually cry."

The thought of Kieran getting a compliment from his favourite android was a funny one. Mickey was always so cool and collected, much like Ayla, it was easy for anyone to forget that Mickey wasn't actually human.

After a few moments, the wait-staff opened a nearby door and the scent of fresh food wafted into the room. One of them raised a finger to get Cleo's attention.

"We're gonna go check on the food," Cleo, Ramona, and Lili headed off toward another room.

"All of you?"

"We may or may not have helped a bit," Lili said before they all disappeared through the doorway.

For the first time since I had arrived at the facility, I

was alone with Mickey. The android always came across nice enough, but it tended to stick to corners, and not offer opinions in a conversation. The buzzed hair and piercings it had helped create a seriously badass look.

"Why are you staring at me?" Mickey asked.

"I just—you—I wanna get to know you—you know, since we're gonna be team members and all, but you seem so—"

"So what?"

"Unapproachable?" I asked.

"And yet here you are."

"Well, I didn't really—"

"Drinks have arrived," Diggs said as he and Pegs made their way over.

"Look, Mickey. Drinks—have—arrived," I said in an awkward attempt to change the subject.

They were all the kind of people I could see myself getting along with. I just wish I hadn't been the one to knock Kiyoshi's brother out of the running. Something told me that after eliminating him on two separate occasions, Kiyoshi wasn't exactly going to want to be my best buddy.

The ladies came back from where they had run off to with a bunch of servers in tow. "Dinner is served!" A couple servers pushed tables filled with food out. "Everybody get your grub on."

"Hey, what happened to Ayla?" I looked around. "Isn't she supposed to be here?"

"Don't worry," Cleo said as she picked up a plate. "The whole process is kinda new to all of us since you're the first person to receive another person's AI. She popped back down to Faith to get ready."

"AI's need to get ready?"

"Not like—getting ready for a date or something. Faith needs to make minor tweaks to her data, so she can do another permanent neural link."

Everyone grabbed a plate and loaded up with a little bit of everything from the long tables filled with food. I expected simple food as Lili had mentioned, but I hadn't ever seen some of the foods on offer before. It was becoming clear to me that the Interceptors received the best of the best for the hard work they did.

"Grab some of those meatballs. Lili made them, they're delightful," Mickey said.

Delightful—there was one of the many words I didn't expect out of Mickey.

I ignored all the questions I had about how an android knew meatballs were delightful and turned my attention to the conversation going on. The team took turns swapping stories about some of the missions they'd been on to catch me up on what had been happening. I filled them in on my life, and what growing up in the slums was like.

"So, about Zeal—"

Everyone became tense as soon as I said his name, but I wasn't quite sure why.

Maybe it had to do with his role in Chase's death. Maybe it had to do with the team not expecting that serious of a conversation during my welcoming party. Whatever the reason, I decided it was best to drop it.

"Never mind."

"Sorry, Rhys. We avoid talking about that human piece of techno-trash if we aren't working. We'll fill you in soon," Diggs said.

"In the meantime, if everyone's done with their dinner, I think it's time for a round of shots." Pegs headed back toward the wooden cupboard.

The fact that the Interceptors were booze-hounds was a bit of a surprise. They always seemed like a deadly-serious group of heroes, but instead, they were a dysfunctional little family just looking to have a good time.

"Are you sure that's such a good idea?" I asked. "Last time I went out drinking—"

"You gotta relax, Rhys," Diggs said as he set his plate down. "One shot never hurt anybody. Besides, the booze-hound is gonna get you to take one at some point. We gotta welcome you to the team with something that's gonna make you feel the burn."

"One quick drink, and you can be done for the night." Judging by the smell of her breath, Lili had already made her way through more drinks than she needed. "We're just happy you made it."

Pegs came back with a round of bright red shots. "This isn't some weird blood-pact thing to induct me into *the cult of the Interceptors* is it?" I asked with a laugh. They each stared at me, expressionless. "Wait is it?"

They all burst into a fit of laughter and Cleo stepped forward. "At least we know we added another weird one to the family. Cheers." She raised her glass, and we all did the same.

After a couple clinks, we all shot back the liquor. It tasted like a handful of fresh berries, but it hit me immediately. Whatever it was, it was way stronger than anything people had access to in the slums.

It may have been a dinner party, but it had already gotten late, and I was exhausted from the fight earlier in the day. I didn't know what time it was, but I suspected it was getting close to when the cameras would stop rolling with how quickly the team had been ramping up their drinking.

Right on cue, all the cameras in the room either shut down or flew off to another part of the facility.

Ayla warped in front of me in a sparkling dress. "Hey, Rhys. Having a good time?"

"It's certainly something else."

"I'm glad. You can head to your new humble abode for your kit. I'll meet you in your room for the neural link," she said before disappearing.

"Actual harmless question this time—anyone know where my place is?" I asked.

"Lili'll show you," Cleo said.

I caught a series of eyebrow raises from Diggs and a wide-eyed look from Pegs.

"Come on." Lili grabbed my hand and pulled me out the door. I looked back as the team snickered. Cleo and Ramona each sent mischievous waves my way.

"We've got more matching kits," Lili said.

"What do you mean?"

"Well, Cleo and Mickey have matching blue—Diggs and Pegs have their matching red—and now the two of us are gonna have matching green. It's like we're all partners." I wasn't sure how to respond and it clearly made her feel a bit awkward. "Not that I'm saying we're partners. I mean—we could be—if you wanted to—oh my god, I need to stop talking—I really just meant the colour of the kits and—"

"You're hilarious," I said.

"Hilarious—and embarrassed."

She led me down the halls of the facility for a while before we came to the same kind of door that Lili's place had. My name was inscribed on a plaque beside the door, and it read:

```
D-Rank Interceptor - Rhys York
```

Chapter 25:
AI Can Feel Too

It felt so official to see it on a plaque, and I might have been choked up a bit if Lili wasn't right next to me oohing and awing about how cool it was.

The place looked like a lot of the rest of the facility. I was a little underwhelmed compared to the common room we had been in, and even Lili's home. I thought it might feel a bit homier.

I must have had that written all over my face.

"Don't worry, I'll show you how to customize it all sometime. What do you think?"

"That's how yours got so much nicer? You can customize it all?"

"Yup, like most of the rooms in the facility, you can choose how you want it to appear. You guys coulda done that for your common room during training, dunno why you didn't."

"Huh, no one told us." Suddenly, the big panel right next to the common room door that everyone ignored throughout training made a lot more sense. "This is so wicked. This is all mine?"

"Yup. Your own home away from home. You don't have to stay here if you want to find a place somewhere in the city, but it's always here if you ever need it."

I walked around the apartment and opened every cupboard to see what they were hiding. It may have been juvenile, but it felt like an adventure exploring the high-tech apartment after living in filth for years.

They were all filled with mundane things like plates and bowls, but I was still in awe. I peeled open the fridge and somehow it had all my favourites. I headed over to the giant holo-TV on the wall and looked at what I had to amuse myself. I had all the latest systems with tons of games to choose from.

"Come with me. You're gonna love this." Lili led me to one of the doors on the far side of the room.

The door slid open and a small boxing gym stared back at me. It had every piece of equipment I could think of, and it far outclassed the crappy gym Kieran and I had been training at for the last decade. The ring looked brand new. While I didn't have Kieran there to spar with me, I had a feeling the ring would be equipped with something to fix that.

"No—way."

"Everyone gets one little extra room in their homes, and I told them this is what you'd like most." Lili walked over to a punching bag and wrapped her arms around it. "Was I right? You can customize this room too if you don't like the look or the layout—"

"One hundred percent. This is incredible." I made my way over and gave the bag a light jab. "Wait, what's your spare room?"

She smirked. "Maybe one day you'll find out."

I didn't even have a guess as to what it could have been. Maybe some kind of fighting dojo of her own, but that seemed like too safe of a guess. I was more partial to an out-there guess, something like a room that housed nothing but a single cotton candy machine. That sounded weird enough to be right.

"Mysterious," I finally said.

"Well, that's not the end of the tour yet." Lili smiled. "You still need to check out your room."

I headed out of the gym and walked toward the door that I assumed led to my room with Lili on my heels.

It looked like my trainee room, only a hell of a lot bigger. The Interceptors could have thrown the dinner party in here. After it was over we all could have climbed into the same bed for a nap if we wanted to.

I looked toward Lili. "This is amazing."

"You think so? Everything you could have ever wanted? Nice big bed—it's pretty comfy too."

"I guess so. I didn't know what to expect to be honest. I never was big on watching the streams of you guys. I caught the big stuff, and I tuned in to Chase's stream sometimes with Kieran. I never really got to see all the slice-of-life stuff with you guys. The only person I'd ever watch was—"

I couldn't tell her that I specifically tuned in to watch her from time to time.

How weird was that?

I never watched any of the biggest heroes in the world, but their hot newer recruit—all the time!

I'm an idiot.

"Me?"

I felt my face grow hotter as I nodded. "But not in a weird way. I'm not some creepy stalker guy."

She giggled. "That's exactly what a creepy stalker guy would say."

"Good point."

"Can I ask you something?"

"I'm an open book," I said with a shrug.

"Why are you here?" She moved closer to me. "Was it just something to do after Cleo added your name to the list, or is there something else?"

"Can I trust you?" I sat down on the bed. "I want to keep this between the two of us."

"Of course. Your secret's will always be safe with me. We're teammates. We all have your back—like you'll have all of ours."

I took a breath. "When I was a kid my whole family was caught in one of Zeals' attacks. An explosion killed both my parents and left my sister with one arm."

"The scar too, right?"

I nodded. The few memories I had of that day filled my head, and it made me angry. My parents died so Lenna and I could live, and we never forgot that.

Lili sat next to me and put a hand on my leg as I continued. "My parents—I guess they shielded us from the blast—they saved us in time, but they didn't make it —for a while, I didn't think Lenna was gonna make it. I thought I'd be left on my own with no family and nowhere to go, but Lenna managed to pull through."

"I'm glad you had her. The both of you were able to take care of each other."

"I promised her—promised my parents," I balled my fist. "That I'd make the person responsible pay for what they did. Becoming an Interceptor wasn't just something to do with a friend or only a way to help those who need it—a big part of it was I knew it would get me closer to Zeal."

I kept my eyes forward. I didn't want to see what Lili's reaction might be. Everyone had their own reasons for wanting to join the Interceptors, but I had a feeling that few had a reason like mine.

"You guys want to stop Zeal, and I want to make him pay for what he did. We're all one step closer to that," I said as I took a deep breath.

There was a moment of silence.

I didn't have anything else to say, and I don't think Lili knew what to say. I knew what I had dropped on her was heavy, and how much she had already had to drink might have made it hard for her to formulate a careful response.

"Revenge," She finally said. "You've gotta be careful with something like that."

"I know."

"But you have a family that can help. We'll stop him —together. Not because of some vendetta. We'll stop him because it's the right thing to do. We'll protect the world and make sure what he did to your parents never happens to anyone again."

I looked at Lili, and she leaned closer to me. She smelled of booze, but I figured I did too. The way she looked at me gave me comfort, and I found myself leaning in toward her. She did the same until our lips were hovering apart.

"Ready to do this thing, Rhys?" Ayla said as she warped in front of us. "Oh—I am *so* sorry."

We pulled away from one another, and Lili stood up. "I—uh—I should go. I'll wait outside until you two are done."

Ayla had shrunken until she was no bigger than an apple. "I totally just ruined a moment, didn't I?"

"I think so, yeah," I said as Lili disappeared behind the sliding door.

Ayla grew back to normal size. "Sorry about that."

"It's okay—probably for the best."

Ayla gave me a look that said she didn't believe me, but it didn't really matter. We were about to be neurally linked which meant she'd know every single one of my thoughts regardless of how I presented myself.

"Anything I should know before we're stuck together for life?" I asked.

"You'll make a woman very happy someday, I'm sure." She rolled her eyes. "Well, for one—don't call it *being stuck together*. We're partners. I guess you should know that your new kit will need a day or so to charge."

"I won't be able to check it out?"

"No, you will. You won't be able to use it for anything particularly strenuous. Hope you weren't planning on bench pressing a skyscraper tonight."

"Is that a thing I could do with a kit?"

"You know what? That's a good question."

"Here's a better question, did you figure out what's up with those data-bits yet?"

"No." She moved closer to me. "I was kind of hoping the neural link might make things more clear to me."

"That sounds like it might help." I looked around for any kind of strange device. "Well, let's do it—*how* do we do it?"

Ayla gestured to a little box sitting on a dresser at the far end of the room. I walked over and opened it up to find another little medallion. It was similar to the one I had on, but I could feel a serious kind of energy radiating from it. I pulled off my necklace and swapped it out for the new one.

"I don't feel any different."

"That's because you wouldn't be able to activate it without my neural link," she said. "You might find it easier to get your element working a bit more effectively for you with your own personalized kit. It's matched to your DNA."

I scoffed. "I have a more than a few questions on how you managed to get some of my DNA, but whatever."

"Well, you bleed everywhere. Little leg blood here, a little leg blood there. You even blew up that one time, remember?" Ayla asked.

"Okay, okay. I get it."

"Good times."

"Not if you're the one bleeding and blowing up."

"Oh, stop with the whining. You ready?" I nodded. "Hold still."

Ayla flew into the medallion, and I could feel the energy pulsating around my body. It was similar to how it was with the trainee kits, but it was way more intense. It felt like all of my senses were dialled up to eleven.

She popped back out of the medallion and spoke without moving her mouth. *We're officially partners. Till death do us part.*

"Am I able to—"

To talk to me without speaking? Yup. I can hear all your thoughts. The cameras will make sure you never feel alone, but with me, you really won't ever be alone.

Weird.

"I know right? Just wait till I get bored and start hanging out in your dreams." Ayla wiggled her fingers. "Did you poop yourself?"

I gave her a confused look until I remembered what the team had said about the shock during training. "No, we're all good." I gave my butt a pat for some extra assurance. "Let's back up a sec. You can put yourself in my dreams?"

"Yup. I used to help Chase train that way."

"That's badass."

I looked in the mirror and let my kit cover my body. The dull grey of the trainee kit had been replaced by the same green Lili wore. It felt better than the trainee kit, and I felt stronger than I had while I was in that one.

My sheathe had finally decided to change into a shade of green that matched my kit. I drew my sword and looked at it. The blade's edges were silver, but it morphed into a shade of green toward the middle. I put it away and turned back to Ayla.

"How do you want me to look?" she asked. I gave her another confused look. "I can appear however you want me to. Do you want me to go through your mind to see what you find most attractive?"

"What? No—"

Ayla's appearance morphed into a mix between how Lili, Fern, and how Ayla had already looked. She had Fern's height with Lili's physical proportions. Her face had all of Ayla's original features except for eyes, which instead looked like Fern's. Her hair had morphed into a ponytail with two strands of hair in the front, a favourite style of Lili.

"Oh my god." I covered my eyes. "This is not okay. I feel dirty."

"What do you mean? I think I look pretty good." She ran her hands along her curves. "You have good taste."

"I don't want you to appear how you think I want you to. We're partners, which means we're equals. I want you to look whichever way is going to make you happiest."

She looked pleasantly surprised by what I had said. I couldn't be too sure how Chase had treated her, but from the way she regarded him, I figured it was pretty well.

I was kinda worried that she might have thought I'd be a dick or something.

"I didn't think you were going to be a dick," Ayla said as she gave me a dull look.

"I really gotta stop thinking when people can hear my thoughts."

"You don't have any secrets from me, bucko. I'm glad you'd say something like that, though. The other Interceptors decided on our appearances."

"Even Chase? Ayla, you might be more human than some of the actual people I've met. There's no way I could tell you how to present yourself to the world."

"Thanks." She nodded. "I don't know—I kind of like how I looked when I was his partner." Ayla morphed back to her original look. "Oh, but with one little change." Her hair morphed from a dark colour to a reddish-brown, and her eyes morphed from green to a greyish-blue.

"That's how you want to look?"

"Yeah. This feels like me."

"It's nice to officially meet the real you, Ayla." I held out a hand, and then gave my wrist a shake to try to play off my goof.

She smiled at me. "I don't know why, but something feels different from when I was with Chase," Ayla said as she brought a finger to her chin. "Oh—here come all your memories." She dropped to the ground and held her head as she groaned.

"Are you alright?" I asked before extending a hand and helping her to her feet.

Both of our eyes snapped to her hand in mine.

I was touching her.

She was touching me.

What?

What?!

Her hand turned back into data, and it passed through mine.

"What—just—happened?" I asked.

"I—I don't know." Ayla stared at her hand.

She tried to touch me again. Her hand passed through my arm, and then through my face. She closed her eyes and scrunched her face as she brought her hand to my cheek.

I could feel her. Her hand felt like the hand of a real woman. I could feel the warmth of her skin and her breath on my face. She grabbed my face and smooched me before leaning back and becoming intangible again.

"Whoa!"

"Sorry. I could tell you wanted to do that as much as I've always wanted to try that. Nice kiss by the way. Whichever lady you end up picking is gonna be a lucky one."

"What? I didn't want to—I mean, I—you can't just kiss someone like that."

My brain was about ready to malfunction.

"Well, you wanted to." Ayla grinned. "I can read your thoughts, Rhys. I know you liked it. It's nothing to be ashamed of. I am pretty hot."

"Uh-huh, not to toot your own horn or anything—not like you can't decide to be the most beautiful person in the world if you wanted to." I rubbed the back of my neck. "What is going on? I have a feeling that you *aren't* supposed to be able to do that."

"No, I'm not. This is new. None of the AI's can do this. I couldn't do that when I was with Chase."

"Maybe it's a side-effect? Something that will go away once we're fully connected, and the kit is up and running?"

"It might have to do with me—"

BOOM

Chapter 26:
Zeal

The explosion shook the facility like the earth had opened up and swallowed it whole—which was a strange thought considering it was floating in the sky. It sounded like it had come from right outside my bedroom, so if it hadn't, the explosion must have been huge. Lili burst back into my room with a panicked look on her face.

"We need to head back there—oh, Ayla. The new-look is so cute," Lili said.

I stared at Lili as I questioned her skewed priorities.

"We'll figure this out later." Ayla nodded before jumping back into my medallion.

"What do you think happened?" I asked.

"I don't know," Lili tore her dress for mobility "But there's no way it's anything good."

It was clear that there was nothing more sobering than a distant explosion. I followed Lili out of my place, and back down the winding halls to the Interceptor common room. We had no idea what was going on, but if the problem was big enough, the Interceptor cameras might start rolling again at any second.

Each step stung the wound on my leg, but I had a feeling it wasn't nearly as bad as it would have been without the advanced medical tech the facility had.

"What if it's Sable or Dorian again?" I asked.

"If it's a fair fight, we'll be fine. Five fully functional Interceptors—you *and* Ramona against those two shouldn't be too big of an issue. They're big and ugly, but we know how to deal with them in a fight."

"A giant explosion doesn't exactly sound like the promise of a fair fight."

Ayla cleared her throat in my mind, *I'll keep you safe, don't worry.*

I tried to scoff at her in my thoughts, I'm more worried about anyone caught in that explosion.

When we burst through the door we stared at a huge hole that had been blown in the side of the building.

Mickey, Ramona, and Cleo were all out cold on the ground. Diggs and Pegs were locked in a fight against Sable and Dorian. I had a feeling none of us had any clue what would lead them to be so bold. It was possible that they figured a night of celebration and drinking would be the night the Interceptors guard was at its lowest.

"We should have detected them before they even got close. How did this happen twice?" Lili said to herself. "Get those three out of here. I'll support Diggs and Pegs against uggo-one and uggo-two."

I wished I could help out in the fight, but Lili had the right idea. If Sable and Dorian thought they were losing —they'd target Cleo, Ramona, or Mickey as some kind of bargaining chip to get whatever it was that they wanted. I needed to figure out a way to move them out of there.

Off to the side, there was a large serving trolley that I could put them on. I could wheel them down to the med-bay and rush back to help out however I could. When I reached it, I tossed everything off the top of it. Mickey was furthest from the action so I rushed there first.

"I didn't realize my first night as an Interceptor would involve becoming the most extreme wait-staff of all time." I rolled the table around a chunk of debris.

"There's the kid." Dorian nailed Diggs with a huge kick that sent him flying into the entertainment area, and his eyes locked right on me. "Do you want him, or shall I?"

Lili jumped at Dorian with a flurry of kicks. There was nothing more hypnotic than seeing the way the Interceptors gracefully moved as they fought. I could have sat there admiring each of their techniques if it weren't for the life or death situation we were in.

She threw a combination of punches and kicks, and while Dorian couldn't quite distance himself from her, he managed to dodge them all.

Lili performed a backward handspring and missed the kick, but the blade of wind she sent out of her feet grazed him.

Before her feet hit the floor she started moving slower. Dorian was starting to use his time abilities to his advantage, and there wasn't anything I could do.

"I want him" Sable rushed toward me and launched a few fireballs.

Speed up, dodge right, and then wait for the third fireball to impact the floor!

Without Ayla's guidance, I would've been done for.

I followed her instructions and none of the fireballs came anywhere close to me. "I'm gonna let you warn me about any and all incoming danger from now on."

That's kinda my job, Rhys.

Sable was closing in on me fast.

"Yeah—" Pegs stopped Sable with a perfect throw of her flaming circle-sword. "How about you don't try to break our new recruit."

She jumped at Sable and seeing Pegs fight was even more mesmerizing than any of the other team members.

She'd spin the sword around different parts of her body to deflect sword swings. While doing that, she'd be landing punches and kicks in the most unorthodox fighting style I'd ever seen. It was like she was dancing around Sable.

"Thanks, Pegs." I called as I kept running.

I reached Mickey and hauled the heavy android onto the table. I was lucky that they hadn't had time to pull their kit on. There was no telling how heavy it would be to try to lift an android in a full kit.

Although, if Cleo and Mickey *had* gotten their kits on, I had a feeling neither of them would be down for the count.

That brought an entirely new question to my mind, how in the world was an android out cold? I chalked it up to Mickey being far more advanced than the average bot, and figured I'd figure it out later.

"I know we never had a chance to connect, Mickey," I said as I headed toward Cleo. "But if you could wake up—or power back on and help me out—that'd be great. How does an android get knocked out anyway?!"

Diggs was in a tough spot. He couldn't use his element without risking accidentally blinding Pegs or Lili. That didn't stop him from holding his own against Dorian with a bit of help. I would have hated to see how their individual fights against the gruesome twosome had been going before Lili thrust herself into the mix.

"If you don't grab the kid, I will!" Dorian roared.

I stopped and separated from the table to keep Mickey safe. I ducked Dorian's incoming attack and rolled away from him. He thrust right up to me, but I dodged a big swing from his right hand. I caught his arm and used the little leverage I had to toss him at the wall.

"Nice one, kid," Dorian growled. He managed to control his spin, and he landed with his feet planted on the wall. "But not nice enough." He looked right at me as he thrust toward me.

I wasn't going to be able to dodge out of the way of it, especially after he slowed my movements.

I shut my eyes, but the clobbering never came.

My movements returned to normal. I opened my eyes in time to see Diggs had intercepted him with one of the biggest tackles I'd ever seen. They launched into the wall, but Dorian was able to get the better of him.

With a violent crack of lightning, Dr. Zeal arrived.

He appeared in the blasted out hole of the building, looking down on everyone. His bushy grey eyebrows looked like they were poorly stitched to his face, and his gaunt features made him look far more intimidating than the average bag of bones.

"Uh—guys?" I said, not having a clue of what to do.

Seeing him made me stop in my tracks. I don't know if it was fear, blinding rage, or something else entirely, but I couldn't will my body to move. I couldn't take my eyes off of him.

"My lord," Dorian and Sable said.

They tossed Diggs, Pegs, and Lili away from them. Without a wasted moment, they each jumped toward Zeal and bent a knee.

Without any water on the ground, Zeal froze the feet of Diggs, Pegs, and Lili to the floor. They struggled against the ice, but the floor beside them morphed into hands and snatched them all in a tight grasp.

I was on my own against three of the most powerful people in the world, and I still couldn't use my kit.

"What are you doing here?" Dorian started. "We have everything—"

"Quiet," Zeal spat. "I thought I'd do this personally. I wanted a good look at him."

Zeal launched bolts of lightning toward Diggs, Lili and me. The bolts struck each of them, and they went limp. The bolt aimed at me hit the table which sent me and Mickey flying.

"Diggs! Lili—Rhys, are you alright?" Pegs asked.

"I'm okay. Ayla—"

They're all still alive—just passed out.

Zeal floated over to Pegs with Dorian and Sable close behind. They knew they had us in a rough situation. I had no idea how long Kiyoshi's operation would last. Maybe if I could hold them off long enough, he could get back here to make some kind of save.

"Stand down," He held a hand to Pegs' throat. "Or she dies."

"Get your hand away from me you old psycho." Pegs spat toward him.

His hand started to glow, and the black mark of poison spread across her throat. She screamed in agony.

I took a step forward. "What do you want?"

"Don't worry about me, Rhys. Back-up should—be here—" Pegs choked out before losing consciousness.

Zeal started delivering small shocks to Peg's body, and her head jerked around. He was torturing her, but thankfully she didn't have to suffer through it. If I could find a way to help her, the Interceptors advanced medical-tech could take care of her.

Ayla, how much power does the kit have?

Next to none.

Enough for me to use my element?

Maybe—once.

Hope that's enough.

I let my kit move to my hand. I summoned a huge concrete pillar right underneath Zeal's feet. It smashed right through the roof of the facility, and we all looked up at it as my kit crawled back away.

"Did he?" Dorian asked.

"No way," Sable said.

I tried to sprint over to Pegs, but Zeal teleported back in and separated us with a wall of fire. He launched a flash, and everything went bright white. I rubbed my eyes in pain, but I knew I was a sitting duck.

Dodge left.

I didn't react in time and took a wicked punch.

Sweep right.

I tried but took a kick in my chest.

This isn't working well, Ayla.

Strike after strike came from what I figured had to be Dorian and Sable. I was like a piece of meat, and they were tenderizing me. Ayla tried to help me out, and I managed to move out of the way of a few strikes, but there wasn't a thing I could do.

My vision started to return in time for me to see Zeal had teleported right in front of me. He was floating still, and even though everything was blurry, it looked like he was amused.

"You bastard."

I took a swing at him, but he disappeared, and I was forced to the floor from a hard shot to the back. I tried to stand up, but the ground below me shot upward and launched me backward. A gust of wind caught me before I hit the ground, and it raised me to the same height as Zeal.

Ayla warped beside us. "Leave him alone, Zeal."

"Ayla—how good to see you. I believe the last time I would have seen you was—"

"You know damn well when it was." The hatred in Ayla's voice was clear. "What do you want with Rhys?"

"So callous—and you all call *me* the villain. Chase tried to stop my population control, and I didn't want him to. It's as simple as that, but what do I want? What I want has nothing to do with Rhys. Unless he's interested in joining my cause."

"No chance of that."

"What a shame. You'll come around," A sinister grin crawled across his face. "I'm sure of it. Back to what I want. I want many, many things—world peace—the destruction of the Interceptors—your data."

He wrapped a hand around my neck and the other on my medallion. I pulled out Trigger, but a jolt of electricity coursed through my body causing me to drop it.

The hand he had over my medallion started to glow, and he cackled in delight. His other hand shook for a moment, and my neck felt like it had been lit on fire. The burning sensation filled my entire body, and I could feel my tired eyes giving up.

I forced my eyes to stay open long enough to see Kiyoshi and General Odon come bursting through the doors. A blast of lightning flew right toward Zeal, and he dropped me to move out of the way in time. I grabbed Trigger and used it to climb to my feet.

"Are you still able to fight?" I heard Kiyoshi ask, but it felt like he was miles away.

"I'm—I got—we." I slurred as I made it to my weak feet. "Pegs—needs help."

I could see Ramona waking up. Cleo must have protected her from the brunt of the blast.

"Rhys. C'mon, Rhys," Kiyoshi said as he gripped his war hammer.

"Ramona is conscious. We have to help her, now," General Odon said.

"But, sir—"

Kiyoshi looked back at me as I fell back to the ground. The last thing I saw clearly was the usual angry look from Kiyoshi, and General Odon approaching Dorian and Sable. Blurred images flashed in my mind, but I couldn't recall any of it if I tried. I stayed awake, but it was a blur.

Someone moved closer, but I couldn't tell who it was or how long it had been. When she leaned closer, I could tell that it was Ramona. She put a hand on my forehead,

but I couldn't hold on anymore.
     Everything went black.

Chapter 27:
Back Here Again

When I finally came to, I was laying in a bed in what I figured was the med-bay. My entire body ached in the same most peoples tended to after a nasty bout with the flu. The burning sensation running from my throat to my chest had to be from Zeal poisoning me, but it was far worse than Rowan's poison.

I blinked the haze from my eyes and turned my head to see Lili and Faith resting in a couple of chairs.

"I really gotta stop ending up here." I choked out.

Lili's eyes opened, and she jumped on me with a tight hug. "You're okay."

"I might not be—if you hug me so tight. What happened? Why aren't I dead?"

I figured the last thing I'd ever see was Ramona. She wasn't the worst last sight to see, but I really didn't want to be killed by someone like Zeal.

"We're pretty sure Zeal and his goons attacked because they were after information," Lili said.

She looked as worn down as I felt, but her beauty still managed to shine through. It did look like she hadn't slept very long for quite a while, which made me wonder how long I had been unconscious for.

"What kind of information?" I asked.

"Well, because of the neural link, Ayla's systems were essentially set to minimum security to ensure your brain didn't get scrambled. I guess they figured they could steal years of secrets from Ayla's data."

"So, everything she did with Chase?"

"Yup. They got it all," she sighed. "His entire life. Your entire life. All the plans, operations, and anything else you could think of involving the Interceptors. Zeal has it all."

That's what that glow on my medallion was.

"And you guys think that's gonna help him with this new Extinction Virus?"

She nodded. "That, and whatever else that bastard's working on. We lucked out when Chase and Ayla managed to wipe all his work on the original virus. Hard to recreate any type of accident if you don't know how it happened."

I hadn't known that. The media always made Dr. Zeal seem like some kind of evil genius. While that might have been true. learning that he had no idea how he developed something that could wipe out the world almost made the villain seem like a bit of a fool.

"Ayla—where is she?" I asked as I tried to sit up.

Lili put a hand on my chest. "Relax, she's okay. If she wasn't—you'd be dead. Faith was waiting for you to wake up to see if she'd be able to come back out of the medallion."

Ayla?

She warped from the medallion and looked at me. "We screwed the pooch on this one, huh?"

"It's no one's fault," Lili said. "We never could have seen an attack like that coming. Zeal's never been that bold before."

"I'm glad you're okay—I'm glad you're all okay," I said as I looked at each of them. "How's everyone else? Pegs?"

"Everyone's okay. No major injuries—aside from our collective pride. Kiyoshi and Odon were able to fight them back after Zeal had already gotten what he came for. You and Pegs were the people we were worried about, but she woke up earlier."

I was glad to hear that Pegs was okay. The image of her jolting around hurt as much as remembering what Dorian had done to Keyshawn.

"What happens next?" I asked.

"You rest up. I'll come see you tomorrow, and the team will get you up to speed."

I remembered something Lili had said during the attack. If the facility had some kind of measures in place to detect attacks before they happened, what had happened during the two attacks?

Was it possible that Zeal's tech was even more powerful than the Interceptors?

I wanted to ask her if the team had looked into what happened, but it didn't feel like the right time.

"We'll have some training drills to work through so we can see how well you mesh with us too. We are a team after all. I'll go let everyone know you're awake." Lili reached the door and turned around. "Diggs told me to thank you for doing what you could to protect Pegs. It really means a lot to him." Lili shut the door behind her as she went.

I was left alone with Faith. She gave me a gentle smile before sliding her chair over to the side of the bed.

She slid her hands into mine. *How do you feel?*

"Like a crazy evil scientist sucked the life out of me."

That sounds about right. What about you, Ayla?

"How does that work? Can you—"

You two have a neural link, it's basically the same thing. I can hear her through your head. Anyway, Ayla?

Ayla scratched her head. "Everything feels fine, but there is one *tiny* thing we should tell you about."

Faith cocked her head and looked back and forth between us. I had a feeling that she wasn't surprised by AI all that often.

What's wrong?

"Something happened with the neural link, and when I focus hard and try—I can do this." Ayla reached out and put a hand on my cheek.

Faith's eyes went wide. *How can that even happen?*

"That's what we were hoping you could tell us."

She thought for a moment. *Have you tried touching other things? Other people?*

"No, Rhys helped me to my feet, and then I laid a big smooch on him."

You what?

"I'd always wanted to try it."

How was it?

"Okay, that's good." I cut in. "It was good—Ayla, try grabbing the blanket or somethin'."

She reached out, but she couldn't touch it. She scrunched up her face before taking a breath and trying again. She managed to nudge it, but that was it. She tried the same thing on Faith, but she couldn't touch her. She focused one last time and flicked my forehead.

"Okay—ow."

Faith brought a hand to her chin. *So she can only easily interact physically with you, and anything or anyone else seems to be possible, but a lot harder.*

She scoffed. "I definitely wouldn't say *easily.*"

"This can't be normal," I said.

I'll look through a copy of the data, but Ayla isn't any different from the other AI's, and I've never seen anything like this before. Have either of you told anyone about this?

"I figured it would be best to keep this info between us," I said as I looked at Ayla. "I trust Cleo and Alfie, but they don't need to know—not yet anyway."

Okay, I agree. Don't tell anyone about this. This has so many implications—what if you're actually starting to become a living being? What if I created life? Living data...

"Living data?" Ayla said as she looked down at her hands.

Faith scurried out of the room without another word, and I was alone with Ayla. For a minute, we just stared at each other, not really knowing what to say.

"What are we gonna do?" I finally asked.

"The exact thing you've always wanted. We're going to make Zeal pay."

Chapter 28:
Wannabe Interceptor

I was thrilled to get out of the med-bay—yet again. What wasn't so thrilling was the fact that I now had my own personal nuisance in the form of a floating camera following my every move. It didn't matter how fast I moved or where I went, it streamed my every moment.

"Welcome everyone to the Rhys York show. Fern—stop checking out my butt. Keyshawn—miss you, buddy. Hope you're feelin' better. Lenna, Kieran—no hanky-panky," I said as I shook a finger at the camera.

General Odon had ordered the team to figure out what it was that Zeal was after. Somewhere within all that information he'd taken—there had to be something that could lead him to a new Extinction Virus. The issue was, there were two lifetimes and an entire facility's existence worth of data to choose from.

They had Faith scrub through all the data that had come into the facility recently. It was a pretty safe bet that whatever Zeal wanted, it was something recent. Unfortunately, the Interceptors dealt with a series of high-profile clients and undertook missions to protect and retrieve incredibly complex pieces of tech.

Zeal could have been after anything that could have helped him with his new strain of the Extinction Virus.

In the meantime, I was finally going to have my first training exercise with the team. Thanks to Ayla, I had become pretty good at finding my way around the facility, so I made my way to the situation room on my own. By the time I arrived, everyone was already set to get started.

"How's it feel having a flying nuisance follow you around all day?" Lili asked.

"Like my adoring public is waiting for me to get yelled at by Kiyoshi again."

"Should we start that now?" he asked.

I flashed him a thumbs up. "Nope. We're good." I let my kit cover my body. "Sorry I'm late. What's the training exercise gonna be?" I looked toward Cleo. "Another hostage situation like back when I was a trainee?"

"Not exactly. This is going to simulate Sellea City as it's under attack by an army of Conks, Dorian, Sable, and Zeal. Diggs and Pegs are going to play the parts of Dorian and Sable. Zeal will be a hologram, and the goal is to capture him. Understood?"

I nodded as I looked up at a facility team watching us from another room. They looked like scientists ready to study their lab rats.

"We're gonna kick your butts," Diggs said as he bumped Pegs' fist.

"Maybe we should make *you* play the role of Sable," Cleo said as she gave him a side-eye.

"Please don't do that. We all know the first thing he'd do." Pegs brought a hand to her chest. "Rhys, don't go thinking we're gonna go easy on you just because you protected me against Zeal."

"Wouldn't dream of it."

"Let's get started." Cleo looked up to the room of facility members and held to fingers behind her ear.

"Ramona, can you have them execute training program two-two-nine?"

"Sure thing." Ramona's voice came through some kind of speaker system. "Brace yourselves."

The entire room morphed into an exact copy of the city below, except it was eerily void of life. Diggs and Pegs morphed into copies of Dorian and Sable before teleporting away.

Cleo, Mickey, and Kiyoshi all pulled out their weapons so I clicked the hilt of Trigger and did the same.

Lili adjusted her gloves and that reminded me about the gauntlets I had grabbed to add to my arsenal. I stuck my sword in the ground and adjusted them. I ran my hand along the arrows and thought back to my fights with Akio. I caught Kiyoshi giving me an angry look as I adjusted the gauntlets.

I hoped he'd get over me eliminating his little brother eventually.

He can't hold a grudge forever.

"I'll go at your pace so that you—" Lili started.

"What? No. This is a training exercise. Go as hard as you would if it were the real thing. I need to be ready the next time we face them."

Cleo turned and smiled. "That's the spirit." She pushed Kiyoshi. "And you said he seemed like a lazy idiot."

"Wait, you said—"

An enormous laser dropped from the sky, and it looked like it had levelled an entire city block.

They each took off toward the event, knowing that's where we'd find Holo-Zeal and his goons. Kiyoshi activated his thrusters and took off like a bullet—while Cleo rode a wolf made of water down the street, Mickey disappeared into the shadows, and Lili used her wind to launch herself high into the air.

I couldn't do anything as cool as the rest of them, so I activated my own thrusters and did what I could to keep up with Kiyoshi.

Conks started appearing all over the city, and they were doing all the damage they could. Every time I had seen them—they'd looked a bit dumb, but here they were vicious. Kiyoshi nailed one with his hammer as he came to a stop, and I sliced one in half as I did the same.

"Ready yourself," Kiyoshi said.

There were more than I had originally thought, and soon we were circled by endless waves of Conks. Different elements were firing off throughout the crowd. I had no idea what kind of damage they could do to us in a training exercise. With how advanced the med-bay was, I had a feeling it was going to be the real deal.

Kiyoshi crushed a Conk that rushed at me with his hammer. "You're welcome."

I glared at him. "I coulda got that."

"If you could have, you would have." Kiyoshi stepped back to back with me, and he gave me a nudge. "I can take my half on my own, but you're gonna need some backup."

"What? I could take out half of 'em if I ran forward with my sword held out."

"If you think that, you need more help than I thought."

"I dunno." I inspected the sleek blade. "This sword's pretty sharp."

Lili and Cleo landed down beside us, and Mickey stepped out from the shadow Kiyoshi had cast. I had never seen Fern do anything like that with her shadow element, so I figured that had to be pretty advanced.

"Mara, give me a scan of the crowd," Kiyoshi said.

His AI, Mara, warped beside us and used her finger to count. "Looks like about five hundred."

"One hundred each it is," Cleo said.

"On three——"

I thought we'd be heading into the fight after Cleo's comment so I rushed forward and started swinging. I cut through a line of Conks and looked back to see the others rush into the fight.

"Wait for the order next time, Rhys," Cleo said as she flipped toward me and took out a Conk.

"My bad." I let out an awkward laugh as I sliced through a Conk.

I always liked checking out the highlights of the Interceptors biggest battles, and there was nothing cooler than getting to be a part of that.

I jumped out of the way of a huge fist from a Brute Conk, and Lili grabbed my arm in mid-air. She launched a gust of wind to spin us before tossing me right back at it. I slammed my sword down into its chest, and the Brute was motionless.

Lili landed next to me. "We are so keeping that move for the two of us."

"Dorian won't be able to power through a move like that," I said as I nudged the sword.

Lili jumped back into the fray as a group of Elemental Conks started shooting electrical and pyro waves at us. I dodged them and started to run along the wall of a building.

Mickey was fighting a group of Brutes alone, but one had perched itself upon the top of a building for a huge sneak attack. I could have delivered a warning on the comms, but I thought it would be cooler to save the day.

Shields.

Ayla activated the two shields on my wrists and she guided me to two perfect throws. They burrowed halfway through the concrete of the building beside me. I stepped up from one to the other and leaped toward the Brute Conk as it jumped down toward Mickey. I caught it with my sword, and the robot's split halves crashed to the street below.

Mickey scoffed. "Alright, show-off."

I flashed a thumbs up. "You're allowed to be excited about this."

Back on the ground, Kiyoshi was being pushed back by two Executioner Conks. It was my moment to get back at him and show him that I belong here.

Rhys, I don't think that's such a—

Thrusters.

Ayla sighed, *Oh boy.*

Ayla activated my thrusters, and I shot forward. I whirled around Kiyoshi and took the executioners by surprise. They split in half and fell to the floor as I grinned at Kiyoshi.

"You're welcome," I said, trying to mimic his voice.

"Do that again, and I'll treat you the same way I treat these Conks." Kiyoshi stomped on a dismembered metallic head.

I tried to tell you it wasn't going to be a good idea.

"I know, Ayla." I rolled my eyes. "Thank you."

Don't you roll your eyes at me.

"How'd you know I rolled my eyes?"

I see everything.

"Creepy."

We finished dealing with the last of the Conks, and Kiyoshi pointed to where the laser had struck down. "Everyone, head there now."

Kiyoshi sped away again. I couldn't catch up to him, but I was able to keep him on the edge of my sight. "Do we have a faster way we can travel, Ayla?"

She warped beside me. "Well, if you got better control over your element, you could launch us toward the battle—oh, or you could stay still, but move all the ground around you."

"Chase whirled around on sand most of the time, didn't he?" I said as I turned a corner.

"That's a lot more complicated than your current skill level—which is basically zero."

We all arrived at the scene of the blast, and as I expected there wasn't a building left standing. Zeal floated high above the crater made by the blast, but Dorian and Sable were ready for our approach.

"Oh no! It's the Interceptors!" Pegs' voice came from Sable.

"What are we going to do?" Diggs' voice came from Dorian.

It was weird to hear their voices come out of two of the evilest people I had the displeasure of fighting against.

"I want Mickey and Lili on Sable, and Kiyoshi and I will take Dorian." Cleo whirled her spear. "Rhys, you can help out wherever help is needed."

Mickey jumped from the shadows beside Sable and launched at her with twin knives. Lili supplemented her attack by adding in a few wind blasts. Sable placed her katana in the ground, and it ignited a small explosion that threw Lili from the fight.

Kiyoshi threw bolts of lightning toward Dorian as he rushed forward, and Cleo launched into the air to throw a series of ice spikes at him. Dorian froze the spikes in time as he swiped his scythe to block the lightning bolts, but he also managed to redirect them toward Lili as she rejoined the fight against Sable. She managed to flip out of the way in time, before hitting Sable with a big kick.

Ayla hopped back into my kit. *Rhys, get to it, dude. You're on this team now.*

"Oh, crap. Right!"

I moved in to help out in the brawl and met Dorian's scythe with my sword. He pushed into my body and swept out my leg. I had to roll to avoid the point of his scythe and I wondered in that moment what would have happened if he hit me.

"On your feet," Kiyoshi said as he sparked the ground beneath me.

It sent me into the air, and I spun with my sword outstretched as I flew toward Dorian. Sable met my sword with a massive swing and Dorian nailed me with a huge jump kick.

I was sent flying away from the action, but I had an opportunity to make a break toward Zeal. If I played the situation right, I could secure Zeal.

To keep the pressure off from the sides I sent an arrow toward Dorian and Sable respectively. They were both able to deflect the arrows, which caused the others to have to think fast to avoid getting hit. They used the separation to rush me, and they stopped me before I got anywhere near Zeal.

I whirled around and blocked a strike from the scythe and the katana in the same stroke. Sable leaned back and opened her palm. She was going to unleash a massive fire attack. I tried to move, but I couldn't. Dorian had frozen me with his time element.

Ayla?

Helmet!

I closed my eyes and let my kit cover my head as a huge wall of flames engulfed me. Cleo tackled me backward into the crater formed by the earlier blast, and when I was clear of the flames I took the helmet off.

I looked up, and Zeal was right above me. Dorian and Sable hadn't come after me, so they must have been busy fighting off the others.

"Rhys, you need to slow down, and—"

I activated my thrusters and leaped into the air. I pointed my hands at the earth from the crater and clapped my hands right at Zeal. The earth rose up and clamped around the hologram. I landed on the earth right next to him.

I did it.

If I could repeat the same sort of thing the next time we faced him, I'd be able to get the revenge I needed.

"No big deal, guys." I called down to the others. "I got him."

I turned around to see Lili and Mickey being held at the points of Sable's katana and Dorian's scythe. Kiyoshi looked furious, and when I looked down at Cleo, she didn't look any happier.

The simulation faded away, and I landed back on the floor. It was nice to see Diggs and Pegs back to normal, but they didn't look too happy about the outcome of training.

Brace yourself.

Ayla wasn't kidding.

Kiyoshi stormed toward me. "DO YOU HAVE ANY IDEA WHAT IT MEANS TO BE ON A TEAM?"

I'd heard Kiyoshi in an unpleasant mood before, but things were different. It was a bit of an overreaction to scream over a training session, but maybe the Interceptors took their training way more serious than I had initially thought.

I looked at Lili for help, but she looked away. "I thought—"

"No, don't give me that. You *weren't* thinking. Do you honestly think you could take Zeal on your own? The man that kicked your ass without breaking a sweat the other night? He turned two Interceptors to his side. That man has a mastery of every element—"

"I get it. He's a bad dude. The point of the—"

"A bad dude? You don't know the half of it, kid. You can barely get your element to work half the time. How the hell are you expecting to take him out on your own?"

"I saw an opening, and I took it." I looked at everyone for any kind of help. "You guys said the point was to capture Zeal. I did that."

Cleo walked over. "Just because there's an opening, doesn't mean you *should* take it. If you tried what you did back there, in a real fight against them, you'd have died on your way up."

"Well, what am I supposed to do?" I asked. "Just let Zeal get away?"

"The first thing on your mind should always be the well-being of your team. Did you even take a second to check on us?" Mickey asked. "You protect your teammates, contain the threat, and then we figure out what to do if Zeal gets away. You don't let yourself become blinded by emotion."

I was taking a bit of a verbal beating. It felt like I needed to stick up for myself, but there really wasn't much I could say. I was the newbie.

"Yeah, but—" I started.

"Rhys, there are no *buts,*" Kiyoshi said as he posted up in my face. "If we beat and contained either Sable, Dorian, or both of them, that's one or two less high-impact players Zeal has at his disposal. That weakens him. You can't expect to stop Zeal tomorrow because of some vendetta you have with him over whatever the hell it was that he did to you."

Only two people knew that, Lili and Ayla. I looked toward Lili, but she still hadn't looked at me. "Lili—"

"Alright, Kiyoshi," Pegs said as she pushed him away from me. "It was his first training exercise. I don't remember anyone ever doing as well as he had before that mistake at the end. Let's not forget, he's the one that kept us alive until you showed up to make the save the other night."

"Yeah, lay off a bit, will ya?" Diggs added.

A little bit of relief from the tongue-lashing was nice.

It did seem like it was only going to be temporary, though. Pegs and Diggs did seem just as annoyed as the others.

"Stay out of this. That's an order," Kiyoshi snapped.

"Your orders sure only seem to come around when you're feeling butt-hurt." Diggs put himself between Kiyoshi and Pegs. "Why don't you take a walk?"

"Diggs—I'm just looking out for this team. If this moron did that during an operation, if *he* didn't wind up dead, one of us might."

There was only so much I could take before I lost my cool. Kiyoshi could talk all the trash he wanted, but I did manage to hold my own against the real Dorian and Sable. Plus, I was the only one left to take on Zeal the other night. It seemed like a serious overreaction to some training.

"Look, I get it," I said through gritted teeth. "Why are you tearing into me like this? You can't expect me to do everything right on my first day of training."

"I don't think you do get it." Kiyoshi bumped past Diggs and stormed toward me again. "You come in here thinking you're going to be the next hotshot. You think you're gonna replace Chase, and be the one to finally stop Zeal."

"Stop it," Diggs and Pegs said, both sounding like they were ready to hit their superior. Pegs moved in again. "You're being unreasonable right now."

"Quiet." Kiyoshi dug a finger into my chest. "You're *nothing* like Chase. He had a brain. As far as I'm concerned, the wrong person won the final round." He shot a look at Diggs. "I'll take that walk now."

Kiyoshi's explosion ended when the doors to the room slammed shut behind him, but the tension still hung in the air.

"I never said I would replace Chase." I stared at where Kiyoshi had left.

It wasn't my fault for how he was feeling. I did exactly what they told me to do. They all had a point, but to me, it felt like stopping Zeal was the most important thing.

Maybe that was small-minded of me.

I flicked my eyes to the camera that had broadcast my embarrassment to the world.

"Nobody said you would, man," Diggs said. "Don't take it to heart."

"I'll go talk to him," Cleo said, before leaning in to whisper something to Diggs and Pegs.

Ayla? Did you say anything to them?

About what?

You know what.

I promise you I didn't.

That means it was Lili.

The team shares everything, Rhys.

I looked at Lili, but all I felt was betrayal. I was pissed.

Everything—or just the things they think could be a liability?

You know that's not fair.

She promised me.

Diggs and Pegs came over. "C'mon, Rhys. Let's go grab a bite to eat."

I followed them out of the room, but I looked back one more time at Lili. For the first time since I met her, I wondered if I could really trust Lili.

Chapter 29:
Chase Dyer

Diggs and Pegs led me back to Diggs' apartment. They'd been trying to cheer me up the entire walk over, but there wasn't much that was going to help. My first official day on the team and I had been reamed out not just in front of the whole team, but in front of the whole world.

I couldn't imagine how I must have looked on a holo-screen, but I bet most people would have described me as a total chump.

Diggs' place was surprisingly—*feminine*. It wasn't the overall design of the apartment, it reminded me of one of those ancient houses I'd seen in those old-timey holo-vids. It was the decorations that filled the apartment that threw me off—the odd vase of flowers and stuffed bears that sat on the couches.

He caught me looking around. "Don't go thinking that's all my junk. It's Pegs' stuff."

"That makes a lot more sense." I let out a half-hearted chuckle. "Here I was starting to think you were a big softy at heart."

"I'm no softy." Diggs flexed.

Pegs squished his face with her hand. "No, you aren't. You're a big strong boy. Let's not forget about you crying by the end of that movie the other night."

"I was not *crying*. I allowed a solitary man-tear to fall. It's completely different."

"Whatever. Sit down, Rhys. Diggs'll make some coffee and grab some snacks, won't you?" she asked, but it was really more of a command.

Diggs held up a finger like he was going to speak, but decided against it and headed to the kitchen. In seconds, the room filled with the scent of freshly ground coffee.

I moved a polka-dot teddy bear and took a seat. "How long have you two been—uh?"

"Together? We are together, you don't need to feel weird about it," Pegs said.

It was hard not to feel awkward. The two got along really well, but also managed to keep things incredibly professional in front of the cameras. If someone didn't know any better they could have been siblings. Somehow, that was an even weirder thought.

"I wasn't sure. Kieran had mentioned it, but I don't think I've ever seen you two kiss or anything. Not that I've been looking out for it." I gestured to the little flying camera that hovered between us. "Last thing I'd want to do is put you in a weird spot in front of the cameras."

Pegs laughed, "When you're being watched by the world for most hours of the day—every day—you learn a couple of little tricks. The biggest one being to try to save the really personal moments for after twelve. You never really think about it, but sometimes privacy is a big part in making moments truly special."

"Plus it drives the people crazy." Diggs called from the kitchen with a maniacal laugh.

"That too." Pegs leaned back. "That's gonna be the biggest challenge for you. When you start dating—the entire world is a part of your relationship, and they'll dive deep into every little thing."

"How've you two done it for so long?" I asked.

Pegs turned around to face Diggs. "Lot's of patience,

but the longer you know Diggs, the more of it you need. That's whether you're with him or not."

"Hey!"

After all the laughter had gone, there was a kind of ugly pause in the room. Pegs looked at me like she wanted me to say something, but the words weren't coming to her.

Ayla warped onto the couch next to me. I wondered about how she managed to look like she was sitting, but I wasn't about to ask about how AI did anything.

"You need to know that they were right," Pegs said. "Kiyoshi was a dick and he went way too far, but he wasn't wrong about what he said."

"It seemed like the right thing to do after what you guys told me. I had the opportunity so I took it."

"I know that, and unlike what Cleo said—sometimes you *do* need to take the shot, but you aren't going to nail it on your first day. The Interceptors—all of us, we've been fighting Zeal for years and the biggest mistake you could make would be thinking any of us could take him down alone."

"If anyone could have done it—" Ayla trailed off.

"If you ask me, ole 'Yoshi's sore about Chase still." Diggs walked over and set down a plate of snack cakes and cookies. The sounds of bubbling coffee came from behind him. "Don't get me wrong, we're all still broken up about Chase in our own ways. It all just—it sounded like pent-up emotion if you ask me."

"Probably." Pegs snatched a cookie. "Everyone knows new recruits are about expanding our mission to be able to keep the world safe."

"Am I allowed to ask you guys about him?" I asked. "Like are you two gonna yell at me if I ask what really went down that day? Or what about everything with Dorian and Sable? What happened there?"

Those were questions that no one had an answer for

to that point. Kieran didn't even know how to answer those questions. They were such critical moments, but not a single person knew how they played out, except for Ayla and the other Interceptors.

"Dorian and Sable is an easy one to answer," Pegs said before taking a bite of her cookie. "Zeal was able to entice them over with promises of power, wealth, and endless life. When the Interceptors started out, the public didn't exactly trust us—hence the constant surveillance."

"We've never asked for the publics opinions on what we do, but it's something we have to deal with," Diggs said as he licked the icing off of a snack cake.

It was hard to imagine a time when a majority of the public didn't like the Interceptors. Sure, the slums weren't the biggest on them, but people from the slums weren't big on anyone.

"The constant trash-talking from the public drove the two of them to anger and madness." Pegs continued with a mouthful of cookie. "Chase and Odon tried to reason with them, but it didn't work."

There was a CLICK. "Coffee's ready." Diggs rubbed his hands and headed back over.

"The day Chase—died. That was the darkest day in the history of the Interceptors. Even when Sable and Dorian defected, Chase was still fighting—still smiling. He didn't give up for one second," Pegs said with a smile.

"He always seemed like a great guy," I said as I looked toward Ayla.

She smiled back at me, but I could see pain in her eyes. I hadn't taken the time to sit down with Ayla and ask her about Chase. She probably could have talked about him for hours—or even a lifetime considering she had every single one of his memories.

"Great guy? Understatement of the year," Diggs said as he dropped off two cups of coffee for us. "The dude was a legend."

Pegs grabbed her cup and a small menu flashed up beside it. She pushed one of the options and her black coffee morphed to a lighter colour. I followed her lead, and thankfully, it worked the same as with the cup of tea.

"It makes me happy to hear how highly you two thought of him," Ayla said.

"I guess if you want the best information you could get, Ayla's the one to ask. She'll be able to explain everything better than anyone," Pegs said.

"Ayla?" I looked over to her, but it looked like she was deep in thought. "Could you do that for me?"

"Of course I can. We're partners."

"I didn't say anything about being partners—this isn't about that. If you don't want to, just say so. You're my friend as much as you are my partner."

It was strange to say that to a computer program, but now that she could interact physically with things, maybe she was more human than I thought.

She smiled at me. "Thank you, Rhys. I—I guess I can show you. It's confidential, though—not something we show the public. Cameras will have to shut off at a certain point."

"Show me?"

Ayla stood up and pointed her hands at the wall. Light rays projected from them onto the walls. The footage everyone had seen a thousand times started to play. I noticed that all the cameras in the room had shut down completely.

"Whoa. Can you do this with anything? Like, could you play a holo-vid for yourself?"

She shook her head. "I can only show things I've experienced. I can help you do something kinda similar with your kit, though."

In the feed, all the Interceptors were down and out after a gruelling battle against some of the most sophisticated Conks anyone had ever seen. A series of hulking behemoths that every team member had to work in unison to defeat had worn them all out.

Chase got the team all evacuated to safety, and then he entered Zeals aircraft alone. He was battered, bruised, and bloody—but he wasn't about to let Zeal win.

It was the bravest thing a person could do.

Something deep inside of me gave me the feeling that Chase knew he was going out to his death, but that didn't matter. Chase knew he was the last person left that could put a stop to Zeal's plan.

The doors to the aircraft closed and locked behind him. I remembered how the world felt like it had collectively held its breath as he limped his way through the halls of the lifeless carrier. The only company he had was Ayla, but that was all the company he needed.

"You'd think the evil lairs wouldn't be as creepy as they are, but nope." Chase rounded a corner and was met with a dark hallway. "This looks like the lair of some sexual deviant, not a mad scientist."

"Is now really the time for jokes?" Ayla replied.

"What kind of a question is that? There's never a bad time for jokes."

I looked over to Diggs as he gestured to the video as if Chase's statement had proved a point. Pegs gave him a pair of dagger-eyes and shook her head before we all returned our attention to the footage.

As he entered the main hanger—the hanger that housed the Extinction Virus, the door shut behind him. He tip-toed through the echoey room until Dorian, Sable, and Zeal finally showed themselves.

The final time the world saw Chase was with a cheeky smile as he said his final recorded words. "Three on one, huh? Doesn't seem all that fair to you guys. Go ahead—I'll let you call a couple more people for back-up."

Even I became a bit emotional after seeing Chase's final smile. He knew what his fate would be—it was written on his face, but he didn't want the world to worry.

Chase would die in that fight, but whatever it was that he did, he managed to stop the spread of the Extinction Virus. A virus that would have wiped out a majority of the living creatures on the planet.

I figured that was where the footage would end, but I leaned forward when it kept going through Ayla's eyes.

Zeal cackled as he blasted Chase's camera. "As insolent as ever. You don't understand what I'm trying to accomplish here. You never have. This is so much—"

"So much more than I could ever know—blah, blah, blah—" Chase made a makeshift mouth with his hand. "This is bigger than time and space—blah, blah, blah— the fate of the thingamajig—I've heard your evil spiels a hundred times before. I could literally write out the bullet points and do it myself."

"Then let this be your final opportunity—" Zeal stretched his hands out. "Join us and together we shall save this wretched world."

"You think wiping out most of the life on the planet is going to save it? You're actually nuts if you think you're the good guys in this situation." Chase wiped a bead of sweat from the side of his head and flicked it toward his enemies. "Oh, and by the way, calling the world *wretched* isn't really ever a sign of good intentions."

"I told you—" Zeal spat. "It's not quite as simple as that—"

"Simple or not, I don't think any good guys would willingly use something called the *Extinction Virus*. *Extinction* isn't usually in the good guy vocab'. Right, Ayla?"

The entire feed jolted up and down. "Right."

"Then we go back to the original plan," Zeal

growled. "You will die—all the Interceptors will die, and there isn't a thing you can do to stop me."

Without a word, Dorian and Sable launched toward Chase. Ayla's view changed to Chase's as she jumped back into his kit to help him. It became clear that for as incredible as Chase was, it was Ayla that led him to overcome Dorian and Sable.

Watch the scythe.

Block the katana.

Chase jumped and placed a hand along the shaft of the scythe. It swung underneath him, and he guided it to block Sable's katana slash. He kicked Dorian as he jerked the scythe from his hands. With one pull he managed to disarm both Dorian and Sable. He tossed the weapons across the room and raised his fists.

"One punch and each of you are goners," Chase said through laboured breaths.

"We'll just have to kill you before you can hit us," Dorian growled.

Seeing the way Chase was moving as he fought, it was hard to believe he had been through an intense set of battles before that.

Chase had no quit in his body.

Jab—incoming.

He caught Sable's wrist after an obvious jab, and he smirked as her eyes went wide. He cocked back a fist and thanks to his gauntlets—he hit her so hard that she dented the wall at the far side of the room when she finally hit it.

"That's gonna hurt." Chase winced.

Dorian swept Chase's leg, and he fell to the ground. A knee was coming right for his face. He launched his other fist into the knee as it came down, and Dorian launched into the ceiling. His body peeled from the dent he had made and he fell back down. Chase caught him with a kick that sent him toward Sable.

Chase opened two small jars he had attached to his belt, and sand poured out. He raised his hands at them, and the sand surrounded each of them. "Aw, c'mon. Is that all you go—"

Chase, behind you!

It was the blindside from Zeal that took him out.

The blade of a sword came through Chase's chest, and blood poured from the wound. The shock of the blade caused the sand surrounding Sable and Dorian to fall to the ground.

He turned around and came face to face with Zeal one last time. He spat a defiant glob of blood into his face before rocking him with a head-butt that sent him sprawling back.

Zeal cried out in pain from the floor as he clutched his nose. Chase could see blood droplets falling from where he held his hand, and he chuckled at his old foe.

He looked to the tank containing the Extinction Virus and took a step toward it. He used some sand to hold the sword steady inside of him. Had he removed it, he likely would have bled out faster.

Sable rushed at him, but he threw up his cyber shield to bounce her back. He molded the sand on the floor into a fist and punched her back into a wall.

Dorian jumped in front of him and tried to stop him with his time element, but he walked through it with nothing but his willpower.

"THIS IS IMPOSSIBLE! WHY THE HELL AREN'T YOU FREEZING!?" Dorian screamed.

"I've got an important job to do, you asshole." Ayla engaged his thrusters, and he hit Dorian with a big shoulder tackle.

I didn't know something like that was possible.

Kieran wasn't able to move a muscle after he got hit with the time element. When Dorian had me under the effect of his time element, I was able to snap out of it with the help of my kit. Chase was so powerful that he could shrug off any effect at all.

After a final step, Chase dropped to his knees, but he tried to stand right back up.

His body wouldn't let him.

He launched his grappling hook toward the virus.

"Ayla, you—you need to destroy the virus—destroy everything. Do whatever you have to—to wreck it. It can't get out. He can't remake it. We can't let him—"

She warped in front of him and looked down at him. "Chase, If I do that you'll be—"

He looked up at her and smiled. "You be the hero—I couldn't be."

Chase willed himself back to his feet before he finally slid the sword out. He coughed up blood as he widened his stance and took the sword in his hand. Dirt trailed along his body, and it did what it could to cover his bloody wound.

"Chase—"

"You can do it, Ayla. I believe in you." She took a long look at Chase, but he was back in battle-mode. "Didn't I tell you jerks that you'd need some back-up to take me out?"

"It's time to say goodbye," Zeal said.

"I'm not big on goodbyes. How about I keep kicking your asses instead?" He brought a hand to his wound. "I —I think I've got a few more rounds in me."

The feed ended. I was speechless. Diggs and Pegs both had tears in their eyes.

I looked back over toward Ayla while they composed themselves, but I hoped they didn't catch what I did— which was a single tear falling down her face, and onto the floor.

I understood why they freaked out at me the way they did. They lost a team member who went out on their own. He saw the opportunity to save the world, and he took it. That caused the team to be a member short—a team without a leader.

"I'm sorry. Excuse me." Pegs rushed into Diggs' room.

Diggs took a deep breath. "Damn, he was ice cold."

"I wish I could have met him," I said.

"I think he would have liked you," Ayla said.

"Really?"

"Yeah, he would've," Diggs said with a smile. "The two of you are a lot alike, and I think that's why Cleo worries so much. It's why Kiyoshi gets so bent out of shape at you as well. It hit us all differently, but it hit us all hard." Diggs stood up. "She okay, Alice?"

His AI Alice warped beside him. "You might wanna check on her. Leo doesn't think she's doing great."

Diggs nodded. "I'll go check on Pegs and calm her down a bit. Be right back—help yourself to anything in the kitchen if cookies aren't your speed."

He headed into his room, and for a split second, I could see what a mess Pegs had become. Chase was special to every member of the team in different ways. Some people saw him as a brother, some as a friend, and others as a crush or a lover. He had managed to make a huge impact on the entire world.

Even in my home section of Sellea City where people bad-mouthed the Interceptors, no one dared bad-mouth Chase.

The other two had their cameras follow them into the other room, so I assumed my camera was finally back on as well—not that I really noticed when they had shut off in the first place. I didn't really understand how they worked, but I needed another private moment.

"How do I do this?" I looked up at my camera and waved at the lens. "Camera—off? Gimme a minute?" The camera's lens closed. "I guess that worked."

I walked toward Ayla, and she looked up at me with

tears in her eyes. She closed her eyes and leaned in toward me. I felt her body push into mine, and I wrapped my arms around her. I brought a hand to the top of her hair and slowly ran my hand through it.

She'd never had a tender moment with Chase, but the neural link I had with her told me that she always wished she had.

"We're going to stop him—all of us—as a team." I let her go. "We're going to stop him for my mom and my dad, and for Chase—for the whole world."

"We're going to be the heroes he couldn't be," Ayla said, looking up at me.

I shook my head. "We're going to be the heroes he'd be proud to call his successors."

Chapter 30:
Catching Up With Friends

I managed to make it through another week of intensive team training without getting yelled at. My element training wasn't going the best, but I could get it working for me when it counted. I'd been longing for the last few days to rush on by because I knew sooner or later I'd be able to leave the facility.

It was my first day out in the city since I had become an Interceptor, and everything was different.

Before, most people wouldn't pay any attention to me unless they were a fan of my fights—mostly, the people of the slums. Most of the time I'd just have people look down their noses at me.

Now, every single person stopped to either congratulate me or grab a picture with me.

I was excited because I had arranged to meet up with everyone from training for a couple of burgers. I hadn't been able to talk to any of them with how busy I had been over the last few weeks, and I had to rely on dinky little visor-messages to plan everything out.

Visor-messages suck.

I asked Lili if she wanted to come along since she had spent so much time training us, but she said it'd be best for me to catch up with my friends on my own.

I had a feeling it had more to do with Fern.

We all decided it would be easiest for everyone if we met up somewhere in one of the poorer sections of the city. Someplace that wasn't too expensive, but also wouldn't cause any problems with a group of hotshots who were looking to start something with an Interceptor.

I showed up early and snagged a picnic table in the lot that dwelled under an overpass. After the over-zealous treatment from the public, I was glad the place was mostly void of people—at least for a little while .

I spotted Fern on a sweet tech-cycle when the engine roared from down the street. It was a sleek black and neon orange bike. On each end were two huge wheels, with the classic thin seat for the rider.

When she pulled into the lot, she stepped off the bike and held up a hand. The bike dripped away into strands of data until a disc was all that was left in her hand.

The smile she had on her face when she looked at me made me feel funny inside. She headed toward me, and as I stood up from the table she wrapped me in a bear hug. I didn't realize how much I'd missed her.

"You look great," I said as the scent of her perfume filled my nose.

"You do too, Mr. Interceptor." She pulled away and looked me up and down. "I'm a little upset you didn't dress a little sluttier for me, but I'll take what I can get."

"Well, I thought about it, but what would the public think of my image?"

Her hair was different. It was a bit shorter with pink streaks on the ends, but she still looked incredible. She brushed a strand of hair away from her eyes and gave me a playful punch in the shoulder. "I've been watching you."

"My first stalker."

"Ha-ha."

"It's nothing to be ashamed about. At least you're kind of cute."

Fern grinned. "Cute, huh?"

"I—uh—I guess that means you saw my first day reaming," I said to change the subject as I gestured to the picnic table.

"Cringed my way through the whole thing." She sat down next to me as I took a seat. "It was brutal."

"You think they were right?"

"I do. I think Diggs and Pegs hit the nail on the head —before all three of your feeds cut out—I have some questions about that by the way. We both had the same problem during training. Everyone has their own shortcomings."

I laughed, "The rest of the Interceptors?"

She nodded. "Even them."

"Like what?"

"Kiyoshi is overly emotional, Mickey is the exact opposite of that—can't fault the android for that, though —Diggs and Pegs rely too heavily on each other, Lili refuses to take the advantage of additional gear, and Cleo has a huge chip on her shoulder. All of that got amplified to another level after Chase died."

I took a minute to take in what she was saying to me. It was a lot, and she'd delivered it all without taking a breath.

She was right.

I always assumed they were the best of the best, and because of that they didn't have weaknesses. The truth was the exact opposite—because they were the best of the best, their few weaknesses were more clear.

"I guess that—"

"Is it weird that I missed you?" she asked.

We lived together and spent just about every hour together for a month, and because of that, we became closer than most people would have in a years time.

I'd never admit it to her, but there was more than one night where I wished I could have spent time with her. I missed the little family we had all formed, and it wasn't easy to be the somewhat unwelcome newbie.

"No. It's not weird at all." Fern looked behind me, and I turned to see Ayla mouthing something to her while nodding. "Ayla!"

Ayla giggled and smiled at me. "I'm just trying to help a partner out!"

She warped back into the medallion, and I turned back to a cheesy grin from Fern. "I'm glad you two have been getting along."

"It's hard not to when your brains are linked—or I guess my brain and her data stream or—whatever," I said as I rubbed my head. "It feels like I'm married."

"I could imagine the whole—having a person living in your brain thing—might take some getting used to."

"That's an understatement."

Everyone in the world took quiet mornings for granted. Each and every day, I'd be woken up by the overly cheerful ball of energy that lived in my brain. Ayla was a lot, but at least she was a lot of fun to be around.

There was a quiet moment between Fern and I. Everything felt a bit awkward, but I wasn't sure why.

"So—now that you're a big shot Interceptor," She put a hand on mine. "Do you think you'll have time for the small folks of the slums?"

I looked from her hand to her face and nodded. "I think I can make the time for a fellow slummer. I'm here aren't I?"

"And would someone like you be able to go slumming with someone like me?"

Spending time with a woman like Fern wasn't close to what I'd describe as slumming, but I understood the sentiment behind the words. Neither of us was particularly good with words, but we did our best.

My eyes kept moving from her eyes to her lips, and she was doing the exact same to me. I couldn't help thinking back to my first night with the Interceptors and how I was with Lili. I glanced over to the camera that constantly hovered around me and knew the entire world was watching—but I didn't care that much.

A loud HONK brought us both back to reality.

I *really* needed to figure out my love life.

The honk came from one of those old pick-up trucks. They were mostly found in the more rural areas outside the major cities, so I knew who it was that had to be driving.

It pulled into the parking lot of the burger joint, and both Keyshawn and Phoebe hopped out. I was happy to see Keyshawn up and smiling. The last time I was able to see him—blood was pouring from the back of his head.

I was worried about whether or not he'd be angry at me, but that worry faded fast when I saw his big goofy grin.

It was just as nice to see him with Phoebe. She had such a big crush on him. It may have taken some of us a while, but we all figured it out eventually. She looked just as happy to see me and Fern as Keyshawn did.

"Have you guys had time to hang out?" I asked.

Fern shook her head. "Everyones been trying to get stuff sorted out at home. We all thought it would be best to wait until you could come back down to us mortals."

I rolled my eyes.

Keyshawn came over and wrapped me in an actual bear-hug, and Phoebe gave me a kiss on the cheek. They each did the same to Fern, and it looked like Keyshawn was squeezing the life out of her in the happiest hug I'd ever seen.

"Keyshawn—"

"Don't even start. Everyone called me saying the same thing. I'm kind of a pro at this, so give me a sec—"

After clearing his throat, he stepped back and lifted his hand. It looked like he was reading from a list. "What happened was in no way your fault. None of us could have seen that coming, and you did everything you could to save my ass." He dropped the act and smiled. "Thank you, and congratulations on becoming an Interceptor. You best believe I'm taking the next vacancy on the team, though."

None of us could have seen the events of that night coming, but of course, Ayla had warned me. She hadn't come back out to say hello, and I wondered if it was because she felt a bit guilty. It wasn't her fault either. She had no idea what her cryptic warning was for. If that's why she'd been quiet, she'd know how I felt.

"Thanks, buddy." I gave him props. "Recovery was good?"

"Stronger than I ever was. I could probably take you out like I woulda in the finals." Keyshawn flexed.

Phoebe rolled her eyes and hit him with a playful smack on the chest. "Your sister and Kieran aren't here yet? I figured they'd be the first ones since it's been so long."

"Yeah—I don't know. Kieran sorta freaked out at me right after everyone left the day of the cuts. I don't even know if he's coming. Lenna said he was, but who knows."

I'd tried to avoid thinking about the whole situation with Kieran. He wasn't interested in replying to any of my messages, and I wasn't sure if it pissed me off more or upset me more.

"What about Akio?" Phoebe watched a few cars go by. "You mentioned inviting him."

"I tried to get in touch with him, but I guess he wasn't interested in hanging out. He didn't take any of my calls or reply to any of my messages."

"Did you talk to Kiyoshi?" Fern asked.

"Unfortunately, yeah. He gave me the classic cold treatment and told me that he didn't control Akio. He said that,"—I turned on my best Kiyoshi impression— "If Akio wanted to hang out, he would answer a call."

"Good to know you and Kiyoshi have been getting along lately."

"I don't understand what his issue is. I mean, I know I eliminated Akio twice, but still. Whatever—"

"Don't look now," Keyshawn pointed down the street. "But I recognize that ride."

The same hover-car that had taken us to that club all those weeks ago was coming down the street. A window rolled down as it pulled into the lot, and Lenna waved frantically at me. I just about jumped over Keyshawn and Phoebe to run over to the car.

It had been so long since I had seen her, and there wasn't a single person I missed more than her. Ever since we were orphans in the slums, we were inseparable, and I always felt a pinch of anxiety while we were apart.

"Rhys!"

She was so happy, and it made me tear up a bit to know she'd been doing well. She hopped out of the car before it came to a full stop, and she jumped into my arms. I picked her up and spun her back and forth.

"You're okay? You've been safe? Happy? Eating enough? I know now is not the best time for a joke, but I swear I'll kick Kieran's ass again if he wasn't taking care of you."

"I missed this crazy big brother energy," she laughed as I put her down. "I've been great. Kieran and his family have been taking great care of me."

"You got the first couple of week's payment, right?"

"Yes, Rhys. Bring it down a notch. Kieran is helping me find a nice house in a safe part of the city."

"You don't need to deal with the crap we had growing up. We can buy you one of those augments for your arm, and—"

"Slow down," Lenna said with a kind smile.

"Where is—"

The door on the other side of the car flung open, and Kieran stepped out. We locked eyes, but I don't think either of us had anything to say. I didn't know if I should apologize, or if I should have asked what the problem was.

"Kieran."

He walked around the car until he was inches away. I couldn't tell if he was still angry or not. I figured that a few weeks was enough time for him to calm down, but I guessed I'd always be the guy that stole his dream from him.

"Rhys. I saw you getting chewed out."

"I'm not surprised. It had to be on replay pretty much everywhere."

"It was."

It was pretty clear that we were both just trying to posture. Neither of us wanted to apologize for our own reasons, but at the same time, it felt like the both of us wanted to set things right.

Lenna cleared her throat. "Kieran, don't you have something you want to say to Rhys?"

He looked out toward the distant traffic. "Nah, I don't."

It hurt to hear something like that. "Then why are you even here, huh?"

"Oh my god," Lenna whacked us one at a time. "Can you two quit with the dumb macho-tough-guy thing? Kieran, you told me you wanted to apologize on the way here. Swallow all your dumb-stupid-moronic pride and say sorry to my brother."

Lenna wasn't the most imposing girl around, but she could get all kinds of scary when it came to the things that mattered to her.

She got even scarier when she turned her fury toward me "Rhys, you swallow *your* pride and accept his apology—then let's go eat some freakin' burgers, because I am actually *really* hungry and I'm only going to get in a worse mood if I don't eat soon!"

Kieran and I stared at each other for what felt like an hour before he wrapped his arms around me. "I'm sorry man. I shouldn't have le—"

I hugged him back. "Don't worry about it. You're my first suggestion next time the team wants more members."

We pulled apart, and he cleared his throat. "Oh yeah. That's the stuff—good 'ole fashion full-hetero bro-hug. I understand, bro. We're so good."

Classic Kieran.

"My sister doesn't care, dude." I rolled my eyes. "No one does."

"Right."

Lenna looked around. "Where's Ayla? I want to meet the girl that needs to keep my brother safe."

Ayla warped next to me. "Right here. Nice to meet you Lenna." She stuck out a hand Lenna went for it, but passed through her. "Gotcha!"

"AI—right. You better keep him from being his stupid self." Lenna flicked me as she finished.

"I promise, I'll do my best, but we both know how hard-headed he is."

"Thanks, Ayla. Really feeling the love," I said. "Let's head on over so you guys can say hey to everybody."

Lenna rushed over to hug everybody else, and Kieran followed me over to do the same. It was great to see everyone carrying on the same way we had before the final round of cuts. It didn't seem like there was any animosity at all between anyone.

"Alright, since he's not here, how sick was it to be the one to eliminate Akio twice?" Keyshawn asked me as he put an arm around Phoebe.

"Oh, you guys are doing that now?" I asked.

"It's new," Phoebe said as she looked up at Keyshawn. "New, but so far so good."

"Damn right. I'm adorable as hell. Just look at me," Keyshawn added. "But seriously—Akio? You took out the golden-boy!"

My miracle usage of my element danced in my mind. Being able to control that boulder really was a fluke, especially considering I'd been yet to pull off anything like it since then.

"I felt so bad," I said as I eyed my camera. "It was such a random fluke—I couldn't believe it worked at the time. I think Kiyoshi's still pretty pissed about it."

"*No kidding?*" Kieran rolled his eyes. "We all saw him blow up at you."

I sighed at yet another mention of my embarrassing moment, "For the one millionth time, It was rough."

"How's things with Lili? The two of you seem to be getting along pretty—" Keyshawn took another smack from Phoebe.

"Not the time, Key," Phoebe said.

I looked over to Fern, and she looked a little bugged by that. I should have assumed that she'd seen our interaction, but it's not like we ended up doing anything. They'd all have their minds blown if they found out Ayla had been the one to kiss me, but I couldn't tell them that.

Definitely can't tell them that. How funny is that, though?

"Shut up, Ayla," I muttered before clearing my throat. "Things with the whole team are good. Everyone's starting to warm up to me—or at least that's what Ayla tells me."

Lenna could tell I was in an awkward situation. "Your camera is super annoying, eh?" She waved my floating camera away from her. "How about we grab some food?"

"That is an awesome idea," I said, jumping at the chance to get out of my current situation. "Kieran, Keyshawn, you guys wanna help me?"

They nodded and we headed in toward the building.

"Gotta watch it, man," Kieran said with a light push to Keyshawn.

"I forgot you and Fern kinda had a thing," Keyshawn laughed. "That's my bad. Forgot you're on Lili now."

"Kinda had a thing?" I said, trying to avoid my camera. "I don't have a thing with either of them."

"But you like 'em—both of 'em, don't you?" Kieran said with a raised eyebrow.

"I mean, yeah. I guess so." I shot a glance at the camera. "That's gonna be everywhere—hello twenty-four-seven news."

"What are you gonna do?"

I sighed, "I have no idea."

I really did have no idea. I never really had issues with girls before, but that was because I never really cared all that much. The territory I found myself in was entirely unexplored.

Keyshawn looked back at the girls. "Hottie from the slums or sexy kickass Interceptor. Tough choice."

"Can we not talk about that—in full view of literally the entire world?" I asked as I swung at my camera. "They'll all know you said that by the end of the day—Fern included."

"What about your adoring public?" Keyshawn asked. "They deserve to know. That's the type of sacrifice I'm willing to make for them." I shot him a dull look and he laughed. "Let's just go get some grub."

I looked back to the table where the girls were chatting as we entered the burger joint. Part of me wished Lili had come along, so she could spend time with them as a friend. Another part of me wondered if the reason she hadn't come along really was because of Fern. Maybe she didn't want to be put in an awkward situation like that.

"So are you allowed to have visitors at the facility?" Keyshawn asked.

"I'm not sure, to be honest." I shrugged. "I guess that's a good question to ask."

"I'm only asking because Kieran and I need to come for a visit to dust you once and for all in that racing game. We're still sitting at three wins apiece."

"You only won that last game when you knocked the controller out of my hand." Kieran nudged Keyshawn.

"A win's a win, brother."

We each walked up to pillars that showed the food the burger joint offered, and we selected our orders. We each transferred our credits for the meals and after a few seconds, small pills shot out the same way they did in the facility cafeteria. The pills each morphed into full meals, and the three of us headed back outside.

Kieran held the door. "Should we have left all the girls alone?"

"Why wouldn't we?" I asked.

"Girls talk, man. Who knows, Lenna and Phoebe might be talking Fern into asking you out."

"Do you really think that'd bother Rhys? Brother's got the pick of the litter." Keyshawn winked at me.

I spotted a crowd of Interceptor fans that had started to grow at a distance. "I'm more worried about that right now."

We reached the table and set the trays down. "Burgers are served, ladies," Keyshawn said.

"Pretty, muscular, and he pays for food? Phoebe, you hit the jackpot," Fern said as she took a sip of soda.

The sudden sound of screeching tires from the overpass caught all of our attention. Whatever was going on up there, it didn't sound good.

CRASH

Chapter 31:
That Was Easy

Something massive had to have happened on the overpass to make a sound that loud. We all shot up from the table and rushed to take a look. Part of a city bus was hanging over the side of the bridge.

"Ayla, are there any people on the bus?" I asked as my kit covered my body.

"One sec." A wave of light shot toward the bus. "Twelve people including the driver. The bus took some structural damage, and the driver isn't going to be able to get the doors open."

"I'm gonna head up there to help, you guys move that crowd out of here—and keep Lenna safe," I said as I readied myself for a jump.

"Got it," Phoebe said as she and Keyshawn headed toward the crowd.

"Wait," Fern said.

"I don't have much time—"

"Take me with you. Wouldn't you rather have some help up there? Just in case?"

There wasn't any time to argue, so I grabbed her and used my thrusters to make it to the top of the bridge.

The sight was more precarious from up on the bridge. The smell of burnt rubber tickled my nostrils in the worst way possible. The bus was teetering on the edge. The slightest hint of movement could have sent it over at any moment.

The sound of tech-cycles roared toward the bus, but I didn't understand who would want to move closer to an ensuing accident like that. I grabbed the front end of the bus to hold it steady as I ripped the door to the bus open.

"Fern, I need you to go in there and help everyone out," I said.

I tried pulling the bus, but I could feel the metal crunching against the overhang. It felt like I could lift it, but if I lifted it, someone could get hurt or go flying out one of the now destroyed windows. Even worse, if I accidentally damaged the power source for the hover function, the bus was definitely going to explode.

"We've got some company," Fern said.

I turned to see a group of Conks as they rushed toward me with swords out. "Fern. Now."

She rushed into the bus, and I readied myself for the shock I'd surely feel when one of the Conks landed a sword strike.

"Don't worry. I can activate your shield remotely. They won't hurt you," Ayla said from beside me as she pretended to hold onto the bus with me.

The roaring of the tech-cycles grew closer, and a storm of bullets stopped the Conks in their tracks.

It didn't sound like any kind of standard-issue police weapon that I had heard. I looked back again, but a group of heavily tattooed people was fighting the Conks.

Leading the group was a chiseled man with a thin beard and a facial scar that was similar to mine. There wasn't a kit in sight, but they were holding their own.

"Remind me to thank—whoever they are, later. Fern, how we doing in there?" I asked.

Fern came out of the bus with a group of people. "Can you hold on a little longer? There's an old woman back—"

"Not a big deal. Less explaining, more old lady grabbing. Last thing I need is a sword in the back from a sneaky Conk."

Fern smirked and rushed back onto the bus. I could hear the sounds of Conks being destroyed behind me, but I had no clue who these people were. It was rare for most people to stand up to Conks but rarer for people to actively seek them out.

A Conk broke loose from the crowd and rushed toward me. I tethered the bus tight to the bridge with each of my grappling hooks and hoped it would be enough to hold it in place for a little while. I whirled around and drew my sword, cutting the Conk clean in half as it approached me.

"Everyone's off the bus," Fern said as she helped the old lady to safety.

The man with the scar approached me and Fern as the battle died down. "Pretty rare to see an Interceptor helping out with a situation in a place like this."

"Rare? It's my job to help people," I said.

"Ha. Hilarious. Maybe your team should make it your job to care about the poorer districts too—not just the rich, and powerful."

"Who do you think—"

"Why don't you lay off him, Jace." Fern leaned into the man's face. "He's new to the team if you haven't noticed."

"Fern—I heard you were all buddy-buddy with the new Interceptor grub."

"Rhys, you're going to want to—" Ayla started.

"Grub? Who're you?" I asked as I moved Fern aside.

"It's Jace," the man said. "The lead hunter of the Vanguard."

"Rhys—" Ayla tried to cut in again.

"The Vanguard?" I asked. "How do you two know

each other then?"

"That's a story for another time," Fern said.

I heard my grappling hooks give out, and the bus tilted downward. Ayla pointed at it as I whirled around. "I tried to warn you."

The bus was heading over the bridge.

Right down onto where Lenna was when I left.

I heard her scream and I activated my thrusters. Ayla gave me as much power to the thrusters as she could, and I made it back down to the ground well before the bus did.

"This is gonna suck," I said as I extended my arms.

Lenna and Kieran were on the ground beside me as the bus fell straight down onto me. I half-expected it to crush us all into the pavement, but to my surprise, I caught it with relative ease.

A bus is nothing. You should see what else you can lift with a bit of help from your kit and your favourite AI.

"Seriously?" I flexed and straightened my elbows and was shocked by how light it was. I waited for the duo to clear the area before I carefully set the bus down in the lot of the burger joint.

Lenna rushed over and threw an arm around me. "Cutting it a little close there, bro."

"I caught it, didn't I?" I asked.

Ayla warped beside me. "I'm going to start flashing warnings in your vision so you know what I'm trying to say—since you DON'T—LISTEN."

"I'm sorry."

"Whoa." She composed herself. "I think that's the first time I've heard you say that. It's fine. You're still learning—and I guess no one got hurt, so it's okay. Good job, Rhys."

"Thanks."

Fern and Jace looked down to me from where the bus had fallen. I cocked my head and wondered how it was that they knew each other, and what exactly the Vanguard was.

A hand on my shoulder turned me around. It was Kieran, and he wrapped me in another hug. "Bro, that was awesome."

I hugged him back, before being swarmed by the crowd that had been lingering from afar. It was a sea of people seeking high-fives, photos, and autographs. I would have been lying if I said it wasn't cool, but I had more important things on my mind.

I wondered if I'd ever be able to have a normal lunch with my friends and family ever again.

Chapter 32:
There Had To Be One

"Everyone geared up and ready to go?" Cleo asked.

"You know it," Diggs said as he high-fived Pegs.

"I'm all good to go," I said.

I looked over to Kiyoshi expecting him to take the lead on something on the mission, but he'd been more quiet than usual.

It was my first official mission with the team.

I figured he'd take advantage of the moment to yell at me for a little bit before we started.

"You better be paying attention." Kiyoshi snarled.

That's what I was waiting for.

Lili gave me a playful bump, and I bumped her fist.

"There's no telling what we're going to be getting into once we teleport down there." Cleo moved to a large white circle in the centre of the room. "There'll likely be civi-scientists so every needs to be careful."

"It sounds cold, but the first priority is to ensure Zeal doesn't get his hands on whatever data he's after—then it's the safety of any scientists trapped inside." Kiyoshi looked down at me. "Got it, Rhys? Repel, not capture."

"Yeah," I frowned. "I got it."

We each stepped up onto the circle, and our kits covered our bodies. It may have been my first mission, but it was going to be a tense one.

A lab in a remote part of the continent had been experimenting with some kind of rogue remnant code and had recently had some kind of breakthrough.

Half the info in the briefing made no sense to me, but everyone else was serious, so I took it seriously.

A distress code-violet had been sent out from the lab to our main facility. Apparently, the team had no idea that there was a lab working on a new form of the Extinction Virus, but for some reason, General Odon had okayed it.

It felt like the longer I was around the team, the more it became clear that they were in the dark on a fair share of things themselves.

"Transferring in ten," Cleo said.

"We're gonna get there in time, right?" I asked.

"If we don't, General Odon is going to have a lot of explaining to do before we go on any other missions for him."

If Zeal managed to get his hands on what they'd been working on, he could synthesize a new virus strand. That would mean the world could potentially end up in the gravest danger it would have ever faced. Apparently, approximately four percent of all living creatures had the necessary genetic defects to survive the virus. If he unleashed it, it would be the apocalypse.

A wave of light covered all of us, and we were teleported into a dark laboratory. I didn't know what I expected, but an eerie silence would have been the last thing I thought I'd hear.

A solitary source of light came from red emergency lights that lined the walls. They'd glow bright red, before leaving us in the utter dark, only to repeat the pattern.

"You want me to scout ahead?" Mickey asked.

"No. We don't know what we're dealing with here," Cleo said.

"Everyone, run a scan of the facility." Kiyoshi looked through the room. "If we can't detect any life, we can at least have access to the facility layout."

Everyone held up a hand, so I did the same. A wave of light passed around the room and headed out two doors on each end. In a few moments, I could see a map of the facility in my hand.

The strangest thing was that a small danger warning popped up in the corner, which showed that the facility had no water left in its reserves. It seemed like a potential problem for Cleo, but I had a feeling she'd be just fine without her element.

"We'll split into two teams," Cleo said, taking the lead. "Kiyoshi, Rhys, Lili, and I will take the door on the left, Mickey, Diggs, and Pegs can take the door on the right. Room sweep for any civvies, and meet up in the large room at the centre of the facility. I have a feeling that might be where the facility's data is—the majority of the back-up power is being routed there."

"You think there's any Conks kicking around?" Diggs started toward his team's door.

"If there are, it'd be Dorian, and Sable with a team of Executioners—no Conks came back on the sweep. Everyone be ready for anything. Radio if you need backup."

The team of three headed through their door first, and we made our own way out. When we opened the door, we saw a creepy hallway that glowed the same way the previous room had. Lili walked with her hand still up —she must have decided to be our navigator.

"It looks like we have a series of offices on the way to that central room, rushed checks or controlled checks?" Lili asked.

Cleo thought for a moment as we made our way down the hall. "We'll do—"

"Controlled checks," Kiyoshi said.

"That'll take a long—"

"I'll scout down the hall and secure the room the power's being routed to for the time being. If anything comes up, I'll call you guys in."

Cleo gave him a strange look, but she nodded. She turned toward me and waved me toward the first door on our right. She did the same for Lili but on the left. I figured Cleo would cover the rest herself.

The eerie sound of the team's quiet footsteps made me nervous. I shook my hands and tried to slow my heart as I approached the office.

I leaned up against the side of the door and turned the handle. There weren't any lights to illuminate the office, so I stuck a hand in for a light switch. I flicked it a few times, but backup power wasn't feeding the office lights.

Put your helmet on, and I can either send night-vision through the screen of your helmet, or flashlights from your kit.

"Night-vision."

I let the helmet of my kit come on and I was able to see into the office through the green and black glow of night vision.

It was small, and the only places to hide would be on the other side of the door, or behind the desk at the far side of the room. There was a small picture of a happy family on a shelf toward the back, and I hoped that whatever had happened, that happy family wasn't now separated forever.

"Hello? Anyone here?" I took a step in. "I'm with the Interceptors. If you need help, you can come out, and we'll make sure to get you out of here safely."

A scream from behind me almost sent me over the desk in fright.

I recognized the high-pitched scream, though.

That piercing scream was Lili.

I rushed into the office she had headed into.

She was being attacked by Dorian.

He must have surprised her in the dark.

She dodged a few punches and pushed him backward. I nailed him from behind with a kick, sending him sprawling to the corner of the room, but he whirled around and came right back at me. The psycho was like one of those stupid old paddle ball games. He'd always come back.

I ducked a punch, and his fist went through a section of wall. He grabbed me with his other hand and rocked me with a head-butt, so I was lucky I still had my helmet on.

Cleo rushed into the doorway with her spear at the ready. "What are you doing here, Dorian?"

He brought a finger to the side of his head. "Three here as well." He paused, and I figured he must either be talking to Sable or Zeal. "Pulling out."

"No, you aren't," Lili said as she launched forward.

Dorian teleported out of the room before she could make it over to him.

"What did he mean by three here as well?" I asked.

"I don't know, but we need to hurry," Cleo said as she brought a finger to her gauntlet. "I'm calling off the sweeps, head to the central room now. We had a run-in with Dorian."

"Damn—" Kiyoshi's voice came over the comms.

"We had a run-in with Sable too, but she teleported out." Mickey responded.

"I don't know what the hell is going on, but I don't like this," Cleo said before dashing down the hall.

Lili and I followed close behind her. We must have passed fifteen different offices, which could have had any number of civilians trapped inside. The issue was that the civilians were the second priority.

We turned a corner, and a large bright room was up ahead. It blinded me, but Ayla reacted quickly by turning off the night vision. I could see the opposite hallway that the other three would no doubt be coming from. We slowed down as we approached the room, knowing that Dorian and Sable could be inside ready for a fight.

Cleo peeked in. "Kiyoshi?"

"All clear in here." Kiyoshi called. "You guys good? Dorian didn't hurt any of you?"

The three of us tiptoed into the room.

"Yeah, Dorian got the drop on me and scared the hell outta me. I'm all good, though," Lili said.

I looked down the opposite hallway and saw the other three. "Hey guys, it's all clear in here."

Before they reached the glass door, it started closing. I looked behind us, and the doorway we'd come through was closing as well. Cleo, Lili, and I looked around in confusion, but Kiyoshi kept typing at some console in front of a large tank. I watched as Diggs slammed into the door.

"What's going on?" Cleo pulled her helmet off and stared at the door. I watched the helmet fade into strands of data as each second went by until there was nothing left.

Diggs tried shouting something through the door, but I couldn't hear him. Whatever the door was made of, it was solid.

He stepped back, and Pegs launched a huge blast of fire at it, but the door didn't budge. I was worried that they may have been hurt by the backlash from the flames, but none of them seemed any worse off.

Cleo spat and and froze the drop of saliva before it hit the ground. She sent it straight for a small hole in a mechanism that was built into the door. I hoped whatever she'd done would be enough to short circuit or dismantle something inside the door, but nothing happened.

I looked around at the room one more time and

noticed something that I hadn't before.

The room was perfectly lit. There wasn't a single thing in the room casting a shadow—the floor was a perfect conductor for electricity—and while there were sprinklers, the warning I saw on my visor said there wasn't any water.

"It's a trap." I tossed my helmet to the floor.

Lili turned. "A trap?"

I was too late. Kiyoshi whirled around and smashed Lili across the side of her head with his war hammer. Thankfully she still had a helmet of her own on, but there was no way she'd still be conscious. I activated my thrusters and caught her before she hit the wall.

Ayla?

She's alive.

Thank God.

"Kiyoshi?" Cleo said.

Three Executioner Conks stepped away from the walls of the room as their camouflage faded away. Their hands morphed into cyber-blades, and they had them at the ready. I put Lili on the ground and pulled the trigger on my sword.

"Cleo? What are we gonna do?" I asked as I pulled out Trigger.

I looked over to her, but she still hadn't taken her eyes off Kiyoshi.

The doors to the room had to be incredibly thick, but I could still hear the ferocious banging from Diggs, Pegs, and Mickey on the other side.

"CLEO! What's the plan?"

She pulled out a silver baton and it morphed into her double-edged spear. "Don't die."

Chapter 33:
The End Begins

Cleo had engaged in a fight with Kiyoshi, while I was doing what I could against the group of Executioner Conks.

They struck toward me in unison, making it difficult to avoid their blades. I'd block one, and turn to see another blade headed straight for me.

I took a slash across my left shoulder and decided I wasn't gonna deal with pain like that again.

I ducked a stab, and swung my blade in a circle, managing to cut one of the stupid assassin-bots in half. It fell to the ground with a small explosion.

"Kiyoshi, stop this," Cleo said as she ducked a swing. "What are you doing?"

One Executioner Conk rushed toward me while the other rushed toward Lili. There was no way I was going to let any of those things near her.

Ayla readied a shield on my right arm, and I rushed toward the Conk coming toward me. I deflected a strike, and booted it backward, using the momentum to turn, and throw my shield. Ayla guided the release time of the shield for the perfect throw. It landed right between the Conk's strike and Lili, sending the bot backward.

I launched an arrow right at it, and I took the Conk's

head clean off. Sparks flew from the place its head used to be and it too fell to the ground in a small explosion.

The final Executioner rushed back toward me, but I took a surprise swing from Kiyoshi's war hammer in the back.

"RHYS!" Cleo shouted.

The feeling was unlike anything I'd felt before. It felt like the kind of pain that I imagined getting in a nasty car wreck would provide.

As tired as I was of the med-bay, It probably wouldn't have been a bad idea to take a trip there if we managed to survive.

I flew across the room toward the Conk. I managed to control my spin, and with Ayla's help, I launched a perfectly aimed arrow from my other gauntlet. The arrow knocked one of the Conk's arms off, and I slashed my way through it.

I landed in a heap on the other side of the room. My back felt like it had been broken from Kiyoshi's strike. The pain I felt was agonizing, but at least I'd stopped the Conks.

I was gonna get that asshole back.

It's not gonna be easy, Rhys.

"I don't think it's going to be."

No—you don't, do you?

I managed to make it back to my feet, but I was struck with awe. Cleo and Kiyoshi were locked in the most violent brawl I'd seen between Interceptors. Cleo was spinning her spear so fast, that it looked like she could have taken off the ground at any moment. One wrong move by Kiyoshi and he'd be missing any of his appendages.

She jumped over a huge swing by Kiyoshi and launched a spit-cicle at his eye. It caught him enough to cause him to cry out in pain as he dropped to a knee.

"You're a disgrace to the Interceptor name." She

pointed her spear at him. "What the hell is going on?"

I sidled my way over to the panel that Kiyoshi had been typing on and inspected it. Whatever it was, something was being sent, and it was about to be finished.

This something you can deal with, Ayla?

Hmm. I don't think so. There seems to be some kind of protection on the data transfer.

Oh, great. Love it.

"Cleo, we have a problem over here," I said as I tapped the screen.

I shouldn't have said anything at all.

The one-second distraction was enough for Kiyoshi to take advantage.

He launched an electricity bolt that caused Cleo's spear to jut away from him. Her spear flew out of her hands with a quick strike, and his hands fell on her, ready to snap her neck at any moment.

"Kiyoshi—relax." I held a hand out. "You don't want to do—"

His grip tightened on Cleo. "You don't know the first thing about me."

Dorian and Sable teleported beside Kiyoshi. "Nice work. Welcome to the team."

I couldn't believe what I was seeing.

Kiyoshi had worked his way to the top of the team. He was a legendary hero, and he had worked side by side with Chase for years.

"How's about we play with *Remarkable Rhys* for a little while?" Sable asked.

"Play?" Dorian asked. "You mean I can't kill him?"

"Well—if he ends up dying on us, I don't think Zeal will be *too* upset. He did say the kid would either thrive or die," Sable said as she passed Kiyoshi. "Hang tight with Cleo, while we have some fun."

They both ran toward me, but neither of them with

weapons. If they disarmed me before either of them started using their weapons, I'd be as good as dead. I put my sword away and readied myself for a fight.

Sable struck high with a kick and Dorian went low with a punch. Her leg came first, so I caught it and wrapped it around Dorian's arm. I grabbed the back of her head and smashed it into Dorians as hard as I could.

It didn't do much, but they backed off for a moment.

"Good job, Rhys." Cleo called. "They may have been S-Rank at one point, but they're out of practice—and crazy as sh—"

"Shut it," Kiyoshi said as he ran a current of electricity through Cleo's body.

The quick distraction was enough for Sable and Dorian to capitalize on. They launched right back at me with a flurry of strikes that I couldn't hope to avoid—even with Ayla's help. After a brutal combo, Sable caught me with a spinning backhand that sent me to the floor.

Cleo's spear was an arms reach away.

I didn't have any real training with one, but I knew where to put the pointy end, so I snatched it. I rose with the spear in hand, and they pulled out their own weapons in response.

"Tsk, tsk, tsk—I thought we were having fun with our hands," Sable said.

I stood there for a moment.

"What? Nothing to say?" Dorian asked.

"I couldn't come up with something quippy for hand-to-hand combat," I said, feeling a bit embarrassed. "Maybe—something about fists?"

"I wouldn't go there if I were you. I think you have to graduate to crappy hero jokes," Sable said with a pompous laugh. "Seems a little out of the D-Rank pay grade."

It wasn't much, but I had an idea.

I was going to take a move from Dorian's playbook.

"I wound you."

Sable gave me a confused look. "No, the expression is—*you* wound *me*—"

I launched an arrow at Sable, but she blocked it without flinching. "Crap."

"Well, that was rude. How's a little light torture sound, Dorian?"

He smirked as they stalked forward. "You don't have to ask me twice."

I pulled the trigger on the hilt of my sword and pulled it out. If they were gonna come at me with two weapons, I was going to do the same.

They rushed at me again, and the spear proved useful in parry Sable's katana while I used my sword to block Dorian's scythe.

I looked up and Ayla activated my thrusters. I hopped upward and spun the spear in my hand, hoping to catch either of them, but they ducked it.

They were so much faster than I was.

I was in the air, and I had nowhere to go.

I blocked another swing from Dorian, but Sable punctured my already wounded shoulder with her katana. It caused me to drop the spear, but I still had a grip on my sword. As I landed, she pushed me up against a wall, and pushed the katana through it, pinning me to it.

"*I-got-you*" She sang as she inched closer to my face.

"Heads up."

She looked up, and then back to me. "You really need to work on the quips. You can't be saying random things—"

I head-butted her, which was enough for her to back off with her katana. Blood poured from my shoulder, but there wasn't anything I could do about it in the moment.

It would have been agonizing, but a part of me wished she ignited her sword to cauterize the wound so I wouldn't bleed out.

I put my back to the console once again. "I'm not letting you finish—whatever it is you're doing."

"That's it. I've had it with you," Sable growled as she headed toward Cleo. "You've already stopped being fun to play with."

Dorian walked over to Lili and pointed his scythe at her, while Sable held her katana against Cleo's throat.

"Why don't you go ahead and finish the transfer?"

"Yes, Sable." Kiyoshi picked up his war hammer.

I held my sword up, but Sable clicked her tongue at me. "If you try to stop him, they both die."

I looked from Cleo to Lili's unconscious body.

It felt like the night of the dinner party all over again, only there wasn't any help coming.

"Don't let them do this, Rhys. Forget about—"

"Shut up." Sable ignited her sword, and Cleo cried out in pain.

"Out of my way," Kiyoshi said at the end of my sword. "Now."

Dorian had a sadistic grin on his face as he chuckled and wiggled his scythe. Sable had the exact same expression on her face as she doused and reignited her katana over and over on Cleo.

"Don't do this, Kiyoshi," I said, looking for a hint of emotion. "You can still come back from this. You can help us take them down."

"You've done a good job." His eyes flicked toward Lili. "Don't forget the things I've told you."

"What?"

Sparks flew from his feet and travelled along the ground to me. The electricity flooded my body, but I still held my sword toward him.

I wasn't going to drop it—no matter what.

The electricity became more intense with each passing second, but I wasn't letting go of the sword.

He swung his hammer, finally knocking it out of my hand. It clattered to the ground and shrunk back down to its smaller form.

I couldn't move thanks to the electricity.

It had shocked my body into a paralyzed state.

Kiyoshi whacked me clean out of his way with his hammer. I slammed into the wall and tried to will myself back to my feet as Kiyoshi started typing on the panel again.

"Kiyoshi, please," Cleo said.

I made it to a knee. "Ayla, is there anything we can do here?"

No...

"It's done," Kiyoshi said.

"Good. Let's kill them and let's go." Dorian spun his scythe in his hands. "We're good to get out of here."

He looked thrilled as he raised his scythe over Lili.

I had to think of something, but I was out of options. I couldn't even stand.

I couldn't protect anyone.

"That's not the deal," Kiyoshi said.

Kiyoshi had made a deal with them?

But why?

What was it that he could have wanted?

"Excuse me?" Dorian asked.

"He's right, Dorian." Sable kicked Cleo to the floor. "We honour our deals."

The three of them nodded, and they all teleported out of the facility. All that was left was a group of broken Interceptors.

The room fell silent as I looked back to the door once again. The three other team members were still doing everything they could to open the door.

I stumbled over to the panel to see what had happened. "Ayla, what was the transfer?"

One sec. It looks like that protection's gone now that the transfer's done. I'll see if I can get those doors open now too.

Ayla hopped into the panel, and Cleo made her way over to me.

"Cleo—"

She slapped me across my face. "You should have let us die. Do you have any idea what you just did?"

"What would have changed if the two of you died?" I clutched my shoulder. "The three of them would have ganged up on me again and gotten away with whatever they did anyway. I did what Kiyoshi told me—what *you* told me—I looked out for the well-being of my team first."

The tension was high, but I knew I was right. If I had sacrificed them, it would've resulted in all of our deaths.

"You could have done something. You could have set the sprinklers off. I could have—"

I launched my grappling hook at a sprinkler causing a spark. There was a puff of smoke big enough to set the sprinkler beside it off, but no water came through.

The metallic clinking of the sprinklers was running, but there wasn't any water in the reserves.

"I saw on the map there was no water in the facility," I said, my vision growing hazy. "They planned this out."

Ayla popped out of the console. "We need to figure something out fast."

"They got it didn't they?" Cleo asked.

"Yeah—everything they need to create a new and improved strand of the Extinction Virus."

I brought my hand to my shoulder. "Improved is the last word I wanted to hear."

Chapter 34:
The War Room

After a few days of recovery, Cleo decided that we needed to have a meeting. We needed to discuss what had happened as a team, but also what steps to take next since we were in panic mode.

We needed to figure out what to do about the impending Extinction Virus.

Lili was the last one to walk into the large command room. I looked around at the various facility workers scrambling to find information and hoped the room wasn't too noisy for her.

She had a tired look on her face, and I imagined it was from the monster concussion she'd suffered. They were able to heal her brain in the med-bay, but I figured there must be some kind of side effects.

"You okay, Lili?" I asked

"I am." Lili smiled and rubbed her head. "A little worn out, but it'll pass." She became more serious. "What the hell happened?"

The energy in the room was at an all-time low.

I figured the only other time they'd been close to how bummed they were at that moment was when Chase died. Diggs and Pegs both looked like they'd lost their best friend, and Cleo still looked like she couldn't believe what had happened. Mickey was more on the same wavelength as Lili and I—angry.

"I don't know. Something must have pushed Kiyoshi over the edge." Cleo leaned against a railing. "He wouldn't have done something like that. Not the man I know."

"He didn't exactly look remorseful," I said.

"No offence, but you didn't exactly know him like any of us did," Cleo snapped.

She was right.

I wasn't sure how to navigate a conversation like that as the new kid.

"You're right. I—"

"Rhys is right." I was shocked to hear Mickey agreeing with me. "I saw his face. He might have been forced to do what he was doing, but it didn't look like he needed *much* forcing."

I'd never heard so much emotion radiating from Mickey. It seemed like the android was heartbroken by what Kiyoshi had done.

"He'd been distant lately—going off on his own missions—a lot," Diggs said.

"Was there anything that happened during those missions?" Pegs asked. "Some kind of contact we might not know about?"

"Not that I know of," Cleo said opened a holo of Kiyoshi in front of the group. "We can't dwell on this forever. What's done is done. Kiyoshi joined forces with Zeal, which adds him to the kill or capture list."

I cleared my throat. "We need to figure out what we're going to do about the Extinction Virus."

That shut everyone up. I knew exactly where everyone's mind went—right to the last time they had to deal with the Extinction Virus. Whether any of us liked it or not, the world was about to be in serious danger.

General Odon walked into the room with Ramona.

"Good. Everyone's already here. It's been a while, and we need to have a discussion."

"You're damn right we do." Cleo marched right up to him. "I wanna know why there was a lab that was working on a new strand of the Extinction Virus. I want to know why you were the only one who knew about it. I want to know why we weren't informed of it—and I want to know all of that *right now*."

With everything that had transpired that day, I had completely forgotten that Odon had okayed whatever research was going on.

Cleo was right to be pissed.

"You'll watch how you speak to me, Cleo." Odon wasn't giving her an inch. "That laboratory was working on a new strand of the virus so that we could synthesize a cure for the real deal. A kind of counter-measure should Zeal ever manage to recreate the virus. I thought it was better if none of you knew because I knew you'd all want it destroyed immediately."

"That's a crock and you know it. The entire world is in danger all over again because of you." Diggs bashed his hand of a nearby desk in a rare fit of anger. "News-flash—Zeal is only going to be able to make a new strand of the virus because you hoped to make an antivirus for something that *didn't even exist anymore*."

As much as I had grown to like every member of the team, I think Diggs had become my favourite. His ability to swap from caring to fiery when the situation called for it was something I wanted to model myself after.

"Oh—and to top it all off, thanks to the research that you decided to allow—on your own—without consulting the team." Cleo started prodding Odon. "This new and *improved* Extinction Virus isn't only going to be able to target *living* beings, but it'll also be able to target *tech*."

"It's going to be a hard reset of the entire planet," I mumbled to myself.

"That's enough. I don't recall being on that failure of a mission." I joined everyone in the dagger eyes they were giving General Odon. "What's done is done. What we need to do is prepare ourselves for the next time he strikes."

"*We*—what *we?*" Cleo had started getting red in the face. "*You* don't do anything. *You* sit in your office and twiddle your thumbs while you read information that you don't even share with us."

"I have a family. People that count on me to come home. You all know that I have no issue joining in the field if the danger is severe. I helped Kiyoshi drive back Zeal to protect all of you before—this mess."

"You're a coward."

General Odon may hav been able to mask most of his emotions up to that point, but that was beginning to fail him. It was clear that Cleo's words stung.

"Like I said," Odon said through gritted teeth. "I have a family."

"So do all of us. Lili has her dad, Rhys has his sister, Diggs and Pegs have each other, Mickey had Kiyoshi, and I—" Her eyes flicked toward Ramona.

"This team is a family," Diggs said as he posted up next to Cleo.

I had no idea how often the Interceptors clashed with Odon, but I had a feeling that even I would have heard about a similar situation if it had happened before.

"We're out there risking our lives every day, and we can't do that properly if—you know what?" Cleo finally got some distance from Odon. "If something like this happens again—I'm bringing your leadership to a vote, and I've gotta feeling things aren't gonna swing your way."

"Excuse me?" General Odon looked at the rest of us, but we all had Cleo's back. "That's not how this works."

"We'll see about that. Maybe it's time for you to retire, *General*. Now if you'll excuse us, those of us that actually risk our asses every day to protect this city—this planet—need to prepare ourselves for the next time Zeal strikes. So that *we* can fix *your* mistakes."

"I don't need this." Odon headed for the door. "Come, Ramona."

"I think I'll be of more use here." Ramona headed over to Cleo. "Sir."

General Odon gave us all an offended look, but his eyes fell square onto me before storming out of the room. It was heavy all over again, but everyone had mischievous grins on their faces. I had a feeling that anyone standing up to General Odon was a pretty rare thing.

Ayla started to cheer. *She's so feisty. I love it. I hope she and Ramona—*

So, they are a thing?

Whoops! Don't tell anyone, okay?

You know I won't.

"I'm so turned on," Pegs said.

"By Cleo or me?" Diggs asked.

"Yes."

"As much as I loved that—" Mickey cracked a toothy grin. "And trust me—censors going absolutely wild—I really, really did—we do need to come up with something. Who knows how long it'll be before he gets a version of the virus up and running?"

"Ayla's been telling me that what the lab had on the virus wasn't enough to be finished anytime soon." I sat on a railing. "It'll take him months or maybe even years to figure out how to finish it, but he's gonna finish it eventually. We need to stop him before it gets to the final hours like the last time."

"Yeah, but how are we supposed to do that?" Pegs asked. "Ask Zeal nicely for the location of his base, so we can destroy all the data?"

"Have you guys ever tried that?" I asked as a round of dagger-eyes landed on me. "A simple *no* would work."

The question was meant more of a joke, but it was half serious. Stranger things had happened, and maybe Zeal would have a change of heart if the team asked nicely. Obviously, that was wishful thinking, but the dire situation called for it.

My eye caught Faith in the corner of the room as she perked up like she had realized something. I held my hands out as she darted toward me. She grabbed me like she'd just been scared by a horror-holo.

It might be the final hours right now.

"What do you mean?"

There's a new experimental piece of tech being moved through the city right now, and—

Ayla warped on the rail beside me. "Rhys. Point your hand at the wall."

I held a hand out and Ayla used it to project a live feed from the city. Dorian, Sable, and Kiyoshi were attacking a heavily armoured convoy of trucks.

"Shoulda known they'd go for it," Ramona said.

"What is *it*?" I asked.

"Ayla, what's being transferred there?" Cleo asked.

"It's Zeals trump card—a monolith-chip."

Everyone's eyes went wide, but I was clueless. "Anyone wanna explain what a monolith-chip-thing is?"

Cleo pulled up an image of the chip. "If Zeal gets his hands on that, it won't matter how long it's *supposed* to take him to synthesize a new Extinction Virus. The chip'll help him do it in a matter of hours."

The thought that our timeline to the potential destruction of humanity had shrunk so much sent my mind into a spiral.

"It's equivalent to a cheat code in one of those video games," Ayla said.

"Less my speed, but I get you."

Ayla brought a finger to her chin. "Yeah, that was more a Chase-style explanation, huh?"

"Okay, so we need to head down there and stop them—plan—anyone?" I asked.

"Well, there's six of us and three of them. Let's just hammer them with double teams," Diggs said.

"I'm glad you can still do basic math, but won't that leave the chip unguarded?" Pegs asked. "What if someone manages to slip through?"

"That convoy seems pretty heavily armed. I'd bet if anyone slips through, they'll be able to at least repel them until one of us catches back up."

I figured that anyone watching the feeds saw our current situation as a team of confident heroes thinking out a plan. Being in the room, things were very different. No one was confident. We were in a hopeless scramble for ideas.

"What about the Vanguard?" I asked.

"Even I can tell you we aren't asking them for help," Ramona said.

"Why not? Wouldn't any backup be a good thing?"

"Maybe so, but we can't go asking a group of vigilantes for help."

Vigilantes or not, any help would have made things much easier. Jace and his crew seemed more than capable of holding their own against the Conks.

It wasn't the time to push my luck.

"It was an idea," I said with a shrug. "Nothing I'm married to."

Everyone felt like they could finally breathe when Cleo took control of the situation. "Mickey, you and I will take Kiyoshi. Diggs, Pegs, you two take Dorian, you'll be able to cover each other best against his time element. Lili, Rhys, you two take Sable, your wind and earth should be able to deal with her flames."

"What about me?" Ramona asked.

"You get your team prepped to teleport in. Wait until you think you're absolutely needed."

Ramona crossed her arms. "Does the situation not look like we're absolutely needed?"

She had a point. It was a bit of a do-or-die moment, and I had a feeling the world's population wasn't in favour of the *die* option.

"I know you want to be more help, but we get one warp out of you and your team." Cleo swiped the image of the chip and it morphed into a map of the city. "If we waste it early while the convoy is moving, you could end up across the city from the fight."

"I hate to ask this, but—what if one of them uses the chip?" Pegs asked.

"If it comes to that," Mickey said. "We have to focus our attacks on whoever used it."

Everyone seemed well aware of what would happen if someone used a monolith chip—everyone, except for me.

"What would happen if someone added a monolith chip to their kit?" I asked.

"There's no way of knowing exactly what will happen, but it won't be good. Let's hope we don't have to find out." Cleo headed for the door. "Meet in the transport room in five minutes. Grab any extra gear you think you'll want or need. We're treating this operation as a world-ending threat. Lethal force is fully authorized."

I could tell Cleo was nervous. As she placed her hand on the panel next to the door, her hand was shaking. I just hoped the cameras hadn't caught that.

What she said next was what made me nervous.

"Take a minute to call your loved ones."

If things were really that serious, we were going to need some help. If the Vanguard wasn't an option, I knew some people who were.

I grabbed Lili's arm as everyone hustled out of the room. "Do you still have your trainee kit kicking around?"

"Yeah, it's in my room, why?"

"Go get it. Swing by the elemental training room on your way to the transport room, and grab one lightning element and one darkness element."

"Rhys, what are you—"

"You told the team the one thing I asked you not to. I don't know if you didn't trust my motives or me in general, but you didn't trust me."

She looked hurt by my words, but I didn't care. If the truth hurt, she deserved to be hurt. Part of me needed to finally say that out loud—it was like a weird kind of closure.

"I—"

"Trust me here. Trust me now. Please."

"I shouldn't have done that—I do—"

I held a hand up and Lili ran out of the room.

I didn't need apologies. I needed a team that trusted my judgement. Especially since I was about to make one hell of a stupid decision.

I turned to Ayla. "You ready for this?"

She whirled around and her clothes changed into army fatigues. "You know it."

"Can you call Lenna for me?"

"Right away."

She spun around and her army outfit switched to that of a secretaries outfit. It was nice to have some kind of levity in the midst of such a serious situation.

I started running toward my home in the facility as the call connected. A feed of Lenna's face popped up in front of me. As much as I wanted to fill her in on everything going on, there wasn't any time for niceties.

"Rhys, what is going on?"

"You need to stay indoors and stay safe okay? We're gonna stop them."

"You better not die. I saw what happened—"

"Wasn't planning on it."

"Seriously, I'll kick your ass if you die."

Her eyes started welling up with tears. It was never good when Lenna got that emotional. I promised myself that I'd never let her cry.

I mustered all the confidence I could. "I got this."

She cracked a smile. "I love you."

"I love you too, sis."

I disconnected from the call and turned to Ayla as I reached my room. "We've got a few more calls to make."

She smirked. "*He* is going to be so excited."

Chapter 35:
Chasing Sable

We teleported into the city, and the sounds of screaming innocents, gunfire, and explosions could be heard all around us.

We had a game-plan, but it wasn't much of one.

Stop the bad guys.

I was worried about Cleo because she had the same look on her face that I always had when I'd make most of my mistakes. A mean look of seriously angry determination.

All of the boxing matches I'd lost had been due to me getting too hot-headed, and not thinking properly—I hoped that wasn't the case here.

"You all know what to do. Get them away from the convoy and take them down. Destroy any Conks you see —if you can," Cleo said before rushing off.

Mickey could barely keep up with her, and I knew I was right to worry about Cleo.

Diggs and Pegs rushed off as well, and Lili and I were close behind them. We rounded a block of buildings and saw a group of armoured vehicles opening fire on the three ex-Interceptors that were pursuing them.

"I'll catch him with my flames," Pegs said as she and

Diggs branched out to line up with Dorian.

"I'll knock her off course with a couple gusts." Lili said as we did the same with Sable.

We managed to catch up faster than I thought we would. Pegs managed to pull Dorian away from the trucks just as she had said.

Lili knocked Sable off course with a huge blast of wind, and I managed to keep her off busy by pressuring her with a series of sword strikes.

We all hoped Cleo and Mickey could stop Kiyoshi.

"So nice to see you again, darling. How's things with the rookie girl?" Sable asked as we clashed swords. "We've been watching you—seems like you're *quite* the ladies' man."

"I'd say it's nice to see you, but I just caught a whiff of something nasty, and I'm starting to think you did one of those fear-farts."

"A lady doesn't fart."

"Well, you don't seem like much of a—" She rocked me with a punch. "Lady."

Lili launched a wind gust to stop Sable from bringing her sword down across my chest. I used the opportunity to move around Sable. If we attacked from both sides, she'd have no way to stay on the defensive.

As I rushed toward her back, she placed her hands on Lili's shoulders and pulled off a rigid handstand on her. My sword was pointed right at Lili, so I whirled the sword around in my hands and swiped upward as I crashed into Lili. It looked like I managed to catch Sable with the slice.

"You good?" I asked as I helped Lili to her feet.

"Let's avoid doing *that* anymore."

I nodded, and we turned to where Sable had landed. "I know we said we'd use it on Dorian, but do you wanna try out that move from training?"

Lili rushed forward and grabbed my hand. She

launched us into the air and started swinging me in circles. After we'd picked up some serious speed, she threw me toward Sable and launched a series of blades of wind beside me.

She had nowhere to go.

Sable planted her feet and ignited her katana. She swung at me as I met her sword, and flames shot toward me. She dodged away as Lili jumped in with a punch.

We kept Sable on the defensive by launching attack after attack in her direction. She was working overtime to dodge our attacks, but despite the double team, we were having trouble landing any hits.

She scraped her Katana across the ground to create a wall of fire, and she thrusted back in the direction that the convoy had gone.

"We can't lose her," I said.

A group of annoying Conks teleported in front of us. It was two Brute Conks with a group of Fighter Conks. We'd have to deal with them fast, or Sable wouldn't have any trouble getting back to the convoy.

"Cut through 'em," Lili said.

We both ran toward the Conks, and each of the Brutes tried to squish us between their hands. We each hopped up onto their arms and ran along them until we reached their heads.

I jammed my sword into the side and hopped down the back of it, while Lili sent two big punches into the side—blowing its head clean off.

As we each landed on the floor the Fighter Conks closed in. Lili launched a kick that sent a crescent wave of sharp wind that took out a chunk of the Conks. I dashed forward and cut through the rest of them with ease as Lili hopped over to me.

"Get ready."

"For wha—"

Lili launched a huge wind gust at our feet to launch

us toward Sable. The force of the wind helped me understand how Lili was able to travel so fast. It was hard to maintain my composure in the air, but with a guiding arm by Lili, we landed right behind Sable and continued our chase.

"Up on the buildings, the debris will slow us down!" Lili shouted.

She was right. The cluttered and ruined city streets were filled with abandoned cars, fleeing people, and chunks of concrete from the surrounding buildings. The entire city was in crisis.

Is that gonna work?

You bet your ass it will.

We both used our thrusters to run along the walls of the buildings that lined the street while Sable made her way through the debris. We were able to stay right in line with her without having to avoid the debris, but we also weren't able to get a clear chance to strike.

"What about the buildings?" I asked. "We're just going to end up damaging them more if—"

"These are pretty structural sound," Lili said. "If they came down, it'd be in whole chunks, so don't worry about damage. It would take a lot for anything bad to happen."

I looked down at my arm. "Could I catch her with a grappling hook from this distance?"

She's just barely out of range.

I caught my camera keeping pace right beside me, and I was shocked it was able to keep up. However they worked, they were made of some intense tech.

I had no idea where Diggs and Pegs were fighting Dorian, but Cleo and Mickey still hadn't managed to pull Kiyoshi from pursuing the trucks.

We were on Sable's heels, but her sudden stop caught us by surprise. We launched back down to the street, but she went right for where we were going to land.

I managed to block a slash from her Katana as I came to a stop, but the pressure pushed me farther down the street. "I was able to hold you and Dorian off without a kit—then I was whooping the both of you on my own with one. How do you think *this* fight is going to go?"

She laughed, "You honestly think you held your own in a *real* fight against me and Dorian? The Lord Zeal was right, you really are something else."

"What?"

You need to back off from her, Rhys.

Why?

Things are about to get bad.

I had no idea what Ayla was talking about, until I felt a pulse of energy radiating from Sable.

Chapter 36:
A Freaking Dragon

Sable's kit started to shimmer, and she shot around as quick as lightning. She slashed at me, but I couldn't keep up with the swings. A lot of her slashes weren't on target, but the ones that were getting through were slicing my arms, legs, and the sides of my body.

If she kept getting swipes in, she'd hit something vital sooner or later.

Lili started throwing blades of wind at her to back her off. In response, Sable's hand started to glow a fiery red, and she brought it to the concrete below.

I tried to force the concrete to swallow her whole, but I couldn't do it. I hated that my elemental skills were mostly relegated to lengthy sessions of concentration—and make or break moments.

Apparently, that moment wasn't make-or-break enough.

The ground started to glow red, and Lili and I prepared ourselves for whatever was coming next—but nothing came.

"Did she mess up or something?" I asked.

"I don't think that's it." Lili looked around.

Sable knew something we didn't.

Tiny explosions—like firecrackers, went off by the

wall of a building beside us. We both turned to face it as an enormous flaming dragon clawed its way out, and flew toward at us.

"Run!"

Lili and I activated our thrusters and started running through the city. "We have no choice—we have to lead this to the convoy!" Lili called.

"What!? Why!?"

"We have no idea how long this thing will follow us." Lili hopped across the roof the bonded cars that littered the streets. "Sable's free to join back up to the convoy and get the drop on Cleo and Mickey."

"Crap. Is she headed there, Ayla?"

Ayla warped beside us. "Let's just say, you two need to deal with this dragon—fast."

We turned to head back on course for the convoy, but the dragon launched an enormous fireball from its gaping maw. The fireball landed in the middle of the street in front of us. It didn't hit any cars, but it caused a few drivers to swerve and crash.

There was nothing we could do for the drivers without them ending up extra crispy, so we continued down the path we had been headed.

"We can't let it push us off course," I said.

I looked back to try to get anything to work with my element. A nice wall of rock could have put out the flames.

I tensed my hand at the ground and lifted it, and a wall of concrete rose into the sky. The flame dragon smashed right into it, and the flames flicked around the edges.

No way.

Apparently, *that* moment *was* make-or-break enough.

"Nice one, Rhys."

You guys are gonna want to keep running.

The flames converged again on the opposite side and

the dragon charged another another fireball.

"Oh, come on."

"I take it back. That definitely wasn't a nice one, Rhys."

The streets had mostly emptied out at that point, but there still were the odd stragglers. I spotted a lone man running down the street. We may not have needed to help people in the safety of cars, but he'd probably get toasted just by being near the heat of the dragon.

I pointed the man out to Lili. "We gotta get that guy outta here."

We ran toward the man with the dragon right behind us. I could hear it getting ready to launch another fireball, so I cut the legs of an ancient mailbox that had been bolted down to the street. I kicked it as hard as I could, and it nailed the dragon's mouth, causing the fireball to explode.

"I've got him." Lili scooped the man up and dashed ahead with her wind. She dropped him off and sent him away from the chaos.

We turned down one of the city streets and spotted Pegs and Diggs as they fought with Dorian. They looked like they were holding their own and keeping him occupied, but that could change with the introduction of a dragon.

They all spotted us—or more likely the giant wave of flaming death behind us, and all five of us fled from the dragon.

Dorian rushed up beside me and struck at me with his scythe. I blocked his strike and replied with a slash of my own. As he came in for another attack, Pegs launched a wave of fire in between us.

"The dragon's after us," I said over the comms. "You two, up and over."

Diggs looked back and nodded. Pegs leaped to the rooftops, and Dorian tried to follow her. Diggs wrapped his ankle with his whip and sent him back in the direction of the dragon as he joined Pegs on the rooftops.

I could feel a wave of energy from behind us—it had to be Dorian using his shield. We wouldn't have time to make sure they were able to stay on top of Dorian.

We dashed toward the next turn we could make, and the dragon shot another massive fireball to block our path.

Lili launched a huge wind slash at it, and the fireball cut down the middle. We made our way through it, but another smaller fireball flew right in front of us.

Lili grabbed my hand and launched us into the air.

"Is this a good idea?" I asked.

"We gotta figure out where Sable is somehow. Hold tight."

The dragon followed us, and started charging another shot while we were defenceless, but as it fired, Lili launched a gust to knock us out of the way. It fired a few more, and I slashed the fire with my sword as it approached, allowing us to pass through the middle once again.

We landed on a rooftop and started leaping from rooftop to rooftop. Our only clue as to where Kiyoshi and Sable had disappeared to was the wall of thick smoke in the distance.

Want me to put a beacon on the convoy's location so you can see them from anywhere?

I rolled my eyes. You could have done that this entire time?

She scoffed at me. *What did I tell you about rolling your eyes at me? You never asked.*

How in the world would I know to ask you about something like that?

A flash of green light swept across the city before it

converged into a pillar and rushed around in the distance.

You know, the fact that you could have—

Oh, quit it. It takes a lot of energy to do something like that.

And you didn't want to tell me that?

We're all human.

EXCEPT FOR YOU.

EVEN THAT MIGHT NOT BE TRUE.

…Good point.

We really needed to figure out what was going on with Ayla—if we survived.

The convoy had been destroyed, and the only truck left was the truck carrying the monolith chip.

To make matters worse, Sable was about to catch back up to the convoy as well.

We locked hands again and Lili sent us flying right back at Sable. We landed a few paces behind her with the flame dragon in tow. She looked back at us with an angry face.

"I have a plan—inspired by Dorian, but I need you to trust me," Lili said.

"Weird that he keeps giving us ideas."

"What?"

"Never mind. A plan is better than my—no plan."

"This is going to work, right Walker?" I hoped the answer was yes. "This is gonna drain the rest of the energy from my kit, but this is going to be our best shot."

"What are you—" She grabbed my hand and pulled me to the ground as she activated her cyber-shield around us.

The flame dragon opened its mouth to swallow us, and the flames consumed the shield. Each of our cameras was engulfed in flames outside of the shield, and I wondered just how durable they were.

The whole scene was an incredible sight to see. An

enormous wall of flame licked the shield.

"That—was awesome."

Lili and I laid on the ground in a heap panting, and looking up at the flames. If the dragon had reached us, we would have been comparable to rotisserie chicken.

We turned and looked at each other. For the first time in a while, there wasn't a little camera to spy on what we were doing.

She looked at me. "I'm glad I have you to watch my back. I really am sorry I told the team about—"

The flames lit up her eyes, and it looked like they were shimmering. Each of our breaths was heavy, but something was drawing us closer together.

I put a hand on her face. "Don't worry about it—"

We had each felt drawn toward each other a few times, but never like that. I leaned closer until all my senses were focused on her. The only thing on my mind, aside from her, was my pounding heart.

Our eyes drifted closed as our lips drew closer.

"This is so cute." We each popped an eye open. Ayla was sitting on the ground, cross-legged with a hand on her chin. "Wait! Crap! I just did that moment ruining thing again, didn't I?"

BOOM

Chapter 37:
Kiyoshi Makes A Bad Call

An explosion from the direction of the convoy snapped us back into action. The fire cleared the shield and Lili lowered it. The scent of burnt chemicals and charred cars reminded me of the day when all the Interceptor insanity began for me.

We stood up to see the convoy ahead had been overturned. I couldn't see anyone other than Sable, but the scene looked like some kind of bomb had gone off.

"What the hell happened?" Lili asked.

Our charred cameras floated over to us, and I rolled my eyes. "Maybe the dragon? How much energy do you have left?"

"Next to none."

"Let me take the lead against Sable." I readied my sword. "You might be able to hit with a hell of a lot of force, but we've got a serious problem if you can't match her speed"

I sprinted toward Sable, but she teleported away as I reached her. Her sudden disappearing act seemed strange. She was right in front of her target.

As I approached the wreck, Mickey was helping Cleo to her feet. I was going to check on them until Kiyoshi ripped the door to the convoy truck open. I rushed at him, but I wasn't expecting him to be aware enough to whirl around, and catch me with his war hammer again.

I flew backward, and my body crackled with a mixture of white and blue electricity. Lili came and helped me back to my feet.

"Cleo, what happened?" I asked.

"Kiyoshi hit the lead truck with a huge bolt. The whole street blew—the truck flipped—and here we are." Cleo winced. "At least that big-ass dragon didn't keep coming."

"Sable must have called off the dragon to avoid incinerating the chip," Lili said.

"We gotta stop Kiyoshi," I said. "He's in the truck."

"I tagged him with a data-stop," Mickey said. "He's got no where to go."

Diggs and Pegs came from down the street. "What's going on? Dorian ditched us."

"Kiyoshi's got the chip."

We all started toward the overturned truck, but Dorian and Sable teleported in front of us. "Not one more step."

"Outta the way." Diggs unfurled his whip. "You can't take all of us."

"You might be right," Sable dragged her katana along the ground. "But we don't have to fight any of you."

A line of fire burst toward all of us, and a wall of flame jutted out from the floor. It looked like it circled the area around the truck. After a few moments, the flames stopped moving altogether, and a blazing orb of still fire stood in front of us. Each of our cameras moved around to get a clean shot of the fire-field.

"What's going on?" I asked.

"They're trying to buy Kiyoshi time to locate the chip and figure out how to disable the data-stop." Cleo sliced a nearby fire hydrant from the ground. "We gotta get in there."

She launched a wave of water at the fire while Lili shot wind waves toward it. They didn't budge the flame's at all.

Mickey disappeared for a moment but came back with a nasty-looking burn on a part of its arm that hadn't been covered by their kit.

"Don't touch it." Mickey winced. "I couldn't even get through the shadows."

"I've never seen anything like this," Cleo said.

I walked closer to it and stuck my sword into the wall of flame. I pulled it out as quick as I had put it in, and my sword had been super-heated. Something wasn't right about these flames.

"I can't do anything like this on my own," Pegs said as she gawked at the flames. "Dorian must have frozen the flames in time."

None of us could push through the flames, but my sword could for whatever reason. It wasn't much, but it gave me an idea.

"Cleo, freeze my sword." I stuck it back in the flames, and Cleo launched a trail of ice at it.

Ice crawled along my sword and pushed against the flames. The ice made me go from sweating from the heat of the sun to being so cold it hurt.

The ice flashed across the rest of the flames, and Lili and Pegs launched attacks to crack it open.

Specks of ice shined through the air, and for a few moments, it felt like it had started snowing for the first time in my life. The beauty of the moment faded when the stakes of the day came back to me.

Dorian and Sable were gone once again.

But Kiyoshi wasn't.

He climbed back out of the truck and surveyed the scene of destruction.

"Stand down, Kiyoshi." Cleo created a series of ice-warriors. "Dorian and Sable ditched you, and you've got nowhere to go."

"You think they abandoned me? They wanted to get out of the way to avoid any collateral damage."

"Collateral damage?"

Kiyoshi opened his free hand to reveal the monolith chip. He tore open the panel on the arm of his kit and placed it in.

"What does that mean?" I asked. "This can't be good, right?"

"It means it's time for us to get the hell out of here," Mickey said.

Clouds formed almost instantaneously.

I had no idea what I was witnessing.

The sky turned a dark grey, and rain started pouring. I held my hand out and felt the cool drops run along my skin. I finally got my wish for some rain, but that was the last way I would have wanted to experience it.

Lightning started striking all around the city. The bolts were striking so fast, it felt like the earth was about to split open. Things calmed down for a moment, and it seemed like the bolts were coming to a stop.

Kiyoshi didn't look happy, or even angry.

He looked like he was full of regret.

A bolt of lightning shot from the clouds above him.

Before anyone could react, it struck Kiyoshi.

The blast from the bolt of lightning threw us all backward. It hadn't hit us, but it might as well have with how worn out we all already were.

Everyone staggered to their feet and watched Kiyoshi's kit start morphing as it expanded to the size of a skyscraper. Kiyoshi had disappeared, and in his place was an enormous armoured kit that was blasting lightning every which way.

"How do we stop him?" I asked.

"We kill him."

Chapter 38:
Help Arrives

I looked toward Cleo hoping it was some kind of dark joke, but the serious look on her face wasn't what I was hoping for. Bolts of lightning flew from Kiyoshi's body, but we all jumped back and hid behind a building.

"Cleo's right. We have to take him out. Anyone have a new plan?" Mickey asked.

Mickey was angry, but I could also see a hint of sadness. The android wasn't doing what it wanted to do. It was going to do what it had to do.

"RHYS!"

I looked down the street, and Kieran and Fern were flying toward me on her tech-cycle. She pulled it to the side of the street, and it flipped back into a disc.

"We made it. What is going on and why is there a giant evil robot-Kiyoshi?" Kieran asked.

"Where's Lenna? Is she—"

"Home safe."

"Whoa, whoa, whoa. We can't have more citizens here right now." Diggs stopped them from approaching. "Clear the area."

I tossed them my old necklace and Lili's old bracelet. "Put those on. We're going to need all the help we can get."

"What? No—no way. You two were great in the tryouts, but—" Pegs started.

"But what? You said no to my Vanguard idea. We don't know how the hell we're going to take him down." I pointed to Kieran and Fern. "That's two more capable bodies that we trust that can help out."

Fern had remained cool-headed, but Kieran looked like he couldn't wait to hop into the fight. I knew he'd love the idea.

Pegs gave me a dull look. "With nothing but kits."

"Oh." Lili tossed the electricity element to Kieran and the darkness element to Fern.

We smiled at each other. I was glad she trusted me, even if my idea was nuts.

"Is that a bit better?" I asked.

They each put on the accessories, and attached their elements. Their kits climbed over their bodies, and the grey suits glowed with their elemental colours.

"We could see Kiyoshi from a few blocks away. He's sending out crazy bolts of lightning and at some point, he's gonna start levelling buildings. You're gonna need us," Fern said as a bolt of lightning struck the street beside us, causing us all to jump. "See what I mean?"

"They're still a huge liability for the team. What if they get hurt?" Pegs asked.

I shrugged. "Let Odon figure that one out."

Cleo laughed, "If those two are good with it, it sounds good to me." She put a hand on my shoulder. "I just wanna let everyone know if we hadn't already decided it before—we're keeping Rhys."

"We need a plan, fast. Ayla, can you scan Kiyoshi for anything that might help?" I asked. "A weak spot—a power source—anything at all?"

"Alfie, assist Ayla," Cleo said.

Ayla and Alfie each warped beside us and nodded before heading over to scan Kiyoshi.

"We'll need to keep his attention split," Kieran said as he created sparks in his hands. "I have a feeling if he hits any of us, we're done for."

"Okay—hold on," Diggs said. "The non-Intercepter isn't the one making the team plan."

Kieran was caught in a constant state of being in between excitement and disappointment. All he wanted was to help his heroes.

"I know you want to help, but—"

"Diggs—Kieran's right. Anyone low on energy?" Cleo asked.

Kieran looked like he was about to cry. "I'm right."

I knew Cleo agreeing with Kieran was enough to trigger a nerd-gasm, but it looked like he was about to trade in his crush on Lenna for one on Cleo.

"I'm pretty low." Lili raised her hand, ignoring Kieran. "I should be fine to fight, but I'll have next to no armour, and I don't know how much damage bazooka fists are going to do to a monster like that."

"I'm in the same boat here," Diggs stepped forward. "But I've got a couple of good flashes left in me."

"List of things you never want to hear a hero say," Fern muttered.

I was a bit worried the team might get annoyed by Kieran and Fern, since they seemed to not really grasp the gravity of the situation, but then I remembered how Chase was. Like he'd said during his final moments, there's never a bad time for jokes.

"Okay. Diggs, Pegs, Mickey—you three go low and try to keep his bolts aimed at the street in this immediate area." She peeked around the corner at Kiyoshi. "I'm going to take the mid-section with Lili to try to find any weak points. If things get too hairy, Lili—Diggs—you two are to move to cover. We can't risk either of you taking a nasty hit. Rhys—"

Ayla and Alfie flew back. "If you can take his right arm off, the chip's supply to the rest of the kit will be cut off. He'll still be huge, but his defences will be minimal for about a minute due to the power cut-off."

Cleo nodded. "Rhys, Kieran, Fern—you three are taking the top. If we can keep his attention split, it might confuse him. When you see the chance for a clean slash at his arm, you have to take it, Rhys. You're the only one with a weapon that can do it."

My heart started racing when she said that. The team was relying on me, and I was only going to have one chance.

I couldn't screw it up.

"What about when his defence is down?" Mickey asked.

"Swarm him. We need to dish out whatever damage we can before his systems boot back up properly. Aim for any and every weak point that you can. Anywhere on the face, the neck, the heel—the groin."

The pulled out their weapons, and I handed my gauntlets to Fern. Between her and Kieran, she was the one who couldn't use her element to launch attacks at a distance.

As she put them on, they resized to fit her hands as the arrows started to load. "I always wanted to try these bad boys out."

"You gonna be good without a weapon?" I asked Kieran

He picked up a chunk of debris and sparked it. "I like our odds."

"I'm just gonna go ahead and not even question how that works."

"Everyone ready?" Cleo asked.

Everyone nodded.

Are we going to be able to do this?

You said it yourself, we're going to be the heroes Chase would be proud to call his successors.

That's what I like to hear—think? What is this form of communication called? Telepathy? Do you have thoughts?

Is now really the time to think about that?

Cleo nodded to me. "Let's take him down."

Fern grabbed Kieran and me, and we watched as she waded through the darkness. In moments the colour flew back into the world, and we were on top of a building.

We emerged from the shadows of a raised section on the roof in time to see a bolt of lightning fly through the streets.

Every time Kiyoshi launched a lightning bolt, the streets reverberated with a massive crack of thunder. I could feel the buildings sway from the force of each bolt.

"You two use the buildings for cover—I'm going to do what I can to find an opening on his arm," I said as I looked out toward Kiyoshi's hulking form.

"Let's give this asshole a headache," Fern said.

"I'm fighting alongside the Interceptors." Kieran gawked. "This is so cool."

She nudged him. "Pretty sure this makes us fully-fledged honorary members of the team."

I rushed from our cover and jumped toward Kiyoshi. He may have been a hell of a lot bigger, but he wasn't any slower. He turned toward me and held out a giant hand. He could have reached out and squashed me like a bug, but Lili sent a gust of wind my way from below.

A lightning bolt flew into the building behind me, but it was so close that I felt a slight tingle run through my leg.

"Thanks, Lili," I said to myself.

I kept trying, but I was sure I hadn't managed to hurt Kiyoshi with any of my attacks. I figured I'd take a shot at where his eyes would have been, but a massive fist punched me straight down the street.

Cleo surfed along a stream of water and caught my hand. She gave me a look to make sure I was okay before tossing me back into the fight. As I landed back on

Kiyoshi's body, a group of icicles flew into his face, but it didn't look like he'd noticed them.

I activated my thrusters and rushed in to chip away at his kit. With every swing, my sword bounced off the heavily armoured kit. Sparks ignited as I scraped the metal of my sword against his metallic form.

There was a tiny opening in the kit's armour at the top of his shoulder. I rushed toward it. I was getting frustrated, and I knew my emotions were making me sloppy.

I just hadn't realized how sloppy.

Kiyoshi caught me with a wave of his massive hand, and I flew through the wall of a nearby building.

Chapter 39:
The Plot To Slay A Giant

"Rhys? You okay?" Cleo's voice came over our comms.

As I stumbled to my feet, I brushed chunks of debris off of my kit. "Still in one piece—I think." I looked around at the ruined office I had crashed through. "Someone is gonna be real upset with me tomorrow morning, though."

Lili wasn't kidding when she mentioned how strong the buildings were earlier. There were scattered chunks of wall everywhere, but a solid portion of the wall I had come through was still mostly intact beneath me.

I shuffled to the hole my body had created and looked out at the battle as my little camera caught up with me. Kiyoshi looked like one of those giant monsters from those ancient movies as he terrorized the city.

We must have all looked like ants to him, but we had all been coming at him full-force.

Ayla warped beside me. "You alright?"

"I'm alive—for now. How's everything—you know— internally?" I asked as I waved my hand over my body.

"You're not currently in danger of sudden death."

"Indirect answer—always a good sign. At least I know my adrenaline is working overtime."

The one good thing in the situation was that

Kiyoshi's hammer hadn't grown in size along with the rest of him. He could have been levelling entire blocks with one swing.

Now that I had a moment to breathe, I could see everyone in action. I watched everyone flail at Kiyoshi, hoping anything might damage him. We'd lose if we kept fighting the way we were.

If we could send Diggs up to Kiyoshi's face, he could blind him—and from my experience, everyone reacts the same way when your eyes are flooded with light.

His hands would be headed to cover his eyes, and if we could catch his right arm, I could cut it off.

Everyone would need to be ready to keep him still.

"Ayla, put me through to everyone's comms."

She hopped back into my kit. *You're good to go.*

"I have a plan. When I say so, Fern needs to head down to Diggs and take him up to the rooftops. Lili, you need to be ready to blow away Kiyoshi's hands as he tries to stop Diggs."

"What do you mean—*tries to stop Diggs?*" Diggs asked. "What is *Diggs* gonna do?"

"You need to hit Kiyoshi with the biggest flash you can create, and as the flash hits, Cleo needs to freeze Kiyoshi's feet to the ground with all the ice she can create. Everyone else—do what you can to keep Kiyoshi stationary."

"If I need to block another swing, I'm going to be out of energy. What are you going to do?" Lili asked.

"If that's the case, do it and run to safety—same with you if you're in the same boat Diggs." I looked down at my shaking hands. "Plan A is to get my element working to hold his arm in place. Plan B is gonna be a work in progress if that doesn't work."

"Let's get plan A to work." Diggs almost shouted over a clap of thunder.

I rushed back out into the street and landed on top

of a sign that lined me up with Kiyoshi's arm.

"It's go time."

Fern disappeared with Kieran from a nearby rooftop and reappeared on the ground where Diggs was. She traded Kieran for Diggs, and soon they were right back up on the same rooftop.

Everyone prepared for their part of the plan as Mickey, Pegs, and Kieran drew Kiyoshi's attention on the ground below. Those three might have been the bravest considering one wrong move would leave them as flat as pancakes.

Diggs rushed out from the building, and just as I thought, Kiyoshi was ready for it. He swung an arm at him, but Lili sent what felt like a strong enough wind to start a violent hurricane right toward his arm. His arm flew back as Diggs reached the centre of his face.

"Cover your eyes, folks," Diggs said through the comms.

Ayla.

Got it.

My kit covered my head, and my vision became pitch black.

Diggs' body became enveloped in a huge white light. I couldn't have looked at it if I wanted to, even with the helmet's help to dull the flash.

I turned back, and Cleo had started working on freezing Kiyoshi to the ground. Pegs threw her circle-sword, and it caught fire as it started to pass around Kiyoshi, locking him in a tight fire tornado.

Kiyoshi's arm was coming in to instinctually cover his eyes after the shock of the light.

I had one shot.

I raised an arm and focused.

—

Nothing was happening.

My arm started to shake as my helmet crawled off

my head. "C'mon—c'mon!"

Kiyoshi reared back and stretched out his arms. Lightning exploded from his body, striking all over the immediate area.

I managed to pull my shield up in time, but I couldn't be sure if anyone else did. The one person I knew who managed to avoid the lightning was Diggs as he used his whip to swing to safety.

I gritted my teeth, and the concrete of the buildings surrounding Kiyoshi extended toward him. Huge pillars of concrete trapped his right arm while it was extended, and I launched toward the weak point in his armour.

"I've got this." I positioned my body and swung with all my might as I passed by his arm.

My blade wasn't big enough to cut his entire arm, but it did enough damage. I caught onto the side of a building as his arm crumbled from the rest of his body, and fell toward the ground. As it fell it reverted back to its normal size.

The strange thing was, there wasn't any blood, but instead sparks.

Kiyoshi's feet crushed the ice as he forced his way out, and he fell to a knee. His kit started glowing, and for whatever reason, his entire body was vibrating.

I took the brief break in the action to rush back to the ground. I figured if I checked Kieran and he was still alive, the rest of them would be too.

As I landed on the ground, I looked out to the far end of the street where a crowd had gathered. They had to be insane to think they were at a safe distance, but there they were—cheering us on.

Kieran was a crazy fan, but even he wouldn't do something quite *that* stupid.

I turned around just as another wave of Conks teleported in front of me. I knew I could take out an army of Conks by myself—but that was when I was at full power. I wasn't sure if I could handle all the Conks alone while protecting the team.

"Leave them to us, Rhys," Ramona said from behind me. "You worry about the giant asshole."

She had teleported in with a small team of armed mercenaries from the facility, but that wasn't going to be enough to handle the army of Conks.

"You and your team aren't going to be enough to take—"

"Well, we're gonna have to be enough."

The roaring engines of an army of tech-cycles came from around a corner. In the blink of an eye, the Vanguard—led by Jace—rushed their way into the fight to even the odds.

Chapter 40:
Kieran Got Some Mad Volts

"Protect the girl," Jace barked to his comrades before walking over to me. "I heard the Interceptors were in need of a bit of back-up."

"I'm not gonna complain." I shrugged. "What girl were you—"

"Working alongside the Vanguard—" Ramona said as she and her team took down a Brute Conk. "What's next? Flying Conks?"

"I'm not thrilled about it either, but if us not helping means the world's toast—I'd rather help you guys out." Jace pulled out a metal stick, and it morphed until a full cyber-saw had been formed.

He charged into the wave of Conks with that in one hand and a gun in the other. Jace was a weird guy, but he also looked like an action star as he rushed into combat.

I ran over to Kieran and slapped his face. "Kieran— Kieran. Wake up. C'mon."

He groaned and coughed as he leaned up, "I'LL ADD GETTING STRUCK BY LIGHTNING TO MY BUCKET LIST, AND THEN SCRATCH IT RIGHT THE HELL OFF."

However the lightning worked, it did a number on Kieran. His eyes were practically bugging out of his head, and he'd lost all control of how loud he was speaking. That was all without mentioning how wild and frizzy his hair had become.

"At least now I know everyone should be alive," I said.

He waved away some of the smoke that rose from his body. "I wouldn't be too sure—pretty sure Lenna'd tell you I'm just too stubborn to die." He leaned closer to me. "I think I crapped my pants when the lightning struck—if you could just not tell your sis, that'd be great." Kieran leaned back and waved at the camera that had been following me. "You've got one shot at stopping this guy. You sure you can take it?"

"I have to be, but I don't know how the hell I'm going to put him down for good."

"I have an idea, but you aren't going to like it." Ayla chimed in as she warped beside me.

"Anything."

"If Kieran lets me route the rest of the power from his kit into you and your sword, I should be able to give it enough power for you to cut Kiyoshi in half, but we're only going to have one chance at this."

"But then he won't—"

"Do it." Kieran grabbed my arm. "I may not get to be the one to save the day, but at least I got to help—thanks to you. You were the right person for the team."

I nodded, and he let what was left of his kit leave his body.

"Put your hand on the medallion," Ayla said.

As soon as I touched it, I could feel a surge of power transfer from it into me. For a moment, it felt like I could have leaped to the moon, but most of the power faded into my sword. I could feel the energy radiating from it, but it didn't look any different.

"Ayla? It doesn't look like anything happened."

"Go for it and I'll let the power rush through it at the

right moment."

I shrugged. "I'm trusting you big time on this one."

"We'll do it together."

"Kick his ass, Rhys," Kieran said from behind me. "I'll lay here—and crawl to safety—whenever my body starts working again."

I launched myself toward Kiyoshi for what I hoped would be the final time. Ayla flew alongside me, and she nodded as our eyes met.

As I reached Kiyoshi, I swung my sword with everything I had.

In the middle of the swing, in the moment right before the blade hit Kiyoshi, it grew to an enormous size. The sword pulled right through his midsection.

I expected a horrible wave of blood to gush from the wound, but again, all I could see was crushed metal and sparks.

Kiyoshi's agonized screams caught my attention as I landed back on the ground. A few more stray lightning bolts launched from his body, and one hit the building on the far end of the street.

The crowd of people below it screamed as it passed over their heads.

I pulled my sword up to block a loose bolt that flew straight at me. The sword absorbed the bolt, but it morphed back into its small form as I shot backward.

I felt like whatever energy still resided in the sword had shot right back into my kit.

Kiyoshi's legs shrunk as they fell backward to the ground, and his top half did the same as it fell to the floor. Both halves landed with a heavy mechanical thud.

I surveyed the body-strewn scene around me as the fight against the Conks raged on. I hoped everyone was okay, but I still needed to secure the chip before Dorian or Sable came back.

"Nice work, man." Diggs limped toward me.

"At least he didn't manage to hit all of us," Lili said as she did the same.

"I'm glad you guys are alright. Kieran's okay too. Immobile for now, but okay," I said.

"We lucked out, I don't know what would have happened if I had missed. That last gust was all my kit's energy." Lili hugged me.

I gave Diggs props. "I'm low, but we should be okay to handle what's left of the Conks. Let's help everybody up, and—"

CRASH

The building that had been struck by lightning had crumbled and a section was tipping toward the street below. A street filled with bystanders. People screamed as they scrambled back and forth, but there was no way everyone was going to make it clear of the huge building in time.

"Crap."

It looked like it was going to be Remarkable Rhys against a falling skyscraper.

Chapter 41:
What Makes A Hero?

It was a situation where there wasn't any time to think—I grabbed Diggs. "Enough energy to help?"

He nodded and my body continued moving forward on instinct, pulling him along with me so he didn't need to use what little energy he had.

"Grab Kiyoshi's arm!" I said as I rushed by Kieran.

I didn't have any time to hear what he said back to me. I needed to figure out what to do about the building.

"Ayla, scan the building and let me know how many people are on the inside."

Gimme a sec.

An energy wave passed over the building.

One group of five people on the sixteenth floor. Looks like they wanted a better angle of the action.

"Could the grappling hooks support weight like that?"

Not for long. A few moments at most.

"Not long is long enough. You're in charge of my gear. Figure out the best points to hold the building up and use everything we've got on the thrusters."

Got it.

"We gotta get those people outta there," I said as I tossed Diggs ahead of me.

He looked back and saluted as he ran forward. "You know it."

As I ran, Ayla guided my arms to a set of buildings. My hook shot into one, and I flew toward it. I launched a hook across to the opposite building, and set my end into the concrete, and repeated the process at another point for my other hook.

I made it back to the ground and threw both my shields so that they would force the building's fall to slow. They flew to the top of the building and hooked onto a raised section.

If I couldn't stop its fall, I could slow it down and catch it.

Catch a building.

Yikes.

Ayla sent the rest of the power in my kit to the thrusters on my legs, and reached the building as Diggs did. I rushed up the side of the building as the falling section tipped into the hooks that stretched across the street.

We smashed in through a window and looked for the group that was somewhere inside. "Hello? We're Interceptors. We're here to help."

Five scared faces pop up from across the room.

The hooks are about to go, and the shields stopped spinning

"Worst day ever."

Rhys, people aren't clear of the building yet.

"What? How? Ayla put all the power to the thrusters again. Diggs!" He gave me a concerned look. "Get all of them out of here as fast as you can!"

What do you mean?

Diggs looked back at me. "What are you gonna—"

I launched faster than I ever had back out to the street. I managed to make it underneath the building as it bent the grappling hook lines toward the ground.

I searched for whoever wasn't clear of the building

and spotted what looked like two people. I ran toward them, but I wasn't going to be able to get them out of the way in time.

Without thinking, I waved my hands and pillars of concrete rose from the ground, but as the hooks snapped, the weight of the building crumbled the pillars.

Everything had helped to slow the building chunk's fall, but it was still coming fast.

Hopefully, Diggs found a way to protect the people inside of the building.

I kept summoning pillars from the ground, hoping the people would run, but they were frozen with fear. I could feel myself getting tired, but it slowed the buildings descent even more as it inched closer.

Rhys, you are not about to do what I think you're about to do.

Well, do you not think I'm going to hold the building up?

Oh my god.

Is it possible?

Maybe.

I started to duck as it neared me, and I braced myself for a hell of a lift.

The moment that I became the only thing separating the building from the ground was the most agonizing moment of my life.

The only thing keeping the huge section of the building from crushing those people in the street was me.

Ayla had rerouted the kit's power again, but there wasn't much left. The only kit left to reinforce my strength was wrapped around my legs, parts of my back, parts of my shoulders, and my hands.

I turned my head in disbelief.

Chunks of debris were coming loose all over the place. They hit the ground with frightening thuds.

On the ground, just a few feet front of me was a woman and a young kid. She was trying to pull him to his feet, but he refused to—probably out of paralyzing fear.

"Ooh—this—sucks," I said through clenched teeth as my little camera flew down and framed me. "You—would be here."

This is a bad idea.

"Not much—of a choice. Everyone in the—building—okay?"

Diggs managed to keep them safe.

"Can't wait to hear—how he managed that one."

He's getting them out now.

"He better be."

"C'mon, kid. We gotta get out of here." The woman pleaded as she tugged the child's arm.

"I'm scared." The kid cried.

Power is fading quick, Rhys.

The kit migrated from my hands, and even though they weren't doing much, it made a big difference. The slight shifting in my kit sent a brand-new wave of force through my body.

"This—really—really freakin' sucks."

Another rain of debris fell loose and smashed into the ground, causing the two people to jump.

I looked down at the kid. "What—what's your name, buddy?"

"Ro—Roddy."

"Roddy—wish I had a name like that. You like the Interceptors, Roddy?" He nodded. "Who—who's your favourite?"

The questions were partially to try to comfort the kid, and partially to try to comfort me.

The weight of the building made it feel like all my muscles were tearing. I could feel the sweat pouring from my body.

Catching a bus had nothing on catching a building.

"I liked Chase before, but now I like Lili."

I chuckled and coughed. "Me too. Any chance you like me at all?"

"I haven't decided yet. You're too new."

"Sounds about right. Well—hopefully after today— you do. I want you to do me a favour—I want you to come grab my sword, okay?"

"Why?"

"You can't give a—" The woman started, but the look I shot her shut her up.

"Because today, I'm making you—an honorary Interceptor."

"Really?" He crawled closer. "You can do that?"

The weight of the building made it feel like my bones were snapping. "Special—special top-secret power of us Interceptors—and I'm using it now, so you can help me."

Ayla flashed an image of how little power I had left in my view. It was a smart way to let me know how hopeless the situation was without freaking out the kid.

"I want everyone to make it out of here, and right now there's just—just one person left to save," I said as I looked at the woman.

"Justice," she said as she trembled.

How ironic.

Not now, Ayla.

You said—

BUILDING. AYLA.

Roddy stood up and put a hand on the sheath.

"It's gonna be a bit heavy, but I know you can do it, okay?" I said. "Give the sheathe a—a pull, but don't draw the sword. A hero—only draws his weapon against a bad guy."

He gave it a tug and fell backwards with the sword still in its sheathe. He hugged it close to his body as he stood up once more. "What now?"

"Now that you have the—magic sword of the

Interceptors—you help me be a hero. It's up to—to the two of us to save Justice, and I can't do it by myself."

Ayla, Ask Diggs how many people he still needs to get out.

Ayla warped beside me, but she took the form of Lili. She pretended like she was helping to hold up the building. "One more."

"Lili? Where'd you come from?" Roddy asked with wide eyes.

"I heard you're a fan. Don't worry about that. We need you to help us out." She smiled down at Roddy. "Think you can do it for me, stud?"

Roddy held a hand out to Justice, and she took it.

"That's what I'm talking about, Roddy," I said. "Alright, I need you to hold—onto her and that sword as tight as you can, and you run right over to the—to the big crowd down the street, okay? Don't look back for one second."

I shifted my body some, and chunks of broken debris fell from the building. A bone somewhere in my body cracked under the pressure from the building. The sound was sickening

"I'm scared," Roddy said.

"That's okay, buddy. I'm scared too," I admitted.

"Really?"

"Even Interceptors get scared sometimes. Beating bad guys doesn't make you a big he—hero—doing everything you can to protect the people around you, especially when it's scary—that's what makes you a hero. That'll make you Justice's hero—that'll make you Lili's hero—that'll make you my hero."

Roddy nodded and squeezed the sword tighter.

"On three, okay?"

"Hold on Rhys, last one's out now," Diggs said over the comms.

"Okay." Roddy nodded and turned to the crowd.

"One."

I could see their hands clasp tighter.

"Two."

Ayla's appearance shifted back to her normal self and she looked at me. "We're almost out of power."

"Three!"

As I hoped, Roddy and Justice ran forward toward the crowd down the street. "That's what I'm—talking about."

"Hold on. I'm calling anyone who's conscious. We're gonna get you out of here," Ayla said as she placed a hand over my hand.

She wasn't just pretending.

She really placed her hand over mine.

"Unless they show up yesterday—I don't think we're getting out of here."

Each moment, the crushing hurt more.

The pain radiated further through my body.

It was a stupid idea to think I could hold up a building.

I looked back to Roddy and Justice. Debris was falling from the building, and I was terrified a stray brick would end my hopes of their escape.

A huge chunk of debris fell into view right over the two of them.

It was all going to be for nothing.

I closed my eyes, but a huge crack made me set my sights back on the scene in front of me.

The debris was intercepted by a huge kick from Lili.

The team was back up and at it.

"Hold on, Rhys." Cleo's voice came through the comms. "We're coming to help."

Cleo shot two huge pillars of ice at each corner of the building. She continued forming more ice than I'd ever seen her create in an effort to alleviate the pressure. Everything I'd done with the pillars of concrete hadn't even come close to what she did.

Diggs and Pegs arrived on each side of the building, and in a few agonizing moments, some of the pressure had been removed. One by one the Interceptors disappeared around the sides of the building, and I could feel the pressure easing back some more.

"Someone grab him," Cleo said.

My body was failing, and I dropped to the ground as my kit ran out of power. Thankfully, the building didn't fall down and crush me into an Interceptor-sized smear on the pavement.

What wasn't so great was me losing my lunch as I crumpled to the floor.

"That—was—the—worst." I managed to wheeze out. "The camera still good?" The little camera flew into my face. "Damn it. Get my good side. Ignore the puke."

My body may have been destroyed, but that didn't matter. What mattered was the Roddy and Justice were safe.

So long as I was an Interceptor, I wasn't going to let anyone die.

Chapter 42:
You're A Hero

I looked toward the crowd of people and watched as Kieran and Fern helped Roddy and Justice to safety. I figured from the lack of Fern's kit that she had given the remainder of her kit's energy to Lili.

I felt a hand on my back, and soon I was out from underneath the building and laying at the side of the street.

"He's clear," Mickey said over the comms.

Everyone's gear shot back to them, and the building crashed the rest of the way to the ground. It kicked up dust and debris, but I'm sure everyone would rather have irritated eyes over being squished.

I tried to stand up, but Mickey held me down. "You need medical attention, Rhys. Your body is in shock. I don't think I've ever seen someone go so pale—you could die. Let everyone else deal with the rest of the fight."

"Kiyoshi. I need to—"

"You look like you're gonna be sick."

Thanks to that building, none of the interceptors would ever see the evidence—hopefully.

"I'm going, Mickey."

"I'll help him," Cleo said as she came over.

"No." Mickey studied my face. "*We'll* help him."

They leaned all my weight across their shoulders as they helped me walk over to the top half of Kiyoshi on the ground. He was still alive, but he wasn't totally human anymore.

"What did the chip do to him?" I asked.

"It destroyed him." Cleo looked down at him. "Changed him from man to machine. He didn't have it for too long, so he probably still has most of his vitals somewhere inside that metal husk."

"If the fight had gone on any longer, he would have been no different from a Conk." Mickey grimaced. "He'll die, and there's nothing we can do about it."

"The Conks. What about—"

"You can relax. The Vanguard and Ramona's team are cleaning up any of the Conks that are still running around. Everything's okay," Cleo said as she turned her attention to Kiyoshi and placed a hand on his chest.

"Cl—Cleo. They—" Kiyoshi started.

"Save it."

Cleo's response took me by surprise. It was a colder response than I expected. I placed a hand on the hand she had placed on Kiyoshi's chest.

"Why'd you do this?" I asked.

"They—they have—Akio. Ple—please—please help him. If you can never forgive me—at least get him home safe. He—he never deserved this. Tell him—how much I love him." It didn't sound like Kiyoshi anymore. It sounded more like he was speaking directly into the blades of a spinning fan.

For a moment, none of us knew what to say. It was clear that Kiyoshi was in the midst of his dying moments, but what was the right way to send him off?

Telling him we'd find his brother, or saying nothing at all after all he'd done?

"Do you think—do you think I'm—going to a better place?" Kiyoshi asked between gasps.

"I can't promise you that, but I can promise you this —we'll get your brother back. I promise you we'll save him." Cleo tapped his chest.

"Thank you." He turned to Mickey. "Mick."

Mickey took his hand. "You told me we are an eternal family."

"We are, and whether—whether androids end up in the same place or not, I'll be waiting for you—it better be—for a long, long time."

Mickey stood up and put some distance between us. I didn't even know it was possible, but Mickey had begun to cry. As far as I knew, Kiyoshi was the only person who'd ever treated Mickey like family before the team.

"Be strong—be ready for anything." Kiyoshi turned his attention to me. "You have no idea what's coming next."

"What's coming next?" I asked. "What do I have to do with Zeal?"

Kiyoshi looked to the sky. "Don't trust him."

The light drained from his eyes.

Kiyoshi was gone.

He was more man than machine, but everything he had done, he did for his family. Cleo had started to tear up, and the other Interceptors gathered around to pay their respects for their fallen comrade.

I looked at Cleo. "Him?" She shook her head. "Guys, I'm sorry. I—"

"It's okay, Rhys." Pegs put a hand on my shoulder. "You did what you had to."

"I knew he wouldn't betray us without a good reason," Diggs said.

"Anyone know what happened to the chip?" Pegs asked. "I haven't seen it anywhere."

Kieran and Fern made their way from the crowd, and he waved Kiyoshi's robotic severed arm. "Guys, I got the chip."

Thankfully, Fern had snagged my sword back from Roddy. I would have hated to have seen how that went.

I felt another hand on my shoulder, and it was Lili. "We need to get you out of here. Your body's been through hell."

I still couldn't stand on my own, but she helped me to my feet. "What about all the people? Is everyone safe?"

"Rhys—you couldn't help out anymore if you wanted to."

"Ayla, any casualties?" I asked, ignoring Lili.

She smiled as she floated next to me. "Other than 'Yoshi, no. A couple injured Vanguard, but no deaths. Thanks to you and Diggs—the whole team—everyone's safe."

The heavy clouds overhead had dissipated, and they revealed the setting sun. I looked down the street toward where the city overlooked a large lake.

It was pristine.

I spotted a bench and forced my feet toward it. I stumbled, but Lili caught me and helped me forward.

"Where are you going?" she asked.

"I need to sit—away from everything—for a sec."

She helped me over to the bench, and taking a moment to sit and breathe made me realize how much pain my entire body was in. A man with a gruff voice cleared his throat behind me, and I turned around.

"I know it's not much, but here," he said as he handed me a hot dog and a bottle of water. "You deserve this."

"Thanks," I said as I took them from him.

"I hope my kid ends up like you one day."

"Hopefully they don't *look* like me one day."

The man chuckled and headed over to a crowd with his hot dog cart.

"Look at you!" Jace sauntered over to me with a gun slung over his shoulder. "The rookie Interceptor is the big-boy of the day. You know you're already looking at a promotion for this, eh?"

I looked at Lili, and she nodded with a shrug.

"I feel like I have to ask this every time I see you—what do you want, Jace?"

"Always so hostile. I came to offer you a job."

"A job?"

"You don't belong with these Interceptors. You may not see it yet, but I can. If you ever feel like ditching these chumps, and hooking up with a real group of heroes, here's my info," Jace said as he brought two fingers to my visor.

"What makes you think I'd ever want to join you guys? You're a bunch of vigilantes from what I can gather."

Jace turned and started to walk away. "We'll see how long that lasts. Let's just say, we're friendlier than you know." He stopped and turned back. "Hey, sorry about your friend."

I nodded and he continued back to his group.

I looked at Lili, but she just shrugged again. "Don't even think about asking me. I have no clue what that was."

I took a bite of the hotdog as I looked around the scene. The small crowd had morphed into a full-on sea of people. My feed was playing on big screens on top of buildings for everyone to see.

The little camera was floating above me, so I looked up to it and raised my hot dog. I had never felt a wave of energy close to what I felt when the crowd of people exploded in applause.

It was a bittersweet day. I was able to stop Zeal from getting what he wanted, but the team lost one of its most important members in the process.

I handed Lili the water and she opened it for me. "I was pretty sure I was gonna get squashed back there," I said before a long swig of water.

Lili put her hand in my hand. "Forget all that for now. Soak it up, Rhys. You're a hero."

Chapter 43:
It's Not Over

From the moment we teleported back to the facility, everything was a blur. I had been rushed to the med-bay to deal with all of my muscles and bones that had been wrecked from holding up the building.

After that, I was rushed from place to place. One day it was a team meeting to discuss Kiyoshi, and another day was helping out with the debris clearing, and the rebuilding effort.

I woke up knowing it was going to be a bit of a weird day. It took most Interceptors a year or two to move up a rank. Due to my actions in the city that day, I was being promoted from D-Rank to C-Rank.

"You sure Lili is okay with this?" I asked Ayla.

"Of course she is. You may be newer to the team, but you proved you deserve it with what you did in a time of crisis. I'm excited for when you make it to B-Rank. I think the blue'll look good on you."

"Thanks. Could you—uh—gimme a few minutes? I gotta shower."

She chuckled. "I already know what your anatomy looks like."

"I'd rather pretend you don't."

"Fine," Ayla said as she disappeared.

I had grown accustomed to the green kit. Switching over to the red kits I'd be sharing with Pegs and Diggs would take some time to adjust to.

They had taken my kit from me to make the necessary upgrades, so I felt a bit naked with nothing but a sword. Luckily, Ayla was still able to stay with me by residing in my sword.

After a few minutes, Ayla warped in front of me in the shower. "It's time, Rhys. Head on out to the front of the facility."

"Dude—really?" I covered myself.

"Oh, relax," Ayla said with an eye roll as she disappeared.

"Hey, don't roll your eyes at me," I said as I realized how crazy I looked talking to myself in the shower.

I finished up and made my way back through the facility. Passing by all the training rooms made me nostalgic for a time that wasn't all that long ago. I was proud of how far I had come.

When I made it to the fountain that held the statue of Chase, I couldn't help but swell with pride. I stopped for a moment to pay respects to the man who had paved the way for the whole team.

"You doing alright, newbie?" Cleo asked as she walked up behind me.

"I'm okay. Just trying to process everything."

"I'm seriously asking. You know as much as I know that you are the one that killed Kiyoshi. You did it to save the city, and probably the world, but still—that's not a small thing. That's a life-changing thing, and it's okay to not be okay."

"I know," I sighed as the emotional weight of the conversation crashed on me. "It feels like the kind of thing that's always going to eat at me, but I know I shouldn't let it. I did what was right. What I had to do."

"You always have this family." Cleo wrapped me in a tight hug. "You never have to go through these things alone, okay?"

I hugged her back. "I know."

We each stepped back and composed ourselves.

"I'll give you some time to yourself before you head out there. The big hero of the day can't look like he's been crying," Cleo said as she poked me and headed for the door.

"Hey, Cleo." She whirled around. "Thank you."

She smiled. "Don't mention it."

"You have any idea who *him* is?"

She paused for a moment and narrowed her eyes. "I think I might—don't worry about that right now. Today is your day."

I looked up at Chase's statue one last time as Cleo headed out of the building.

"You know he would have been so proud of what you did." Ayla put a hand on my shoulder.

It still felt strange that she could touch me if she concentrated hard enough. At that moment, it didn't seem like she was trying all that hard.

"Thanks, Ayla. Faith figure anything out yet with the whole—you being able to touch me thing?"

She pulled her hand from my shoulder and looked at it. "No."

"Hey. What are you doing? Everyone's waiting for you out here," Diggs called as he burst through the doors. He made his way over and placed an arm around me. "Everyone's here. The mayor, the police chief, just about every news outlet you could think of. This is a big deal man—you're the fastest ever candidate to be promoted."

"Yeah, I don't know how thrilled about it General Odon is, but—"

"Ignore him. He can be a hard ass, but he's probably equally as impressed as the rest of us. Oh, before I forget, I was supposed to give you this." He placed a single-use kit in my hand and a small brown power core.

"What're these for?"

"It's a precaution. Danger has seemed to gravitate toward you so we thought it would be best if you had some way to defend yourself if Dorian or Sable decide to attack. You know what a single-use kit does, but that little core will let you use your element whenever you want without a kit. We use it to train, so it's weaker, but it might make it a bit easier for you to use for now."

"Huh, cool. So, when am I going to stop being surprised by all the insane gear we have?"

"Probably—never. Every so often one of us is surprised by something neat we haven't experienced before—plus Faith is always coming up with some cool stuff."

We walked through the front doors, and Diggs led me up to the stage to a huge round of applause. It was rare that the Interceptors allowed the general public up to the facility, but Promotions were as rare an occasion.

I shook hands with and hugged each of my team members before moving to the front of the stage with General Odon and Ramona.

All my friends cheered me on from the front of the crowd. It was weird to have them all cheering for me, but I was happy to see how proud that they all were.

After a small speech from General Odon, the crowd exploded with thunderous applause. I wasn't used to people gushing about me, but it was something that I could get used to.

General Odon shook my hand and leaned into my ear. "I want to see you in my office."

He turned and waved to the crowd with a smile before heading back inside the building. I was left alone in front of a microphone with nothing to say. I felt like there wasn't anything I could say that didn't sound overly hammy.

I decided a warning to Zeal was the best option.

"If you're watching, Akio, we're coming for you, buddy. Hold on."

The crowd didn't cheer.

How could they?

I'd delivered a message to someone who, at best, was being held hostage, and at worst, wasn't alive anymore.

Diggs shot forward. "Let's hear it one more time for Remarkable Rhys!"

The crowd burst into another round of applause as if they were a group of trained monkeys. I made my way off the stage and into the building.

"Can't forget Ramona and her wonderful team of Mercs either." Diggs continued as the door to the facility shut behind me. "Give it up for 'em."

I didn't know what General Odon wanted, but from the way he had spoken to me—it couldn't have been anything good.

Chapter 44:
Another One?

The door to General Odon's office slid open, and I stepped inside. He was sitting at his desk but turned around to face a window.

To my surprise, my camera halted outside the door.

"Take a seat, Rhys."

"Sure," I sat in a leather chair facing his desk. "Is everything okay, sir?"

"I'm not going to lie to you, Rhys. Things have been better. Not too long ago we lost Chase, and now we've lost Kiyoshi. Two of the greatest heroes this world has ever known in far too quick of succession. Not to mention this whole situation with Akio."

I had no idea what that had to do with me.

I thought that me improving so quickly, and being promoted would be seen as a good thing with something like that having happened, but maybe I was wrong.

"I was meaning to ask, and I don't mean this in any kind of disrespectful way, but with Kiyoshi being gone—does that mean we'll be holding another tryout for a new candidate?"

"I suppose that is what that would mean, yes."

I felt bad being excited by that. It was horrible that all these people lost someone they had grown to cherish, but now Kieran would have another shot at becoming an Interceptor. He had been so close before, and I knew he could do it if he was given another shot.

"But that's not what I'm here to talk to you about." General Odon continued.

"Wait a sec. I don't think I ever mentioned anything about—"

"Apparently you've been deemed a bigger threat than initially thought."

"Deemed a bigger threat? By who?"

He looked me dead in the eyes. "Kiyoshi was trying to take the fall for the new recruit who Zeal had managed to twist into a traitor."

"Sir—I don't know where this is coming from. That doesn't make any sense."

"That's good. Denying it will make you look even more guilty."

I shot up to my feet. "What are you talking about?"

"Rhys, you are being placed under arrest for conspiring with Zeal against the Interceptors. Submit quietly, or you will be dealt with—by force."

"I've never worked with him. I wouldn't ever work with that madman. I joined so that I can get back at him for what he did to my family, I—"

It all hit me.

"You—you're working for him, aren't you?"

He'd gone out of his way to let me know that he never watched the feeds. He didn't stay up to date on the day-to-day operations of the team, no one ever reported directly to him, and he had already headed back inside before I said anything about Akio—how would Odon have even known anything about him.

"How ridiculous of an accusation—"

"How did you know about Akio?"

"Well—Cleo informed me—"

"That's a load of crap. She's a few days away from putting your leadership to a vote. She wouldn't tell you anything."

Odon struggled to conceal a smirk. "Enough of this foolishness."

"You sick bastard." I balled a fist. "We all trusted you. The attacks on the facility, you're the reason they weren't detected before hand, aren't you?"

I expected some kind of surprised look, but his expression turned sinister instead. "I'd be careful what you say, and who you decide to say it to."

"What are you—"

"Say, for example, you decided to try to tell Lili any of this—well if that were the case, I'd be forced to deal with her for conspiring with you."

"I'll tell the whole team."

"Who are they going to believe? The new rat they aren't quite sure they can trust, or the last remaining original Interceptor?" He slammed his hands on his desk. "I'm a war hero. I'd bet a few of them are secretly sour about your quick promotion. Anyone you tell—I'll kill. Even worse—maybe Zeal will want to torture them for information first."

"Why are you doing this? You protected me from Zeal—the whole team. You could have just let us die."

"Things are a tad more complicated than your little brain could ever comprehend. Let's just say that Zeal has decided you might end up being a liability."

"Liability?"

I was in a corner.

There was no way Odon was going to let me walk out of that room. I couldn't go to the team without risking their safety. The one option I had was to somehow make it off that floating rock, and figure things out in hiding.

Ayla? What's going on?

I can't get through to Delaynie. He has to be working with Zeal. We need to get out of here.

What about the other AI's?

I can't patch through to any of them.

"You can quit your conspiring. Ayla's loyal to a fault. I've already severed her connection to the rest of the facility and the other AI's."

General Odon stood from his chair and readied his staff, but my elemental skill was ready to go.

It might have been due to the seriousness of the situation—or maybe the power core really did help, but I managed to shoot the earth from the potted plant on his desk at Odon's hands. It knocked his staff away and stuck him to the wall.

He laughed as it solidified, "Congratulations, Rhys. You're officially a traitor to the Interceptors. Delaynie, activate the emergency siren with the announcement that Rhys has been labeled a renegade. Be sure to let the team know."

I turned and darted out of the office as an alarm started blaring. The camera that had followed me into the office didn't seem interested in following me anymore since I was labeled a traitor.

"Ayla? Are you with me?" I panicked.

She warped beside me. "I'm with you. We need to get out of here and find someplace safe in the city."

"What are our options?"

"Pretty limited. I can do anything for you now, but if we manage to slip away my functions will be minimal without them being able to detect where we are."

"Let's get the hell out of here."

I rushed back into the main corridor of the facility right as the rest of the team rushed in through the front doors.

"Hold it, Rhys," Mickey said as the fully kitted team readied their weapons.

They all looked shocked and hurt, but Cleo had a different look on her face. Something about it reassured me, even though I was pretty sure she was about to try to kill me.

"Come quietly and we won't have to hurt you," Cleo said as she pointed her spear toward me.

"Ayla. Find me the quickest path out of here."

"You got it."

"You guys need to know that I didn't do anything."

"He really didn't," Ayla added.

"Put your weapons on the floor and explain yourself," Pegs said.

"I can't do that."

"We couldn't trust Kiyoshi, and now we can't trust Rhys. Who the hell can we trust?"

I looked right at Cleo. "Not *him*."

I pulled the trigger on the hilt of my sword and stared at my ex-teammates. If I was going to make it out of here and figure out how to clear my name, I was going to have to make it past the Interceptors.

I could feel my sword pulling me in a direction as if it were magnetized by something. "Follow the sword's pull whenever you're ready."

"Alright," My eyes bugged at Ayla. "We seriously need to sit down and you need to explain to me all the weird things you can do for me."

"You don't want to do this, Rhys," Pegs said.

"No, I don't," I said as I removed Trigger from its sheath, feeling the slight pull coming from it. "Looks like I don't have any choice, though."

Me versus a team of Interceptors.

I raised my sword and sprinted forward as the Interceptors rushed toward me. I've had some bad days, but that one was going to be among the worst. There was nothing I could do—I needed to stay alive, clear my name and show the team General Odon was the real enemy.

Step one was going to be the hardest.

Enjoy more novels from Cameron Stewart Miller:

(Available in paperback and EBOOK on Amazon)

Scallywags

Is this ship sinking?

That's what Finn thought right before learning one of the most closely guarded pirate secrets ever whispered across the seas.

When Finn was just a boy, his sleepy village was ravaged by a band of horrific pirates. The destruction they left behind was nothing compared to what they had taken – Finn's mother. After years of wondering what happened to her, Finn finds an opportunity to set out in search of his long-lost mother with some help from the most notorious pirate captain to sail the seas, Captain Fortune Palmer.

Finn's only problem is that Fortune isn't exactly what he'd imagined from all the stories he'd heard.

With his furry companion by his side, Finn sets out into the exciting and dangerous world of swashbuckling adventure. Between Pirate Hunters, scorned ex-lovers, and ancient warriors with magical treasure, Finn has his hands full as he works to discover what became of his mother the day she was taken while also proving his worth to his legendary captain.

The Glass Flowers

The Travelling Islands

Mahlurma, Cerulea, Flurris, Mulos, and Voxal. After two young boys find themselves transported to this strange new world, they embark on a journey to find their way home. The adventure won't be easy, because getting home means a trip to all of the islands, each stranger than the last. From occasionally wise frog wizards, dishonourable hog kings, and hungry harpy ladies, Wake and Desi must rely on each other and the kooky friends they make on their quest.

In this heartfelt tale, Wake and Desi must each learn what it truly means to grow up, and just how important it is to protect the vibrant nature of the world before it's too late.

Getting Locked Down

On what was supposed to be the happiest day of his life, Brain Berkley gets ditched at the altar by his fiancee, Sarah for one of the douchiest guys around.

Sappy, I know, but a chance meeting with a mysterious and exciting woman known as Holliday leads Brian into a life he never would have pictured for himself, a life of crime. The neurotic young man has to deal with a woman that's way out of his league, a childhood best friend turned police detective, and the heist of a lifetime, all while Brian does his best to not brown his trousers.

Brian and Holliday may have only just met, but if things don't go as planned then they might be spending the rest of their lives together, whether they want to or not.